The Arbor House Library of Contemporary
Americana is devoted to distinguished works of
fiction and nonfiction, many of which have long been
out of print. Included are a number of novels, highly
praised and warmly received at the time of
publication, that have secured a permanent place
for themselves in the literature of twentieth
century America.

THE
GALLERY

THE GALLERY

John Horne Burns

Introduction by John W. Aldridge

ARBOR HOUSE
LIBRARY OF
CONTEMPORARY
AMERICANA

ARBOR HOUSE · NEW YORK

Manufactured in the United States of America

10 9 8 7 6 5 4 3 2 1

Library of Congress Cataloging in Publication Data
Burns, John Horne, 1916-1953.
    The gallery.

(The Arbor House library of contemporary Americana)
    I. Title. II. Series.
PS3503.U6385G3   1985   813'.54   84-28390
ISBN 0-87795-709-6

In Memory of
ROBERT B. MACLENNAN
Germany, 7 April 1945
and for
HOLGER AND BEULAH HAGEN

INTRODUCTION

by
John W. Aldridge

I read *The Gallery* for the first time in the summer of 1947, a few months after it was published. I remember the occasion very clearly not only because the book excited me, but because I had at the time something more than a casual interest in what Burns and the other new writers were trying to do. I had myself returned from overseas with some strong opinions about the kind of war fiction my generation would produce, and I was eager to find out whether my expectations were being confirmed. I therefore made a point of reading all the war novels as soon as they appeared. By late 1947, I felt I had sufficient evidence that I was on the right track to put together a critical essay, my first, which the editors of *Harper's* saw fit to publish in the November issue, and which turned out to be the earliest assessment of the emerging postwar fiction. In it I offered, with the insufferable assurance of youth, my predictions about the shape that fiction would ultimately take and just how it would differ from, and might even be superior to, the fiction produced after World War I by such elders and inferiors as Hemingway, Dos Passos, and Fitzgerald.

Today much of that essay seems arrogant and immature, and all of it was clearly premature. In 1947, the most ambitious novels of the second war—Norman Mailer's *The Naked and the Dead,* Irwin Shaw's *The Young Lions,* and James Jones's *From Here to Eternity*—had not yet been published. And indeed if they had been, they might have changed the emphasis—although not, I think, the essential argument—of my essay. But at the time the only novels I could offer in evidence were, with one important exception, minor works—mostly first books by writers as young as I was and not likely to deserve more than passing reference in the literary history of the postwar period. They were Gore Vidal's *Williwaw,* Calder Willingham's *End as a Man,* Thomas Heggen's *Mr. Roberts,* Alfred Hayes's *All Thy Conquests,* Robert Lowry's *Casualty,* and the one important exception, John Horne Burns's *The Gallery.* This was a book that seemed to stand out as something very different from the others and very special. I recognized it then as a remarkable piece of work. But I did not recognize, as I do now, that it was the first distinctly major novel to come out of the war.

The Gallery can, I believe, justly be called major, first, because it displays the full range and depth of Burns's immensely compassionate understanding of the tragedy of war, an understanding equaled by no other writer of his generation, and, second, because it is a triumph of literary language. Burns had an extraordinary gift for striking an exact metaphor, the ability to evoke in a phrase or paragraph the subtle mood of a time and place or the psychological character of a human being. With the exception of Mailer, who was later to show a comparably original talent for descriptive language, Burns's contemporaries seemed to have learned more than they should have about how to write from reading Hemingway. I think particularly of Hayes, Lowry, and the early Merle Miller, all of whom produced novels that had the obligatory terseness of style and that curious effect of frigidity in the face of any emotion too intricate to be expressed in monosyllables. Yet they all lacked the quality that contained the secret of Hemingway's special magic: the impression he gave when he was at his best that there were violent emotions kept barely under control just behind the facade of that iron prose, that chaos had been temporarily subdued by the sternly imposed rigors of form and could be kept subdued only if the right words were put down in exactly the right order.

Burns, by contrast, seemed to write out of an altogether different tradition, one that bequeathed him not a hamstrung economy of language but a splendid prodigality, not a fear of emotion but an almost wanton eagerness

viii

to embrace and celebrate it. Yet his style, while full and free, was always precise, always functioning as the efficient servant of his subject. Here, for example, is his description of a morning street scene in Fedhala:

I remember how the dawn begins. . . . Out of the heavy uterine dark a violet light begins to swirl like a soft turbine. The color mottles into gold, the sea dies still more, and something seems to swish through the air like yellow torpedoes. There's a reveille of braying from all the Fedhala donkeys, as if, fearful of the sunrise and the workaday world ahead of them with its blows and kicks, they tore off a last chunk of donkey love. When the sun is up, the Medina opens its walls and out stream the Ayrabs who work in the cord and sardine factories. . . . They converse together like turkeys gobbling. They play tricks on each other. They use the French telephone poles with considerable liquid spite. . . . The faces of some of the men are as hawklike and refined and supercilious as a ballet dancer's; they have a feminine walk and a way of holding themselves aloof from the others. Some of the women have mashed noses and wide-set eyes like Nubians. . . . But there are a few Ayrab girls of sharp hurt beauty, flowers manured in a rich and poignant soil. These too walk apart from the others like the beautiful slight men. The handsome ones of the Ayrabs link hands as though from some lore inside the Medina they had learned of an aristocracy of body and face given to few in their generation. . . .

And here is a description of Major Motes and his wife in the "Portrait" called "The Leaf":

He spent his time in his laboratory at Roanoke. He was a petroleum engineer. By nature he was a dreamer. He thought of himself as a catalyst of the aristocracy of the Old South who'd somehow made the conversion to the world of 1930. . . . And he'd married a dreamer too. She was a belle of Roanoke, belonged to the DAR and the Methodist Church. She wrote poetry with the rapt efficency in which most women cook. And when no editor took her verses, which fluttered and sighed like herself, she published them herself. Though she had no children, each year she Brought Out a slim lavender or ocher or mauve book containing her thoughts on love, flowers, and life. She said she loved life with a fierceness known only to the elect. She'd married him because great loves, unlike butterflies, can be pinned down.

Yet they saw little of each other in their Roanoke apartment. She wrote her poems and read them at women's clubs, where she was applauded by wrenlike elderly ladies who then drank iced tea and champed on shortcake. He in his laboratory brooded on the possibilities of gasoline.

The materials in this passage are not at all unusual. The major and his wife might even, in a different context, be considered stereotypical: two mismatched people locked into their separateness in a marriage without passion. Yet Burns rescues them from cliché—as he does the other characters in the "Portraits"—by the freshness of his language and the extremely gentle touch of his satire. Such passages—and there are many others just as fine— make it possible to argue that his is quite simply the best written of the war novels.

But *The Gallery* is different from those novels in another and perhaps equally important respect. Nearly all of them follow the classic thematic pattern of war fiction going back at least to Ambrose Bierce and Stephen Crane: the individual soldier undergoes a process of violent initiation in combat and is forced out of his innocence into an often traumatic confrontation of the brutal realities. He comes to learn that war is the worst of imaginable hells, and that there is finally no idealism, no romantic fantasy of heroism or noble crusade, that can disguise its hellishness. The soldier's manner of facing this truth, his deportment before the unspeakable, may become the measure of his courage or of his talent for self-deception. He may—although this happens rarely— be transformed, like Crane's Henry Fleming, by a new and redemptive vision of his manhood and the world. Or—and this is most often the case—he will come to perceive himself as the dupe and scapegoat of those corrupt and lying institutions within his country that have sent him out to die a meaningless death.

There is undoubtedly much truth in Yeats's observation that "we begin to live when we have conceived life as tragedy"—if, that is, we don't die in the course of the tragedy. But Yeats presumably meant that we come to engage life more vigorously when the tragedy of inevitable death, even of meaningless death, becomes part of our bearable knowledge of life. As so much of our war fiction has shown, such knowledge often proves to be unbearable and, therefore, destructive of life. But it may also serve to engender a new and more compassionate understanding of the pathos and injustice of all human existence.

The latter seems to have happened to Burns, with the result that *The Gallery* is virtually alone among war novels in arriving finally at an affirmation of the humanizing effects of the view of life as tragedy. Burns appears to have begun to live when, as an American soldier in North Africa and Italy, he saw that the horror of war is not represented solely by the death of men in combat, but may be even more starkly displayed in the suffering of the civilian population in countries occupied by victorious armies—in this case, our own and those of our allies. There is only one brief combat scene in *The Gallery*. But there are a great many other scenes that express Burns's anger and sorrow over the plight of the conquered, exploited, and dispossessed.

Burns's development from a state of relative innocence to a recognition of the evils perpetrated by the victors in war is a less violent but no less traumatic form of the front-line soldier's initiation by combat. The novel's narrator—who is Burns speaking in his own person in the "Promenade" sections—becomes increasingly aware, as he moves from North Africa to Italy, of the ugly disparity between the professed high-minded intentions behind the Allied occupation and the cruel exploitation of the civilian populace by the occupying troops. He sees that the air attacks and artillery bombardments brought unavoidable misery and death to the people we sought to liberate.

xi

But we then compounded the tragedy by treating them with the most abject cynicism and contempt. He tells of well-brought-up Italian girls forced to become prostitutes in order to eat, of others who are seduced by soldiers with promises of marriage and then deserted, of decent young men who become pimps and thieves because their families are starving. And all the while the Allied military plunder and ravage without remorse and entirely without need.

These atrocities force Burns to a conclusion reached by so many writers in the past and somehow always reached with a shock of the bitterest revelation: that modern America is a military and industrial giant but an emotional dwarf, that we have achieved our massive power at the great cost of spiritual impoverishment, and that in our worship of the purely material we have lost all sense of honor and human decency. In the seventh "Promenade" Burns says:

> My heart finally broke in Naples. Not over a girl or a thing, but over an idea. When I was little, they'd told me I should be proud to be an American. And I suppose I was. . . . I did believe that the American way of life was an idea holy in itself, an idea of freedom bestowed by intelligent citizens on one another. Yet after a while in Naples I found out that America was a country just like any other, except that she had more material wealth and more advanced plumbing. And I found that outside of the propaganda writers . . . Americans were very poor spiritually. Their ideals were something to make dollars on. They had bankrupt souls. . . . Therefore my heart broke.

But to balance and finally outweigh this unhappy conclusion is the affirmative lesson the war and Europe have taught him: that there exists in the suffering victims of the Allied occupation an essential dignity and humanity that no amount of misery or exploitation can destroy, that it is still possible for them and for him to find the power to love.

The Gallery is thus something far more unusual than an indictment of the evils of war. It is finally a passionate declaration of faith in the ability of human beings to survive and prevail no matter how much pain they are forced to suffer. In other hands this could easily become a sentimental, even a mawkishly wishful conclusion. But Burns does what by definition a sentimentalist cannot do: he presents concrete justification for the intense emotions he feels through his vivid and precise rendering of the factual details of his experience, details that powerfully reinforce the conclusion he could not help but reach.

Burns died tragically young, at thirty-six, of a cerebral hemorrhage on August 10, 1953. He published two other novels, *Lucifer with a Book* in 1949 and *A Cry of Children* in 1952. But neither had the power of *The Gallery,* his masterpiece. In it he seems to have said all that he had to say about his experience of the war in Europe and what he learned from it. And clearly that was all that needed to be said.

All characters whose portraits hang in this gallery are fictitious. Any resemblance to persons living or dead is pure coincidence. Only the descriptions of Casablanca, Algiers, and Naples are based on fact.

Floorplan of THE GALLERY

How are ye blind, ye treaders-down of cities!
—*The Trojan Women*

Entrance

~~~~~~

THERE's an arcade in Naples that they call the Galleria
Umberto Primo. It's a cross between a railroad station
and a church. You think you're in a museum till you see
the bars and the shops. Once this Galleria had a dome of
glass, but the bombings of Naples shattered this skylight,
and tinkling glass fell like cruel snow to the pavement.
But life went on in the Galleria. In August, 1944, it was
the unofficial heart of Naples. It was a living and sub-
dividing cell of vermouth, Allied soldiery, and the Italian
people.

Everybody in Naples came to the Galleria Umberto.
At night the flags, the columns, the archangels blowing
their trumpets on the cornices, the metal grids that held
the glass before the bombs broke it, heard more than
they saw in the daytime. There was the pad of American combat boots on the prowl, the slide of Neapolitan
sandals, the click of British hobnails out of rhythm from
vermouth. There were screams and coos and slaps and
stumbles. There were the hasty press of kisses and
sibilance of urine on the pavement. By moonlight, shadows singly and in pairs chased from corner to corner.

In the Galleria Umberto you could walk from portrait to
portrait, thinking to yourself during your promenade. . . .

1

FIRST PORTRAIT

The Trenchfoot of Michael Patrick

HE LIMPED hurriedly along Via Roma, bumping into the swarms coming the other way. He kept saying scusate because he wanted to make amends for the way the other doughfeet yelled at the Neapolitans and called them paesan. Meanwhile his chin kept peeling back over his shoulder, for he had the feeling that two MP's were stalking him. In his pocket there was a hospital pass to which he'd forged a name. He had butterflies in his stomach from last night's Italian gin, and the sun and his sweat weren't helping things much. The speed with which he was moving hurt the feet inside his boots: it was all too clear why the medics wouldn't have given him a Naples pass until it was time to send him back to the line. This was why, limping more than a little, he'd taken off to Naples every night this week. The nurses couldn't figure out why his feet healed so slowly.

Naples. The name spelled a certain freedom and relief to him, in opposition to that other idea of being flown up to south of Florence. . . .

He saw two little concrete posts that made a stile into a covered arcade. Inside there was a crowd loitering, almost as big as that pushing along Via Roma. He sighed to be out of the relentless moving on the sidewalk. It seemed cooler in this arcade. He couldn't see an MP, and there were a lot of bars. He preferred not to sit at one of the tables on the pavement. What he was looking for was some bar as small and tight as a telephone booth. There he could wedge his chest and swallow one vermouth after another. The butterflies would go away, and he could dwell lovingly on what he would do after the sun went down.

To do? The important thing was to forget that tomorrow or the next day his feet would be well, and he'd be waiting for that plane at Capodichino. After the

2

truck ride toward Florence, with the sound of the guns getting stronger. . . .

Perhaps his trenchfoot was something sent him by Saint Rita of Cascia, to whom his mother used to have special devotion. Saint Rita had been pierced with thorns during her ecstasies. And he, after standing in his wet foxhole for weeks and listening to the artillery go screaming toward Florence, had been pierced with trenchfoot. Perhaps it was some subconscious cowardice that had broken out in his feet. He'd thought for a long time anyhow that he was going to crack, and trenchfoot was a more honorable way of doing it than becoming a psycho. So he smiled down on the CD patch on his left shoulder and thanked Saint Rita that he'd been able to take the cure in Naples.

First he wanted some vermouth. Then some music. At the GI Red Cross he'd picked up two tickets to the San Carlo while working a little sympathy out of Betty, rapid and abstracted behind the information desk. She was thinking about her date with a colonel tonight. She didn't have much time for him except her hospitality song and dance. But she'd introduced him to music in Oran. So tonight he would hear *La Bohème*. And after the opera he hoped for that last release. He'd never been a lover in his life, but tonight he'd like to have somebody kiss him, to feel somebody's disinterested hands going all over his body. He didn't much care whom the hands belonged to, but he cringed at the idea of paying on Via Roma for such a rite.

In the middle of the arcade he came upon a bar that was nearly empty. On the marble counter were two shining boilers of the coffee machines. He ripped out of his chest pocket a beatup hundred-lira note and bought some chits. His hands were quivering under their Ayrab and Italian silver rings. The fat Neapolitan behind the cashbox didn't miss this jittering of his fingers.

A double vermouth was set at his elbow by a girl wearing a furpiece. She was proud of this and kept emphasizing it by stroking it in the August afternoon. She missed being pretty because she was so mouselike. As she served him, she looked at him, but then her eyes darted away. Then he decided he wouldn't take off his cap, for he was getting bald at twenty-seven.

3

"My red face," he said, "isn't from drinking, but from those C-rations they feed us."

The look she threw at the fat Neapolitan made it evident that she was as strictly brought up as Neapolitans could be in wartime. Then her eyes went down to the two wrist watches strapped side by side on his left wrist, like twins in bed.

"Tedeschi watches," he said, unstrapping one for her. "I figured they couldn't use them. Stiffs can't tell time. . . ."

Her father slithered around from behind the cash register, came over, and held out his plump hairy hand for the watch. He weighed it, smelled it, tapped it, and listened to its pulse with a flicker of love in his eyes. The deal was on.

"You speak, Joe. Quanto?"

"O my back! Sure you don't want to buy my cigarettes too? But I smoke two packs a day. So I can't help your black market, except to get rid of a Tedeschi watch or two."

The signorina's eyes began to sparkle in a pleased way, as though her father had telegraphed her to play up to him. He began to wonder if perhaps she might come to the opera with him and how it would feel to touch her hair. Her breasts pressed the counter as she leaned over to look at the watch her father was appraising. He thought that no GI had touched her—yet.

"Quattro mila lire," the fat Neopolitan said. "Forty dollar, Joe."

"O my aching back. And for a Tedeschi watch too."

His elbow gave a jerk and the glass of vermouth splintered on the floor. Its smell arose in the hot air—sweet, dry and wistful. The signorina looked disdainful but served another glass. From his cash drawer her father counted out four thousand-lira notes in Allied military currency. That left only one Tedeschi watch to be sold. He toyed again with the idea of taking the signorina to the opera, of sliding the Tedeschi watch on her wrist in some darkened box. She had slim hands with nails a little gray under their chipped vermilion paint. He leaned on both his elbows, thrusting his face a little closer to her furpiece. And the second glass of vermouth hit the floor.

"My mother said I was very high-strung."

4

The Neapolitan flounced out with a broom and swept up the splinters. The signorina drew another double vermouth, setting it quite a length from his elbow. He watched the cold superiority creep over her face as pettishly she stroked her furpiece. She looked at him the way a nun regards the convent cat who has just made a mess in the parlor. He laughed to cover his chagrin, but he didn't care much for the sound of his laugh. It trailed into a cough, and he started thinking up some more ways to get in touch with the signorina. She was only a foot away from him, but she seemed to be receding into an icy planet. He had the impression that she'd continue to sell him double vermouths till closing time, but that she considered him just some maggot in boots and suntans that had wriggled out of the cracks in the arcade. And with this thought his elbow flinched into a spasm that sent the third glass jingling to the floor.

"I guess the point is to drink it," he said, laughing again..

Out came the broom; a fourth vermouth was poured. Panicky, he lifted it to his lips, noticing that his whole arm vibrated like a drunkard's who laces a towel round his neck to guide a pick-me-up to his mouth in the morning. He closed his eyes and swallowed three doubles in a row. He waited, leaning his red face in his hands, till he could feel the stuff flickering in his gut with an uneasy flame. The tremors in his muscles gave one final flip and ironed out into a kind of feverish peace. He lifted his glance to look at the signorina, but she'd moved off to wait on some New Zealand soldier at the far end of the bar. Where she'd been standing, he now saw his own face in the mirror behind the tiers of wine bottles.

"Michael Patrick," he said, "how even your own mother could have loved you? . . ."

For his was a face pretty much like everyone else's who isn't anybody in America and less than that in the army. His eyes were raw from a week's drinking; his cheeks looked burnt from the inside by a fire without point or focus. And his body, slim and lithe, was good enough to draw fire from Jerry and to dish it out in return. His cap was set on his head, not at the jive angle that young parachutists love but strategically, to mask the fact that at twenty-seven he was losing his hair, but fast. He couldn't bear to look at himself, and he didn't

5

see how anybody else would want to either. Naturally this signorina had moved away. He was just another GI who'd been on the line and was going back to it. There were thousands in Naples like him, except that they pretended to be surer of themselves. They had the ability, in place of his tired negation, to dramatize themselves for the appropriate minute. They hadn't yet seen the pointlessness of themselves.

Nevertheless he moved toward the signorina with his empty glass. As long as he could afford to buy her rotten vermouth, she'd have to serve him. He pushed his glass almost imperiously into her folded hands. This brought a smile to her face, her small pointed teeth looking as though they'd nip her own lips, or whomever she kissed.

Michael Patrick had an envy of Italians, seeing a certain kindship between them and the Irish. But the Irish stayed hurt all their lives; the Italians had a bounceback in them. All his life he'd been silent, waiting and listening for some cue that would set him off on one of those oily harangues that people vent at wakes, twisting their rhetoric and loving it for its own cadence and invention. But after months of being alone with himself a reserve of chatter had been dammed up in him, punctuated with shellfire. He so wanted to talk on and on just for the joy of creating sentences! But he couldn't talk to himself. Nor did he want what is known as polite conversation. He wondered if in all Naples tonight there was someone to whom he could address himself, in whom he could find the function of an Ear, an Ear that would listen him out of himself till there'd be nothing more to say. Actually he had nothing special to say—a mere loving recitation of facts about himself, the flight of the plane from the evac hospital, his thoughts while circling over Rome. And after that he might start on the old days in Easton, Pennsylvania, on his brother who always did him dirt in their partnership in the seed business. His life was bursting to be released to someone, someone who would really listen to him. Words—they meant so little, but he felt like a bottle with a narrow opening that must be drained drop by drop. He wanted to purge himself by talking. After that he might feel like reaching forward with his mouth opened for a kiss. . . .

She poured him another vermouth. In grabbing for the chit to pay her, he spilled everything he had in his breast

6

pocket over the top of the bar. The two opera tickets lay face up before her.

"If you'd like to come tonight," he said in a rush. "If your father would let you. . . . It's *La Bohème*."

A quick delight coursed over her face, like all the women in the world when a treat is offered them.

"Ma . . . ," she whispered back, "senza papà non potrei."

The fat Neapolitan made a clucking noise in his throat.

"O my back," Michael Patrick said, raising his voice. "You Ginso girls are all alike. You automatically assume that every GI wants to get in your pants. . . . And of course you're right."

He put out his hand and touched the wolf's head that bit its own tail and clasped her furpiece. She straightened up, and he saw that she was looking at his fingernails, bitten back so far that they formed mangled halfmoons.

"Listen," he said, trying to force the stridency out of his voice. "I'm not pulling any hero stuff on you. But this is my last night in Napoli. Do you know where I'm going tomorrow? I don't look forward to it. . . . Oh I know you've all been bombed here. But this is different. . . . I'll be out there all alone with the noise, running through hell all by myself. It's different. You have no idea of how alone it is. And while I was there last month, I dreamed of all the things I'd do if I ever got back to Napoli. . . . And here I am, and nothing's panning out the way I hoped it would. . . . I feel like a kid reaching for jam on a shelf that's too high up. And I don't know what it really is I'm reaching for. Maybe life itself. . . . Do you suppose maybe I'm already dead? What would you do if I touched you? I'm in a dream from which I can't wake up. . . . Capeesh?"

"Cosa?" she asked, and he realized that coquetry wasn't atrophied in her.

"Now if I was an officer, you'd be nicer to me. I haven't got any gum or chocolates. Just me and two opera tickets and some cigarettes."

He knew he was hitting too gloomy a strain. So he drank another vermouth and lit a cigarette. He carried his butts in a small plastic case. Inside the transparent cover was the picture of a dark girl he'd found when his company looted a farmhouse near Poggibonsi. He'd never had a steady girl in his life like all the other GI's.

7

"È bella *La Bohème,*" she said, stroking her fur speculatively.

"No, I don't know whatall about music," he said, reestablishing himself on her plane. "In the States I was too busy for it. Then when I hit Oran, all the cravings of my life caught up with me. Like a disease when you stop treatment in the middle of the cure. One day at the Red Cross in Oran I found out that the music expresses all that I look for and never find. . . . I don't see very much to our own music. You see, it doesn't give me that feeling of watching someone die, and you can't do anything to help."

She began to sing "Pistol-Packin' Momma."

"O my back!" he said excitedly. "That's what I mean. I hate that goddam tune. It reminds me of a fat old bitch jigtiming on the edge of her grave. She's wearing black lace stockings, she's tearing off her corset, she's kicking off her shoes, and the paint is running down her face."

"È bella, però, la musica americana," she said, and sang it through again.

With another vermouth in his hand Michael Patrick walked to the entrance of the bar and looked out into the arcade. The hour was close to sunset and the place was humming like an anthill. A lounging kid screamed, "Wanna eat, Joe?" Old ladies in black passed on the arms of their daughters. Neapolitan doctors and lawyers swarmed by arm in arm from their offices gesticulating and complaining. And Michael Patrick saw that sunlight in this arcade had a thick swooning texture like tired gold melting. The vermouth was now well into his brain, his nerves no longer snapped. He began to taste that half-mulled feeling of time deliciously unrolling before him. This reaching out in vain was only felt when he tried to mesh himself with the gears of other people. When he was drinking alone, he was aware of certain untapped potentialities in himself. But when he talked to others, something in him went limp and kept sneering at him that he was alone alone alone and wrapped in some inaccessible womb, that nobody else really cared, or that they were doubled up with secret laughter at the sight of him.

These long-felt nibblings of defeat so enraged him that he spun round in his boots and went back to the bar. The signorina had been watching him where he stood between her and the setting sun. This time he broached her almost in ardor.

"Tell me the difference between your life and mine. Don't answer, even if you could. . . . It's a question of time. . . . But how important that is, like looking back over a hundred years after you've lived through them. . . . I suppose you've got a fidanzato? A little Ginso who's a P/W in Africa?"

She stared curiously into his eyes, having caught the word fidanzato. And she seemed to catch some of the virus of his desperation, for her hands lay quiet where they'd been fretting her furpiece.

"You lucky lucky girl. . . . And that long stretch you've got ahead of you. . . . He'll come home to you when the war's over. Then you'll have one of those Neapolitan weddings, which will be the last thing you'll have to look forward to till a big black hearse pulls you through the streets. . . . O that long long time you've got ahead of you! You'll both go walking arm in arm on summer evenings on Via Chiaia. You'll stop for ice cream or caffè espresso. And each year there'll be one more kid by your side. . . . How many rooms will you have? Maybe two, and one big bed with a picture of the Madonna of Pompeii over it. She'll watch you two kissing and fighting at night, and she'll hear your cries when your kids are born. . . . I can see them now. . . . Neopolitan kids I kind of liked even when they stole from me. . . . That'll be your life. It's not very much, but it's life. And it's more than GI's think it is. . . ."

Michael Patrick had started to flail his arms about just like a Ginso. But his voice hadn't risen out of that low weariness that always sounded as though he were going to cry. The signorina's father had come out from behind the cash register, put both hands on his hips, and was watching them with a kind of sly benevolence. Neapolitans take their theater wherever they find it. The old man had a stomach that rippled and creased under a GI belt fastened into a rattail along his shiny pencil-striped pants. Then he made a motion, graceful and insinuating, that his daughter should serve a drink on the house.

"Sometimes," said Michael Patrick, wiping his mouth with an olive-drab handkerchief, "I like you Eyeties better than I do my own. There's something . . . good . . . and gentle in most of you. . . . Where are we going in

9

this war? . . . I don't know, for all the orientation talks they used to give us. . . . There's something about Italy and you Eyeties that gets me. There's dirt and poverty here. . . . But there's something else that gets me. Seems to survive your battered towns and your bitter men and your degraded women. . . . Why is all this? Why must it be? Something terrible has come into this world. . . ."

There was a small Kiwi listening now at the back of the bar. He wore tight shorts and a crazy beret. He leaned against his Marsala and cheered feebly:

"Give em whatall, Yank!"

"Hi, Dig," Michael Patrick said listlessly.

"Grazie, Nazi."

"Prego, Dago."

In his life Michael Patrick hadn't said three sentences in a row. Yet here he was like a priest at the time for the monthly collection, ringing all the changes on a theme. The signorina'd been watching him with penetration. He took his vermouth and paced again restlessly to the door of the bar, where the iron shutters were rolled up over his head. His gait was easy now in those same polished boots in which he'd got trenchfoot.

Through a sudden gap in the crowd he saw to the other arch of the arcade, to a flight of stairs down into Via Verdi. Up these bounded three Alpini lieutenants in their shorts and feathered sugarloaf caps. He mused on what it must be like to be an Italian soldier in August, 1944—half of them walking shyly around Naples, unable to have a girl because the Allies were paying twenty hundred lire; half of them in P/W stockades scattered from India to the States. Italian soldiers of a vanquished army, inured to the idea of patria and screaming throngs in Piazza Venezia and their names among the fallen on a bronze plate in the municipio. . . .

And Michael Patrick saw the posters with which the arcade was spattered, urging the Neapolitans to join a hundred political parties, to drive out the king if they wanted white bread for their babies. And there were some hammer-and-sickles daubed in red on the walls. And there was a quotation from a Mussolini speech on the heroism of the people of Naples. The hysterical block letters had been half scratched out; there were mud and liquid streaks blotching the Duce's ranting words.

Office girls padded by him in their makeshift sandals.

10

They had no stockings to wear. The fuzz and the sandfly bites showed on their dark legs. They crooned together in a misty passion, resting their heads on one another's shoulders:

> "*Core, o core 'ngrato,*
> *T' aie pigliato 'a vita mia;*
> *Tutto è passato,*
> *E nun 'nce pienze chiù . . .*"

It was time to move on someplace else. The opera didn't begin for another hour, yet an infantry itch was in his legs. He hadn't found the Ear he wanted. The vermouth had heated him to the bubbling slow gold of the broiling sun in the arcade. The tune that the girls had sung invaded him with a yearning stronger than his tentative desire for the smug little signorina with her furpiece, pitiful as an Easter hat on a hungry whore.

Michael Patrick set down his glass with a gesture that he strove to make as calm as possible. He took the girl's hand. Her father sighed noisily behind the cash register. She didn't withdraw her hand, though a remoteness which veiled her eyes showed a disappointment that he hadn't played her game her way.

"Good-bye to you and your lousy vermouth. I don't know what I'll do with the other opera ticket. . . . And when I say good-bye, I mean addio. . . . There'll be so many others who'll come in this bar and plank down twenty-four lire for vermouth. . . . But how sick you must be of all of us, the whole goddam crowd with their trousers tucked into their buckled boots, their shoulder patches, their yelling, and their cussing. . . . But anyhow I never rumpled your hair or made a pass at your breasts. . . . I'll remember you longer than you'll remember me. . . . Why? Because you'll be one of the last things I saw in Naples. . . . Next week, a few hundred miles north of here, there's something waiting for me with my name on it. . . . I feel it." The father raised his hands to heaven with the soft horror of a Jew.

"Well," said Michael Patrick, avoiding his own smile in the mirror, "there are worse places to be buried than in Italy. In the summer the ground is warm and dry, and the GI mattress cover seals in the rot and stink. . . . But . . . I wish someone would tell me why I must go

11

up to Florence when life's all around me here."

He clapped his hand over his mouth, tasting the dank tobacco on his blunt fingernails. This was the same hand that had sold seed packets to housewives in Easton, Pennsylvania, that had jerked the trigger of his carbine, that had slipped Tedeschi watches off the sprawled hushed bodies of Feldwebels, that had cooked a chicken in an OP at Frosinone. He pushed his cap a little farther back on his head—to where the hair began to fade out —and went off into the arcade.

The sun knifed his eyes, dilated from vermouth. Blinking, he hated the fierce Neapolitan sun. Until he hit the light, he'd been at just the right stage, but he knew how margins are: you exceed them because you're always reaching for a horizon.

Pigeons were scooping down through the domed skylight of the arcade, scudding mockingly through the grates where the glass used to be, dropping their white excretions on the stone parquet. They had a meditative way of calling one another that carried like a ground bass under the squeaking hurrying human beings below them.

The vermouth he'd drunk was pressing on his abdomen, so he nosed out a dark slit opening off the arcade into a garden with a fountain. It was cool in this court within a court. And since no housewives were screaming to one another across the balconies, Michael Patrick stood on the rim of the fountain, unbuttoned his trousers, and drilled the dead water in the pool.

"Mamma mia!" a voice cried behind his shoulder. "Ecco le porcherie pubbliche che fanno gli alleati!"

Hastily he righted his fly and tottered back off the fountain. A woman in a soiled house dress was scolding him from a balcony. She had a baby by the hand and a smile on her big face as though the whole world was among the category of her children. Her child wrapped its little legs around the gratings and waved at Michael Patrick, whose face got redder than ever.

"Joe! Gimme caramelle!" the baby called.

"Ma stai zitto!" the woman shrieked, slapping its little head.

Then with another wave the two whisked behind the long shutter of the balcony door.

He'd have liked to call them back to talk to him for a little while, yet he was ashamed that they'd surprised

12

him going about his business. Something in the woman's
face had been so innocent of meanness, something easy
and strong in the sloppy braid of her hair about her
temples. She reminded him of all the good mothers he'd
ever known, who go about their childbearing and cooking and slavery with a comic abstraction and a delight in
what they are doing. He knew that she loved her child.
And something told him that at the very moment of her
railing, she'd loved himself too. But now she'd gone back
into her house. Probably on the stove she had a kettle
of pasta cooking, making supper for her man and the
other children. Anyhow she'd gone.

He went back into the blaring arcade, the grilling sun,
the crowds. An American parachutist lounged against
one of the columns, his knee arched so that a boot was
off the pavement. He was chewing gum and wiping away
the sweat from under his cap. This parachutist was arriving at a price agreement with a small girl in a tight
blue dress. Her body was skinny, on her bolero she wore
officers' insignia, wings, and divisional patches. She also
chewed gum. Beside her stood a scabrous urchin pre-
siding as auctioneer, screaming out a sales talk, the
specifications of her charms. The parachutist had his eyes
half-closed and worked lazily on his gum while he reached
out for the girl's waist. He muttered slowly:

"I said vieni qua. Ya know it's all a crocka shit."

Michael Patrick in passing attempted by some secret
glance to show the girl that he understood and apologized.
But she spat her gum on his shoes. He blushed and entered a little shop where rows of bottles stood like soldiers at attention. He knew very well what he could buy
here—Benevento alcohol at five hundred lire a bottle.
It carried labels of Scotch, cognac, and gin, but it was
all the same stuff with different flavoring. You weren't
supposed to buy it because it went to your liver or to
your eyes. But it did hit you with a hard bright drunkenness, and that was what he was seeking. He came out of
the shop with the bottle propped like a ramrod inside
his trousers. It couldn't fall to the ground because his
pants were tucked into the tops of his boots.

He went back to the courtyard with the fountain and
sat down on the rim. Perhaps the woman who had called
out the friendly lambasting might appear again. But
most of all he wanted to get the sun out of his eyes.

13

Sprawled along the lip of the fountain, he wondered whether he should pull out his bottle and taste it. He put his head between his thighs. Almost at once a dark heaviness passed over him like a wing, and he fell asleep.

No dreams visited him: he blacked out for an hour or so. Often when he tried to sleep sober, he'd hear the shriek and thud of artillery or screaming and lamenting that seemed to seep up from a rocking chair. But this was a sleep of negation in which he ceased to be for a while. On the line sleep had been the one pleasure he'd had to look forward to.

He twitched up suddenly with the beginnings of a sick headache. The Tedeschi watch told him it was time. His chin had been scraping the blue infantry badge above his heart. He got up and dragged along with a new sort of limp, for the bottle stiffened his right knee. He barged across the arcade with his head down, in that same feeling of apprehension when he'd crossed the New York streets with a hangover, the feeling of a frightful doom suspended over his head.

There was a portico running along the outside of the San Carlo Theater. There was also a traffic island and a green-lighted pro station. The opera crowd reached in a queue out of sight, except for a few who waited for their opera guests outside the arches. Or those who were more than usually lonely waited here to invite or to be invited inside.

Michael Patrick managed to get across from the arcade in blind lunges that carried him to the doors of the San Carlo. At first he thought he'd give away his extra ticket to somebody in the waiting line, but instead he ran up the stairway and shoved his ticket at one of the Neapolitans. They wore dirty powdered wigs, brocade crimson coats, knee breeches and stained white stockings. As his ticket was torn in half, he laughed and looked down at the splayed pumps of the ticket taker.

"Trade ya my boots," he said a little thickly, and watched the bowing flunky bounce back from the impact of his own vermouthy breath.

Michael Patrick climbed to his box in the sixth tier at the right-hand corner of the proscenium arch. There was no one else in this palco. The box door was unlocked by yet another character in eighteenth-century costume. Michael Patrick dug out a tip of one hundred

14

lire and settled himself in a high-backed poltrona by the railing of his box. He could look straight down into the orchestra pit, where sweating gossiping men and women were tuning up or chaffing their friends who had dropped in casually on them in the pit. The San Carlo orchestra pit was as friendly and communal as a bomb shelter. Over the burr of the oboe and the running scales of the strings, the players and their guests chattered and fanned themselves with the evening newspaper.

Looking again with relief to see that there wasn't anybody else besides himself in the box, Michael Patrick loosened his belt and extracted the bottle of cognac from his trouser leg. As he took his first swig, all the lights in the theater blinked out. Red glows appeared over the exits. The flutter and movement in the house abated, giving way to a noisy shushing by the audience. Only the orchestra in their cellar gave off a nimbus of phosphorescence; the footlights stained the velvet curtain as rich and dark as blood. Michael Patrick gasped with delight and leaned far out over the barrier of his box.

A tired old man, a turkey wearing a frock coat, came into the orchestra pit from under the stage. He groped his way among the crowded music desks until his grizzled skull jutted over the podium and the wall of the pit. A hand reached out of the prompter's box and diddled with a mirror. For a while the old Neapolitan talked to the orchestra, dispensing wisdom and sadness to them like a Dutch uncle. He seemed intolerably weary, sternly kind. Then he lifted his stick and the trombones blatted out a hectic and cynical phrase. The strings muttered and swayed, and the curtain went up on a skylighted garret overlooking the frozen roofs of Paris.

Like a child Michael Patrick peered and listened to the persiflage of the painter with green smock and easel and the writer who burned his manuscripts to keep warm. He heard the tenor and the violins in unison lift and drop in long tender melodies that were both sad and gay. Sometimes Michael Patrick would raise his bottle to his lips, never taking his eyes or his ears from that sweet world on the stage.

There was a rap on the door of the garret.

"Chi è là?"

"Scusi."

"Una donna!"

He watched the violins plug on their mutes. The old maestro concertante leaned over them cajolingly. An aching perfumed strain rose in the darkness till Michael Patrick felt his heart begin to ache with a wild wistfulness. A shy little seamstress came onto the stage carrying a lighted candle. At this moment Michael Patrick ceased to be anywhere particular in this world, least of all in Naples of August, 1944. He was happy.

What was there here in the sweetness of this reality that he'd missed out on in America? He'd opened a door into a world that had nothing to do with merchandising and selling, with the trapped four-four beat of boogie-woogie, with naked girls shaking their navels through cigar smoke on a runway, with nervous old ladies totting up their insurance, with the fact that he wouldn't live to be twenty-eight, with the gum-beatings of topkicks, with the smell of a world like a slaughterhouse, with groping and misunderstanding and cruelty. He felt himself inundated with the loveliness that men seek in a woman's arms, that old nuns sense on their death-beds. He saw for the first time in his life that the things which keep the world going are not to be bought or sold, that every flower grows out of decay, that for all the mud and grief there are precious things which make it worth while for us to leave our mothers' wombs —if someone shows us these priceless things. Before and after this truth, he saw, there's nothing, nothing at all. . . .

"O soave fanciulla! . . ."

His body was racked with a delight from outside himself. And when the lights came up again at the end of the first act, he fell from his paradise. The applause, the simpering curtain calls had nothing to do with what he'd felt—for the first time to be abstracted from his own sweating tired body, from a regimen that tormented him because it had no meaning he could decipher. So he retired sulkily to the rear of the box, sat on the floor out of range of the theater lights and the chatter of the audience, and drank slowly and methodically. There were no odds in walking down to the foyer and making a pretense at a social promenade. Besides he was pretty drunk.

Near the close of the third act of *La Bohème* Michael Patrick had emptied his cognac bottle. It lay by his boots like a spent rifle. He leaned heavily on the barrier and stared out at the stage. He couldn't see too distinctly now,

16

but the music and the voices came up to him in a vortex that carried him along in its conical eye. His sight was blinking and bloodshot.

> *"Se vuoi . . .*
> *Se vuoi serbarla per ricordo d'amore,*
> *Addio, addio . . . senza rancor . . ."*

He laid his head on the plush railing by his arms. His tears fell on his knees. He wept very quietly but at length. It was okay to cry because he knew with clarity and brilliance exactly why he was crying. For his own ruined life, for the lives of millions of others like him, whom no one had heard of or thought about. For all the sick wretchedness of a world that no one could, or tried to, understand. For all who passed their stupid little lives in the middle of a huge myth and delusion.

At the end of the opera Michael Patrick felt and reeled his way down the five flights of stairs. He leaned bemused and lost in the portico of the San Carlo till the shrill crowds had gone away. The moon was out above Vesuvius. The bay shimmered out toward Torre Annunziata and Salerno. The night still had the hot heaviness of the daylight hours. Naples was a murmur of sound, the river-rushing of people fleeing and seeking and pretending and betraying.

Then he noticed a girl with a birthmark standing close beside him. Her hands were folded under her breasts. She seemed intensely aware of him. There was a red flower in her hair, and she smiled at him as though she beckoned across some unbridgeable distance. He was too drunk to string ideas together, but it was perfectly clear what they must do, and each understood it in a kind of mute joy. He took her arm, warm and almost weightless in its cotton sleeve. He led her into the arcade and to that quiet fountain place where he'd slept this afternoon. He placed her against a wall out of the moonlight. He kissed her hands and her throat and the mauve birthmark on her cheek, pressing himself gently against her. His fingers went through her hair the way children wander in a dark forest, numb and crying and lost.

"Oh I think I love you," he said.

Their tears mingled; he felt she was nodding her head.

FIRST PROMENADE

(Casablanca)

I REMEMBER the smell of the air in Casa, a potion of red clay and the dung of camels. That was the way the Ayrabs stank too.

A Liberty ship in convoy brought me to Casa from Camp Patrick Henry, Virginia. In the nineteen days of crossing the Atlantic, I remember that something happened to me inside. I didn't know what adjustment to make for where I was going, but I think I died as an American. I'd climbed the gangplank with some of that feeling of adventure with which all soldiers go overseas. All the pacifist propaganda of the twenties and thirties couldn't quite smother that dramatic mood of well-here-we-go-again-off-to-the-wars.

I remember the endless foul nights below deck, with the hatches battened, and the clunk of the depth charges, and the merchant marine eating like kings and sneering at us and our Spam-twice-a-day. We GI's were like pigs in the hold, bunks five-high to the block, latrines swilling and overflowing, and vomit or crap games on the tarpaulin-sheathed floor where we huddled. The sergeant was on the bottom tier, one inch off the floor, with his nose jutting into the rear end of the joe sleeping above him. The pfc was on the top trying to sleep with his face against a ventilator. And everywhere a litter of barracks bags and M-1's, with every man making up deficiencies in his equipment at the expense of his neighbors. It was the first time I'd seen American soldiers stealing from one another. There were three hundred of us in that hold, looking down one another's windpipes. We lived off one another like lice. I'd believed that Americans liked to give one another elbow room, except in subways.

I remember the enforced calisthenics on the deck of the Liberty ship, the drill with the Mae Wests, the walking guard on deck lest Neptune should arise from the waves and goose the ship with his trident, the crap game that ran night and day throughout the voyage, the listen-

18

ing to the ship's guns spit out practice tracers. There were nurses and Red Cross girls and State Department secretaries on the boat deck, which was off limits to us. They took sun baths and dallied with the officers and screeched when the depth charges detonated. If a starboard wind blew it my way, I heard their laughter, stylized like a sound track for bobby-soxers.

I remember the harbor of Casa at 0700 hours. At first when I saw the cranes and the berths, I thought it was all a joke, and that we were really still at Hampton Roads. It took all day to disembark us replacements because the cargo security officer couldn't find a case of Coca-Cola and was worried about his date with a Casablancaise that evening. He had the one-up-on-you wisdom of one who's already been overseas, and he peddled his wisdom to us gratis:

"I tell ya, French gals can teach the American ones a trick or two."

We got two days' supply of C-rations, and we carried our M-1's and A-bags onto the soil of North Africa. The smell I'd sniffed out in the channel was now strong, like the tart sweatiness under the wing of a dying chicken. And the Ayrabs stood around our two-and-a-half-ton truck. They were wearing GI mattress covers. They held out their hands, smiling as cagily as poor relations. They had white teeth and red fezzes. We tried to buy some of those Ayrab chapeaux.

I remember the Place de France and the Boulevard de la Gare and the billboards of Publi-Maroc. There was a secret yellow bell tower I'd seen as photomontage for Humphrey Bogart. And the long cool Hôtel in the Place Lyautey, near palm trees, fountains, and an MP motor pool. However they might deal with the Ayrabs, the French had hit on a colonial architecture that seemed to grow naturally out of the pink soil of Morocco. There were stained stucco walls around the two Medinas, all of which were off limits to us.

Why is it called Casablanca? Because for all the smell there's a ghostly linen brilliance about the buildings clustered on their terraced levels. This White City is best seen at noon or sunset. I knew that I couldn't be anyplace else but in Africa. There's something festering here, something hermetically sealed. With the exception of the indigenous Ayrabs, all Caucasians here seem to be corpse intruders, animated by a squeaking desire to be somewhere else. The restlessness of Casablanca is of the damned. It's a place where all the tortures of the twentieth century meet and snicker at one another, like Ayrab women under their veils marketing in the Suk.

"What I mean to say is, I'm going to start chasing some of this French stuff tonight."

"And I'm plenty pissed off at Miss Lucy Stout, who taught third-year French at Coolidge High. Ya need more than a bongswahr in this town."

"J'aime le jambon quand il est bon."

I think it was at Casablanca that the bottom dropped out of my personality. Americans profess to neatness of soul because their country is Protestant, spacious, and leery of abstracts. Now I'm an American uprooted. I'm in a foreign land where I must use a ration card, where there's no relation between the money in circulation and the goods to buy with it. This was the only way I could explain to myself the looks I got from the French and the Ayrabs. That housewife who protested she was born in Lyon was thinking about the difference between my lunch and hers. That foxy old Ayrab selling leather wallets knew I was almost as rich as the Caïd. That splayfooted garçon who brought me Bière la Cigogne, tasting like straw soup, wondered whether he might have sniped at me in Fedhala on November 8, 1942. For the first time I saw the cancer of the world outside of the United States, where we put nice sterile bandages over any open sores, and signs of Men Working by sewers.

I remember that a truck carried us to a staging area outside Casa. Around this camp was barbed wire to keep us and the Ayrabs on our respective sides. But such arrangements never work, because of the x factor of human curisoity.

"Yas, ya're repple-depple boys now. Ya'll get to know these sandy tents so well. Beds made of planks and chicken wire. Ten percent pass quota. Rushes to the pro station. Details we dream up just to keepya out of mischief. . . . And don't ya dare try to write ya mom about ya sorrows. That's what the army has censorship for. . . . The slip of a lip may sink a ship, but the slip of ya pen may upset the Congress of the United States."

I remember the Old Man of our repple-depple. He was a major. Once he'd been a lieutenant colonel. We heard

20

that at Salerno he got the idea of marching his battalion in parade formation up the beach. The battalion didn't exist any more, and neither did his lieutenant-colonelcy. So now he toughened up infantry replacements. He used to walk all over camp waving his stock and wearing his campaign ribbons. He loved to make inspections. He always wore leggins. Sometimes he carried a bull's pizzle to beat the Ayrabs with. And at all hours his voice came over his personal public-address system, through the whirling sand and the flapping lonely tents:

"Men, I know what war is . . . you don't . . . yet . . ."

Evenings he might be seen at the Automobile Club in Casa with a French WAC officer built like Danielle Darieux. But he had trouble with the parachutists in our repple-depple. They'd shoot holes in their tents when they couldn't get out on pass. Then our major would drive through the areas in a jeep, with a tommy gun pointed out of his sound truck.

At midnight the parachutists would take off under the barbed wire for Casa, for at reveille everybody answered to everybody else's name. In repple-depples the noncoms were only acting, with brassards pinned sheepishly to their arms. Even our first sergeants were only casuals themselves—privates. So they couldn't chew us out too much because we'd get them later at the Bar Montmartre or at the Select or at Pepita's, and we'd fix them up with Marie the Pig, who was malade.

I remember that at Casablanca it dawned on me that maybe I'd come overseas to die. Thus I was put for the first time in my life against a wall which I couldn't explain away by the logic of Main Street or the Weltanschauung of Samuel Goldwyn. I'd read of the sickness of Europe and shrugged my shoulders—Oh those furreners. It didn't occur to me that they were members of the human race. Only Americans were.

And I remember finding myself potentially expendable according to the Rules of Land Warfare, trapped in a war which (I said) was none of my making. So I began to think of my Life with the tenderness of a great artist. I clasped myself fondly to myself. I retreated into my own private world with the scream of a spinster when she sees a mouse. And I remember that I saw the preciousness of the gift of my Life, a crystal of green lymph, fragile and ephemeral. That's all I am, but how no-

21

accounting everything else is, in juxtaposition to the idea of Me! What does anything else matter? The world ceases to exist when I go out of it, and I have no one's assurance but my own for the reality of anything. Those who were machine-gunned in 1918—it's the same as though they had never been.

I remember that I began to think these things in Casablanca, though I didn't utter them. Therefore in a sense I went mad. Those who brood on death in wartime find that every pattern of life shrivels up. Decency becomes simply a window-shade game to fool the neighbors, honor a tremolo stop on a Hammond organ, and courage simply your last hypocrisy with yourself—a keeping up with the Joneses, even in a foxhole.

Oh my sweet Life, my lovely Life, my youth—all destined for a bullet. . . . Perhaps it were better if my mother hadn't borne me. I wondered whether my father really wanted children, or was feeling sorry for himself after a rough day at the office.

I remember in Casa going to the Gare on MP duty from the repple-depple to see that some of our joes got loaded on the forty-by-eights—forty hommes and eight chevaux. They were going to Oran, then to Algiers, then to Italy. We'd heard that General Patton had GI's walking about in the Algiers summer in OD's and neckties. Even the French could tell what was cooking.

"Forty American men in a boxcar, like cattle. Wish I had my camera. The American people ought to know about this. Wish I could write my congressman."

"They look like the French Foreign Legion."

"Are your canteens full, men?"

"The Ayrabs sell vin rouge all along the route."

"And buy the shirt offn your back."

"This is an outrage to American manhood."

"Americans are dying in Italy right now. The American people know that, don't they?"

"Yes, but do they care as long as we preserve their standard of living for a few more years? D'ya think they give one healthy you-know-what when they get up in the morning?"

"See the chaplain. . . ."

O my Life, my green ignorant dreaming Life! I said so long to them as the forty-by-eights left the Gare at Casa.

22

And when I remembered that soon it would be my turn to go to Oran, I didn't go back to the repple-depple, even though my pass said I should. We kept on our MP brassards, and big-timed it through Casablanca in our leggins. The bars didn't open till 1700 hours. So we went to the Vox Theatre, which the Red Cross was operating, and saw a movie in technicolor. It was all about the glory of the Army Air Forces, those same ones who at the repple-depple bitched about the calisthenics and the sleeping on chicken wire.

I remember waiting for it to get dark in Casa because as an American I'd all sorts of ideas about the Romance of Evening. I wanted a girl, but it was the American code to pick them up in twos, with your buddy. From high school on I'd doubledated. Going steady and gettin' a little lovin' weren't private affairs, because they were done in parked cars. I couldn't understand how a French sailor, and cold sober too, could walk up to a girl by herself, talk to her, and take her arm. No sense of shame at all. French love and all that. I thought that love, till you get married, was a business of foursomes. Otherwise it seemed something rather sneaky. You were expected to kid back and forth at some bathing beach or rollerdrome. Eventually you reached over somewhat sheepishly and the foursome broke up into twosomes.

"Nossir, nothin' in the world like American wimmin. Maybe a little independent, but then ya can't spend all ya time in bed."

"I never did understand those Lysol ads and all that talk about keeping yaself dainty."

"I knew a Polish beast once. She loved it."

"French girls do things that no decent American woman would.

"A chaplain once explained to me the difference between love and lust. But I can't remember exactly what he told me."

"All I know is, boy, when you're in love, everything you do together seems beautiful. . . ."

Those Casablancaises—it wasn't hard to get myself invited to their homes if I came armed with half my PX rations. Maman always claimed she wasn't born in North Africa, but of course France after June, 1940, wasn't fit to live in. Her girls went to the cinéma and to bicycle

23

club and to dancing school. They loved to be taught American songs by rote. That was one way to kill an afternoon. They liked to be called Jackie.

But I remember that the surer bets were in the bars. There the widows of French officers sipped crème de menthe. Not a one that didn't claim mon mari had been killed in Tunisie; not a one whose rank had ever been lower than commandant.

"Je suis seule ce soir avec mes rêves. . . ."

I remember how the fetid fragrance of Casablanca let up in the evenings. The oleanders came out with the bats. There was a hum and clatter from the New and Old Medinas. Little Ayrabs ceased their operating and promoting. The sound of donkeys wheezing and snorting and stalling died with their clop-clopping in the streets. Then I knew that I was far, far from the States, and that nothing I had brought with me of my own personal universe would make Casa anything other than Casablanca, a hinterland of secrecy, where German submarine captains came ashore in civvies and drank by my elbow in bars.

I remember that I first knew loneliness in Casablanca, the loneliness that engenders quietism. I was stripped of distractions and competitions since I no longer was a citizen of my own hermetical country, with ideas on progress, better homes, and sanitation. These thoughts often assailed me on the benches in the Parc Lyautey after sunset. My loneliness was that of a drunken old man sitting in a grotto and looking out on an icy sea at world's end. Then, sinking under a weight of time, I'd be constrained to draw down the head of her on the bench beside me. I'd kiss her in an attempt to focus all my longing and my uneasiness.

"Demain sans doute il fera beau, et après-demain, et la semaine prochaine."

"L'ombre s'enfuit. . . ."

Through her hair I counted the spines of barbed wire in the enclosure of the tank park. There the French kept old tanks lined up for a surprise review by General de Gaulle.

Along with the barren names of Cazes and Mogador and Mazagan I remembered birdlike ones, Henriette and Marie and Suzanne and a chorus of others who rode their bicycles by me on Saturday afternoons and made

24

me teach them to jitterbug. They were almost like pretty boys, those Casablancaises. They had the pinched brilliance of old paupers' garments, lovingly mended and darned.

"Darling," they said, "il faut gémir quand nous faisons l'amour. Et la prochaine fois je te prie de m'apporter un peu de chewing gum."

I remember Casa. . . .

SECOND PORTRAIT

Louella

HER PERMANENT was always a wreck in Naples. It was hard to retain either her dignity or her crispness in the simple act of walking along Via Roma.

She'd arise every morning with just a soupçon of hangover and lower herself tenderly into the fat green Fascist bathtub in her apartment. There she'd float among the perfumed suds till her head cleared and she could think lovely thoughts of all the good she was going to do that day. (First she'd put on her blue uniform of sveltest cut, stroking the Red Cross patch on her left shoulder. The other girls allowed themselves to get wilted during the day, to wear junky jewelry and divisional patches on their lapels. But not Louella. She was proud of her volunteer status, and she always tried to conduct herself the way an American officer should.)

Louella lay in her bathtub. A line of Emily Dickinson's sang through her head: Success is counted sweetest by those who least succeed. . . . Actually it hadn't much to do with the sultriness of a Neapolitan morning, but it gave her a lift. In her work, keeping up the morale of American GI's and officers, she had to be vital. Some of the other girls weren't. They'd done too much settlement work in Hartford slums; they'd come overseas with too starry eyes; and they'd collapse into Vassar cynicism when some lonely lieutenant colonel tried to make them in a jeep. Louella maintained that her sort were like the pioneer women in covered wagons who followed their men into the West. Names like Nancy Hanks, Ann Rutledge

25

and Jane Addams came to her mind. Thus at thirty-nine she'd learned a secret most American women were in danger of forgetting; war strips everyone down to their (his or her) essentials. Louella was fighting her own private war in Naples—just being a woman. Perhaps she'd never be a great one because she had too much heart and let people walk all over her. But Naples was her battlefield, and her American Red Cross uniform made her a modest Jeanne d'Arc with a smile and a coo for all comers.

Louella's apartment had belonged to a Fascist lawyer before AMG stuck him in the internee camp at Padula. He must have been very vain, like all Italian men, because he'd fastened a mirror over the bathtub. Louella looked up from her ablutions and smiled at herself. She'd been told she looked like Billie Burke in 1900. It was true. The dark gold hair she spent so much time keeping crisp, the too generous mouth, the slightly querulous chin. The circles under her pale blue eyes were deeper this morning. Louella wanted so much to go on the wagon, but then that would diminish her effectiveness as a morale factor. After all, when some poor flier came up from Foggia to see her, she couldn't very well ask him to see the town on lemonade. And she knew perfectly well that those little half-moons under her eyes were because she couldn't sleep, worrying about the state of the world.

She'd made airplane drivers her especial province. They were so pitifully young and lost, lemon-haired kids of twenty-four. And they seemed to be grateful for the stabilizing influence of a maturer woman. Younger girls would have abandoned themselves to mad fun on equal terms with fliers, but Louella instead played the part of one of those eighteenth-century women (just past the first flush) who held brilliant salons and had a profoundly moral influence on the young men who sat at their feet. She knew, with pardonable pride, that she was fulfilling a function unique in the Red Cross. An American woman is a symbol in the mind of any American soldier in Italy, but an American woman divorced of all selfish aims was unique in Naples of August, 1944.

When she first came to Naples, she'd tried to interest herself in the GI's because she felt it was her duty to do so. She'd read that they were the underprivileged, the proletariat of a democratic army. But somehow she

26

couldn't quite get to the GI's. All they wanted was to hold hands and talk about nothing. So gradually a conviction was born in Louella (which she never whispered to her dearest friends) that, though they were good kids and all that, the GI's were just a little . . . vulgar. Perhaps God had intended her for something, well, on a little higher level. And then the officers were much lonelier because their commissions had put them into unnaturally exalted positions. Wasn't she perhaps helping those who were the worst off? GI's have buddies and signorinas all over the place, but most American officers are isolated and sensitive. Which reminded her of that ineffable line: If I can stop one heart from breaking. . . .

The war had been the consummation of Louella's life. Like most people who are a teensy bit out of the ordinary, she'd waited thirty-nine years for something into which she could throw herself wholly. She liked to compare her life up to now to a high-powered engine wasted in lifting matches. And now (changing the metaphor) she was living in the most sorrowful time the world had ever seen, a time to sink her teeth into. She'd started her Public Ministry by having officers to her lovely home in Cambridge, giving them those little snacks they couldn't get at Fort Devens. The way they'd smiled at her during her candlelight suppers had given her a priestesslike ecstasy of sacrific and service. She was forgetting herself in the sorrows of others, than which there is no more cathartic annihilation of self.

But gradually the type of officer who came to her Sunday Evenings at Home began to give her qualms. She'd always been a woman of unusual sensibilities, and she smelled something phony. Instead of the gallant second lieutenants who used to come around for her lobster salad, who had high ideas and talked vital things till electric currents chased up and down her spine, she'd observed that she was now entertaining rather smug older officers with big rear ends. They were forever talking about how they'd give their eyeteeth to get overseas, but they never seemed to go. They cursed the Pentagon, which (they said) had emasculated old warhorses like themselves into the chairborne infantry. Now Louella, whatever her faults (and she was by no means perfect), wasn't exactly slow. She decided that these officers were cowards who were making a good thing out

27

of the war. They had all the protected prestige of the uniform and none of its trials. In fact, they were having the time of their lives in the foxholes of the 1st Service Command, drawing per diem, eating C-rations at the Copley Plaza. And all the while they cursed draft dodgers and strikers and criticized the slow conduct of the war in North Africa. She got so that she couldn't look at them without that nausea that visits women of scruple. They were nothing but thugs got up like an Arrow collar ad. She'd close her eyes at the head of her buffet, clutch her napkin, and think that the boys *she* could serve weren't in the United States any more. They were dying in Africa and looking at the dirty Arab women and wondering if everybody had forgotten them. Louella felt faint with pity.

So she'd joined the Red Cross as a volunteer, with the stipulation that they send her overseas immediately.

Louella got out of her tub, dried herself, and stepped into her immaculate uniform. Dry cleaning in Naples was unpredictable, but they loved her so at the QM laundry that she got priorities on all her garments. She'd pointed out to the officer in charge that, whereas a Negro truck driver didn't have to bother about his appearance, it was *her* stock in trade. He'd agreed with her feelingly because he came from Alabama.

She decided to look in on her roommate Ginny, a pitiful little thing from Detroit. It was Ginny's job in the Red Cross to serve coffee and doughnuts to all airplanes landing wounded at Capodichino.

The shutters weren't down in Ginny's room. The implacable light of Naples streamed in. Sandflies made a dancing nimbus before the open window. Louella guessed that Ginny had probably got drunk when she'd come off duty at the airport, had poured herself into bed, and was now in the troubled sleep of a hangover. Ginny lay under her mosquito netting, her hair over her face, Tears lay in the pools under her eyes. That was just like Ginny, to go out and get tight, give herself to some GI she felt sorry for, then come home and cry her silly little eyes out. For a long time Louella had wanted to have a good taking down of hair with her roommate, but Ginny'd always shied away from woman-to-woman confidences. Perhaps she'd been scared by a big Negro while doing settlement work.

28

Louella stood at the head of Ginny's bed, aware of how trim and spruce she herself looked, while that dizzy little thing lay there with her tears leaving gashes in what rouge she hadn't washed off.

"Morning, stinky," Ginny said, reaching for the handkerchief beside her cigarettes on the night table.

"Hullo, darling. Did you pour coffee for your basket cases at the airport last night? Then did you meet some strapping staff sergeant and go off and get tight with him?"

"I wasn't drunk," Ginny said.

She lit a cigarette and offered Louella one, which was gracefully declined. Louella never wanted her roommate to feel she had to be nice to her. After all, she'd made the first overtures, which Ginny had repulsed in the most pleasant manner. But Ginny began to cry in earnest now, puffing on her cigarette and sobbing in a manner that reminded Louella of Italian opera.

"I'm about due for a section eight," Ginny said. "If I can get one from the Red Cross. Stinky, I can't stand it much longer. . . . Those poor little bastards. Flown in from the evac hospitals. . . . They've got legs off . . . arms off . . . wounds all over them. . . . And they just lie there on the stretchers and grin at you. . . . I've never seen such eyes. . . . I try to pour the coffee, but my hands get shaky, like I had d.t.'s . . . and I haven't. I don't drink as much as you do, stinky."

"Some girls can hold it better than others," Louella said softly.

She was of the opinion that a reproof can be delivered in the mildest tone. That was part of the tradition of a great lady. But then anything subtle would be wasted on Ginny.

"God, I'm not soft," Ginny said, her sobs strangling off. "But it just knocks hell out of me, stinky, what I see on those hospital planes. I'd settle for an assignment in Rome, giving instructions on shopping tours from behind a counter. . . . This is something I just don't understand. They're so *good*, those kids. What harm did they ever do? And they lie there, terribly, terribly hurt. And if they're able to talk, all they want is to discuss upstate New York and the crops and their mothers and their girls. Such sweet faces . . . not at all bitter . . . American men are so good-looking."

"American men," Louella said, "have understood very

29

little about the world in which they live. They're new to anguish. Europeans have already lived with it. Europeans are concerned simply with existing. Americans have always had enough and to spare. . . . Naturally Americans are baffled by combat. It doesn't have much to do with the stock market ticker and that dash for the eight-ten after kissing your wife. . . . But they'll get over it after a time. There have been wars before, and men have recovered from them."

"That's not my point, stinky," Ginny said. "The whole business seems so wrong . . . so fiendish. No human being should have to suffer the way those kids do. Life itself is so natural and so good. Those kids love life as much as you and I . . . more maybe . . . I don't know why you came overseas, stinky. I did because I was bored in the States. Well, I'm not bored any more. I bit off more than I could chew. Now I understand how Jesus Christ felt on the cross. . . ."

"Watch that talk," Louella said, tapping her foot clinically. "First thing you know, you'll be in the nut ward of the Forty-fifth with a Messiah complex."

"No danger," Ginny said, squashing out her cigarette and tucking in her mosquito netting. "I'm a tough nut, stinky. I don't cry much. And I don't know what it is to feel sorry for myself. . . . But I'm troubled . . . terribly troubled."

"You probably gab and think too much while you're serving your coffee and doughnuts. Wounded men like quiet. Just smile, squeeze their hands, and pass on. And are you quite sure you don't permit greater familiarities?"

"If it would help them any," Ginny said, raising her voice, "I'd let them put their hands inside my blouse. Some of them try to, you know. And if anyone who isn't out cold wants to kiss me, why, I let him. Wouldn't you?"

"Dear, it's possible to excite wounded soldiers more than you help them."

Ginny sank back on her pillow and looked through the netting at the ceiling. She'd stopped crying now, and her sleepless little face looked like rice pudding fallen on a dirty floor.

"Go away, stinky. We don't see eye to eye. What the hell do you think you're doing in Naples, anyhow?"

"Each has her own ideas of service, darling," Louella said, turning. "And at the Last Judgment we'll all get a
30

chance to state our cases. . . . Don't presume to judge
other human beings, dear. I myself have frequently been
mistaken. Get some sleep."

With a sigh she went around the room picking up
Ginny's slip and bra and uniform that seemed to have
been stripped off her by a cyclone. She put them neatly on
a chair and shut down the blinds. At her approach the
sandflies broke apart from their cloud. The hum of
Naples reigned in the now shadowed room. Ginny turned
over on her face and entombed her cheek in the crook of
her arm. She had a wispy little body and skinny shoulders. She appealed to the GI's the way a signorina does
on Via Roma—a certain one-night-stand air about her,
a certain shrillness in her voice that chimed in with the
stridency of wartime Naples in August, 1944. Louella was
big enough to pity Ginny. Others would have slapped her
face and told her to go back to where she belonged. But
Louella'd learned something of frailty and charity. It
took all kinds, even though the saying was a desperate
cliché.

The vein in her left temple was throbbing when she let
herself out of her apartment. Ginny's selfish tirade had
got her worked up a little. That was one of Louella's
major faults, that she was more sensitive to situations
than they demanded. She always tried to descend to
other people's levels instead of insisting that they meet
her on her own. It was an exhausting philosophy of life,
but she had an inkling that, after she'd left them, people
gave vent to an admiration and a veneration they never
dared show to her face.

The Italian elevator carried her dubiously down into
the cortile. She pulled down her blouse and marched out
into Piazza Carità. The heat at nine in the morning was
like a club in her face; she had difficulty breathing. In
spite of her feeling of incipient suffocation she put on
her bravest smile. It was this smile which some of the
air force had called a violet floating in a tornado. Louella
strode along. She carried her head and its blue overseas
cap like a filly she'd loved and ridden as a child. There
was a spring in her step. Neapolitan women turned and
looked at her. This had been one of Louella's few grati-
fications in Naples, that homage paid her by the Italian
women.

Before crossing Piazza Carità Louella had to wait a

31

moment. Crossing a street was about the most dramatic thing a woman can do in modern life. Louella felt that to traverse a street in Naples of August, 1944, was almost as heroic as crossing the Volturno. Finally she spotted an open space in the truck convoy that made daytime in Naples one long roar. She took a long and dainty run. She'd always been fleet-footed, but this time she simply skittered across the street.

There was a screech of brakes. Louella thought her last moment had come. A tech five leaned out over the windshield of his jeep; there was a panicky grin on his face, and he was steadying himself against the wheel.

"Ya almost went to join my late Aunt Minnie, baby," he said.

Louella braced herself for a gentle but forceful reply. But then she saw the name stenciled below the windshield of the jeep. Most of the legends painted on jeeps amused her—names of girls and little maxims in English, French, or Italian. But this jeep bore the two simple words Wet Dream. So she hunched up her shoulders and marched into Piazza Carità. She now knew what she'd long felt from conviction—that many American men, especially the GI's, had frightful manners. She hoped they'd learn something from Europe. She saw finally that she was intellectually justified in preferring the company of officers.

She entered the cool corridor of the Red Cross Annex. One thing she would say for Italian architecture was that they certainly knew how to build—and to last. The palazzi were iceboxes in winter, but in summer they had solidity, coolness, and spaciousness. Red Cross girls working in Naples were billeted in this annex. Except Louella.

She climbed the stairs and entered the snack bar, which was just opening its screen doors. Here she always started her day with coffee and buns. She pulled down her blouse and pushed the screen door to. The room was dark and calm. At the ticket desk Adriana, the Neapolitan who sold chits, sat with her usual squaw frown. She was a dark hunched little thing with a soupçon of a mustache.

"Buon giorno, Adriana," Louella said cheerily.

Louella'd learned six or seven words of Italian, which she sprinkled into her conversation like paprika. She didn't really care for the language, which made her think of gooey kisses pressed by some greaser on the neck of his sweating mistress. And she saw no good reason to learn it because the Italians were a conquered people. The sooner they learned the clean intricacies of English, the better for them. There was also something sinister about Italian, in which they could spit out ten words to your one and talk you down by sheer breathing power. Louella had nothing against Italian culture; that was fine in its place, but she didn't need to learn the language to appreciate *Rigoletto* and look at a painting by Botticelli. Yet somehow it seemed to her a gracious gesture to fling out a few words in his own language to every Italian she met. It would remind him that noblesse oblige wasn't quite dead in the world, even if the Neapolitans didn't wash regularly and had far far too many children.

"I said buon giorno, Adriana."

The girl looked up from pressing her brown forehead.

"Good morning, mees," she said.

Louella smiled and walked to a near-by table. All the Neapolitan waiters loved her. She had only to sit down and one of them would bring her coffee and a bun. She never had to stand in line the way the officers and nurses did. And now Pinuccio brought her a potsherd cup of coffee and a dry raisin bun. He'd told her he was a student at the University of Naples, but of course she hadn't believed a word of it. Italians were always telling her in broken English of what they had been and of what their army might have done. She didn't see why they had to lie to her that way. Pinuccio had one of those long olive faces that seem already dead of weariness and grief. This lack of spunk was what Louella loathed in Italian men, especially the good-looking ones. They were much too effeminate. And they had the kind of cringing good manners of a Negro, when he's afraid you'll push him off the sidewalk—which you won't if he knows his place. Louella guessed the reason why Italy'd lost the war. Too much inbreeding and not the virility to support their culture.

"Grazie," Louella said. "And cheer up, Pinuccio. It's not as bad as you think it is."

He left her with a look that she knew how to interpret only from her long reading of the classics. She suspected Pinuccio of secretly desiring her. He had a passionate mouth and slender hands lightly coated with hair. Louella knew that Italian men weren't to be trusted sexually. His

33

cankered look told her that he'd like to posses her, then put a knife between her shoulders. She shivered slightly and sipped her coffee. She wasn't at home in the arcana of love; she preferred the way American men had of laying their cards on the table. They got drunk and threw themselves all over you, and you could say either yes or no.

She drank her coffee slowly, with a sense that energy for her day's catalogue of good works was beginning to flow back into her body. She watched the Neapolitans mopping up the floor. They wore small mustaches, by which they attempted to ape matinee idols of twenty years ago, some in their green fatigue coveralls that they'd begged or stolen from the Americans. She'd never think of the word parasite in the future without modifying it by the adjective, Italian. She hardly ever saw a Neapolitan on the streets without American shoes. And those who weren't fully dressed had an OD GI undershirt. Louella laughed a little bitterly and wondered what the American taxpayers would think if they knew where their money was going. Not on the backs of American soldiers. How Karl Marx would have loved Naples in August, 1944! Practically a universal distribution of the world's goods—and upon people who would bite the hand that fed them.

Louella sighed. She saw bearing down upon her, like a corvette with shortness of steam, the American Red Cross field director for Naples. Bessie McCloskey symbolized to Louella the sort of thwarted old maid who sublimates all her repressed love urges into a passion for organization, a delight in seeing other people made miserable by bureaucracy. Bessie plumped her jittering body into the chair opposite Louella, adjusted her pince-nez, and began her old act of finger shaking. Louella put on her most patient smile and thought to herself that Bessie deserved a lecture fellowship in the Cathedral of Saint John the Divine.

"Oh here you are," Bessie panted. "How in God's name does a body get hold of you? Do I have to make an appointment with your receptionist? Why don't you go to Capri if you want to take a vacation?"

"Having trouble with your asthma, darling?" Louella said.

"Asthma, hell. . . . Now you listen to me, Louella.

34

. . . Your club at Aversa is a shambles, a perfect shambles. If you don't want to work for the Red Cross, why don't you pack up and go home?"

"I believe you called my club a shambles?" Louella said with tender hauteur. "Perhaps you'll explain. There are lots who claim it's the prettiest little club in Italy. . . ."

"Through no fault of yours, my fine lady. You've got good assistants and Italians who aren't afraid of working up a sweat. . . . But you don't seem to realize that Red Cross clubs run on programs. You can't expect American officers to entertain themselves. They're not that far civilized. You must schedule events and keep scheduling 'em till you're blue in the face. Otherwise you're going to find all the air corps joes shooting crap on the front terrace, as I found them last night."

"Oh, spying?" Louella said, looking out from under her lashes.

Nothing was easier than to lash McCloskey into mania by needling.

"It's my job to spy. . . . And now this spy will tell you a mouthful, since you're asking for it with your nonsense. You're the worst Red Cross worker in Italy. You're using the Red Cross, which God knows receives criticism enough, simply for your own joy ride. You think you're running a house party here and that you can invite your own guests. . . . I'm just an old hen with no illusions, but I tell you that it's immoral of you to use the Red Cross to play Lady Bountiful. As a program director it's your business and your duty to have something doing all the time at your club, specifically stated on your bulletin board, even if it's only tiddly-winks in the lounge. If you're not resourceful enough to do that, by God I'll take steps to have orders cut shipping you out of this theater. Now how about it? You've really put me on the spot, I can tell you."

"Louder, please," Louella said, pushing back her cup and rising. "You've missed your vocation, darling. You'd have done better in a nunnery, shoving around a lot of tittering novices. Then you could wear a swastika on your veil and an SS brassard on your sleeve . . ."

"I want your answer tomorrow," McCloskey shrilled, still shaking her finger.

Louella left the snack bar at a speed greater than she'd have liked. Adriana at the desk looked up from counting her chits, and Louella fancied that a spiteful smile crossed that muddy face—just the way Italy had stabbed France in the back. Louella descended the stairs around the glass elevator shaft. She felt something inside her crying, the way French poets say it does. Yet she'd suffered before and probably would again. It was the lot of every extraordinary person to be misunderstood and harassed by the ordinary. The more you were capable of giving to the world, the more the world picked at you.

She went back to her apartment and laid herself down on her bed. The heat of Naples pressed like a vise round her head, and the coffee was making her heart pound till she could feel it in her temples. She got up, went to the bathroom, and took a dose of phenobarbital. A stout graying little major at the Fifth General dispensary had given it to her for her sleeplessness when she first came to Naples.

With the phenobarbital Louella poured herself a glass of vermouth because she never trusted Neapolitan drinking water, even when it came out of the udder of a Lyster Bag. She knew that the sedative would soothe and relax her the way love and music did others. Returning to her bed, she lay down on its fully dressed. She wished she could cry the way the other girls did, but she was incapable of feeling sorry for herself. Soon she fell asleep.

Like most intelligent people, Louella rarely dreamed. Since her training in psychiatry in college no symbols ever visited her in sleep. She slept the sleep of a little girl who has nothing on her conscience. People had told her that while she was asleep her face took on an expression of incredible rapture, and Louella had modestly replied with her theory that when people were asleep or drunk their souls came to sit like shy wrens on their faces. This was the only flight into fancy she'd ever permitted herself.

When she awoke, her watch said three o'clock. The torpor of afternoon Naples was at its peak; the hum in the city below had subsided because the Latin population gets off the streets from the sun, as they did from bombardments. Louella's body was drenched. There was still a slight aftertaste of the vermouth she'd swallowed, and a muted jangling in her nerves from the opiate.

Nevertheless the bitterness of her morning had died, and she thanked God for some vitality in her that allowed her to cast off ugliness. Otherwise she'd have long ago been dead. She guessed she had that magnanimity of mind that Shakespeare must have possessed—the ability to come through any situation, understand it, but retain intact the integrity of her soul. What had she learned overseas? To forgive. She lifted her arms with a soft smile and lit a cigarette.

She bounded out of bed, washed her face, and redid it. In Naples she was allowing herself a brighter shade of crimson on her lips than she'd thought permissible at home. When in Rome . . . and Naples wasn't so far south. . . .

Ginny had gone out, her room had been straightened up by the signorina. Louella never could find out where Ginny went after sleeping, before it was time to return to the airport and serve coffee and doughnuts to the hospital planes. Possibly Ginny tied a bandanna round her head, put on sandals, and went out and leaned carelessly on Via Roma, pretending to be an Italian girl. Perhaps it was a trifle unkind, but Louella had too broad a knowledge of the world not to see that those women who affected an unbounded love of humanity were simply disguising an indiscriminate and insatiable sexual appetite. This could be the only explanation of why Ginny had so many GI friends from every state in the Union and from quite a few parts of the United Kingdom. She'd even brought a French soldier to the apartment. It rather looked like the vast humanitarianism of Mary Magdalene.

The signorina housemaid was still loitering around. Louella knew all her tricks: she'd pretend she wanted to clean up the room. Actually what she did was to help herself to Louella's cigarettes, bathe in Louella's bathtub with fragrant American bath salts. And possibly the signorina spied on all Louella's activities, of which reports were then sent to the Germans in North Italy.

Seeing that the signorina was watching her golden pencil of lipstick, Louella took pains to hide it. Then she went out. She knew full well that ten minutes after she'd locked her apartment door the signorina would be entertaining some fisherman from the Bay of Naples on the couch. They'd jabber at each other in dialect, laugh at the Allies, hang Mr. Roosevelt's picture upside down, and have one another till supper time.

The crowds on Via Roma made it seem like pushing your way into a haystack coming at you full tilt. Louella knew that the harbor was full of LCI's, that three American divisions were in rest areas around Naples. Everybody said that there was to be an invasion of southern France, though for military security they never discussed this, except with their best friends. Naples was always a tense hot city, but in the past week Louella'd been aware of a lull like that before a twister.

Though she loved the carnival movement of Via Roma, she never walked on it unescorted after dark because all the Allied soldiery were drunk from sundown to curfew time. You got propositioned twenty times in one block or were in danger of being hauled up an alley, and the CID found your body a week later and said it was the work of black market operators.

But Louella preserved her entity on Via Roma, walking like Saint Elizabeth of Hungary, looking neither to right nor left, but scattering hypothetical roses. She was whistled at, but she smiled understandingly—after all she was an American woman, and these boys were lonely. It indicated that if Bessie McCloskey didn't appreciate her, there were lots who did.

Yet an Olympian pose of Via Roma in August, 1944, would have exhausted Katharine Cornell, and Louella found herself wilting by the time she'd reached the Galleria Umberto. She turned in at the little concrete posts and trod the pavement of the arcade. She'd always liked the Galleria. Even if all the glass had been bombed out of it, there was something sort of darling about the place, like a baroque subway station. She'd often done the shops, though of course she'd never bought any of the crude oils of Mount Vesuvius or the junky jewelry that GI's bought at twenty times its value for their girls in Montana. Louella just doted on the horrible blotchy pillows and ottomans lettered with MOTHER (sometimes misspelled by the Neapolitan seamstress) or great vulgar samplers stitched with the red bull of the 34th Division or the mosque of the Fifth Army.

She sat down in an outdoor café and ordered a vermouth. Near her were some GI's in combat boots, their shirts open, wearing, against their sweat, neckerchiefs studded with their divisional insignia. They all had their feet up on the cane chairs and were cursing and railing.

They deliberately tried to look like Bill Mauldin cartoons. Louella'd tried to understand combat infantrymen, but she found them unnecessarily bitter and unappreciative. They seemed to think that they were the only ones suffering in this world. Once she'd tried to talk to a second lieutenant of the 45th about the world and the times, but after groping all over her daintiness he'd subsided into his gin and passed out.

She saw the seamy side of life in the Galleria Umberto. It was the burning glass of Naples. Louella sat and drank her vermouth with an adventurous little thrill, thanking her stars she'd been put on earth in 1944, with cultural background to appraise all this. Life, Life was what she got in the Galleria Umberto.

Stimulated by the sun and the crowds around her, she ordered another vermouth and went into a sort of ecstasy. It was a delight known to oriental mystics, at which one arrives after all fear is conquered and one resigns oneself to the idea of being just a drop of human consciousness. One's heightened perceptions give one a superior detachment, and one watches the other drops with a clinical scrutiny, knowing that all this has been before and will be time and again.

Louella snapped out of her raptus. By her table an Italian child was standing with the shy yet intense presence of one who asks alms. It was scarcely more than a baby. It was wearing what looked like a potato sack, had a wilted flower in its gummy hair, and its tiny dirty feet had already been spread from pressing the scorching pavements of Naples. In its smeared fingers it extended a placard:

THIS GIRL IS AN ORPHAN BECAUSE OF ALLIED
BOMBARDMENTS. WILL YOU HELP HER?

Now Louella had social consciousness. She wasn't one of those Boston old ladies who refuse to go to movies or read books which show the world as it is. She hated people who shove their noses into the sand of illusion and say that the war is none of their affair. But one had to make distinctions in one's charity. Nine out of ten beggars are panhandlers. Louella found it an excellent rule of thumb that the really needy are too proud ever to do what this little girl was doing. So she summoned up her sweetest smile for the little girl, returned her stare, and said:

"Poor, poor moppet. You see, dear, you're not old enough to realize that the Allies *had* to bomb Naples. The Germans were here, and Naples is a very important port. Some day when you grow up, you'll see how cruel and complicated the world is, dear . . ."

The little girl approached her placard to Louella's face and began to wrench at her uniform. Something like tears formed in the huge black eyes, but Louella wasn't taken in by this act. Not a bit. But rationalization wasn't much use. Louella always ended by being guided by her heart, no matter how intellectual she tried to be. She clicked her tongue sympathetically several times, dived into her shoulder bag, and took out one lira.

Still the little girl remained, holding out her hand and examining the one-lira note speculatively. It always embarrassed Louella when the recipients of her mercy hung around. She hoped the little girl wasn't going to make a scene and start kissing her skirt or anything lurid like that. Louella liked to do good works and keep them a secret between God and herself.

"Gimme sigaretta," said the little girl suddenly.

"Now, dear, really! Don't try to pull that on me. You're already stunted and wizened enough as it is. . . . And isn't that the Italians for you? They haven't got enough food, but they're scrounging chewing gum. They have no cigarettes, but every last one of them has an American lighter. . . . Now my dear, I advise you to go back to the good nuns at the orphanage. Tell them the nice American lady said to give you a good bath and put you to bed . . . buona sera . . . run along now, dear."

When the waif had gone, Louella treated herself to another vermouth. Her family used to talk about how the Other Half lived. In Naples everybody was the Other Half. Her sympathies had been stretched like an elastic band, and she'd return to the States with a depth of understanding and a compassion that might startle a few of her friends, who were still fighting for nylon hosiery and getting up concerts for ship-wrecked merchant seamen.

She observed a feverish activity in the bar, behind the metal coffee machines. A cluster of Neapolitans were bartering and gibbering and making with their hands and

40

exchanging lire with someone at the center of their circle. Louella stood up with her glass in her hand and saw that it was an American GI. Out of his haversack he took bars of Palmolive, cigarettes, chewing gum, flints and wicks, lighter fluid, a fountain pen, a watch, and two boxes of K-ration. All these he sold covertly and swiftly to the Italians, who scattered when his small store was exhausted. Then he had a drink at the bar, counted his receipts, and left. He was a typical joe in bright combat boots, with that smooth easy way she liked in American men.

"How much'd you make?" Louella hailed him.

"Quiet for Chrissakes! Twelve thousand lire."

She sat down with the gay laugh of a conspirator, applied herself to her vermouth, and fanned herself. Yes, here in Naples the economic unbalance of the world was being evened out, and by the business acumen of the GI. This private was getting sixty dollars a month, a pitiful pittance for facing gunfire and for buying anything at the frightful Italian prices. And yet he had a typically American kindness: he'd seen the stark need of the Italians for things he could buy at his PX for next to nothing. It was this speculative free enterprise that had made America great. She made a mental note to write her Wall Street friends how finally she'd come to understand economics better than it's taught in the colleges. Now she could be reasonably sure that there were two great laws at work in this world—the moral law, and the law of supply and demand.

A plump Neapolitan woman came sweeping around the tables with a broom such as witches ride. She wore a dress of frayed black cotton which by the afternoon sunlight silhouetted her pregnancy. In her pierced ears she wore rings and a chain with a cross hung around her doughy neck. Occasionally she would spit on the pavement of the Galleria to lay the dust. Her shoes were clogs of roped cord which kept slipping off her ankles. She worked slowly and haphazardly; otherwise Louella would have been upset at a woman so far gone exerting herself in the brutal August sunlight. Louella didn't think it very hygienic the way the woman, for all her condition, would sink grunting to her knees and pluck up the cigarette butts under the tables. These she would consign to her pockets and continue sweeping. Louella wondered if she smoked them or sold them. She knew of the fantastic Neapolitan practice of breaking down thousands of cigarette .butts into a can and selling the result as pipe tobacco. But this sweeper with the brown face and the knotted hair had one touching compensation in her drudgery. As she worked she sang unembarrassedly one of those tender Neapolitan songs that are weighted with poverty and love. Louella knew that great art comes out of sorrow. On this score she worried for America. We must guard ourselves in America, Louella knew: when we banish poverty and disease, we must take pains not to banish genius too. This idea struck her as so original that she ordered another vermouth.

It was getting toward sunset. And in Louella's drinking there was something almost Persian. The poet Hafiz tells us that whoever can't drink can't love. If perhaps overseas Louella drank a little too much, alcohol brought to her an outlet and an expression that were perhaps the only things her nature lacked. In conversation she was eloquent, and her fruition had been reached in the very human act of being surrounded by a small coterie, exchanging stimulating ideas with them over full glasses in which the ice chimed a punctuation to her conversation pieces. That was Louella's world and she knew that out of such worlds of people getting together and drinking and talking every worthwhile thing had been born. She hadn't much patience with the lonely and recondite spirits who pretend to rare gifts in order to camouflage this essential inability to get along with the rest of the human race.

Two figures bore down on Louella, slicing across the orange motes that makes sunset in the Galleria a flood of orange dust. One was an old violinist with only sockets where his eyes should have been. His body was sheathed in unclean pitted flesh suggesting that his youth hadn't been circumspect, or that he belonged on Molokai. He was guided by a boy in shorts and sandals. The son had a mysterious dark beauty that made Louella uneasy, since she felt that no man had the right to look that way. Beauty in men is only embarrassing. The music of the blind violinist was frightful to Louella's ear. Children who stretch a catgut string across a cigar box get better results. Louella found gross fraud in anyone's attempting

42

to fob such dreadful sounds off on the public, preying on its sympathies because he couldn't see. She tried to keep from shuddering as the scrawny scarecrow leered at her from out of its empty caverns, and as a special tribute scratched out Stardust. She felt herself in the presence of something obscene, at the revels of a kobold and a pixie. Her stomach turned, and she was about to rise from the wicker table and leave her vermouth when two newcomers slumped at her table. They waved away the blind fiddler and his son, who started to pass a plate. They threw fifty lire into it.

"Via!"

The musician padded off led by his boy and Louella turned to thank her new companions. They were both airplane drivers, and they smiled at her a little drunkenly because the setting sun hit them square in the eyes. They wore their caps on the backs of their skulls, sloppy squashed caps that looked as though they'd been jumped up and down on. Both were captains. Little silver Capri bells jingled on their leather field jackets. On their backs was stenciled a nude girl in color who flew through the air dropping bombs. On their feet, which they'd trussed up on neighboring chairs, were boots of softest leather, such as cowboys wear. Ginny used to say that airplane drivers never looked like human beings, but like goggled men from Mars. Louella knew better. Uninhibited children on the ground, at their controls they became serious technicians controlling colossal steel birds that dragoned through the air and dropped death on Jerry factories. She loved the faces of airplane drivers, so fresh and smiling, unsoured by their grim task. They were never bitter like the infantrymen, and they were never over twenty-four, even if they were full colonels. They were the sort of kids you saw in drugstores who drank cokes, listened to juke-boxes and whistled at the girls. They were *good*. They'd been thrust out of high school fraternities into a war. They were the sort of tow-headed fellows who are the backbone of American manhood. Thinking was a pussy disease of modern life but the fliers of the United States Army Air Force hadn't caught the contagion.

Louella felt so old and mellow and wise and she leaned forward over her vermouth and smiled at them.

"Roger," the first captain said, and called for three vermouths.

"Flak, flak, flak," his buddy said, and reached over and patted Louella on her wrist.

She didn't flinch or go prissy because she knew she was in the presence of that sacred and awful thing, American Loneliness, akin to the face of Abraham Lincoln. She knew that Americans were the saddest people in the world in time of war because they were Magnificent Provincials. That was why every American soldier who wasn't queer had to have his buddy with whom he shared a stream of consciousness in itself meaningless but which added up to all the nobility and isolation of a young and idealistic people thrown into death and destruction.

"Wilco, Roger."

Airplane drivers had a language all their own, a patois compounded of machine vocabulary, of the tension and relaxation alternating in those spells in which each tried to work off his nervousness between missions. Louella understood it with the reverence of a scholar. But this was a living language with a syntax of agony. She beamed at them both as though to say she wanted them to feel right at home with her, consider her their big sister.

The first captain was pretty high. He slumped into his chair and inhaled one vermouth after another, mumbling "flak" and "Roger" like an incantation. He was obviously the more poetic and sensitive of the two, and the more passive, since equals rarely mate in friendship or in love. But he was also at a plane of self-communion and negation into which Louella was too perceptive and reverent of human isolation to thrust herself. There was nothing she could do for him tonight. So she applied herself to the second captain who was looking at her appreciatively. Noticing the gold band on his finger she asked him about his wife.

"Oh that bitch, that lovely little bitch," he said. "She hasn't written for three months. And I'm over here in this arsehole of the earth eating myself out and wondering what she's doing. Is she turning into a Victory Girl? I'll kill the slut if I ever find out anything. . . . Three months she hasn't written, and she used to write twice a day. . . . One V-mail and one air mail. . . . I'm going crazy. . . . I'll turn myself in for pilot fatigue and get myself sent home. . . . If you could see her, baby."

"Louella," she corrected gently.

She was working herself into a sweat of empathy. All
44

day long she'd longed for an airplane driver for whom she could do something unselfish.

"Louella, she worked in the PX at Luke Field. . . . If you could have seen her, the way she used to stand behind the cash register. . . . Just like a cute mouse. And when the jukebox came on, the way her eyes'd sparkle. . . . All she wanted was to dance and eat ice cream sodas. . . . But what a bitch not to write to me in three months."

"She's true to you. I know it," Louella said, laying her hand on his leather sleeve; he put his own over it and moved a little closer to her. "I swear she's true by all that's fine in American womanhood."

"Three months," the captain said. "I married her quick. I was graduating from flight training, and I didn't want somebody else to snap her up. . . . Three months she hasn't written. . . . But if I find she's using my allotment checks for something else than that little house . . ."

"She couldn't, she wouldn't," Louella cried in a passion of righteousness.

The captain buried his face in one hand and tightened his clutch on her with the other. His sleeves were half-rolled to the elbows; the Capri bells on his jacket jingled mockingly. Louella knew that he was sobbing inside. He was a handsome lithe man. And the situation came clear in her mind, and her pity for him moistened the edges of the whole sorry portrait. And Louella decided that the greatest of war crimes is the bitchery of a wife when her husband is far from her. Louella imagined stunning scenes in which she gave the cheap painted little wife a piece of her mind, a piece of the mind of all the decent American women in the world. Right now the minx was probably out in an Arizona roadhouse, spending the captain's money on some new OC out for an evening's kicks. She saw them laughing through the din of the band, drinking champagne and kissing. . . .

It was dark now, and all three of them walked unsteadily along Via Roma with their arms about one another's necks. They were all crying and wondering who started this war anyhow. Louella was the steadiest of the three. She steered them through the crowds. Both kissed her good night at the door of her apartment in Piazza Carità. They wanted to come up and have a party, but Louella didn't want Ginny to start thinking things.

45

In her bedroom, after draping her mosquito netting with an insouciant hiccough, she poured herself a nightcap of vermouth and shook a phenobarbital capsule into it. She lay quite motionless in her bed and felt two tears scamper down her cheeks. There was a roaring in the merciless Neapolitan night, and she saw the red and green lights of a transport plane track through the sullen air out Vesuvius way.

"Roger," she said, and hiccoughed again.

SECOND PROMENADE

(Fedhala)

I REMEMBER that there's an American cemetery at Saint Jean de Fedhala, twenty-seven kilometers up the coast north of Casa. The graves are plotted in neat rows. I saw how close and still bodies can be laid together in the earth. Over each rectangle a white cross spreads its rafter arms. Most of the crosses have dogtags affixed to them, giving each its relief from anonymity. But walking lightly among the crosses and looking for the names of my friends, I found some unmarked. Underneath must be the bodies of those who were blown apart by artillery or drowned while still wading ashore, or who didn't wear their dogtags. I remember that the body of a priest lies next to a pfc.

The sky at Fedhala is the color of slate, and the air of Fedhala is of that musky heaviness I knew only in North Africa. The atmosphere lies like a shroud over the continent. Perhaps from this comes the thick lost mystery of Africa, which teased my mind, particularly after sunset. It's a strange air to lie in for all the time when your nose was used to the damp of New England or to the winds that congeal the Loop. With X-ray eyes I pierced the layer of loam blanketing the bodies and saw them lying there, each in his mattress cover, staring up at me. They didn't have the finished peace of ordinary dead, embalmed in funeral homes. There was a rigidity and bitterness about them as though a cop had surprised them in the orgasm of life. There was something of un-

46

finished business about all of these Fedhala American dead. To their spirits, smothered underground, the air there, as in all military cemeteries, was charged with question marks. I knew that the air could never be static above Saint Jean de Fedhala. A military cemetery never knows peace.

Near the American section the provincial French of Fedhala have buried their dead—daughters who died of the whooping cough at eight, old women who came from France for expansion and trade after Maréchal Lyautey's landing in 1907, wives named Suzanne who didn't survive childbirth. Little Rouget lies in the same grave with Odette. Over the French graves I remember the marble angels in little niches perpetually green with flowers, crucifixes with marble Christs bent over them. For the French like the sentimental statuary of death just as much as the Irish. And the French of Fedhala bring flowers for the graves of their dead ones. But I remember no flowers on the American graves, clean and bare as the tombs of old misers who died unwept. For who would deck these American graves? The hands that would itch to are on the other side of the Atlantic. They have never seen the still cemetery of Saint Jean de Fedhala. And even if they came, bearing flowers, they'd have to dry their tears long enough to give two American cigarettes as an admission tip to the gardener of the cemetery.

I remember Fedhala because it had the fairest bathing beach in the Casablanca area, a crescent without popcorn stands or roller coasters. There was only a ring of fresh sand (the recent American blood was not to be seen on it) and a high sea wall that looked toward the sunset. Farther down I remember the docks and cranes that the provincial French charged us for the use of during our landing operations—that is, after the landing was an accomplished fact. I remember that the casino which made Fedhala an African Lido had been a little scarred from the shelling, but we Americans made it first a hospital and then a service club.

Along the sea I remember villas and copses of palm trees where the rich French shut themselves in and brooded. Then you came to that square white pearl, the Hôtel Miramar, out of which American officers peered at the sea after dark. In 1943 the Miramar had been requisitioned by the Americans, but actually it was in the hands of a combine of French and Ayrabs, who soaked the Americans for cognac and Meknes champagne, and sold our Spam out of the mess cellar to their friends. I remember making friends with the madame and her husband, who were resident in the hotel, representing the proprietors. The husband was a Casablanca corporal who worked in the Shell Building. And Madame used to pace the Miramar sun porches all day long in her high woolen socks, wringing her hands in the Moroccan sunlight:

Hélas, mon cher, vous autres américains, vous êtes tous trop riches!"

The other French in Fedhala told me that Madame, born in Lorraine, hadn't always been a great lady. She'd been a chambermaid in Fez. One night she'd made Monsieur le Caporale into a bed.

"Qu'est-ce qui se passe, madame?"

"Rien, rien, mon enfant. C'est seulement ma douleur."

I remember the center of the beach town of Fedhala. It was a lush and classic park with geometrical walks and squares. There were palms set out like chessmen, begging to the eye to go on along the squares to the sea or to the hills back of Casablanca. There were stone benches in the alcoves of this park, where after dark we sometimes chased the Ayrab maidens who did our washing. Their names were Hadouche and Busheltits. And there was also the largest woman in captivity, the French secretary to Fedhala's doctor. We called her Blockbuster. Each payday there was a ratrace in Fedhala park, a shag lineup coming out of the bushes or under the sea wall in the bathhouses, and Busheltits' snortings and gigglings:

"Me professeur ziggyzag. . . ."

Sometimes we suspected that Busheltits was malade, but nobody could ever prove anything on her. Her Ayrab tendency toward speculation in her prices was offset by the behemoth dignity of Blockbuster, who pranced by daylight through the streets of Fedhala with her parasol and the doctor's baby in a perambulator. She carried her hundred and ninety pounds with the offishness of a Caucasian among Mahomet's followers. She insisted on deferential treatment to discriminate her from the Ayrab wenches who were far more natural and amenable to reason.

48

I remember the church in Fedhala that white half of a tin can lying on its side and stuccoed over with creamy plaster. In the sun it rolled and sparkled visible from halfway to Casablanca. Its pastor a white Father often walked in the courtyard in beard and cassock. They said he had taken to the hills when the Americans landed. And back of this church was the school Relai de la Jeunesse. General Patton had used it for a hospital but now they read P/W mail there.

But I remember best the Hôtel de France. Madame Jean was the hostess there, of quick step and quicker tongue. She could handle us and she could handle the French sailors off the *Richelieu* or the *Jean Bart* when their pompons got out of hand.

"Bonsoir, mes petits américains! Pour ce soir je vous offre un magnifique menu-marché noir. Mais vous mangerez! . . . pommes de terre en robe de chambre, un biftek merveilleux . . . et . . . si vous êtes très mais très mais très gentils, il y'aura du homard."

Madame Jean counted her delicacies on her fingers, screaming them at us with flashing eyes. All day long she worked the black markets of Casa, and every night there was a meal at the Hôtel de France such as we couldn't get in any army mess. And she'd a little bar in the bowels of the dining room, waited on by a glistening Ayrab who looked like a Negro. In this small room we met all the adherents of La Boule Joyeuse, who bowled their Sundays away on the terrace and drank anise at night, and all the Septième Régiment de Tirailleurs Algériens, and the workers in the cork factories. They bummed everything off us, but after the vin rouge and the Grand Marc around 2300 hours we looked at them through a mist of affection:

"Après tout nous sommes de bons Alliés."

Before Madame Jean threw us out for the evening, she allowed her husband to sing just one song. We thought that he must have worked as a female impersonator in Paris before 1940. He did soubrette songs with gestures that gave the idea he was singing about things we'd like to try:

> "*Il fit ce que je voudrais faire*
> *Si j' osais faire le soixante-neuf . . .*"

49

Most of all I remember a small Bordeaux sailor who came on certain nights to the Hôtel de France. He never had any money for the vin rouge that he loved. He used to sit at the end of my table, shy and alert till I'd bought him some. He had the huge eyes of a girl with a bedroom look and a mouth such as Frenchmen don't legally wear. And I'd buy him one drink after another till his pompon began to slip over his ear, and he'd seek out my shoulder till it was time to go back to his batterie. In his cups he used to thunder like Clemenceau:

"Tu vois, mon cher, c'est très simple . . . les anglais, les italiens, les allemands, les japonais. . . . C'est plus que simple, la guerre."

And I remember that he'd clutch my arm and weep as I walked him back to his batterie. He'd be beaten, he said, by his capitaine. I used to watch his shining tears under the stars of Fedhala, and then I knew I was surely in Africa. He wasn't in Bordeaux and I wasn't in the States. He'd forget me till next time he wanted some vin rouge, for he spent his Sundays off from the batterie in the arms of an espagnole who was secretary to the Comité de la Libération. She gave him for love what she peddled for her living. But here now in the Moroccan moonlight Jean worked on me to give the impression that he was alone in this world, that I was his only friend:

"Ah, que tu es sympathique . . . ton nez, tes yeux, ton sourire. . . ."

I remember that this was the first time I'd come upon the European idea of being *sympathetic*, an idea which doesn't exist in the American language. It came to mean much to me—sympathique, simpatico—anything, so long as that sympathy existed. I thought it must mean that the emotions and the deepest feelings were involved, even though they were being bought and sold and bartered for in American money and PX rations. It was the beginning of my initiation into the economics of the world, a gradated graph of moonlight and romance on one peak and the struggle to exist on the other. They weren't intermingled here, as they were in the States. And perhaps the discovery of this cleavage was fatal to me. I remember that I drank more and more because I was trapped in the problem that confronted me. It was this coming to know people who spoke another language, whom the war had already pressed flat. Naturally they preyed on me, though at first I thought I was going to see Life without paying for it. In North Africa I thought I could keep a wall between me and the people. But the monkeys in the cage reach out and grab the spectator who offers them a banana.

I remember that there's nothing like a North African hangover. When I was used to Canadian Club and a stop after midnight for a hamburg and milk at the White Tower, the liters of vin rouge and vermouth and cognac that I poured into myself took a toll. In the morning I'd awaken to a nervous and palpitating world in which myself seemed to have died. The night before was remembered like the negative of a photograph; I'd overreached myself in attempting to step into the picture. Ah misery, thy name is Grenache or Moroccan marsala! So I was never free of the vapors till noon. I used to black out on the red and white wines of Morocco. But though I couldn't remember what I'd done, they told me that my body went right on functioning. I began to realize facets of my personality I hadn't plumbed on Main Street or in the First Baptist Church.

"Ooooo, what you did lasnight! You walked right up to her an said voolayvoo cooshay aveck mwah? Ya're a bad baaad boy, and I hope ya tell ya mother in ya next V-mail."

"The human body is a wonderful thing. You walked around just as if you were walking in your sleep, took off your shoes, and put yourself to bed. You answered all our questions, just like you'd been hypnotized. I said to myself: That's my boy, and I'm proud of him. . . ."

I remember how the dawn begins in Fedhala: the murmur of the sea drops like chained wolves. (Why is the sea louder and more insistent in the night?) And out of the heavy uterine dark a violet light begins to swirl like a soft turbine. The color mottles into gold, the sea dies still more, and something seems to swish through the air like yellow torpedoes. There's a reveille braying from all the Fedhala donkeys, as if, fearful of the sunrise and the workaday world ahead of them with its blows and kicks, they tore off a last chunk of donkey love. When the sun is up, the Medina opens its walls and out stream the Ayrabs who work in the cord and sardine factories. It's

51

a stretched-out file of a thousand persons walking in the streets and on both sidewalks. They converse together like turkeys gobbling. They play tricks on each other. They use the French telephone poles with considerable liquid spite. The Ayrab men wear battered caps and jackets that perhaps they took off the beach on 8 November 1942. Others have mattress covers and cotton breeches. But they don't look like a background of extras for Marlene Dietrich in technicolor. The faces of some of the men are as hawklike and refined and supercilious as a ballet dancer's; they have a feminine walk and a way of holding themselves aloof from the others. Some of the women have mashed noses and wide-set eyes like Nubians. A few show blue slits above their noses where the facepiece meets the veil. But there are a few Ayrab girls of sharp hurt beauty, flowers manured in a rich and poignant soil. These too walk apart from the others like the beautiful slight men. The handsome ones of the Ayrabs link hands as though from some lore inside the Medina they had learned of an aristocracy of body and face given to few in their generation. The calling out and the horseplay are always from the uglier and coarser Ayrabs, as though to distract attention from their own thinking. The Ayrabs of delicacy and wistfulness commune only with themselves or their likes and walk with downcast eyes, aware of their spell. For they've sucked up out of filth and squalor the wisdom of the Suk—that to be born is the greatest misfortune that can befall anyone. Ayrab beauties make their whole life a lament that all but escapes us Americans. The handsome Ayrab men and women never beg; and when I catch their eyes I know that they feel a mistake has been made in their caste: it is I who should be begging from them.

The procession passes from the Medina to the cork factories with a swiftness as though the Ayrabs had a secret determination to get off the streets before the Americans and the French are abroad. I note Busheltits and Hadouche in the streaming files. They smile at me, thinking themselves already set apart from their own people by the favors they've conferred on the Americans. And last in the parade is Oombah and his wife, locked to him with an invisible manacle. For he has married well in the Medina because of his profits on vin rouge to the Americans. He's wearing his encrusted Omar Khayyam

slippers and a turban such as Rudolph Valentino introduced to the movies when Ayrabs were romantic. The
clucking of the Ayrabs and their spoiled smell fade as
they pass to the sardine and cork factories or to the
brick kilns of Fedhala. They've gone beyond the huge
windows of the Brasserie du Parc. Oombah goes in and
starts setting the tables. But first he locks Mrs. Oombah
in the ladies' latrine, where she will sit and cry all day
long till he takes her out in the evening.

I remember the varieties of breakfasting around Fedhala. I had almost never to eat in my own mess, where
the KP was done by Ayrabs, and later by Italian P/W.
Sometimes I was invited by a French family with whose
daughter we took turns in shacking, depending on the
results of last night's crap game. The breakfast was frugal
and accompanied by French provincial homilies and im-
precations against the times. Madame watched every sip
of coffee I took, as though the guillotine were too good
for the world's men. Better fare was provided by Martin
the Spanish barber, who'd escaped (by various versions
of his own) through Tangier and Gibraltar. He'd make
coffee on a hot plate he'd begged of me, and I'd sit on his
bed while he cut dark bread and moaned of his little
daughter and the Falangists:

> "En el fondo del mar
> Nació una perla . . ."

Martin had rimmed mad eyes, and his hands always
shook except when they held a razor. But the best Fedhala breakfast was to be bought in the Brasserie du Parc,
where the flies spiraled over the fruit and the wine bottles.
I remember that I used to buy a long black loaf cut in
two and stuffed with spicy granulated pork. With this I
would drink white wine so cold and bitter (the Brasserie
had a frigidaire) that I stumbled out from my breakfast
more than a little crocked and with a churning in my
belly as though the pork and flies were wrestling on the
mat of my stomach. Then I'd go back to bed, for often I'd
stayed up rolling them all night long. My eyes would be
stinging from the sun and the wine, for Fedhala at 0900
hours has the hard brilliance of a Spanish landscape at
noon. Or maybe I'd go out to the Fedhala golf course
over a rustic bridge. Sometimes I could buy American

beer there and bat the breeze with a corporal from Texas who'd been a pro and didn't want to be anything else. He had his special racket because colonels and brigadier generals would come out from Cazes airport and from Casa to take putting lessons. This corporal therefore had that liberal immunity about him, a large looseness of spirit found in great gamblers and in the bodyguards of presidents. Sometimes he'd let me use a colonel's club for a few holes of the course. And I would correct his French and look at him over my cold beer with a gee-whiz delight. So far from America, from Saratoga, from Balmoral, and here was golf and that air of controlled opulence that hangs like cigar smoke around bunkers and country clubs.

I remember the long afternoons by the beach wall of Fedhala. Was that the Atlantic Ocean? Yes, and three thousand miles on the other side was Virginia. Along the sea wall the French had gun emplacements and barbed-wire entanglements. And the sailors were always oiling these pieces as though they weren't quite satisfied with the way they'd functioned on 8 November 1942. These were the sailors who came to Madame Jean's bar in the Hôtel de France. By daylight they looked seamy in their pompons and dungarees, outside the dull glow of Picardan wine and the moth-eaten gentility of the salle à manger. Tonight they and I would meet on a different plane, and we would fly to one another like estranged lovers.

The Fedhala beach season begins at noon. The provost marshal of Casablanca fined us for going in swimming without a lifeguard, without our dogtags, or at other than stated hours. I lie in the sand and watch the rich French and Spanish families come out like lizards from their cabañas. They are as eager to offer me hospitality as they were gracious to the German Armistice Commission caught in their pajamas at the Villa Miramar. The wives in their sleek bathing suits are all studied and wise, their daughters are all fifteen and studying with the nuns of Casa. The Spanish wives of the cork magnates are especially luscious and cordial. One of them loves one of us, and he uses her love for her benedictine and her fruit-cakes. She looks like Dolores Del Rio. He hasn't told her that he's married and has a kid. After all, that was

54

back in Charleston. She waits for him on evenings when her husband is away in Rabat, leaves her patio gate open for him, and sits hushed and cool in her silken wrapper. She's an accomplished mistress, he tells me. But he enjoyed even more seducing her daughter, to whom he taught the secrets that her mother taught him, and which are not dispensed at the convent school in Casablanca. At midnight sometimes (he says) mother and daughter sit up with him while he chews chicken and swills Chablis. Mother and daughter look at one another slyly, conspirators with one another, against Papa. They don't know that they are against one another. He takes all that they give. After all, he's on vacation from Charleston, South Carolina. They are foreigners, aren't they; and who conquered this desert oasis of Fedhala?

I remember the afternoons on the beach at Fedhala in French Morocco. It wasn't crowded like Coney Island. It seemed the seascape of a dream, where bronzed French and Spanish and American bodies cut into the water and splashed and laughed and called out to one another. There was the jingle of dogtags on our chests or mothers warning their children in French to beware of the undertow. . . .

THIRD PORTRAIT

Hal

HAL SAID, fastening the gold bar to the collar of his shirt:

"Nothing can hurt you now, dear . . ."

He looked at his face in the mirror of the latrine. It was that same latrine in which he'd scrubbed toilet seats with Bon Ami for Saturday morning inspections. Last night he'd clipped the officer candidate badge from the pocket of his blouse. Now he was a second lieutenant in the Army of the United States. Perhaps this was the moment in which he was to come into his kingdom.

Hal thought that something had been omitted from his nature—some gland, some gonad, some force possessed by all the other men and women in the world. He

55

knew it when his Viennese mother used to look at him by candlelight as she played *Der Rosenkavalier* waltzes on her piano in Greenwich Village. He knew it in his first scrap at Public School 13. He knew it in the Bayonne office of the Standard Oil Company.

Hal's secret was a great emptiness within himself. He believed in nothing, often doubting his own existence and that of the material world about him. Some evenings when he was drunk in Greenwich Village, he'd stretch out his hands and say:

"Yes? That's what all the girls tell me down at the office. . . ."

Everybody was his friend. He was six two and had such magic of face and body that people looked at him when he came into rooms. He was held to be a wit because the vacuum inside him made him envelop like a bell jar every personality he met. Everyone said he was a genius, but Hal thought himself a zombi, one of the undead. Consequently everything in life was quite clear to him, as it is to one who lives for ninety years and then allows himself to be buried alive because he can't put up with human beings any longer.

His commission had put him into the first stable spot of his life. It was the first time that he knew exactly where he stood. His pinning the gold bar to his collar had the same effect as if the President of the United States had chopped off his head, pickled it, and set it for display inside a gilt frame, as whiskies are advertised in *The New Yorker* magazine. For Hal it was a relief to have the horizons of his mind planed down, with certain conventional fences erected in their stead. He would be saluted by all enlisted men, and henceforth his mind must move along neat little tracks, greased by order of the secretary of war. It was the first breather Hal had ever had from coping with things.

"And you'll be overseas soon, dear," he said to himself, turning away from the mirror. "Perhaps you never belonged in America at all."

He walked out of the latrine and into the squad room. They were busy putting straight their bars, because after the general had handed you your commission at graduation, you put on your insignia any old way and rushed out to give one dollar to the first officer candidate who saluted you.

56

Hal had been popular at OCS. He'd agreed with every-one and understood them all. For one week he'd been acting company commander. On week ends, like the rest of them, he'd tear into Washington, take a room at the Statler, and get drunk with all the cliques. There was the Brilliant Crowd, the Swishy Crowd, the Empire Builders, and the Drugstore Cowboys. Hal knew them all, even those fringers who didn't belong to cliques.

And now he was leaving them with the same smiling casualness as he'd come into the company twelve weeks ago. He'd always had this sense of isolation: he loved his Viennese mother when he was with her in the Bayonne apartment; he loved people when he was drinking with them. But when he was alone, it was as though all his life with others had never been. They were all shadows thrown on the wall of his brain. Hal was just a raw piece of sensitized paper. And no one would ever develop the pictures he'd taken. . . .

"Hal," said a new second lieutenant, grabbing his hand. "Look me up in New York. And stay out of the Astor Bar, hear?"

"They're making Hal security officer at Fort Hamilton," another said. "Then the Germans will never know what is sailing out of the harbor. . . ."

They all milled around from their packing and looked at him with sentimental old-school eyes. Their new bars glistened like jewels on paupers. Hal knew that it would be months, if ever, before their uniforms, for which the people of the United States had given them each two hundred and fifty dollars, would look natural. At heart they were all still corporals or sergeants.

Hal towered over them all as he shook hands. He'd been close to every one of them. Each had expressed his personality in Hal's company with the license of a spin-ster before a mirror. But not one had ever made to him the gesture of surrender. They were simply happy that he'd understood them and accepted them. They had loved him for the reflection he gave them back of them-selves, for he knew how to make people shine in their own eyes.

He went out of the barracks and took the bus for Washington. The undergraduates were getting out of their classes, and his arm got stiff from the unaccustomed saluting he had to return rather than initiate. And the

57

undergraduates saluted him in tribute to the commission that they themselves were still sweating out. They'd be gigged if they didn't salute. The Adjutant General's School was almost like the movies in its conception of the Army of the United States. Its new second lieutenants were the cream of something or other. Hal smiled to himself as he thought that he was the most pasteurized of them all.

He got on the long bus, pulling in his legs, which never fitted anywhere. He leaned back in a dreamy way, deceptive of relaxation. Two WAC's across the aisle nudged one another. Hal knew. They were telling each other he looked like Gary Cooper. The bus began to groan off, and he slitted his eyes, feigning sleep.

"Gee, sir, congratulations, you graduated today."

It was a little officer candidate behind him, from class twenty-one. All the way into Washington he talked Hal's ear off, of how in another month he too would be a second lieutenant. At the Adjutant General's School there was a relation between students and already commissioned officers that tickled Hal. The barrier between them wasn't quite that of officers and enlisted men, but the incestuous byplay between the upper and lower forms of a large private school. The officers called the enlisted men *gentlemen* with the sniggering deference of a dowager toward a pantrymaid who is about to come into a fortune. But Hal said nothing of this. He wished the little man well and got out of the bus.

It was the Washington of June, 1943. There was a hysteria here that ran underground from the Pentagon to the Statler, Mayflower, and Willard hotels. The sun was as tyrannical as it can be only in Washington, but everything was air-conditioned. Everybody drank a good deal and everybody talked about bureaucracy and the windup of the Tunisian campaign. Brigadier generals flounced along the street like democratic abbesses. All the enlisted men who weren't sweating out a commission at Fort Belvoir or Fort Washington wore the shoulder patch of the Washington monument. Near the navy buildings soft-cheeked Waves strolled in an innocent pride. WAC's tore efficiently through the streets. Thousands of sailors and marines were on the loose with cameras strapped to their shoulders. Civilians groaned about the housing problem, but everybody beamed at everybody

58

else, particularly on Pennsylvania Avenue after dark. To Hal it seemed as though America had grown sharp and young again after the years 1929-1939. They all thought of themselves as part of an adventure, so for the first time in a decade they were united, proud, and rather gay. Washington was a garden party listening to communiqués from Europe. Then the shining frocks and the seersucker suits would have another drink, and the talk would bubble up again. There was plenty of shrimp at O'Donnell's Sea Grill. The only people who looked at all uneasy were a few British and French officers who'd come over for infantry training at Fort Benning. For this was Washington of June, 1943.

Walking through Washington steeped Hal in a Schwärmerei he'd inherited from his Viennese mother, who'd wept all through his childhood in Greenwich Village. Last week they'd had words, so she hadn't come to his graduation from OCS. Hal thought himself wiser than she. Every time she tried to put the silver cord around him, he'd cut it with a tender rueful smile. Their relation hurt them both. But Hal had read too much at CCNY and had had one bout too many with smawt young psychiatrists. Their fingers were all over his soul, the way the flesh of a salmon is maculate from the angler's fingers. So in Schwärmerei Hal floated through the world as today he walked through the streets of Washington. He smiled and was oh so gentle with all. And he read and reread the New Testament and Harry Emerson Fosdick and Monsignor Sheen and Rabindranath Tagore and Omar Khayyam and Elsie Robinson and Clare Boothe Luce. And this was why Hal said, as people hung over him at midnight:

"You must understand yourself, kid. Then you'll get to a point where you're as solid and limpid as good hot jazz in a dive at four o'clock in the morning."

"But you help us understand ourselves," they said, putting a careless arm round Hal's shoulders. "We talk to you, and everything seems clearer. Then we go away, and everything is as snafu as it ever was. Tell us your secret."

"They always ask me for my cake recipe down at the office," Hal said.

Confronted with the peripheries of his own personality, he became frightened. It was like walking down a long corridor, every door of which bore his name. Yet he was an alien in all those rooms. He could open door after door, but in each he was as ill at ease as he'd been in the last. Thus he often wondered what it was he had, that everyone came and talked to him and assured him of a wisdom that he never sensed. To himself he was a magnificent and brilliant zero. Yet he'd have had everything if God had given him a single creative impulse. Instead he'd been put on earth simply as five hair-trigger senses in a gorgeous shell of flesh. He was incapable of taking anything and molding something out of it. . . .

Hal entered the lobby of the Hotel Statler. It was twenty degrees cooler than the streets outside. A rush of sweat came under his gabardine shirt stretched taut over his wide tanned back. He grabbed off his cap, feeling faint and giddy in the icy damp air. He tucked his cap under his belt; the gold bar on it swung like a neon firefly from the lope of his long legs and his tight neat hips. As usual people lounging in chairs gave him the lookover and looked once again. A naval flier winked at him. And a wilted mother swooning in the midst of two quarrelsome little girls fanned herself harder as Hal passed. He went into the men's bar and drank three rum cokes with the quick precision that had made him famous in the bars of the Village.

It wasn't possible for Hal to be five minutes in a bar without being invited to join someone. He saw the usual overtures beginning from a table across the room, where sat a catlike man in an open shirt, looking like a State Department secretary on his afternoon off. So Hal settled for his drinks and went out into the elevator. He'd been one of the great drinkers of the Village, even when he was at CCNY. Alcohol made him colder and more compassionate and more penetrating than ever. When he arrived at the state which in others would be drunkenness, the last veil of illusion was torn from him. At such moments he saw nothing to life but a grisly round of eating and sleeping and talking to others until your heart stopped beating. His huge physical charm heightened under alcohol. He'd hold himself up like a locket before the dazzled eyes of whomever he was with. And then he'd excuse himself and go away to sleep. He never had hangovers because the alcohol never gave him any plus for which to exact a corresponding minus.

In the elevator Hal lit a cigarette and looked at the operator, waiting for him to speak first. The boy's head rose out of the high collar of his Statler livery.

"Today you're a new lootenant, ain't ya?" the boy said with 4-F wistfulness.

"Mother, mother, pin a rose on me," Hal said. "For today I yam a maaan."

The boy laughed and slid open the door. Hal walked along the corridor. He passed himself in mirrors. He knocked at the door of 2023 and leaned his head against the jamb. The door opened.

"Ho-ney!" she said. "Take off your rubbers and come into this house. . . . He's in the shower . . ."

Hal took her by the elbows and tried to hold her off from him and look into her face. Instead she edged across the barrier and kissed him, her breath sweet with rum. Her lips skidded across his mouth. Sometimes she even kissed him in the presence of her husband. It made Hal sick and sad because he knew she loved him and had flaunted the mistake of her marriage from the first night that Lyle had introduced them. She used to come down from New York every week end that Lyle was free from OCS. Then she would experiment in getting Hal drunk till she found that his essential chill became ice by midnight.

"First of all," she said after the kiss, "you're going to share our New York apartment. Lyle won't hear of anything else."

He released himself softly and walked to the window. She poured him a drink and sat on the bed to watch him. From the shower came the hiss of the spray.

"Why don't you act like a native of Oklahoma, Helen?"

"Because if I did, I'd go around in Indian costume and sing songs by Charles Wakefield Cadman."

Helen was crisp by Nature and Helena Rubinstein. She worked at a large department store, drawing hard stylized mannequins for ads. She claimed to no illusions, but Hal believed that she was fuller of them than most New Yorkers. Actually she had a nature simple and passionate, secretly dreaming in terms of the *Idylls of the King*.

"Honey," she said, "you're still yearning for the Blessed Virgin."

"Let me alone, Helen, and straighten up your own attic."

"Why do you pretend to be a saint?" she said, kicking off a shoe. "You're a bitch on wheels."

"Let's get away from personalities," he said. "I'm sick of them. . . . Everybody's playing on me like a harp. And you're not happy till you've pulled off all my strings."

"All jazzed up, aren't you? You've enough energy to put the lights on again all over the world."

A screaming sort of singing came from the bathroom, and they both knew that Lyle was toweling himself. Presently he came out in his shorts. He was a little fat, and hairless as an Eskimo. He talked constantly about the theater in a high strident voice and was miserable outside New York.

"He's here he's here he's here he's here," Lyle shrieked and swung Hal three times by the hips. "Stand by the mirror, child. . . . Helen, I just see it, I visualize it. . . . Better than Danny Kaye. Put him on the stage in gold foil, and have Gertie Lawrence singing to him in a violet light."

"You've both been stabbed to death by New York," Hal said, walking again to the window.

"Listen to the likes of that!" Lyle shrieked. "He covers the water front and he's eating in chophouses and he's doing Pennsylvania Station at five in the morning and he's biting the hand that feeds him. He has pernicious anemia every time he gets out of New York."

The old song and dance, Hal thought. They were all three like hamburg chopped fine from New York. They all professed to love her, yet New York had pressed them down with her rhinestone steam roller . . . too much speed, too much automat, too close proximity, too many manufactured values, and no humanity in the anthill. Every New Yorker a doll with flashing eyes and expensive gestures. They all drank too much and smoked too much, and no one really enjoyed himself in anything he did. They read the *New Yorker* and went to all the first nights. They had high blood pressure of the soul and petrification of the heart. Machines for sex and money and furs. That was all. Hal sat down on the chaise longue and put his hand to his head. The other, holding his glass, went slack.

62

"Oh that body," Helen said to her husband. "The kind you cherish in settlement house boys."

She worked on the theory that to oxidize her desire for Hal at all times when they were together was the surest method not to give offense to her husband. Thus (she figured) no dam of Victorian inhibition would build up inside her and break, to everybody's embarrassment.

"That body," Lyle said, "should be up against a ballet bar every morning at ten o'clock."

"To hell with the New York stage," Hal said. "I look enough like a chorus boy as it is. I don't dare go to the beach at Fire Island."

"That's his Li'l Abner pose," Lyle screeched and laughed his harpy whinny.

At moments Hal found a desert of horror in Lyle, shrieking for irrigation from the heavens. No rain ever fell on that parched face. Lyle's eyes protruded when he talked. Nearly everything he yelled forth in his monologues had a quality of dry pumice in it—shrouds like the linen on night club tables, smiles like Italian waiters on roof terraces above Central Park. There was a thirst in Lyle madder than a morning after. The whore and the mystic were at odds in Lyle's heart, and writing copy for perfumes hadn't helped him any. Yet he came close to believing in anything that was smawt. Though sometimes, when the dawn came up over the subways, Lyle would be visited with an epileptic ague, and he'd babble about a little farm in Vermont.

"Hal," said Helen after a pause, "is in the position of Jesus Christ attending Radio City Music Hall."

"The most tragic remark of the year," Hal said, and poured himself another drink.

They drank all afternoon and evening in that air-conditioned hotel room. Helen switched on the Philharmonic concert and lay back on the bed with her shoes off, one arm under her head, a glass in her hand, and stared at the ceiling. She said that the designs in Mozart's music brought her back to sanity, yet there was a fever in her eyes as she pretended to listen to the Jupiter. Lyle talked over and through all music, shouting like the mistress of a ballet troupe counting out the time. He talked of the advertising business after the war, of how—now that he was commissioned—he was going to talk his way

63

into army PRO and sit out the war in the Pentagon. The music made Hal as nervous too. He sat on the floor and wondered if the room would close in on him. When the sun set outside over Washington, they rang for lobster salad and sandwiches and melons. Then they continued to drink till midnight. Lyle passed out reminiscing of Maria Ouspenskaya and was laid on his bed. His face was as pasty and wrinkled as an old squaw's.

Hal turned to go to his own room. By the door Helen caught him and reached up to his shoulders.

"You know we might be together tonight," she said.

Her body shook, for Lyle had never given her anything profound or warm. The veneer cracked on her mouth. He saw that she was as lonely and outlandish and simple as a cactus. Her kisses, to which he couldn't respond, searched all over his face.

"Please, Helen," he said.

His monosyllable tinkled like ice dropped into an empty tumbler.

"But you need a woman, Hal," she said. "You need love because you're afraid of life. . . . You think you're subscribing to ideals of nobility and selfishness. They don't exist any more . . . if they ever did. People have become petty and horrid . . . if they ever were anything else. . . . This is the age of toothbrushes and war bonds and depilatories. Shakespeare and Dostoievsky are dead . . . spirituality was something to console people when they couldn't buy medicine and life insurance. . . . If you don't stop chasing shadows, you'll go nuts. You're far enough out of this world as it is. Very few can still get to you. I can . . . imagine that I love you."

"I know you do," he said, turning away his face.

"All right then, I do," she said. "Do you think of yourself as some redeemer? If one were to show up in this day and age, he'd be crucified by more horrible methods than Pontius Pilate ever dreamed of. . . . Let go of yourself, for God's sake. . . . You're in a bad way."

He pulled himself from Helen's arms and shut the door in her face. In his own room he looked again at himself in the mirror—the bright bar, the striped shield on his left collar. All he needed was an eagle to perch on his head. He took off his clothes slowly and lay down naked on his bed. His body stretched along under the sheets like a lank and flexible flagpole.

Then there came upon him the old vertigo of his childhood. Noises sounded ominous in his ears. The very air became a maelstrom of fear to suck him down. Even the whispering of his hair on the pillow promised a menace and a shudder too dark to contemplate, The final stage in the attack was that the darkened room shot backwards in his vision to one-quarter its size, as though he were looking through reversed binoculars. The chair by his bed was a piece of furniture for a doll's house. Hal lay and trembled and tried to pray in the soft dialect of his mother.

While waiting for orders to sail from the New York port of embarkation, he worked at Brooklyn Army Base. But the eight hours of toil inside the area guarded by glistening MP's was only a hiatus to his nights. He simply did what he had been taught to do at OCS and waited till 1630 hours, when he would slip by the white-leggined sentinels and take the subway from Brooklyn to Times Square.

Sundown was for him a time of passionate questing. After dark New York opened up like a sticky lily. He courted every stamen and pistil of this flower; he knew it with the loving horror of a naturalist who has succeeded in evolving a frightful fern which he keeps and fondles by moonlight. So after dark Hal could be seen slipping through avenues and squares of New York City from Central Park to Greenwich Village.

He was seeking something missing in himself, something like his own double, which would confront him with the image of something positive. He was always alone. He would listen to people at the Astor, at One Fifth Avenue, at little beer joints off the Bowery. They all had much to say, as most people have, and Hal would bend over them listening and smiling his shy brilliant smile and encouraging them to pour out everything that was in them. He'd drink two to their every one. Then he'd slide away from them and go out into the summer night. For it was the old story of his life: everyone discovered that Hal understood him and was elated, the way a man is when he buys a perfect mirror at an auction.

Hal usually wound up drinking beer and sucking pickled eggs in flyblown bars of the Village. Then he'd walk about from four o'clock in the morning until it was time to return to Brooklyn Army Base. Just before dawn in Brooklyn the air was sweetish with baker's buns and the sweet brown smell of roasting coffee.

One day in July, 1943, Hal received ten mimeographed copies of a movement order by which he was assigned to permanent overseas station By Order of the Secretary of War. He looked at the purple dittoes of the adjutant general's seal and signature, and something cool slithered in his spinal column. So he made his will on the quiet blank form, increased his insurance, and decided to make up his differences with his mother. It was a month now, this their latest spell of ignoring each other. She would have spent that month in her flat at Bayonne, sending out her mind in panic over the universe, and having it return to her lap like a whimpering pigeon. Two months earlier she'd been toying with the Catholic Church. This month she'd be convinced that Basic English was the solution to the world's problems—and hers.

He left Pennsylvania Station for Bayonne. At first he thought he might go carrying his new carbine so that his mother could see the facts for herself when she opened her door. But then, she had a Viennese instinct for disaster, by her unaided imagination. He knew his father would still be at the office. So he went directly to the apartment, having armed himself with a bunch of jonquils and sweet peas at a corner florist's. He rang the bell, let out a sigh, and drew himself up to his six feet two.

His mother was wearing her housecoat as she answered the door. She'd always wanted him to call her Eugenie, but her name somehow never reached his lips —only her function. She'd once been beautiful but the weight of his father's body and of his father's personality gave her the appearance now of a lily snapped in a press. Eugenie was so tiny that Hal wondered how anyone as big as himself could have come out of her. He kissed her cheek and then her hands, which she most often wore folded on her breast. This gave her an attitude of a piety counterfeiting her inner resignation, because no other pose availed her anything. He knew she hadn't nursed a hope since he'd left her breast.

"Mother," Hal said, "I'm going overseas. You know we aren't allowed to tell exactly when."

"And I had a feeling you would come today," she said. Traces of her Viennese dialect still remained.

She relieved him shyly of his flowers and led him into

66

the parlor. She had a Jacobean piano covered with shawls, and pictures of himself at all ages on the shawls. She never opened the piano when she played Grieg songs and Strauss waltzes, so her music whimpered like her voice. By the tea caddy he observed a pot and two cups.

"Are you expecting someone, Mother?" he asked.

"You know who," she answered and seated herself to pour him tea.

Her eyes floated before him like flowers in oriental rice paintings. She tucked up her little feet under her housecoat and pulled on the cigarette he offered her. The loose bracelets by her wrists tinkled to her elbow.

"I'd like a shot with my tea," Hal said, turning to his father's cupboard. "How's Dad?"

"It's his ulcers again. And he has eight new deals . . . is that the word? . . . and talks with his mouth full at table."

Hal stirred whisky into his tea. There was a secret odor of his father's tobacco through the flat. He remembered that same whiff when he used to reach up to his father's knees and cry; that same bittersweet pungency that seeped under the door of his parents' room when they lay awake after midnight and shouted at one another about the rent and the difficulties of the English language. Hal's father's tobacco was Hal's father, gross and mordant. Even now he saw the saliva bubbling about his father's mouth as he smoked his after-dinner cigar. He saw the jut of his father's stomach under those rich pencil-striped vests; he heard that grating voice scolding in his ears:

"Dummkopf, was nun? . . ."

"He talks much about you lately," Eugenie was saying, stirring her tea with a waferlike spoon. "Oh how proud he was of your commission! The other night he had some people in to supper. . . . He said that the reason why his son was not here was because you couldn't leave Fort Hamilton."

"He never thought he'd have a second lieutenant in the family. He thinks this is his reward for making me play basketball at the Y. He's made an American man of me finally . . . one that a stockbroker needn't be ashamed of."

"If you could leave a picture of yourself in your uniform . . . with your visored cap and green blouse . . . I think it would please him."

67

"I'll have one taken," he said, swallowing the tea and whisky.

"Habe Dank," she replied.

The whisky gave him an almost instantaneous lift. He got up and walked to the bookcases. Eugenie belonged to all the monthly book clubs and got limp boxed Shakespeare and classics with ornate covers and illustrations. His father read only the papers. His mother had even taken a subscription to the Sunday afternoon concerts at Carnegie Hall. She'd been seen entering the auditorium fearfully in her pince-nez and studying her program notes in the intermission. She was always alone. He'd heard too that she used to jump out of her seat at the Beethoven sforzandi. And Hal remembered her too when they still lived in the Village, sliding through the streets with her shopping reticule, out of reach of the gangs playing baseball up the alleys. In those days she still spoke German, and she seemed to hold for support to the tenement walls as she walked along. Sometimes she would take aside a crying Italian child and slip it a piece of candy. . . .

After Hal had walked around the room once, it seemed to him that his father was following him, telling him not to break anything because it cost dear. His father's conversations had always been inventories of prices, admonitions of what boys not to speak to at school, and lectures about young men who'd Got Ahead in America. They'd never once talked to one another.

Hal sat down beside his mother on the couch and reached for her hand. A smile came to her lips as though there were some stricture in her left breast that made her catch her breath. And he remembered that when his father had first started to make money, she'd taken himself for little treats to the movies—uptown. And coming home in a wild enthusiasm she'd sometimes suggested that they splurge and take a taxi. Settling back in the seat with her eyes closed, she'd nearly always reached over for his hand. She used to run her fingers along the hair on his wrists. So this was the first time Hal had ever actively caressed his mother, other than in greeting or in parting. . . .

"I have a feeling," he said smiling and forcing a bubble into his voice, "that I'll see Vienna before the war is

68

over. . . . What would you like from there, Mother?"

"You must just write and tell me how the city is . . . a long long letter on how the people are dressed. You can write such good letters."

"I'll write every day when I'm overseas," he said ponderously.

"And so will I," she said, closing her eyes.

If he felt an agony of emptiness when he walked about the outside world, looking handsome and omniscient, Hal knew only a flatulence in his own home. He'd rarely come there since he'd left CCNY and had gone to work for Standard Oil in Bayonne. And every time he entered this apartment, he seemed to run square into the big stomach of his father. His father's hats always bulked on the rack. And once having fought through his father's abdomen, he'd meet another image bumbling around the walls by that candlelight that Eugenie always preferred to electricity. It was a moth with a woman's face. It flew around his head in tenderness and terror, beating its own antennae with its wings. Often it would swoop at him and he would recoil in childish horror, to discover then that the moth was at the other side of the room, thrashing against the wallpaper. . . .

His mother held tightly to his hand. Her fingers went tentatively a little way up his wrist.

"I have never seen you look so hübsch," she said. "There's something in your face that's improved by the severity of the uniform."

"The melancholy appeal of the warrior leaving for the wars?"

He felt sorry he'd said it and took away his hand as softly as he knew how and went and poured himself some more of his father's whisky.

"You'll stay to dinner?" she asked. "When something told me you were coming, I went wild with all my red points. Mr. Liedermann is very good to me at the market."

"I shouldn't even have left Fort Hamilton," he said, "to come here. We're what they call alerted. . . . I can't stay, Mother."

The cruelty that was forever rising between them strangled him. They were constantly groping toward one another. But everything they could say had a smothered overtone of: Oh, what's the use? We were together for

69

nine months, and we never can be that close again. . . .

"I understand," she said, putting down her teacup to go to the piano.

She began to play.

"Mausie, schön warst du beute nacht, ha, ha, ha, ha! . . ."

Hal watched her from the doorway. It was the last musical comedy she'd seen before leaving Vienna. Eugenie's back was toward him. And remembering that her eyes were shut while she played, Hal decided that he'd go now. He knew that was the way she expected it to be.

Leaving New York harbor and easing out to sea in blackout to join the convoy, Hal had a sense of something being lifted from him, as though his umbilical cord were cut anew. He seemed at last a free agent, responsible to no one. He put out his cigarette and went up on deck. The East River had a slow humming in it. He could smell the oil on the water and hear the fumbling of the tugs. He looked up at the stars and leaned his head against a davit. The ship trembled under him, but he couldn't see the water that buoyed her up. Atavistically he felt that he must have experienced this same security and warmth when he lay on his mother's lap, when thinking was only a registering on his brain of the first impressions of his five senses. Now this concept of ocean made his mind go faint and blank in annihilation, the concept of the mother.

He felt his long thick thighs against the railing of the ship, twined about the metal in loving support. And he thought about the current of his life, which had not yet been quickened thirty years earlier. He thought, This world and this sea aren't so very much bigger than I. They're all inside this head of mine. They didn't exist thirty years ago when I was not. And some time in the future they'll all go again for me, like a moving picture when the arc lamp fails. . . . I can have a profounder influence on my world than I have hitherto had. Since the whole thing is nothing but a shadow in my brain, there must be some secret how I can make the reflections dance the way I want them to . . . I should like to meet the Man with the flashlight. . . .

He spent the endless days in the convoy reading and taking sunbaths on the officers' deck. His body got to be

70

the smoky hue of coffee except for the small white circles around his eyes where he wore his sunglasses. Hourly changing the position of his body as he sprawled on his GI blanket stenciled with his name and serial number, Hal read and read the New Testament, especially the Gospel of Saint John. From this evangelist he got the taste of a bright sweet fruit such as he'd never experienced from allowing anybody to make love to him. And at nights he began to dream of a love not to be found in the bodies of men or women, but a love going forth from his own mind to all the human beings in the world, since actually they existed only in himself. For him to refuse to love them would be as cruel as if God were to shut off the sun and sit back to watch the results. To Hal in his sleep there came often a line that would cause him to start up from the bed in his stateroom, tingling with sweat as when he was fourteen:

"I am the Resurrection and the Life. . . ."

One Sunday in the middle of the Atlantic the transport chaplain took to his bunk with a bout of seasickness. The merchant marine master of the ship canvassed all the officers aboard for a volunteer to conduct church service. Hal heard his own voice lifted. So on a foredeck while the gun crew looked down from their nest Hal addressed several hundred GI's and officers who had nothing else to do but come to church. They sat around him on the tarpaulins in a big half-circle with their hands clasping their ankles.

He was nervous and exalted as he talked. He put his hands behind his back and paced about in a tiny ring. Often he had to lift his voice because a starboard wind kept blowing his words out into the Atlantic. Everyone was keyed up because the convoy had been tacking all night long. The escort destroyers had been zigzagging, and the depth charges had been thudding below them. They hadn't slept without their life preservers. Hal spoke to them of the power of prayer and of the mind of God, in which everything is beautifully ordered (even if it wasn't to them), and the delicate discriminations God made between a sparrow's falling in the air and an airplane's diving to the ground. He told them that each had a little of God in them, and how some, by using that inkling of something beyond them as a firefly to guide them, got closer to God than others did. Finally he spoke of the

71

mystery of death, of how we were all afraid of it instead of being resigned to it.

"Imagine," Hal said, and he found that his voice was choked, "that you're all just drops of rain. I know you all think you're pretty wonderful. But a drop of water isn't much, is it? But maybe a drop of water has its thoughts too. The important thing (and he waved his hand toward the plunging bow of the ship) is the sea itself. It's just as easy to die as to be born. . . ."

After this sermon he left them quickly, for he'd moved himself farther than he'd intended. He couldn't bear to face anyone. He walked swiftly to the open space below the bridge and watched the water swell and scud under the bow. Presently someone came and stood beside him.

"Thank you, suh, for that sweet message from the Spirit. Just as movin as any ah ever got at revival meetins in Shelby, South Calina."

It was a small freckled pfc, wearing his helmet liner against the sun. He kept peering at Hal and running his tongue over his goat-teeth, a rich mocha from chewing tobacco.

"Pahdon, suh," said the pfc, "but ah you a minister of the gospel?"

"No," Hal said. "I'm not. And in South Calina they'd say I drink too much."

"Well now, that's sin," the boy said, winking and seeming to be fighting a temptation to nudge an officer. "You git you there some of that mountain dew and then you git you a nigger gal, and fore you know it, you have to confess Jesus Christ as your savior. . . . When ah'm thiry ah too am gonna git saved by confessin Jesus Christ as mah savior. Jest now ah figure ah'm a lost sinner. But ah read a piece in mah Bahble every night."

"Try the New Testament instead of the Old," Hal said, and walked away.

The boy snapped out of his dream of equality between their ranks and saluted him. Something told Hal that he should have stayed with this boy. Just a little longer.

After noon chow he found the bulkhead to the engine room open and went down the flights of stairs cutting through the runways on the sides of the amphitheater compartment in the center of the ship. When he reached the Diesel engines, he leaned on the railing to watch the walking beams pump and the pistons slash through the

72

air with their slow murderous fists. They were oiled and burnished. The heat of the engine room was fierce. Hal wondered if great American industrialists went to a hell like this. Through the tube under his feet passed the thick axle that turned the ship's screw in the water outside. He felt faint from the temperature and began to wonder if the engines that man had made caused God any jealousy.

A finger made a hole in his back, so he turned to face the engineer officer wearing oil-spotted blue dungarees. He was young and affected a certain brusqueness, perhaps to offset the lush nude tattooed on his chest.

"What a character to be talking about God," the engineer said. "You make me laugh. If I looked like you, my Polish pig at Newport News wouldn't be ditching me every time she gets drunk. I buy her furs and I buy her flowers. I buy sateen-covered chairs for her dive. And what for? So she can hold open house while I'm at sea and give away for nothing what I'm paying for. . . . Perhaps you can tell me what I ought to do, Mr. Anthony."

This engineer had cold Swedish eyes that pierced nonsense. He played the game his own way. He showed Hal the engines and the salt water purifiers and the boilers, touching each fondly with his red arms. And Hal thought that the sea gave men a certain immediacy to reality and an insight. This was the reason for the wisdom all sailors had. They were more and less than other human beings. They could laugh at the women in whose arms they were lying, and they laughed at all earth-rotted men secretly, but with great good humor, pitying them a little, the way one pities those who've never been able to learn to walk.

"Engines," Hal said, wondering if it would get a laugh, "give me more of a feeling of power than I get from the men who made them."

"You talk like I do when I get rummed up. . . . You're slightly off the beam, but I like you. And I can size up my man, don't think I can't. . . . Say, why don't you come up and live with me for the trip? I got an empty bunk. And you know goddam well that the merchant marine lives better than you poor doughfeet below deck. You wouldn't have to eat Spam three times a day. And I got beaucoup rye. . . . Whaddya say?"

"I've never learned to live with anyone," Hal said. "I'd be a disappointment to you. I have my moods. I get ornery."

73

"Well, so do I," the engineer said, taking hold of Hal's arm. There was a kindness and disinterestedness in his squeeze. "When we got ornery, we could bat the hell outa one another. Do us both good. . . . Whaddya say?"

"Maybe it would be better if we met on deck at night and talked once in a while. You see, I keep telling myself that I need one close friend. But I know I never can have one."

"Anything you say, bud," the engineer said, walking away. "My error."

For the second time Hal knew he should have listened more.

One midnight he stood on the officers' boat deck and watched small lightnings play on the horizon. Every fifteen minutes he'd duck inside the blackout curtain and have a cigarette. The thunder had a dull unsatisfied rumble. And certain things had come clear in his mind after thinking all afternoon. He had a tempo different from anyone else's in this world—whether faster or slower he didn't know. And all his current was imprisoned in himself in insulation of his own making. He'd never be able to make contact with people on their own grounds because he couldn't accept those conventions of timing and pacing that made conversations possible. Only in moments did his spirit reach out to others' like a flash of lightning. For the rest he was destined to be alone, like a twin whose double has died at birth. . . .

The antiaircraft guns on the turrets opened up with a spit of tracers, sending ribbons out into the sky. A rain began to fall. Lightnings soft and cozy began to play about the ship's funnels. It occurred to him that maybe no one else on earth heard this thunderstorm except himself. In the flashes between the tracer antiaircraft and the streaks of summer lightning he could see the other ships in the convoy rolling over the horizon. Nevertheless they seemed sure of their own reeling fates, like drunken people on a merry-go-round. And then Hal had an intuition that in these muddy heavens a bolt was being prepared especially for him. He dropped to his knees by the railing, frightened and alone.

In the gummy city of Oran he was visited with something that in the old days at CCNY would have sent him to a smawt psychology student. It began as a malaise,
74

a feeling that his heart had been broken crossing the Atlantic. He'd thought to carry his soul intact out of the States, but he seemed to have dropped a piece somewhere, possibly in the ocean. He would wake in the mornings with a feeling of the most intense displacement. He didn't know where he was or why he was here. Something in him seemed to be chasing another part. Often this hunt between sections of himself became so vicious that he had to put his head between his hands, as a man with a hangover expects his heart to stop in the very next moment, and prays for even the distraction of a bowel movement.

Or at the beach of Ain El Turk, lying in the sun on his days off, drinking Grand Marc, Hal would look anxiously at the sky with the presentiment that some vulture was up there wheeling over him. These anxieties he sought to escape by being with his men as much as possible and seeking to trace his own uneasiness in his GI's. But they only laughed among themselves and got drunk and went AWOL and picked up diseases from the women of Oran.

One day in an attempt to uncoil himself from his paralysis, Hal asked to be made officer of the day. There was to be a formal guard mount in the Place. It was the first time in the history of the American Army that a second lieutenant had requested a detail as officer of the day. A French band played two national anthems. Hal, standing in the Oran sunset by the flagpole, wondered if his leggins were tight, whether the bar of paper from an Old Gold package he'd pasted on his helmet liner had slipped off. He did a smart about-face and walked to the opened ranks to inspect their pieces. He had a pressing feeling in his head and his heart beat so that he thought he was going to fall on his face in the loose sand of the parade ground. The guard for the evening was composed of Oran MP's, tough and cynical, because they'd been wounded in Tunisia. But instead of being sent home they found themselves patrolling the streets of Oran and arresting GI's with loose buttons. In between these functions the MP's operated and promoted with the bars and the ladies of the evening, arresting them or possessing them as the mood struck them. This was Hal's guard. Yet in formation they were magnificent, nazi-looking. Their eyes glittered snakelike under their varnished liners. Their brass and weapons and cartridge belts were impeccable.

75

Hal stepped up to the flawless files, knowing that though they kept their eyes front they were appraising him and sniggering to themselves. He hadn't been in Tunisia or in the landing on Gela. He was just a base section chickenshit second looie. He heard the breathing of each man as he inspected him up and down, cracking the rifle as he snatched it from each. By the second file he all but slipped in the sand as he did his right face. But he got through the whole guard without a hitch. As he was grabbing for the rifle of the last sentinel, he dropped it. He had to stoop over and pick it up. He tilted it and peeped down the bore.

"Your piece is filthy," he said to the sentinel.

"Wasn't before you dropped it, sir," the man answered, never flickering his eyes from attention.

Somehow Hal got through with the guard mount, the closing of the ranks, the lowering of the flag. While the bugler blew retreat and Hal stood at parade rest, he felt their eyes and the setting Oran sun gouging at his back. He posted his first relief and reported to the adjutant, asking to be relieved as OD because he wasn't well. He was shaking so that he had to wedge his knees together as he stood at attention before the adjutant.

"Lieutenant," said the adjutant, "it isn't good policy to drink in hot weather, especially just before you have a guard mount."

"I haven't had a drink since last night," Hal said.

"Then use your mosquito netting and take your atabrine, hear? . . . You're relieved as officer of the day."

Hal saluted and did an about-face. His heart was going like his knees. The adjutant must have heard it. He didn't bother with chow. But when he'd removed his side arms and leggins and had put on fresh suntans because the leggins had creased the others, he went at once to the officers' club, stood at the end of the bar, and ordered one brandy and soda after another. Already in the lounge were majors with nurses or with French WAC's of the Corps Féminin Auxiliaire de l'Air.

For some time now Hal had been noting in himself symptoms unknown to himself in the bars of New York, where he used to stand for hours alone, listening and appraising and throwing down the drinks. It had always been the same with him in bars: the joe next to him struck up a conversation. But in the bars of Oran some

76

gap had arisen between him and all other human beings. It seemed to him that anything anybody else had to say was too prosaic, too factual, or too obvious to the situation. Like a bad exposition at the beginning of a play. It amazed and horrified him how people could talk for ten minutes on such subjects as how they couldn't get the cigarette brand they wanted at the PX; what they said to their first sergeant; or the Oranaise who wouldn't. Hal's mind had become like an idling motor; he could foretell what they'd say ten minutes before they said it. In everything they wished to communicate there was something like a stale joke. And Hal found it difficult, after a few drinks, to look them straight in the eye. There was some vast and deadly scheme in which they were all working; only they didn't know it.

Hal himself had an inkling of what was upsetting him. Casting about for a rational explanation of why he felt so *odd* in Oran, he decided it was because the war was beginning to seep into his bones. This war was the fault of everybody, himself included. Therefore he couldn't bear to hear them jabbering at him, opaque to another reality more bitter than their own. They were enmeshed in their own tyranny of fact, insensitive to the dreadfulness of their own natures and to the position in which they happened to be—squirrels of fate in a slimy North African town, having the time of their lives. And Hal wondered if all the Americans rolling in the materialism of the base sections were living like bloodsuckers off the deaths of those at the front, which were their only excuse for being here at all. And gradually, pondering on his new inability to come to grips with people in their domain of PX rations, office hours, and no mail from home, Hal found himself swimming in a wild and lonesome lake of semantic irrelevance. Nothing made any more sense to him. There was nothing anybody could say to him to lift the weight of unreality that was crushing him. He felt like a sleepwalker among all these grimacing marionettes. He wondered if overseas in wartime there might be some dark vortex of death that sucked back from Salerno even to the city of Oran. His desire was to tear himself away from all who tried to monopolize his ear. Something in him kept saying, Come away, dear. Your place isn't here. . . . But where?

By evening, with no dinner in his stomach, Hal was

still at the end of the bar. He was slightly stupefied. The brandy of North Africa didn't give him the compassionate calm that he got from the rye of the States. It was only a poison that anesthetized whatever censor was in his mind. In the mist of the fumes of Grand Marc things crawled up through a trap door in his brain. They were nameless little incubi with no bodies or faces, but they scuttled around inside his head squeaking in furry voices of doubt and doom. They played with one another like a litter of kittens, but it was the calculated play of children putting on a show for their parents. Hal knew that actually they were playing with him—that each of these vague animals was himself in pieces.

The bar filled up with officers and nurses and Red Cross girls. They wedged themselves into their niches and attempted to impinge their private worlds on one another. By now Hal knew also all the solitary drinkers of Oran. But if they looked his way or motioned to him to join them (he'd been father confessor to them all), he'd study his glass or look at the wall. Others would immerse themselves sufficiently to float what they imagined were their troubles, then they'd forage about the club for someone to talk to, carrying their individual obsessions in their arms like abortions being hustled to a sewer. Only Hal had no particular release. Alcohol simply shut tighter the gates of his prison, spraying the air of his jail with something deathly sweet. He saw himself beating about in the fumes and fanning, trying to create air where none was.

A figure slipped into the empty place at the bar on his left. He didn't look, as he used once to turn welcomingly to newcomers in New York, as though they were keeping an appointment with him. He merely ordered another drink. But straightway he was aware of a seepage between himself and whoever stood next to him. It was as though they'd already entered into conversation. The elbow touching his own on the bar was eloquent though motionless. At last Hal couldn't stand the atmosphere any longer. He narrowed his eyes and slowly turned his head to look out over the club terrace.

At his left was a parachute captain who seemed to be looking through him. Apparently he too had been waiting till the psychic charges he'd been hurling at Hal would energize him into turning, as the sun eggs on a sunflower. The captain was shorter than Hal and slighter. He had a tension as exquisite as the fake repose of Greek athletes in marble. His jet hair was so tightly curled that it had an energy all its own. He was dressed in combat fashion. His sleeves were halfway up to his elbows. He wore no tie. The hair grew up his throat and on his neat tight arms. His eyes were set at a slant, and his teeth were white and daggerlike. He seemed a monarch of some race of cats.

"Look at them, will you?" he said to Hal, as though they were resuming a conversation.

"Whom?"

The parachute captain put one of his boots on the brass rail and kicked it. Then with a lazy tension he made a gesture including all the other people leaning on the bar:

"This race of straphangers and human adding machines. . . . Look at the faces of those nurses. Sleek inanity sleepwalking in a beauty parlor. Look at the paunches on those majors. . . ."

His vituperation came out slowly, with the detailed passion of an expert at murder.

"You don't like Americans?" Hal said. He was fascinated by the green eyes and by the parachute insignia, wings suspended like a bat's at dusk.

"Who does, except themselves? Automatons from the world's greatest factory. . . . They have no souls, you see . . . only the ability to add up to one million. Did you ever hear them try to carry on a sensible conversation? . . . Oh, they've got quite an ingenious system of government, I grant you. But none of them gives a damn about it except when it gets them into a war. . . . They've got less maturity or individuality than any other people in the world. Poetry and music to them—why, they're deaf to anything that isn't sold by an advertising agency. . . . They don't know how to treat other human beings. With all their screaming about democracy, none of them has the remotest conception of human dignity. . . . Listen to the sounds that Negro band is making. That's their American music. Sexual moans and thumps. . . . They don't know how to make love to a woman, and all their hatreds are between football teams or states of the same Union or for people they don't understand. Victims of the mob spirit and regimentation. . . . They've never really suffered. But when they get the first twinge of toothache of the soul, they start feeling sorry for themselves instead of learning any wisdom from pain."

"You're talking treason," Hal said.

It was almost his old manner of listening and advising in the bars of New York.

"Truth is always treasonous," the captain said, clicking his glass with a soft ferocity on the bar. "And now these poor dears are involved in a war. This war is simply the largest mass murder in history. Theirs is the only country that has enough food and gasoline and raw materials. So they're expending these like mad to wipe out the others in the world who'd like a cut of their riches. In order to preserve their standard of living for a few more years, they've dreamed up ideologies. Or their big business has. So they're at war with nearly everybody in the world. The rest of the world hates Americans because they're so crude and stupid and unimaginative. . . . They will win this war. They'll reduce Europe to a state of fifteen hundred years ago. Then their businessmen and their alphabetical bureaucracies will go into the shambles of Milan, Berlin, and Tokyo and open up new plants. . . . International carpetbaggers. . . . Millions of human beings will be dead, and most of the human feelings will be dead forever. . . . Hurray for our side. . . . We're destroying all the new ideas and all the little men of the world to make way for our mass production and our mass thinking and our mass entertainment. Then we can go back to our United States, that green little island in the midst of a smoking world. Then we can kill all the Negroes and the Jews. Then we'll start on Russia."

"Not pessimistic, are you?" Hal asked feebly, watching the glowing green eyes.

"Me?" the captain said. "I'm the most optimistic man in the world. I see what is happening to the human race. It gets worse all the time. . . . What an obscene comedy."

The parachute captain had an almost effete way of speaking, like poets in the Village. This contrasted with his agile body and the violence of his passion.

"When shall I see you again?" Hal said, disengaging himself softly.

"I am buried near Taormina on the island of Sicily. I wish I had a few flowers on my grave. . . . When I was alive, I loved flowers."

Afterwards Hal often thought of the parachute captain. His life in Oran became a round in which he did his work, enclosed in himself. He made no further attempt to enter into the lives of others. Nor did he visit any army psychiatrists. He knew he'd arrived already at a point where no one schooled in Freud or Jung could help him, any more than a bespectacled young psychiatrist from CCNY could have helped Jesus Christ in the Garden by psychoanalyzing the bloody sweat.

Nevertheless Hal went at the problem with a simplicity finer than any with which he'd ever attacked the enigma of his life heretofore. He went on the wagon from January to July of 1944. Stopping his drinking had had particular effect on him for better or for worse. He smoked a little less, and the evenings dragged more. That heightened awareness of his was still with him. After a deep night's sleep, sweltering under his mosquito netting, he could never be sure whether he'd really slept at all. He seemed merely to blank out for eight hours. Awaking, he was neither better rested nor less fatigued than when he went to bed.

He knew no French, for some block arose in his mind whenever he tried to learn a Romance language. Yet he made the acquaintance of an Oranaise who worked in the officers' PX. This girl never forced an issue. She was as cool as a mannequin. From some secret source of supply she had a jeep—she'd been loved by a brigadier general in the ATC, by an American ensign, and by a French colonel from Sidi-Bel-Abbes. When Hal's work was finished, she'd meet him with her jeep and relinquish the wheel to him. On these outings she wore polariod glasses, wedgies, and a blue silk bandanna about her hair. Unlike most French girls she seldom spoke; and when she used her French on him, she pantomimed everything without a trace of nervousness. Evenings, he'd stay at her apartment and sit drinking fruit juice while she played "Tristesse" on her piano.

"C'est ton destin," she said once, " 'aller au bout de toi-même." Hal understood what she meant.

He often slept on the couch in her apartment. Sometimes at sunrise she'd come to his side in her blue kimono. She'd sit on his couch and watch while he passed without a jar from the depths of his sleep into full wakefulness. Then she'd take his hand. Sometimes she kissed his wrists or the lobes of his ears.

"Je t'aime pour ton angoisse indéfinie."

He understood what she meant by that too.

In a sense he was happier with Jeanne than he'd ever been. She had all his sensibilities plus a fortitude he didn't own. She was the first with whom he had the certainty that anything he needed would be found in her, and with an abundance that would stop flowing only with her death. Jeanne was like a tube reaching into eternity that sucked up a grace of oxygen to one asphyxiating. She never seemed much moved by anything except when he took her hand or when she read aloud to him from the *Jour de Colère* of Pierre Emanuel. Hal caught very little of this poem. But often he thought that his only salvation would be to marry Jeanne. For she had that awareness and resignation of spirit that has sipped everything lovely in life, letting such values be her guide through some mortal experience that has purged her. The focus of her compassion was in her breasts, geometric as cones. Her nipples seemed to see.

In June, 1944, when Jeanne had brought him to a tranquillity like a magnetic field pointing all one way, she left him to visit her mother in Casablanca for a month. When he drove her to the station in Oran, he knew and she knew that they'd never see each other again. It was terminating in the silvery casualness with which it had begun. As she mounted the battered wagon-lit, she turned back and kissed him on the forehead saying:

"Et je dis, en quittant tes charmes,
    Sans larmes:
    Adieu! . . ."

The cadence of her voice told him what they were both thinking. For three days her spirit remained with him intact. He continued to sleep at her empty apartment, to which she'd left him the key. But on the fourth day his old sickness seized him with redoubled violence, as though Jeanne's nursing had only caused its virus to become dormant. Hal now couldn't bear the company of other Americans at all, particularly of his brother officers. It was difficult for him to sit still in one place without chain-smoking to distract himself from a compulsion to keep in constant motion. He couldn't look anybody in the face. While giving orders to his GI's, he'd walk up and down his office wringing his hands and feigning to concentrate. Sometimes it took every gram of control to keep from telling his first sergeant to please go away and let him alone. And he decided he'd have to fall off the wagon because at least having a glass of something numbing in his hand gave him an excuse for remaining stationary in one spot. When these fits were at their height, Hal had a feeling as though he'd like to dash the whole twenty-five thousand miles encircling the world. Then he'd come back to his point of departure and find himself standing there leering and saying, "Welcome home, old goon. . . ."

He meditated putting in for a transfer to Casablanca to be near Jeanne. But he knew and she knew that she'd done everything in her power for him, that her therapy was only a breathing spell in the denouement. Even now at the Hôtel Anfa or at Villa Moss she'd be allowing someone else to possess her cool body, the while she covered her eyes and thought of Hal and shook her head sadly. There'd been nothing cloying in her pity for him. But what Jeanne had given him was a sip of life, for which he had no thirst. He'd read enough romances to know that he'd already entered, through no fault or desire of his own, into league with those who are on the other side of the looking glass.

He got a five days' leave forced on him, for his CO had noticed his removed emotional state and had chalked it up to overseas blues. He booked passage on a plane to Cairo and stopped off in Algiers, both to see the city and to renew the acquaintance of some of his friends from OCS. He left the plane at Maison Blanche and hitchhiked into Algiers. It lay before him in the July afternoon, sprawled on its hillside like the segments of an amphitheater. Dozens of barrage balloons floated above the harbor like silver sausages on a blue plate.

In the offices of AFHQ Hal sat on his friends' desks and cocked a critical eye to see whether possibly some new insight or mercy had been born in them as a result of being overseas and brooding on the war. They cursed the Ayrabs and said that the French were laying us for all they could get. All their meannesses, latent in the States, had only been crystallized by a year in Africa.

So Hal declined their offers to dinner at a dozen sump-

tuous messes and went out to walk along the Rue d'Isly.
There were more British than Americans in evidence,
clumping along in their boots and gaiters and shorts. And
at 1800 these British all left the streets for a few minutes
to put on their long trousers. On a ramp near the Hôtel
Aletti Hal found a transient officers' mess. The meal was
good. Discovering that he could buy a bottle of wine, he
fell off the wagon. Along with the brown pork chops and
the greenery on his plate the strong white wine began to
work upon him. He knew what was coming—the old
desolating anxiety and heartache stirred in his bowels.
He knew he oughtn't to finish the whole bottle, but he
did and lit a cigarette.

The P/W lieutenant in charge of the mess had been
leaning against a column and looking at Hal with a lumi-
nous interest. This Italian resembled a little the parachute
captain, but there was also in his brown triangular face
a print of the wildness of Reggio Calabria. He treated
his waiters with a gentleness, unlike the domineering
of the Italian officers over their soldati in the P/W enclosures around Oran. This Italian lieutenant knew some
secret of relaxation, for he nestled his thick hair in-
dolently against the column and crossed his bare legs. He
was wearing his old Italian khaki shorts, but his shirt
was American suntan P/W issue, with stars attached to
the tabs of his open collar.

Finally Hal lit another cigarette and held one out to
the P/W lieutenant. The Italian bounded toward him as
though he'd been preparing this movement for the past
five minutes. The flare from Hal's cigarette lighter threw
into relief the brown eyes and the sleek head. The Italian
took a puff and came to attention.

"Grazie tanto. . . . Lei mi sembra così gentile. . . . Se
tutti fossero come Lei."

"But I don't know a word of Italian," Hal said.

The Italian kept at rigid attention by Hal's table. Now
it was hard enough for Hal to keep up any intercourse
with people whose language he could understand. Therefore a huge tension reared inside him when he knew he
couldn't get a word across to the P/W lieutenant. Hal
wasn't one of those extroverts who could shout in English at someone ignorant of the language, and use violent
gestures, hoping thereby to force some semantic rap-
port. Nevertheless he motioned the Italian to sit down op-

84

posite him. The lieutenant in his turn motioned one of
the waiters to bring another dish of ice cream. Hal had
to eat it. The ice cream didn't belong to the Italian, but
there was a miraculous graciousness in his bounty as he
smiled his melting smile and talked a soft stream of
compliments of which Hal didn't understand a word. Yet
it wasn't so difficult as he'd feared. He didn't have to *cope*
with the Italian. When an American started to talk, Hal
always felt like asking him to please shut up. But there
was nothing offensive about this elegant little man. Perhaps he was lonely after thirteen months of imprisonment.
Perhaps Italians, being gregarious and rhetorical, became
even more melancholy than British and Americans.

"Mi permetta, signor tenente. Mi chiamo Scipione. E
Lei non può immaginare quanto mi piacerebbe avere un
amico sincero. Beh . . ."

"If I were going to be in Algiers long," Hal said, "I
could distract myself by teaching you English. I'd like to
do something for someone."

"Quindi," the P/W lieutenant said. He spread his
hands in a deprecating shrug as though to say that their
friendship was already a sealed testament. "Ho una bel-
lissima stanza qui in un albergo d'Algeri. . . . Sono tanto,
tanto bravi con me gli americani."

"All you need is a girl now," Hal said.

"Sono quattordici mesi che non tocco una donna,"
Scipione said. "Ho quasi perso il ricordo. Ma . . . cosa
vuole? È il nostro destino."

Hal was aware of the official stand on fraternization
with prisoners of war. But he waved for another bottle
of wine.

"Caro tenente, mi dispiace. Ma la lunga prigionia mi
ha rovinato lo stomaco. Il vino non lo posso più bere."

"In short," Hal said, "you won't drink with me. Lucky
people. No rough edges in your relations with others to
be lubricated with the grape. I envy you."

Rising abruptly from the table, he shook hands with
the gleaming little officer. A look of sodden dismay and
regret flooded the brown graceful face.

"O Dio mio, L'ho offeso? . . . Mi dica, La prego, che
fastidio Le ho dato?"

"It's nothing, nothing," said Hal.

Though something told him not to act this way, he
turned away with a surgical smile and went out into the

85

city of Algiers. It was beginning to grow dark. He went
and drank at the Center District Club where Italian P/W
dispensed a potent rum. At midnight he went walking
along the Mediterranean and picked up a girl. But he
discovered that the rum or his own mind had finally
made him impotent. He lay beside her weeping and
thinking through the old tale of Narcissus.

On July 26, 1944, Hal left Africa. He carried with him
its silt, since no one can be on that continent long without
forever being marked with something shadowy, brooding,
and evanescent as the Ayrabs. He sailed on a British
steamer onto which had been sardined the last remnants
of Allied Force Headquarters. Everyone said that as
soon as the ship sailed the French would clip the hair of
all Algerian grisettes and machine-gun the Ayrabs to
boost their own sagging prestige. They sailed on an old
cruise steamer converted into a troopship. There were
sumptuous meals, and the British were most obsequious,
as though from some policy of gratitude for lend-lease.
The passengers were a garish lot. They'd been swept out
by the last broom to clean AFHQ: French captains
involved in some misty liaison, American signal corps officers still carrying telephone wire and switchboards, and
unidentified Desert Rats who'd been waiting transportation to the Italian front since the fall of Tunisia. Every
night the ship blacked out, for who knew but what Jerry
might fly down from southern France and bomb the day-
lights out of them? Reconnaissance planes had been over
Algiers every night in July, 1944. If he bombed this troopship, some of the stoutest old lumber of the Allied armies
would go to the bottom.
    After Hal had swung his bedding roll into the hold,
where he bunked in the five-high arrangement, he stood
on deck and watched the lights of Algiers shimmer away
from him. The barrage balloons still swung aloft in the
moonlight. He was leaving Africa forever. There he'd
spent almost a year of his life. Some of the aridity of the
desert had been blown into him. There his personality had
learned of limitless horizons and the sickening mirage of
eternity. There he'd been sliced by the French perfection
of detail, but soundlessly, as glass under water can be
sheared by a scissors.
    He tried to sleep a lot on the trip to Italy, but the hold

was an inferno in the daytime. And at night the venti-
lators sounded as though his head were being held under
water. So he spent the hours of light hiding under funnels
on the deck. To read there were only improving books
put in the ship's library by British pietistic societies seeking to turn the traveler's mind to his salvation. Most
often Hal read the Gospel of Saint John.

He knew he was going to Italy, though security forbade
his knowing where. The dopesters were all certain they'd
land in Naples. And Hal, just after a rich English breakfast, when with coffee and a cigarette his spirits would
rise to what would be normal in most men—numbness
and resignation—used to wonder what he'd find in Italy.
Perhaps his African sojourn had been a time of testing, a
dark night of the soul. Perhaps in Italy he'd finally blos-
som out. But in his midnights he knew that Italy would
be just one more new place to adjust himself to. And
his powers of elasticity were now about as good as a
rubber band's that has lain in a sunny attic.

In those midnights when he couldn't smoke on deck
because of the blackout, Hal used to lean over the rail
and glare at the phosphorescence of the Mediterranean.
He'd seen it from Oran and Algiers. Now he was on it.
The Romans rode on it, Shelley was drowned in it, Mussolini thought it was his sea. By sunlight it was an
aching blue. At midnight it was just another body of
water on which a ship could float. Sometimes, in the dark,
anonymous figures in shorts came and stood beside him
and shared his glances over the black water glowing
in the wake of the ship. But even though they stood at his
elbow, Hal made no attempt to enter their worlds, as he
might once have tried to. Once, accosted by a word of
greeting, he left the rail and descended swiftly into the
sweltering hold. Anything was better than to be talked to.
It was his achievement that in crossing the Mediterranean
he never said a word to anyone except the gentle Cockney
table waiters.

He saw the Cape of Bizerte shrouded in its ghostly
triangle of sunset. He saw the island of Sicily jutting like
a palace. Over those escarpments the spirit of the parachute captain flew. Perhaps at night his spry hairy figure
sucked the blood of Sicilian children abroad late in the
streets of Palermo.

With the dawn of the third morning he arose heavy

and sweaty to find birds flapping alongside the ship and a hammerlike mass of ocher rock lifting out of the sea. He saw the eyeless sockets of caves in its sides and many pretty villas perched over crevasses.

"That's Capri," someone said to someone else, accenting the last syllable. "We'll go and see the grottoes. The airplane drivers do a lot of their shacking there."

By noon they were sliding into the harbor of a city.

"That's Naples," said the voice that accompanies all travelers. "I'd know it from the postcards and the pitchers in the barbershops. Look, that's Vesuvius. . . . Yessir, the old anthill's smokin. Ain't got over the shock of Anzio yet. . . . And see that big thing that looks like a country club at the top of the city? That's Castel Sant'Elmo. . . . I been readin my guidebooks."

Hal thought, See Naples and die, wondering if he really might. It had the same open-fan formation, spread on the hills and sliding into the harbor, as Algiers. But it was vaster, Naples. Hal thought of the million lives squirming in that crowded dihedral; of the spray of dialect, of the typhus and DDT, of the flash of colors in the streets where boys slept on their bellies. An odor such as he'd never whiffed before was in the air, a stink and a perfume of dead flowers and human matter and the voice of Saint Thomas Aquinas at the University of Naples, and Enrico Caruso dying at Somma Vesuviana and all the spaghetti in the universe. Already the tugs were slithering them into their berth like patient worried little daughters leading a blind old mother. And tiny fishing skiffs water-bugged it over the bay and careened alongside the British troopship. The fishermen showed their teeth and called out in an indescribable dialect.

Nearly all the berths in Naples harbor were twisted like the machinery in a petroleum yard after an explosion. Blasted and bombed cranes clawed wildly at the sky. A few ships still lay on their rusty sides. They looked like fat women who'd committed suicide in water too shallow to drown them. The acres of devastation along the water front were something Hal had never imagined, except in the rubbled castles of his own brain. For a mile along the port area the houses lay in their gray dust. Here and there a room stuck out of a second story where a bomb had split a house in half. Some were like dollhouses, in which a side can be hinged away for a cross section of all the rooms. Here was half a staircase leading nowhere, a flapping shred of blue wallpaper. In one blasted room the pictures still hung askew on the wall, waiting for some housewife to come and straighten them. The dock area and beyond it were mostly blocks of rubble and segments of balcony and girders thrusting out in pointless punctuation marks. In these ex-houses people had been born and loved and begotten and died. Eggs dropped from the sky had blown them apart.

Hal leaned his head against the railing. Now he understood the difference between being and no-being, there in the silence and the heat and the mess of Naples at high noon. The lovely, the cruel, and the opportunist were all entombed here in this shambles around the Bay of Naples. Himself, trembling and weary and reduced to a zero before the horror of it, saw the aftermath. He saw clearly what he'd been feeling dimly for twenty-nine years —that to human life and striving there's no point whatever. That we are all of us bugs writhing under the eye of God, begging to be squashed. That as evidence of our mortality all we leave behind us is the green whey of a fly that is swatted to death.

There was a dispute over the order of debarkation. Finally the British infantry were marched off first. They were going straight to the front, so there was no need of their idling on deck. They clunked down the gangplank with their rifles.

"Ees doon bloody well ere. Blimey, whot eel do to oos or oos to im!"

Some of the Americans got bored watching the stream of Limeys debarking, so without authority they scaled the rope ladders, grabbing their barracks bags and bedding rolls and tearing across the hinged bridge to land. They pre-empted little Neopolitans to tote their luggage. These were dirtier and more vociferous than anything Hal had seen in Africa. He'd expected a Neapolitan would look like a chef in a Second Avenue restaurant, standing on the pier in an apron and mixing a dish of spaghetti and garlic.

"Eyeties," said the voice of the Eternal Tourist. "Ginsoes. There they are. The Ayrabs of Europe."

The barracks bags and the bedding rolls were put into piles with armed guards. Nobody trusted the little Neapolitans. Hal heard explanations that one would be three

89

miles away by the time he'd hoisted your baggage to his shoulder. He heard that if a jeep were left unattended in the streets of Naples, the Neapolitans would pick it clean to the chassis.

He obeyed all the landing instructions and found himself in a two-and-a-half-ton truck with all his baggage inviolate. The small Neapolitans swarmed all over the truck, not at all fazed by having empty or loaded carbines pointed at their heads. Over all the confusion at the port their dialect twittered and buzzed like a hive of hornets. Hal sensed that for all their dirt and thievery they also stole a zest and a passion for life.

He was driven through the port area, past tetrahedron air-raid shelters, past files of crumbled buildings, to his billet on Via Diaz. He lumped all his junk in the center of the floor and went out to see Naples. It was 1600 hours; the sun was like a white-hot thumb pressing on Castel Sant'Elmo.

In the first words he'd spoken in four days he inquired the way to the main drag. On Via Roma he found moving in both directions on both sidewalks of the narrow street a crowd thicker than anything in Times Square. The Allied soldiery all had a sour look. The Italians were selling cameos. They catered also to every bodily need in shrill idiomatic English. Pimping was the province of very tiny boys. Hal walked for five minutes and came at last to a spacious arcade opening off Via Roma. The crowd just pushed him there. It was like walking into a city within a city. There was no glass in the domed skylight. He asked an idling GI for information.

"This is the Galleria Umberto, lootenant, sir. Everybody in Naples comes here."

Hal looked around the Galleria as he walked through it. It was like all outdoors going on inside. He liked the feeling of being roofed over without any coffin sensation of claustrophobia. The Galleria was jammed with Allied soldiers and sailors, women sweeping, bars, art shops, small booths selling jewelry, columns, tattered flags and standards, lights suspended from the vaulted roof as though this were some vast basketball court.

"These people," he said to himself, "are all in search of love. The love of God, or death, or of another human being. They're all lost. That's why they walk so aimlessly.
90

They all feel here that the world isn't big enough to hold them. And look at the design of this place. Like a huge cross laid on the ground, after the corpus is taken off the nails."

Hal walked around the Galleria. He stuck his hands into his pockets, swaggered a little, and tried to smile at everyone. Often his smiles were returned. But he didn't follow them up. His was the disinterested smile of God the Father surveying the world after the sixth day. And Hal had never seen so many soldiers whose free time hung like a weight on their backs, as their packs had hung in combat. They sat at the outside tables of the bars and drank vermouth. They wore shoulder patches of three divisions. Their faces were seamy or gentle or questioning or settled or blank. No other people in the Galleria Umberto had so many nuances on their lips as the Americans Hal saw there.

After looking in all the shop windows and all the posters and traversing both sides of the X-shaped pavement that bisected the Galleria, Hal sat down at one of the tables. He knew that he was in the tiniest yet the greatest city of the world. But it hadn't the fixed pattern of a small town. It was a commune of August 1944, and its population changed every day. These people who came to the Galleria to stand and drink and shop and look and question were set apart from the rest of the modern world. They were outside the formula of mothers and wives and creeds. The Galleria Umberto was like that city in the middle of the sea that rises every hundred years to dry itself in the sun.

An old Neapolitan in a greasy apron was standing beside his table. Hal ordered a drink, giving the old man two cigarettes and the fee for a double vermouth, which tasted like fruity alum. And then, looking again through the Galleria, which had enraptured him as a circus does a child, Hal saw a figure bearing down on him. And he knew that he had been waiting, had been summoned to the Galleria for this. The figure came through the mob with the surety of a small boat picking its way through shoals.

The parachute captain took one of the wicker chairs and sat down beside him without saying a word. Hal felt the bright bitter eyes going over his face. The Neapolitan brought another vermouth. Then Hal spoke with the studied casualness of one who seeks to show that his thoughts are elsewhere:

"How's your grave?"

"Blow all that," the parachute captain said. "You've always stalled with me. That's caused your ruin. You're a dishonest man, chum. You think of yourself as the center of the universe. . . . And anything that doesn't fit into your scheme of things gets rationalized away like a piece of rock found on the wrong geologic stratum."

That vague sword was already beginning to pierce Hal's heart, but he paid no attention and said:

"Look at these people around us . . . the same as you and I.'

"The same?" The captain threw back his head and laughed. "Your pity goes too far, boy. Or not far enough. You've never learned the difference between seeing humanity and getting smothered by it. The more you feel you *must* love humanity, the more you indicate a certain deficiency in yourself. . . . Jesus Christ must have been a misanthrope deep down inside, who tried to offset his truer characteristics. Love is the most natural thing in this world, you see. A lover never feels he *must* love, because he does. Only the harf-arsed poets invented love as a force that has nothing to do with anything, because they had to cook up something to write about, as propagandists cook up causes to die for. . . . I'm talking of the sorrow of those who think, rather than those who do. . . . In wartime the greatest heroes are the sensitive and shy and gentle. They're great because they have to live in a world which is dedicated in wartime to an annihilation of everything they stand for. They're the unsung. No one will ever sing to them. Except us, the dead. Their theme's too secret, like masturbation. . . . If a man all his life has oxidized his every mood the moment it entered his glands, if he insulted and slugged his way along, it's not a much greater effort for him to go into battle. The gentle die in battle. Your crude extrovert comes out of his ordeal more brutal and crass and cocky than when he went in. That's the way civilizations die, gradually. A premium is put on physical courage in wartime which kills off the gentle, because they're too noble to admit of cowardice. So they die. . . . Death to them is terrible. And it's just another of

92

those things to people who aren't aware of life, except as a current of vitality that carries them along."

"And yet," Hal said, leaning forward and hearing the thumping of his own heart, "you fought and died in Sicily a few months ago. What are you so bitter about? Your ghost should mount a soapbox in Union Square. Perhaps you could finally teach the world something."

The elegant and mocking figure looked at him and laid its shining high boots across an adjoining chair. This parachute captain had the scorn of a demon, who knows that he can very well afford to thumb his nose at God because he will burn through all eternity no matter what he does.

"My death in Sicily," the captain said, sending a graceful hairy claw through the air, "was merely a compensation for my life. My life was a mess. I was a Broadway chorus boy. Do you think I liked swishing my way through the American theater? Do you think I enjoyed the fascism of great stars and booking agents and elegants who thought they were writers? Jesus, no! But in my jump training I was able to exorcise all this nonsense. In the crazy camaderie of silk and geronimo I achieved reality to my life. . . . Oh, there was nothing solemn or dignified in the way I took my exit. It was a bullet in my face, just after I'd landed, and was looking around for my men, to urge them on in the way that cameramen like. My death was the expiation of that ridiculous society for which I danced, painted and epicene behind a proscenium arch. I was a very jerky marionette on the stage and a very still one as a corpse. . . . But let me tell you one thing, Joe: the ecstasy of death is a greater one than I found in love or the dance with a capital D. . . . I pity you for all your struggling and whining to yourself. For I'm free, free! . . . Out forever from under all this pitiful shit of human life!"

"How you hate," Hal said, covering his face with his vermouth glass.

"Your imaginary troubles," the captain said, crooking a finger and smiling almost tenderly, "are far more serious than mine ever were. At least I was able to lump all mine in one ball."

Hal looked away into the sunny Galleria. The captain's words clattered in on him. And there was that old sinking sensation of having a world on his shoulders without asking for it.

"The wisdom of death," he said, trying to strike a tone of banter. But his teeth showed like a skull's.

"The French," the captain said, striking a tone of preciosity, "speak of the expérience mortelle. We've both had it . . . but it seems to have paralyzed you, boy. You must either live or die. You're trying to do both. . . . I died. . . . But my spirit is congealed into one knot of fury. I left this life angry, but not hurt, whole, even though mangled. . . . I see through you. You're trying to conceal that your soul is a perfumed jellyfish. You've tried to wrestle with the larger issues when you're not sure whether you can read and write. . . . Wise up to yourself, buddy. It's not too late."

Hal arose and knocked over the wicker table.

"I don't care to drink with you any more. And please, please don't visit me again. Let me alone. You're the essence of all that's evil in the world. You're the evilest person I've ever known. There's something about your mouth, the way it works, as though this world were just your orange, to be sucked dry. . . ."

"Ah, mysticism and metaphor," the captain said softly, also rising. "There's no place for that crap any more, chuck. It's outworn, like the Middle Ages trying to smoke out syphilis with incense. Certainly there are faith and spirituality, but this time there's no applying the old creeds and schemes. You have no right to seek God directly. You must do it through other people. They're all small pieces of Him. If you know and love all the people of your time, you know God."

"Let's go down on our knees together," Hal said, "and pray because we're both so proud and cold and heartless."

"Less proud and cold and heartless than most. . . . I prayed as I was dying. And I died at twenty-two. . . . But my death was part of the scheme and the deception, that's all. . . . You don't want to learn anything, do you, kid?"

"Pray to Our Lord and Savior Jesus Christ," Hal said.

He was terrified at the rabid insistence in his voice.

For the next five days he lay in his billet and looked at the ceiling. For five nights he couldn't close his eyes. In his head he heard a continual crashing, as of buildings falling down irreparably. Often it seemed to him that he was capable of everything, but especially of the great and

94

the good things of life. It seemed he had only to stretch out his hand and the sorrowing world would be remade and every tear dried in every eye. He wanted so to help, to help, to help. . . .

Then they took him in an ambulance to the Forty-fifth General Hospital, where he was given a knockout drug for paranoia and delusions of persecution. A nurse there was a first lieutenant, a Russian Jewess named Luba. She said to the psychiatrist, a major:

"Gee, sir, nuts are all so individual. They're not ordinary people. . . . Now you take that tall good-looking one who thinks he's Jesus Christ. . . . Why, damn it, if he grew a beard, I'd believe he *was*. . . ."

THIRD PROMENADE

(Casablanca-Algiers)

I REMEMBER the Sixth General Hospital in Casablanca. It was stuck, as they seem to stick all hospitals, in a school with large windows and many floors. Its doctors and its nurses were mostly from New England, so that the place had an air of efficiency and cold kindness that struck me strange in Casa. The nurses lived in a high apartment like a silo. The GI's had a tent area near Parc Lyautey. On one side was a clearing of French tanks drawn up in rows, the way military force is deceptive and orderly—on review. Between the tanks and the tents there was a cement road where the French used to walk arm in arm in the evenings. Ward boys and dental technicians leaned over their barbed-wire enclosure on nights when they weren't on duty. They called out to all and sundry, as though they felt it necessary to reaffirm their being in a strange land. Their tents were pyramidal. In the daytime the flaps were tucked up, and I could see the mosquito netting looped up over the frames of the cots in a tight ball.

I remember that the nurses at the Sixth General Hospital were plumper and saltier than most ANC's. They talked wistfully of Boston and Taunton and Waltham and Cambridge and Worcester. Army general hospitals are incestuous. They're like a little town in which everyone spies on everyone else, and everyone dates everyone else. The surgical captain has his favorite nurse, while the anesthetist looks on and gnashes his teeth. The patients are well cared for, but they're outside the charmed circle; they're like guests at a summer hotel in the Adirondacks. They never get to see the inside. They lie on their beds and watch the life of the general hospital. They're not a part of it at all, unless some nurse takes a fancy to them on her ward, or some doctor bucking for his majority takes a special interest in their rare disease.

The main ward at the Sixth General was the biggest in the whole world. They'd taken over a lumber shed and a printing plant, and the beds just went on and on. In those acres of beds they could have laid all the sick and wounded of the war. I remember lying in my bed in this ward. I had the GI's because I'd neglected to scald my mess gear with one soapy and two clear. My illness gave me a time schedule all my own. I'd feel the dry spasms of peristalsis in my belly and I'd go tearing to the latrine. Everything came out of me in an agony over which I had no control. Then I'd go back to bed, cured of everything, including my energy and the will to live. Two hours later it would happen all over again. I turned from side to side under my mosquito netting and watched the going and comings on the big ward, the visits, the flirtations. I envied the Georgia ward boys for the easy way they had with the doctors and nurses, the kidding, the rushes with the bedpan, and the goose-necked jars of amber. And because I was an ambulatory patient, I had to make my own bed every morning.

I remember best one of the nurses. She told us to call her Butch. She was from Dorchester and she was the biggest gal I'd ever seen. When she bent over to take my temperature, I thought from her wide breasts and bulging belly that a witty and motherly cow was ministering to me. We loved the lieutenant for her laugh that was cynical and rich. She specialized in making the appendix patients laugh until they all but burst their stitches. There was a smell of cologne and soap about her. One night she had a baby on the stairs of the nurses' quarters. The colonel had to deliver her himself; it was the first time he'd practiced obstetrics in thirty years. He was so mad at her for waking him out of a sound sleep that he shipped

96

her and her baby back from Casa to the States. We smiled in our beds, for after she'd cared for us all, she now had something all her own to love. A parachutist in a near-by bed bet that an Ayrab was the father, but none of us laughed. We were ashamed of the parachutist and devoted to the lieutenant. She'd been the nurse of the Sixth General who'd mitigated for us the somber impersonal excellence of army medical care. She'd had a good word for each of us. Often when we couldn't sleep in the Casablanca nights, she'd given us that pink pill. A truck driver three beds over said that if he ever got back to Boston alive, he'd take out our lieutenant and her baby and set them up to supper and drinks. He added that women like the lieutenant are the salt of the earth.

I remember also the nut ward of the Sixth General in Casa. Not that I was ever in there, except for a visit. It was called the Parker House after the nice old psychiatrist in charge of it. Lieutenant Colonel Parker never knew why so many people smiled at him on the streets of Casablanca. He kept the nuts in a separate building, locked and grated and barred and remote from the other buildings of the Sixth General. Beaucoup GI's and officers ended up in the Parker House. From there they usually went home on a boat, under guard. The officers and GI's were together in one ward. I guessed that when you went off your trolley, you didn't care much whether your insignia was a bar or a stripe.

I remember going to the Parker House to visit a buddy who blew up after a week's sitting and staring at the wall of his tent. He took his tommy gun and fired it at the canvas. Then he lay, after he'd fired his bursts, in a slit trench of his own making until our major came:

"What are you trying to do, Perkins, k-k-k-kill us all?"

And Perkins was taken to the Parker House. It was his theory that his heart was going to stop in the very next minute. Old Colonel Parker told him there was nothing the matter with his heart. Still he moaned and stared at the wall for hours on end. He wasn't the same, I remember, when I went to see him the last night before they shipped him back to the States. He sat on a bench with his head in his hands. He was wearing GI pajamas and a red bathrobe with 6TH GEN HOSP stenciled on the back. They'd taken away the belt of his bathrobe so he couldn't strangle himself. But when he saw me outside

97

the grating, all his apathy dropped, and he came over
and hung on the bars, smiling and cavorting, like a monkey praying to be fed.

"They're ZI-ing me. It's one way to get out of all this
crap."

He told me about the new truth drug they gave him,
and he wondered what he'd talked about under its influence.

"Just like you do when you get crocked," I said reas-
suringly.

"Well, anyway, I'm getting out of all this crap," he said
over and over.

After a while the MP told me I must go. The MP's at
the Parker House were a strange gang, gentle and gan-
gling and tender. They used to kid the nuts, and they
told me on my way out that many people outside in the
army were crazier than some locked up in here.

I remember that outside on the streets of Casa I wondered which of us would go next to the Parker House. I
got lower and lower because I knew Perkins wasn't just
pretending. So finally I went into the Select Bar and started
throwing them down. I got bluer and bluer in spite of
the phonograph playing "L'ombre s'enfuit" and the luscious Casablancaise hanging over her cash register and
the pigs sitting buxomly on the green leather chairs and
waiting till I'd buy them a drink. It was a new sort of
drunkenness I hit that evening. I seemed to be a ghost in
a roomful of yelling people, all aliver than I.

When they threw me out of the Select at closing time,
I lurched through the streets of Casa and got lost. I'd
go a few blocks, lean against a doorway, black out, come
to, and then blunder on again. It was the only time I'd
ever wanted to meet an MP. Once I came to and looked
up to see the stars of Casa flickering. I was lying on my
back in the rue, and an Ayrab was bending over me. He
was removing my cigarettes and franc notes from my
pockets. I began to laugh in my stupor as I thought of
the GI legend that the Ayrabs will cut off your balls
and sew them in your mouth. I laughed although the
cognac had paralyzed me. The Ayrab stopped his frisk-
ing and kissed me on the forehead.

"Je cherche ce soir un copain du genre féminin."

And knowing I was about to black out again, I gath-

98

ered up all my forces and yelled. The Ayrab fled laughing into the blue shadows. I remember being trussed into the MP wagon. And I remember waking in an immaculate bed at the Sixth General.

"I want Lieutenant Duffy to give me a pink pill."

"Oh hush your mouth," the nurse said, reversing my ice pack. "You're still as drunk as a skunk."

I remember when it came our turn to go in the forty-by-eights. We sat by the long stubby train in the freight yards of Casa, swatting flies. The officer in charge of the movement bustled about counting noses. We lay on our barracks bags swigging from our canteens.

"This is it. We're going to Italy to fight."

"Ah, blow it. . . . I figure we're going to Oran or Algiers for more of this base section life."

I remember that our officers had two cars of their own up front. We were put with all our equipment into the open latticed horsecars. Guard details were posted in each car. Through the slats the Ayrabs could stick their fingers and remove anything, for we heard that the train went through Morocco at a speed less than a man could run. We made our beds on the floor, where there were still leavings of hay.

I remember how strange and autonomous it was to scud slowly through Morocco in a boxcar. At one end we had a pile of C-rations and a gasoline can of water. On the floor were our packs and blankets. We slept like a litter of kittens. The brown cleft hills swam slowly past; I sat on a ledge with my legs swinging. The crap games started up. The train would stop in the middle of desert spaces where there was nothing to halt for. And Ayrab kids would come out of the nowhere as though they'd inched up from the sand. With them, since we'd been red-lined for months, we did a thriving trade in mattress covers, shirts, and trousers. They brought us vin rouge in leather bottles. At night, lying on the floor, it was hard to sleep. In the moonlight the sandy hummocks drifted past as though I watched them from a magic carpet. Or sometimes I remember that the duty officer would come to our car when the train was taking on water. He wore fatigues and carried his carbine slung on his shoulder. After six months in Casa he figured that these were genu-

99

ine combat conditions. Who knew but what the Ayrabs would ambush us all by the full of the moon when we were stalled out in the middle of nowhere?

"Remember it's a court-martial offense to sell anything to the Ayrabs, men."

"Yessir," we said in chorus.

In his barracks bag the mess sergeant had beaucoup vin that he'd laid in before we left Casa. He had also a small spirit lamp, a present from his last shackjob. He was a Polack hunky and knew all the angles. He knew how to lick around officers with a bold obsequiousness that made them think he was treating them as a rough and ready equal. With us he was like an SS man in the movies. When drunk, which was always, he'd knock our heads together and let loose on us a stream of obscenities. He said that these phrases excited a shackjob more than loving words. Then when we were black and blue, he'd fall into a sort of motherliness towards us and make coffee. He was in his element in that forty-by-eight. Made us bring him his breakfast box of K-ration as he lay yawning in his sack. His buddy the second cook Jacobowski was growing a mustache on the trip.

I remember the sorrows of our officers in their two wagons-lit up front. The French locomotive sooted all over the cars so that they had to sit all day with their windows closed while they read their cases or did crossword puzzles. Our officers fell into types. The Sporting Set had their musette bags full of rum and didn't come out of their haze till we hit Algiers. The Girls had pneumatic mattresses which they inflated every evening at sundown. On the second day out of Casa the officers ordered the French engineer to put their cars at the end of the train. Said they were tired of looking like Negroes. But French engineers take orders from no one but Maréchal Pétain.

Outside of Oran at Mostaganem I remember we stopped on a siding near Prisoner of War Enclosure 131. Shipping to Algiers were all Italian officer P/W who'd decided that they were no longer fascist but wanted to collaborate with us Allies. We got out of our forty-by-eights and stretched our legs. We were warned by the duty officer that we mustn't fraternize with the P/W.

"Fraternize, my arse," the mess sergeant said after the officer had gone. "Who wants to fraternize with an Eye-

100

tie? They fired on our boys in Africa, didn't they? And they're doin it now in Italy."

"They did it because they were told to," the pfc said. He was a liberal and wore horn-rimmed spectacles.

"I say, put the bastards against a wall," the mess sergeant said.

He always shouted his opinions.

"You forget the Geneva Convention," the pfc said gently.

"Sure, we treat em white!" the mess sergeant said, looking at his buddy Jacobowski. "So in twenty years they can declare war on us again. What have they got to lose? They'll live better'n they did in the Eyetalian Army. . . . Friggin wops . . . Dagos. . . ."

"Polack," the pfc said, almost inaudibly.

I remember how the Italian officers approached their cars with the MP guards. I thought of the Guineas of Brooklyn and Joisey City with their pimpled faces and their oiled hair and the aggressive spite that made them boxers and corner toughs. For I'd never seen anything of the Italian Army except the explosive tiny Sicilians from Camp 101 who used to wait in the officers' messes of Casa.

"Christ!" screamed the mess sergeant, waving his lumpy fists. "They're gettin parlor cars!"

"The Geneva Convention," the pfc prompted under his breath.

"Those Ginso bastards are gettin parlor cars while we sleep like pigs in a forty-by-eight! Will someone please tell me what this goddam war is about?"

We walked a little closer to have a look at the Italian officers, waiting to mount the train with their gear.

"Gosh, they *are* good-looking men," the company clerk said.

He read the pomes in *Stars and Stripes*.

I remember that the Italians struck me with marveling. They looked neither like movie gangsters nor like the sad barbers of Brooklyn. These carried themselves with a certain soft proudness, though I remember arrogant ones among them. A few were blond. But nearly all wore a delicacy of feature and a dignity I'd never seen before. Their noses and their mouths had a different look than Americans'. The Bersaglieri officers had sugarloaf caps

101

with feathers in them. The Alpini officers wore shorts
that showed their fine long legs, like the limbs on wres-
tlers in old statues. And all had sewed, below the left
shoulder, a metal boot.

"Well, Musso did all right in his men," the company
clerk said.

"Wait till we see the wimmin," the mess sergeant
promised. "I'm keepin my C-ration till we get to Italy.
Those Ginso signorinas will do anything for food."

"Damn good-looking guys," a corporal said. "But I
s'pose they'd put a knife in your back as quick as they'd
look at you."

I remember that one of our officers talked Italian.
His old man had left Naples and had made a mint in
the meat-packing business in Chicago. This was the moment Lieutenant Figarotta'd been sweating out for years,
a chance to crap all over the folks from the old country.
He stepped forward and offered a cigarette to an officer
of the Alpini. When the officer reached out with a smile
and a bow, Lieutenant Figarotta tittered and twitched
the cigarette out of reach. The Italian officer flushed
and stood at rigid attention. This scene angered some of
us.

"If you ask me," the pfc with glasses said, "they make
some of our officers look sick."

But no one had asked him.

"Pretty boys, ain't they?" the mess sergeant ranted to
his following, but not too loudly. "How'd ya like to have
ya sisters goin out on dates with them? Because that's exactly what them P/W are doin back in the States. And
our wimmin are fassenated with that Dago stuff."

And I remember that, as he was getting into his
car, a captain of the Bersaglieri dropped his portfolio at
my feet. I hesitated an instant, then I bent and picked it
up and handed it to him.

"Grazie infinite," he said.

There was something old and warm in his voice such
as I'd never heard before. I felt that beyond all pretense
he liked me, that he was lonely and lost. On his lips was
a neat mustache. He had clear gray eyes behind lashes
longer than any I'd ever seen, except those that girls
buy in the five and ten. His breath was sweet. He wavered
an instant before me, then vaulted into his car.

The Italian officers hung out of the windows of their

cars, talking excitedly to one another like vacationists on an excursion train. Most had blue-gray caps like Mussolini's, with the earflaps tied up over their heads. Some waved cordially to the MP's.

"Addio al reticolato, a quel benedetto recinto!" one called.

The mess sergeant was beside himself with fury. He raved at all the cars of Italian officers:

"If ya hadn't declared war on us, I wouldn't be here lookin at ya goddam sissy faces."

"They had no more to do with the war than you did," the pfc confided to his spectacles.

I remember that as I lay down again in my sack in the forty-by-eight, I mused on the faces of those Italians. They had fewer lines, fewer splotches than the young men of America. I wasn't quite convinced that their sorrow came because they were defeated. It must be some agony that we as yet knew nothing of. . . . But then they'd declared war on us. They were our enemies. Yet in those young men of Italy I'd seen something centuries old. An American is only as old as his years. A long line of something was hidden behind the bright eyes of those Italians. And then and there I decided to learn something of the modern world. There was something abroad which we Americans couldn't or wouldn't understand. But unless we made some attempt to realize that everyone in the world isn't American, and that not everything American is good, we'd all perish together, and in this twentieth century. . . . My mind kept reverting to the captain of the Bersaglieri. And under different circumstances he'd have ordered me to my death. . . . Something stirred in me that touched me more profoundly than ever before, even in love. And I fell asleep. . . .

FOURTH PORTRAIT

Father Donovan and Chaplain Bascom

IN AUGUST, 1944, the Galleria Umberto echoed like a bowling alley to the noise of the truck convoys going north to the front. Father Donovan and Chaplain Bas-

103

com used to stroll afternoons through the din and the
heat. Sometimes while window-shopping they'd take off
their khaki caps and mop their brows. Chaplain Bascom
wore a gold oak leaf, but Father Donovan was still
that same first lieutenant who'd left a South Philadelphia
parish with the blessing of his bishop and the Military
Ordinariate.

Chaplain Bascom was commenting on the heat. He was
a stout man, used to the sun over his turnip patch in
Spartanburg, South Carolina.

"Hope we never git closer to hell than this, padre."

"Beware of sins against the Holy Ghost, chaplain,"
said Father Donovan.

For two years now he'd been indoctrinating his friend
with Catholicism. He did it gently, for he was a mild sort
of priest who replied you're welcome when a telephone
operator thanked him for his number.

The two chaplains often walked arm in arm. They
were the only officers in the 34th Division who did so,
sober. They were reasonably fond of each other. And
their friendship was high propaganda for the chief chaplains, showing how all faiths worked together in the army.

Chaplain Bascom withdrew his arm to light a briar pipe,
his only vice.

"These Neapolitans," he boomed jovially, "could do
with a shoutin baptism by immersion."

"But they've already been baptized once," said Father
Donovan. "Though not in the Baptist Church, chaplain."

"Well, I've written to Charleston," Chaplain Bascom
went on doggedly. "I told them that Naples is an un-
plowed field for Baptist missionaries with a will to work.
. . . Bibles instead of cameos of Via Roma. Prohibition to
cut out all this devil's drink of vino. And good friendly
Barathea Clubs on Wednesday evenings to keep these
signorinas off the streets."

This was the focus of their differences. The division
chaplain had introduced them in the staging area, and
they'd been friends ever since. To Missus Bascom and
Lavinia, Chaplain Bascom reiterated by V-mail that Padre
Donovan was almost a white man. And Father Donovan
had offered up many a Mass and rosary for the conversion of Chaplain Bascom and his South Carolina flock.
Both were popular chaplains in the 34th. Men who had
knocked up a signorina came to Father Donovan for con-

104

fession. Those desiring advice on their life insurance came to Chaplain Bascom. They complemented one another. Chaplain Bascom at the end of a meeting yelled for every man to get away from the sides of the tent and come up and be saved. Father Donovan was still as shy and efficient and button-eyed as when he played quarterback at the seminary.

Father Donovan looked up at the glassless dome of the Galleria, at the lordly angels sounding their trumpets from the cornices.

"Spacious as the Vatican," he mused. "I'll get you to an audience with the Holy Father next time we're in Rome."

"H'm'm, padre. A body has to draw the line at some things."

Chaplain Bascom stumped along huffing on his briar pipe. He'd underestimated the papist till the division went on the line. Then he'd seen why even Protestant colonels of regiments tried to requisition Romish chaplains. For along with his combat boots and neckerchief, Father Donovan wore a Purple Heart. He might have looked like a mouse, but the Italian-born mice at Cassino hadn't been so much in evidence as Father Donovan ministering to the dying under a helmet that made him look like a child playing soldier.

And Father Donovan also whisked along thinking his own thoughts. Often he looked slyly at Chaplain Bascom. How much he thought on Chaplain Bascom while reading his breviary! What a find this man would be for Holy Mother Church! That swollen voice, how eloquent it could be pouring out in praise of Mary, instead of inveighing against dancing and cardplaying and likker! Father Donovan would have given his Purple Heart for the conversion of Chaplain Bascom. For this grace he importuned every saint in heaven, including his dead mother, who'd scrubbed floors all her life.

Father Donovan bent down and fastened a buckle on his combat boot. He paused to mop his thin pale face. He spied some GI's sitting at tables on the terrace of an outside bar.

"In the mood for a cool drink, chaplain?"

"None of this vino for me, padre. You should take the pledge yourself."

105

"And what would I do at morning Mass?" Father Donovan laughed plaintively.

They sat at one of the wicker tables under the dome of the Galleria Umberto. All about him Father Donovan spotted GI's of the 34th who waved to him and went back to their sprawling. He ordered a glass of vermouth for himself and a tumbler of flavored gaseous water for Chaplain Bascom.

"Our boys mustn't think I'm guzzling," Chaplain Bascom said, holding up his orangeade to show everyone in the Galleria that he was taking the Neapolitan equivalent of an ice-cream soda.

"It would only increase their esteem for you," Father Donovan said primly.

Now Father Donovan didn't smoke. He always said that the fumes of Chaplain Bascom's pipe were enough for two. In spite of his wispy body he was in fine condition, and combat had made him like a grasshopper. Chaplain Bascom's steaky belly had gone down during these two years of Africa and Sicily and Italy when he wasn't getting Missus Bascom's corn bread for supper. Father Donovan used to spend Sunday afternoons in South Philadelphia playing touch football with the kids of his choir—after he'd peeled off his Roman collar and rolled up his cassock till it was a black towel around his waist. Father Donovan loved baseball, candy, and the movies—after he'd assured himself that they'd been certified by the Legion of Decency.

"There's one favor you could do me, chaplain," said Father Donovan, leaning softly over his vermouth.

Never in his life had he raised his voice except to call for the murder of the umpire.

"Anything, anything," the chaplain said, clearing his throat of orangeade with a lordly gargle.

"Why won't you call me Father? I'm a priest. Padre sounds like Teddy Roosevelt. . . . Oh I know it's regular army and all that . . ."

"Army Regulations," said Chaplain Bascom, assuming the rapt pose with which he ended his prayer meetings, "provide that all chaplains, regardless of denomination, shall be addressed as chaplain . . ."

"But they also state that there's no objection to calling a priest Father. Don't tell me that at this stage of the
106

game you're jealous of the prestige and affection in the word Father?"

"Always a slight chip on your shoulder," Chaplain Bascom said, gathering his weight up behind his orangeade. He smelled brimstone.

"Just thought I'd ask," Father Donovan said in his meekest tone, which he always lapsed into when piqued.

Chaplain Bascom glowered around the Galleria. His veinous porcine eyes stared, as though he were looking for some shrinking GI to work on with the magic words: All here from South Calina raise their hands. . . . He relit his pipe. Father Donovan, who knew all his moods, waited but said nothing. He looked at the other chaplain's cap with its gold oak leaf and wondered why all the priests in the army except the chief in Washington seemed to be first lieutenants. Soon Chaplain Bascom would be a lieutenant colonel, at which point he'd begin to consider himself a staff officer, with command functions. In vain did Father Donovan keep telling himself that he was a priest, commissioned in the army only to keep souls in the way they should go, to give the last rites to the dying, and to return the living to their dioceses without loss of faith or strain or mortal sin. For sometimes when he was saying his rosary or reading his holy office, he'd find his fingers straying to his cap and feeling that lone silver bar. It was a sin of vanity. But in his examinations of conscience he admitted to himself that to be promoted to captain would delight and appease him. . . . He deserved it. He'd done just as much work as Chaplain Bascom. . . .

And Chaplain Bascom, watching his mild friend out of one corner of an eye throbbing with rage, thought: They're all alike deep down inside. The same who started the Inquisition, the same who held back all scientific progress, the same who still wield a world dictatorship.

"Look there now," said Chaplain Bascom. "Most interesting. . . ."

An oily Italian priest came cruising into the Galleria in black cassock and brushed round hat. He zoomed among the GI's like a water bug, wheedling, panhandling, trembling with holy zeal for alms. He had a card in English which he thrust under the faces of the GI's.

"Almost a different church here," Father Donovan said under his breath.

The Italian priest arrived over an isolated GI who'd passed out in his chair. He looked quickly around the Galleria, then bent over the hunched form.

"Most interesting," Chaplain Bascom said gleefully.

As Father Donovan watched, saying a Hail Mary under his breath, the greasy Italian friar began to pry at a wad of lire and a pack of Luckies protruding from the unbuttoned breast pocket of the GI. Father Donovan leaped from his chair, crossed the Galleria, and barged up to the thieving brother. He didn't know any Italian, but he used the Latin that came into his mind:

"Hoc est enim corpus meum."

Then as a sort of exorcism he shook the silver cross of his collar insignia. The hustling friar, unshaven and smelling of his last meal, whirled about in his cape, gathered it about him with grimy fingers, and went streaking away into the crowds of the Galleria Umberto. Father Donovan woke the sleeping GI gently and returned across the arcade, wondering what in this world or the next he could find to say to Chaplain Bascom in excuse for this most unpleasant incident. Through his mind flashed all the dialectical training of the seminary, long since all but forgotten now that his sermons had become a matter of the monthly collection and choir rehearsal. Father Donovan prayed madly for the gift of tongues, for Jesuitical casuistry to fence off the question his Baptist friend was preparing for him. Though he seldom did it, except when pounding the chest of a section sergeant who'd forgotten to make his Easter duty, Father Donovan rallied all his shyness and determined to take the aggressive. After all, the Church was facing a greater opponent than she'd had at Anzio.

"Shocking," said Father Donovan, seating himself. "Probably not even a priest. Naples is full of them. Impostors . . ."

"Oh, I don't know," Chaplain Bascom said silkily. "Looks kinda like the Good Samaritan rolling the man who lay by the side of the road, don't it? Or Christ asking Mary Magdalene for a handout. . . . You have a very rich church, padre. Money rolls into Rome from all over the world. . . . I think I begin to understand the capitalism of the Roman Church. I'm only a Hard-Shelled Baptist, but I guess I realize that a big political machine don't pay its expenses on hay. . . . No sireee."

108

Father Donovan felt a white flame of rage rising in him. Then he saw something and said in a choked voice: "Look. . . ."

Two nuns were entering the Galleria in that way they have of seeming not to walk. No GI yelled at them. Each nun had by the hand two little girls in the chaste black dresses of Neapolitan orphans. The children laughed to one another and to the GI's. They had the glowing faces of southern Italian babies. The nuns beamed down on them, keeping a firm grip on their small hands. Then Father Donovan thanked Our Lady for answering his prayer.

"You must consider this side of the question too," he said, relieved.

"Ah yes," said Chaplain Bascom airily, "mother love. . . . How nice to find it even in Naples. It's the one great constant òf our mean little world."

"But you miss the point, chaplain. . . . Those nuns have no natural tie to those orphans. They function in accordance with the Church's exalted idea of parenthood, which goes back to Our Blessed Mother. . . . And you Protestants seem almost ashamed to admit that Christ had a mother. You make fun of our devotion to her, as though you were uneasy at the function of the love between man and God . . ."

"It's a scorcher today, padre," Chaplain Bascom said. He finished his orangeade, fanned himself, and loosened the shirt about his thick neck.

Chaplain Bascom brooded sulkily to himself. It was quite clear to him why the Roman Church had failed in the modern world. In a time when men wanted something positive to cling to, she offered them only the lacy traceries of an old theology. The twentieth century was too rapid for arguments on the navel of Adam. Especially Americans . . . they wanted that good solid old-time religion, which was precisely what the Baptist Church was giving them. Plenty of tangible things for Americans with common sense. Good shoutin' of hymns, fear of hell, and tables heavy with food at church suppers—that was religion. Deep down inside Chaplain Bascom suspected that Christ was more than a little of a red; this was why He'd been done to death. No American need examine too deeply the nature of Christ. This was what the Baptist Church offered them: a renewal of the spirit on Sundays

109

and Wednesdays, excellent business contacts, and keeping the young away from sinful habits. It was all so down to earth. Chaplain Bascom thought of Thomas Aquinas visiting Spartanburg, South Carolina, and had to slap his chunky thigh. . . . No, the Roman Church was Europe and the past and a dirty slice of history to boot. He'd seen enough to know how uneasily Romanism sat on Americans. Whereas your good southern Baptist *was* his religion walking and in act. So was his good comfortable wife, who cooked for church socials and taught Sunday school. So was his immaculate prim daughter. Practical Christianity. . . .

Over the kettledrumming of the truck convoys moving to the front, the crowds in the Galleria Umberto were like all the crowds of the world, drifting and inert except under stimulus. But this crowd had an uncrowdlike tendency to break up into its individual components. Their only common bond as a crowd was that they were all in Naples in August, 1944. Their focus shifted. Since most of these people came to the Galleria to lose themselves and therefore to find themselves, their flavor was more strongly marked than that of a crowd assembled for a specific purpose. The chaplains noticed isolated elements more easily than they might have at a race track or on a city street. And both chaplains thought to themselves that this crowd, perhaps more than any other on earth, showed the agony of the individual and of society, that some peculiar problem of the age was here mirrored.
Presently, in the crushing brilliance of the August sun and the buzzing of the convoys the chaplains found themselves dozing. A burr of laughter brought them sharply to in their chairs. For the laughter that they heard was intended to pierce even an unconscious man. Two Italian girls skipped arm in arm through the Galleria. There was an intimacy in their leaning on one another more flagrant and saucy than the friendship between school chums.
The girls spied the two chaplains, but they danced easily through the Galleria, in no hurry, exclaiming over the shop prices, casting swimming eyes over the lounging GI's. And they sang. Both chaplains knew that they were singing not out of high spirits but as a call to all interested to come and buy, as a fruit vendor hawks melons
110

in the street. They sang in English. It was an American song learned by rote from many darkened rooms with rumpled beds and empty vino bottles:

"You'll nevair know just ow motch I mees you,
You'll nevair know just ow motch I caaaare . . ."

"Those girls are wearing crosses on their necks," said Chaplain Bascom, clucking with his tongue.

"Aren't they entitled to pray?" Father Donovan asked, setting down his vermouth.

The Neapolitan girls paused by the two chaplains' table and stood there swaying enticingly, arms around each other's waists.

"Why, allo, major! Buy me a drink?"

Chaplain Bascom for the first time in his army career, instead of flashing the gold oak leaf on his right collar, took hold of his left and wriggled his silver cross at them. Father Donovan began to giggle.

"What would you have done if you'd been a rabbi?"

"I'm thinking of my wife," roared Chaplain Bascom. "Believe me, padre, I've reached such a maturity of married love that those two women seem to me vile Jezebels."

"You are a cute one, lieutenant," the other girl said. She sat genially down in the chair at Father Donovan's right. The waiter brought two vermouths without being asked. Chaplain Bascom reddened as the other girl sank into the wicker chair at his left.

"I think we should leave at once, with dignity," said Chaplain Bascom.

"It would be the first issue I ever knew you to avoid." Father Donovan said to the girl on his right:

"Are you hungry?"

"As hungry as the devil for Christian souls," cried Chaplain Bascom. "Padre, let's end this comedy and get out of here. You can't touch pitch and not be defiled. . . . I think my wife's ears are burning back in Spartanburg, South Carolina. . . . Padre, think of what you represent."

"That's exactly what I'm doing," Father Donovan said. "You and I were in tighter spots than this at Cassino, chaplain."

He looked at the girl, who was now nervously stroking her vermouth glass and shivering a little, though it was August. Then she reached out to lay her hand on

111

his arm. But before his fingers descended, she seemed to reconsider and dropped her hand to the beaded bag in her lap.

"You don't like me?" she said, making a face. "Whassamatta, Joe?"

"But I do like you," Father Donovan said, taking a thousand lire from his Ayrab wallet. "Now listen to me. You take this and go to a black-market restaurant and buy all you want to eat. Then go to confession, hear? Then go home and get a good sleep. You look very tired. . . . Promise me? . . . Sacerdos sum. . . ."

Both girls went quickly away, covering with one hand the jeweled crosses on their necks. They went out of the Galleria into Via Roma.

"They should be horsewhipped by their families," Chaplain Bascom said testily, mopping his beety brow.

"No," Father Donovan said, replacing his wallet. "Their sin is partly the world's."

"The world," Chaplain Bascom said, blowing his nose with an olive-drab handkerchief. "Women go on the streets because they're just plain ornery and refuse to settle down . . . and Italian women are much more immoral than our own. One minute they're crossing themselves in church, and the next they're on Via Roma. The only way the world is concerned in this filthy business is that public opinion doesn't have the power in Naples that it has in our own country. Here nobody cares what those women do, because all the Italians are that way."

Father Donovan thoughtfully spread his ringless hands and ordered another vermouth. He didn't try to answer Chaplain Bascom directly. He spoke more shyly than usual:

"We must be cautious in judging impurity because it's such a natural sin. Not everyone murders. Not everyone robs. But impurity springs from the natural impulses of our own bodies. A deed which under one set of circumstances brings a child into the world becomes under others a mortal sin. Impurity comes from an impulse that we all possess."

"Then we must wrestle with that impulse," Chaplain Bascom cried in triumph, slapping the table so that the glasses jumped to attention. "We must marry if we don't want to burn, as the Apostle Paul says. . . . I don't mind

112

telling you, padre, that as a young preacher I wrestled mightily with the lusts of the flesh."

"Then you should be more charitable towards those who are still wrestling," said Father Donovan gently.

Chaplain Bascom always got riled up in his arguments with Father Donovan. Secretly he feared that the priests of popery got a more subtle and cunning training in propaganda than they gave you at the Baptist seminary. He saw why people feared the Roman Church. You could easily dismiss the run-of-the-mill Catholic as a superstitious fool living in the past, but Father Donovan not only had faith but could explain why he had it. Chaplain Bascom explained it to himself this way: Catholicism was a secret society whose aim was just barely eluding him. He was sure it was up to no good. This aim was known only to the Pope and to a few of the inner circle. Even the average priest didn't know it.

Chaplain Bascom was also honest with himself. He knew he wasn't Christlike. Yet that name was always in his mouth because it was the open-sesame of his profession. It was a name which had a strange hold over people, possibly because they thought it should. The name Jesus Christ could open more hearts than a skeleton key. Nor was Chaplain Bascom quite at ease with the personality of Jesus Christ. His mind was teased by the concept of a carpenter who allowed Himself to be crucified and was remembered and invoked for the next two thousand years. Chaplain Bascom sometimes went so far as to ask himself whether he'd honestly have liked Christ. Perhaps He was just a little . . . effeminate. All this talk about love. . . . Chaplain Bascom acknowledged no other love than one took in the arms of a good woman. Any other love seemed to savor of unmentionable vice. . . .

Father Donovan broke the silence:

"You're thinking hard, chaplain. Isn't it a painful sensation?"

"Not at all, not at all, my boy. . . ."

And at this moment Chaplain Bascom realized that for two years Father Donovan had been playing with him, in that savage affection with which a cat tortures a mouse. He felt the blood rising under his crimson skin. And he knew at last that there are other forces in the world than the fists of a red-blooded American man. So he changed the subject.

113

"I was thinking of the future of the church."

"Which church?" Father Donovan asked coyly.

"Christianity, of course," Chaplain Bascom growled. Then something inside his burly soul swung outward like a rusty lock after it's oiled. He called to the waiter to bring them each a vermouth. Father Donovan looked at the vermouth in front of the Baptist and began to laugh in the high-pitched relieved manner of a boy who has passed an examination he expected to flunk.

"Thank God I've lived to see this, chaplain! Vermouth! The blackmail I could collect from you if I had a camera! What would your South Carolina congregation say?"

Chaplain Bascom took a huge swig of the vermouth. He made a face like a maddened bull and called for another.

"Why, I like you so much this way," Father Donovan said still laughing. "And there've been times when you depressed me no end."

"The fruit of the vine isn't altogether strange to me," Chaplain Bascom said in a mellow voice. "In my youth . . ."

"I'm not hearing your confession," Father Donovan said, raising a hand and smiling.

It was getting on to the time of sunset in the Galleria Umberto. The arcade was swelling up with people.

"I'm worried," said Chaplain Bascom, resuming, "for the future of the church. You and I both know, padre, that there *are* atheists in foxholes. And many of these fellows will go back to the States and attempt to sweep away the heritage of the ages. They'll call all faith simply dead lumber which has survived because people were stupid and afraid."

"And I'm of the opinion," said Father Donovan, "that good things, like the poor, will always be with us. It's an article of faith with me that my own church will last till the end of time. As for the others, unless they have something to offer the returning veteran that is free of bigotry and sectionalism, those other churches will go down in defeat."

"Just what do you mean by that?" cried Chaplain Bascom.

"Just this. When an American has seen Naples and death and the wretchedness of the whole world, he may

114

try to forget it when he goes back to the farm in Illinois. But he won't forget it completely. Malaria and sorrow temper the blood. And do you think that such a man will be satisfied again with a religion which says he may not smoke or drink, which offers strife for peace, which bases its commandments on little stupidities he has outgrown? . . . After this war we're going to see either an age of complete barbarism or a gradual return to the simplicities and felicities of Our Lord's life, adapted of course to the time in which we live. . . . And I, chaplain, have faith in human nature, which isn't intrinsically evil. There are many things in human life that you and I have almost forgotten since we put on these uniforms. It's natural to lose sight of these things in a war so vast and horrible as this one. And there are reckonings to come for all this slaughter. . . . But as surely as I know there's sin in the world, I know also that there's that in us which makes us desire to bring up our children in love and peace, which makes us shield our wives and daughters, and which occasionally makes us capable of the noblest sacrifice. . . . You can't tell me that these virtues will ever utterly disappear. . . . You remember how far the striking of a match carried in those black nights on the line? So tiny but so bright? Well, just like that match, whatever is good will survive till the end of the world. Otherwise human life becomes the cruelest joke and the figure of Christ on the cross the hollowest gesture that anyone ever made."

"Let's have chow," Chaplain Bascom said, wiping his eye.

They arose together and replaced their chairs as though they'd been at a formal dinner. Chaplain Bascom took Father Donovan's arm. Together they walked through the Galleria Umberto. Father Donovan took pride in his uniform as he had pride in his Mass vestments, so he looked down to see if his trousers were neatly belled out over his combat boots. In this same spirit he called Chaplain Bascom's attention to his protruding shirttail.

The Galleria was filtered with air currents. At the transcept crossing from the San Carlo Theater to Via Santa Brigida a column of cool air swam on the heat.

"Say, I feel that vermouth," Chaplain Bascom said heavily.

"There are worse things to feel," Father Donovan said brightly.

He loved the Galleria because it was always full of Neapolitan children—children begging, children selling, children looking, children shuffling barefoot. What caught at him most were the little children pimping. They'd learned a perfect and Saxon English for the pleasures they offered for sale, and their obscene phrases smote Father Donovan more brutally than the worst sins he'd heard in the confessional, where at least he could be impersonal. But when a Neapolitan child played the bawd, the ugly sentences shrieked out as though a parrot spoke them, and they seemed all the fouler because the child understood their import. Father Donovan wondered about Americans who were capable of teaching such things to little Neapolitans of seven and eight. Sometimes when he lay awake at night, he thought of the tragedy of the children of Europe, born and passing their formative years under a rain of bombs, keeping alive by catering to the desires of soldiers. What would these poor children be like in maturity, who had never known the innocence of childhood? If these children grew into cold bitter reptiles, then the world would really have lost the war. . . .

"Next week," said Chaplain Bascom, "if we're still here, I mean to bring some soap and wash these children's mouths out."

"There are better uses for soap in Naples than that."

These children, Father Donovan thought, are the same as those in South Philadelphia. They're the same as kids all over the world. I wish I had them all to teach them baseball and buy them popcorn.

"Italian children," he said aloud, "are the saddest spectacle of the war."

"But we have slums in the States too."

"Oh I know that, I know that. But these children have no escape at all . . . not even a settlement house."

The chaplains went down the steps of the Galleria that led to Via Verdi.

"What a place that arcade is," said Chaplain Bascom. "A great novel could be made of it. I suppose the market place in Jerusalem was like this arcade. Except that Christ isn't here."

116

"Oh, I disagree with you," Father Donovan said. "I think He is . . . very much so."

They waited for a truck convoy to pass them with a roaring and a streaking. Across Via Verdi was a transient mess for American officers. In August, 1944, it was busier than a Childs. In shifts officers ate a soup, a plate of warmed-up C-ration, and a saucer of canned pears. It seemed as though every officer (except airplane drivers) out of combat took his meals there. It had a screen door that swung and clattered. On this door always hung one of two signs—OPEN or CLOSED. When this mess ran out of C-ration, the CLOSED sign went up like a storm flag. Winding out of the entrance was a queue of officers, a depressed little concentration of nurses clutching their shoulder bags, and civilian secretaries of the State Department and the War Shipping Administration. Officers paid ten lire a meal, civilians thirty-five. Ducking the bobbing screen door was a hag in a torn black dress who sold *Stars and Stripes, Yank,* and *Time.* She saluted all officers who bought a paper and beamed on them with jagged gums. One rumor had it that she was born during the Vesuvius eruption of 79 A.D., another that she was the sybil come in from Cumae because business was better in Naples, another that she was Eleanor Roosevelt in disguise gathering material for her column.

Father Donovan and Chaplain Bascom went to the tail of the line and mopped their faces and their necks in the Neapolitan afternoon. As four people came out of the mess, the line would inch up four places.

The tables in the mess were like those beds where people sleep in shifts. An old Neapolitan was wiping the untidy table top, stacking plates, and talking threateningly to himself. Chaplain Bascom seated himself and beat on the table jovially so that all the glassware vaulted.

"Mangiare, Joe. And be presto about it too."

The old Neapolitan retreated and was seen no more. Father Donovan turned his quick timid smile on a young Neapolitan in a drenched white coat who brought them two plates of soup.

"Buona sera, Joe. Come state?"

"Ehhhh!" the young Neapolitan said, relaxing and smiling. "Non c'è male. Ma c'è troppo lavoro. . . ."

"Dago-lover," said Chaplain Bascom. "These people are good for nothing but to sing operas and work in barbershops."

Father Donovan didn't answer. He was making the sign of the cross prefatory to saying grace before meals.

"You know that embarrasses me in public," Chaplain Bascom continued.

"I thank God even for C-ration," Father Donovan said when he'd finished his brief prayer.

Chaplain Bascom plowed into his soup. He continued to watch suspiciously the slight brown hands making their second sign of the cross in front of the Purple Heart ribbon on the priest's left breast. Father Donovan then applied himself to his soup. He ate demurely, never looking at what he was eating.

"In the seminary," he said, "they used to read aloud from pious writings while we were at our meals. So naturally I expect nothing but edifying thoughts from you until dessert."

The chaplains looked distrustfully at the second course, which was what they knew it would be: diced pork with beans, dehydrated potatoes, spinach, and a leaf of lettuce.

"I keep thinking of Missus Bascom's fried chicken."

"But just taste this iced tea," Father Donovan cried gaily. "You're having qualms because you drank three glasses of vermouth. Don't. Saint Thomas says we may drink till we feel hilarious."

They both arose as two nurses prepared to sit at their table.

"Ya don't mind, boys?"

"Not at all, not at all, girls."

With women Chaplain Bascom was almost feudal. In the slight glow of the vermouth he was still enraged that he hadn't scored one this afternoon on Father Donovan.

"Oh, padres," one nurse giggled. "We could use a little salvation, Tessie."

The nurses were older than most ANC's. They had an air of edgy misanthropy of women overseas too long. They had also a certain pride in their captaincies, since every nurse above the rank of second lieutenant considers that she has jumped the Rubicon.

"And where are you girls from?" Chaplain Bascom purred.

118

It was a theory of his that people could be put at their ease by any of a dozen key phrases.

"Oh lands," said the nurse named Elsie, "let's not go into that. The only thing we're sure of is that this is Naples, Italy, and that we wanna go home and can't."

"You girls have the most Christian mission in this war," Chaplain Bascom said.

"Oh we know that," Tessie said. "But, since Salerno it's been goddam . . . beg your pardon . . . wearing."

They smoked while eating, holding their cigarettes in painted fingernails which nevertheless betrayed how often those hands had been in hot water.

"There's nothing pleasant about overseas assignments," Father Donovan said, slicing his preserved pear.

"You can say that again, Father! As soon as I looked at you, I knew you was a priest. . . . Remember me in your prayers so I can stay outa the booby hatch."

"I promise," Father Donovan said.

The chaplains finished their meal and said good night to the nurses.

"If they didn't smoke like stoves," Chaplain Bascom said on the way out of the mess, "they wouldn't be so nervous."

"Well, I expect they're lonely and very, very tired."

On the sidewalk outside the transient officers' mess they put on their caps and peered at one another in the sunset that streamed down through the dome of the Galleria. Father Donovan yawned in the hot light.

"Shall we go back to our tent in the Dust Bowl?"

"Look," said Chaplain Bascom. "What's that?"

Between the two stairways of the Galleria that cascaded into Via Verdi there was an entrance they'd not noticed before. Over the doorway hung a sign in yellow and red.

Now Father Donovan couldn't imagine what Arizona was doing in Naples. But since he was fond of western movies, he thought this might be worth looking into. Chaplain Bascom said:

"Since you put me on the path to perdition with vermouth, we might as well look in. Maybe they have cactus plants and saddle horses."

The corridor of the Arizona was leaden with smoke. A girl sat in a checkroom the size of a telephone booth.

119

She reached out as they passed and flipped their caps out of their belts.

"But we won't be staying long, girlie," Chaplain Bascom said, reaching for his cap.

"Hundred lireee, pleeese," she shrieked and put their caps on an inaccessible hook.

"Must be a clip joint," Father Donovan said out of his movie vocabulary.

Inside there was nothing but a small room swimming in smoke. Tables were crammed about a cleared square no bigger than a checkerboard. Officers hunched over these tables, a few French, a few British. But most were American airplane drivers with their high soft boots ensconced also on the tables. Everybody was drinking steadily. But somehow the chaplains sensed that nothing had really begun yet. On a dais smothered in greenery a small Italian band was playing dance music. They did it self-consciously, as though they were imitating phonograph records. Steered by Chaplain Bascom, Father Donovan sat down at a table on the edge of the cleared space. Trying to feel at ease, he tapped his boot to the music.

"Everybody's looking at us queerly," Chaplain Bascom whispered. "Our insignia must stick out like a neon sign."

"No one's looking at us."

A waiter shambled up and regarded them with menacing timidity. Evidently something went on at the Arizona which made the Neapolitan personnel regard the Allies as an honest-to-goodness conquering army.

"Now this will be on me," Father Donovan said grandly, bringing out his Ayrab wallet. "Will you bring us a bottle of . . . champagne, please?"

"Good Lord," Chaplain Bascom said.

When the wine came Father Donovan blanched at the price, but to make good his gesture he paid up without a murmur. An airplane driver with swollen eyes leaned over chummily from the next table:

"It ain't the champagne ya payin for here, kids."

"Atmosphere, I presume?" Father Donovan said, feeling quite worldly. He'd learned much from the movies.

"Well, ya can call it that," the airplane driver said. He was on the wrong side of the chaplains to see the crosses on their collars. "I keep comin here night after night. I call myself a beast, but I keep comin. . . . Roger."

"What's he talking about?" Chaplain Bascom whispered. "He's drunk. No wonder they have so many casualties in the air force."

"I heard that," the airplane driver cried. "Lissen, Jack, I come here to fergit my troubles, not for fights with doughfeet. But if ya spoiling for a bruise, wait till my buddy gets back from the bobo, and we'll mop up the floor with the botha yez. . . . Roger."

"We're not in the infantry," Father Donovan said, laying a hand on his arm. "We've just worked with it a little. And since we're both in the same army, there's not much sense in a fight, is there?"

"Roger," the airplane driver said.

He settled back mollified and beamed on Father Donovan's Purple Heart. He pointed to his own, to his wings, and to the Twelfth Air Force patch on his left shoulder. It had been crocheted in rhinestones by some Neapolitan. He winked at Father Donovan and reached over to put an arm about his shoulders.

"Y'are all right, lootenant. But who's that ole beagle with ya? Shoulda left him home."

With a warm swell of good feeling Father Donovan set the two glasses precisely in the middle of the table and poured out the champagne. It bubbled so cool and golden that even Chaplain Bascom assumed his Something Special air. They clinked glasses. Father Donovan was a host for the first time in his life. Being curate under a bitter brooding pastor in South Philadelphia had somewhat pinched his naturally hospitable nature. All he'd ever been able to do for anyone was to teach kids baseball. Only in saying Mass had he ever been in a position to do something grand for other people.

"Delicious," said Chaplain Bascom, smacking his lips. "I see the point of Solomon's warning against wine. Look how it giveth its color in the cup."

"That guy talks like a chaplain," the airplane driver muttered, emerging from a funk in which he'd laid his head on his chest.

"I am a chaplain," Chaplain Bascom said loftily.

"Then what are ya doin in this place, Father?"

"I am not a priest."

"Well, ya should be."

Father Donovan blushed. There was a cyst of delicacy in him that made him itch and sweat when things didn't run smoothly.

"Some of our champagne?' he said to the airplane driver.

The flier had been regarding them with a confused affection and hostility, like a dog making up its mind. He tottered to their table and seated himself with the help of Father Donovan.

"Thank ya. My buddy musta died in the bobo. Since last month at Cerignola, all ya have to do is yell flak, and we all start shittin . . ."

Chaplain Bascom twitched.

"An now my missions is all done, Roger. I'm goin' back to the States."

"Well, I advise you to watch your language when you get there," said Chaplain Bascom. "There are ladies in America."

"If you wasn't a major, I might be tempted to tellya to blow it. In fact, I think I will anyway."

"I'd hate to pull my rank on you," Chaplain Bascom said.

"That's all you Protestant chaplains is good for is to pull rank. Ya get GI after leavin a little piddlin church in Georgia that pays ya five bucks a Sunday . . ."

"We're all friends here, boy," Father Donovan said.

The flier gave a windy sigh, said "Roger," and went to sleep on Father Donovan's shoulder. He removed the dead weight softly from himself and settled the head on another table.

At this moment some glasses and bottles went whizzing through the air and crackled against the orchestra stand. A fight began in the farthest corner between three airplane drivers and two combat engineers. The noise rose in level as though an invisible hand had turned up the volume control on a radio. What was going on the chaplains couldn't see clearly for the billowing smoke and the crowds pushing in from their tables. The disturbers of the peace were lured out the door by the Italian manager into the arms of waiting MP's.

"Nice place," said Chaplain Bascom, sipping his champagne.

Then girls appeared and sat down invited or not at various tables. The din rose. This was what everyone had been waiting for.

"Why," Chaplain Bascom said, "this place is a taxi dance hall."

122

The airplane driver came to and straightened up. He identified the girls for Father Donovan:

"That's Lola with the green handkerchief. . . . That's Gina with the earrins. . . . That one there signalin the waiter is Bruna. . . . That number in red is Bianca Stella. . . . Most of em is married to officers in the Italian Army that are prisoners of war. All these cheesecakes have bambini. But a gal has to make a livin. . . . Mamma mia, what a covey of quail. . . . They all got a union rate of two thousand lire a night . . . an don't tell me that us airplane drivers have inflated the prices. . . . But O Roger, Roger. . . ."

Father Donovan and Chaplain Bascom turned on one another as though they'd just met and were sizing one another up.

"Look," Chaplain Bascom moaned hoarsely.

A girl had come out in front of the orchestra. She got an ovation. In a low rasp she sang "I'll Be Seeing You in All the Old Familiar Places." A carnation was stuck in her hair. She wore a dress that seemed to have been sewn from pieces of lace and silk rooted out of ashcans.

"That's Lydia," the airplane driver said, his eyes blood-shot. "An she don't gimme the time of day."

"It seems," whispered Father Donovan, rising from the table, "that Lydia is about to take off her clothes."

The two chaplains retreated through the maze of tables where the officers leaned forward toward Lydia through the iron-gray smoke. Some had girls on their knees who incited them to drink deeply, to forget everything but This Moment Now. Through the fumes eyes looked out at Lydia with weariness and desire and fever. There was an air of daze and bestial futility cut by the mechanical-saw voice of Lydia. The chaplains got their caps. The MP at the door leered at their insignia.

Outside it was dark. Evening had come to Naples, but the heat stayed on as loving and deadly as a pillow over a sleeper's face. Down the steps of the Galleria Umberto came buzzing evidence of trafficking going on up there in the blackout. Chaplain Bascom was sweating and panting as he put his cap on his head and set it de-terminedly at a forty-five-degree angle.

Father Donovan said nothing but bent down and tucked his trousers over his combat boots. Then he noticed a little girl sitting on the curb. She had blond hair, so rare

123

in Neapolitan babies. She seemed so tiny and alone. She
was peeling a stick of American chewing gum, her mouth
already open in anticipation. And her eyes glowed like a
kitten's at dusk. Father Donovan walked over to talk to
her. He had another stick of gum in his pocket to give
her. But she, fearful of her treasure, darted out into the
street. He laughed and ran after her.

Around the corner from the San Carlo an English
lorry turned in. It slid like a huge coffin behind the blackout lenses on its headlights. These cast a sick pencil of
glow on the little girl's bobbing hair, on the pursuing
legs of Father Donovan. Chaplain Bascom saw what was
happening. He shouted and leaped into the street after
them. The lorry bore down. His ears exploded with the
scream of brakes and the crunch of bodies, as collies are
mashed under heavy turning wheels.

On the opposite curb the tiny Neapolitan girl watched
the truck back off. The two bodies lay there quietly, one
with a bit of purple silk ribbon over his heart. She put
her gum into her mouth. Americani. For it wasn't the
first time she'd seen the dead lying in the streets of Naples.

FOURTH PROMENADE

(Algiers)

I REMEMBER learning all over again how to walk. My gait
was something between a sailor's and a mountaineer's.
For Rue Michelet winds and grinds to the top of the city.
Walking in Algiers means going either uphill or down.
Consequently I was forever leaning forward or backward. I got to be uneasy on a level stretch, the way a
drunk's nerves twitch till the bars open.

I remember that Algiers was more European than
Casa. In the summer of 1944 there was a quality of reaching out. It was the old Paris trying to find itself. Most of
the people in Algiers were refugees from Paris and were
waiting to get back there. They rejoiced over the Nor-
mandy invasion because it was the beginning of an attri-
124

tion they'd thirsted for since June, 1940. Sometimes I thought it was we Americans who were getting Paris back for them, but I didn't say so.

I remember that in Algiers many French soldiers wore our uniform. It was easy to tell that they weren't Americans—something narrower about their eyes, something contracted and concentrated in everything they did. Nevertheless they wore our uniforms, and the Mediterranean Base Section decided that a discrimination must be made —possibly to keep us out of the Kasbah and out of certain bars and areas smelling of bed sheets and strange foods. So we had to affix to our caps the little brass circlet US. Then it was clear to us and to the MP's who was a French GI and who an American.

It was the first time I saw British soldiers. Till July of 1944 Allied Force Headquarters was at Algiers. In the AFHQ offices there was an Englishman to counterbalance every American. Thus the streets of Algiers clomped with British hobnails. The British wore shorts till 1800 hours. Through the leafy heat their legs bobbed like brown pistons. They wore canvas gaiters and short sleeves and berets designed after the queen's own tam. On Rue Michelet and Rue d'Isly I remember the signs in the windows: WO'S & SGT'S CLUBS. The OR's had theirs too. But the British said that we Yanks were better off than they. They'd been a long time away from Blighty, as long ago as Tobruk, and they resented our rations and our cigarettes and our theaters. ENSA was never like this, they said. They scratched their bare legs, bitten by the anopheles mosquito.

I remember my first pass in Algiers. I knew just where I wanted to go. I walked out into the twilight where the barrage balloons shimmered over Algiers Harbor like silver kidneys. The port was teeming with hospital ships, the air buzzed with planes flying into Maison Blanche. I walked down Rue Michelet, leaning backward. Along my way were green public gardens, but their iron gates were locked at sundown.

"Why, myte? Because you bloody Yanks used to myke a shambles of them after nightfall."

Through the heat of Algiers I looked inside the scrolled gratings. I could see the fountains playing and the statues with inscriptions in French. What, no walks there after dark? At noon French girls walked on their lunch

125

hour from the office. They were crisper and cooler than the Casablancaises.

"Closer to French love all the time. The wimmin in Casablanca have seen too many Ayrabs."

I remember how few Ayrabs there were in the city itself, as though the French had put guards at the entrances. I saw Ayrabs only when I was out in trucks, along the roads to Maison Carrée or Maison Blanche or spying on the Tamaris Hotel at Ain-Taya. That too made Algiers seem less an African city. It was also the French everywhere spoken. I stopped many times as I strolled along, trying not to seem a country cousin just in from Casa:

"Oosir troove l'Hôtel Aletti?"

"Il n'est pas trop loin, monsieur."

The Hôtel Aletti. Only colonels and generals and foreign correspondents lived in it. But everybody flocked to its gardens and terrace, and not to look at the colonels and the generals and the war correspondents.

Nearly every GI in the city of Algiers converged afternoons on the Hôtel Aletti, like the rays of the sun in heraldic designs. I'd go to the Place d'Isly and turn right toward the harbor. I'd pass the street of the peppermint columns of the Bar Pigalle, where people in white linen drank vermouth and talked of Paris. Then I'd turn left on a ramp and go downhill again, leaning backwards.

"That there's the Aletti, kids. The Passion Pit of Algiers. . . ."

I remember that in front of the hotel there was a terrace of different levels with metal tables and umbrellas. There was constant movement here of people with glasses in their hands, swarming on the different planes like drunks at a garden party. It was almost a terrace restaurant where people idle and look for and at other people. In the Aletti garden there was an excitement seemingly without reason. Occasionally a brigadier general would issue martially from inside the hotel, picking his way among the tables and the Ayrab shoeshine boys. GI's would lower their eyes to their drinks. But the ladies would appraise the general's mistress. Sometimes it was a Red Cross girl. But often it was an Algérienne whom he kept in lipstick and an apartment near the Saint Georges. The BG's lady sometimes flew to Italy with him in his plane when he made inspections.

I remember that persons with a purpose never stayed long in the outdoor garden of the Aletti. They'd go into the lobby, which looked as though it should be cool. But it never was. It was like the lobby of a New York flop joint, with hundreds of rotting leather chairs. On these GI's lolled. Past their relaxed bodies flitted the corps of mademoiselles, about fifty in number. They had union hours and union prices. The rules of courtship weren't strictly observed. The GI's just lay in their chairs drinking, while the girls moved from one cluster to the next, making their sales talk. They knew instinctively where to do their promoting, working from the bar to the farthest recesses of the lounge. They spoke to as many as two hundred GI's in the two hours that the bar stayed open. I remember their French social sense. Even if I wasn't interested, they'd make a social call on me lasting five minutes in return for a drink, a cigarette, and a stick of gum. For ten francs the bar offered white wine with a block of ice in it. It was a strong and melancholy drink.

I remember the Duchess, who always sat alone in a pink straw hat, drinking and smoking and thinking. She never made the advances, having high ideals of her profession. She knew French poetry, the opera, and the gossip of the haut monde. If I bought her a drink, she accepted it so that I understood the great favor she was doing me. Nor did she ever entertain a proposal till closing time, since goodly fellowship was more important to her than her career. She viewed her lovers with a mellow cynicism. I knew she was out of her century. But I didn't tell her, for the Duchess knew it herself.

"Hélas," she said, picking up her gloves at closing time, "qu'ai-je fait de ma jeunesse?"

I remember the most sought-after, Emilie the tigress. She was an exhausting girl. She'd fling herself on me in a rage of delight, chewing her gum madly, her eyes spewing forth little sparks of coldest fire. She nudged me, prodded me, kicked me, pulled my hair, nipped at my ears. She'd get hold of my waist and squeeze and tickle and maul:

"Ah, chéri, que tu es timide! Crache-moi dans la bouche et dis-moi que tu m'aimes!"

Then she'd get bored with me and egg the other girls

127

on to fights. I remember discovering that this was an epileptic fit that she sustained for two hours because she was, as it were, on the stage in the Aletti.

I remember that the prettiest of them all was Claudette, who'd come in with her suitcase from Tunis for the pickings. Because she was as fresh and straightforward as an American girl, she was the most popular. Claudette talked a rolling salty English. She made it quite clear that with her stipends from the Allied troops in Algiers she could retire a rich woman in another year.

"And I won't be a beatup old bag, either!" Claudette said.

She never allowed herself to be sampled in public, which was part of the selling propaganda of the other girls.

At the bar of the Aletti stood a circle of misanthropes, officers and people who wanted to look at the circus without standing in the ring..They drank their white wine and listened and gazed at the ground. What conversation they made to one another or to me heightened my sense of the mania and irrelevance of the war. Nothing they said registered with me at all. It was as though a comedian were to describe death to an audience in a burlesque theater. They all simply lectured when they talked. In the things they said there wasn't an attempt to establish contact with another human being. They raved like people coming out of anesthetic. They'd built their walls around them for the duration.

I remember that the only person who dared intrude on these solitary drinkers was some girl who wasn't doing too well for herself in the Aletti lobby. But she too soon saw how these anonymities had been frightened, how they came to the Aletti bar merely in order not to lose their hold on humanity. It was that vague escape from misanthropy in which one frequents crowds in order to assure oneself one hasn't lost the way.

I remember that sometimes I'd grow weary of drinking and of being pushed around by the Aletti Victory Girls. So I too would stand at the bar with the zombies. I'd take a token white wine and wedge myself in with the rest of the dying pack. When the wine nibbled at me, I sometimes caught psychic currents I couldn't explain. I'd look up with a sudden uneasiness and see someone at the other end of the bar communicating with me by signals that seemed to have been already agreed on between us. And then I sensed that I could talk out of this world, as one sometimes does with total strangers on railway trains and in confessionals. Sometimes I was close to believing that old crud about the wigwags human beings send out to others when they're lonely, as insects are said to talk with the scraping of their wings. And I too began to slide around in the dihedrals of time and space, slipping in and out of being like a ball bearing in a maze.

I remember that sometimes my life in that sweating bar of the Hôtel Aletti looked like a separate and removed bubble inching along a thread. Then my mind would start gyrating like a corn popper and I'd have to quiet myself by reasoning that I'd been away from the States a long time, that I was drunk, and my mind was playing me dirty tricks. It was trying to be God and come face to face with itself. But why? why? why? At these moments I'd see myself rocketing out into space, seeing this world from the viewpoint of eternity. How tiny we all were, how like fleas dolled up for a pageant.

I remember that a second lieutenant of the engineers used to drink every afternoon at the bar of the Hôtel Aletti. For a week I watched him. He fled the girls and leaned in the farthest corner of the bar, holding onto his drink as gods clutch at their membra in orgies. I wondered why he never had a buddy. He had hair as white as the snow that Algiers never sees, and a thin sunburned face. He looked like the social young men in *Life* magazine's dances, but he didn't act like them. If anyone spoke to him, he'd reply in just as many words as they'd used on him, smile as though to tell them they didn't see the farce of it all, and return to his wine. If after this an attempt was still made to continue the conversation, he'd smile again and softly change his place at the bar. His encounters with Emilie and Lucie and Bettine used to make me wonder. I think they were afraid of him. He'd disengage himself from their arms and their nipping teeth with the slippery coolness of an invisible fish.

One evening, I remember, when the white wine had taken a communicative turn in me, I slipped into the place next him and waited shyly, tingling a little. I ordered another white wine with the Aletti ice cube bobbing in it and looked at my boots. It was odd to feel him close

129

by me. It seemed as though all air had been sucked into the place where he stood so aloof and silent. He smelled of Lifebuoy soap and shaving lotion, as though he strove to be impersonal.

I know my army officers pretty well, having observed them for years from the perspective of a pebble looking up and squinting at the white bellies of the fish nosing above it. Americans usually go mad when by direction of the President of the United States they put a piece of metal on their collars. They don't know whether they're the Lone Ranger, Jesus Christ, or Ivanhoe. Few Americans I ever knew could sustain the masquerade of an officer. Their grease paint kept peeling in unexpected places. I heard that in combat the good officers simply knew their men well and did them one better in daring. But to be a good officer out of combat demands a sort of shadowboxing between truth and posing. Europeans know the secret. But few Americans can play the nobleman without condescension or chicken.

American officers fall into three easy slots of the doughnut machine. The feminine ones, I mean those who register life and are acted upon by it, become motherly, fussy, and on the receiving end from the GI's under them. If they rule at all, it's by power of their gentleness, which can fasten a GI in tight bonds once his will consents and admires. Second, there are the violent and the aggressive, who as commissioned officers assume a male and fatherly part ranging from drunken pas who whale their sons on Saturday nights to the male and nursing tenderness of an athletic coach. Yet these most masculine men aren't always the best officers in a crisis or showdown. Third, there are those commissioned nonentities who as civilians were male stenographers, file clerks, and X-ray technicians. They are neither masculine nor feminine. They move through the army in polyp groups of their own sort. They're never alone. I can be in the same room with such officers without feeling the presence of anything or anyone. Touching their personalities is like poking at a dish of lemon Jello. They smile and assume another shape.

I remember standing beside the white-haired second lieutenant of the engineers. I thought that if he didn't speak soon, I'd scream, as the saying goes. I didn't

130

know into which of my three slots he fell. He seemed a coin with the milling rubbed off.

"Don't be so goddam condescending, corporal."

"Pardon, sir?" I said.

I jumped at the sound of his voice. I realized that his mind had been tracking mine for the past five minutes. This lieutenant had a voice that began at his navel and got muted in his sinuses. As he leaned toward me, his breath was mixed with wine and peppermint.

"You've been watching me for the past week, corporal," he said.

"A GI looks up to his officers, sir. Or wants to. . . ."

"Ah . . . you hoped to prove to yourself that I'm a sad sack. Well, I am. Completely lost. . . . How do *you* know you're in Algiers? Or for that matter what proof can you give me that you're alive?"

"One at a time, sir," I said, gulping my wine so that I could buy him one and establish some ground between him and myself.

"Your curiosity will be the death of you, corporal. Play safe and retreat into some sort of role. . . . It's wonderful how in a war you can purge yourself and become nothing or everything. . . . I for example have lost my touch with life. I'm like those basket cases in combat. A man still alive but limbless and deaf, dumb, and blind. I just lie in a great white bed, my brain still functioning, but able to make no impression on the world outside me. . . . Do you understand me? You have the face of a ferret or a weasel. . . . But knowing too much will sicken you. Just go back to being convenient and optimistic and slick and conventional."

"The lieutenant speaks a fine English," I said, gulping.

"Don't address me in the third person. You're like the Ayrabs saluting me when they want a bonbon. You're an American corporal, and you have confused ideas of democracy and independence and the four freedoms. You loathe saluting me on the street. You think, that sonofabitch shavetail. . . . So don't think you're kidding me when you address me in the third person. It's not respectful. It's fawning. . . . So for God's sake just cut out that crap. . . . You came here to talk, and I'm giving you what you asked for. You'll never want to talk to me again, which will be healthier for both of us."

131

"Shall I go away now, sir?" I said, bridling and trembling at the same time.

"If you like, but you won't. . . . I'm your experience for today. Well, I'll give you a dose of me."

"Well, I try to give everybody an even break," I stuttered.

"Except me, corporal, except me. For one solid week now you've been staring at me when you weren't allowing yourself a free grope from these putains. . . . Did it ever occur to you that I have a right to privacy? Is your own life so small that you must enlarge it by listening in on my party lines?"

"You've got me all wrong, sir . . ."

"Mother of shit," the lieutenant said, his voice as cool and removed as ever, "how I envy you mediocre people! Since I came overseas I've been in a position where nothing has squared with the education I got. I have a good mind. And it's disciplined. I know Shakespeare and Mozart and calculus and how to hold my moxie. But nothing I learned at Yale has given me any preparation for the mad world in which I find myself. . . . Do you all think you're playing a game with high stakes? Are you happy to be a Joiner? Are you happy moving in herds and thinking as the newspapers and the radio commercials tell you to? What sweet consolation to be able to say to yourself: I'm an American, therefore better than anyone else in the world! . . . You see, corporal, the human race is getting worse all the time. Each year we know less than we did in the preceding. We're more no-account now than we were five hundred years ago. Five hundred years from now I doubt that there'll be any of us left on earth. Just thousands of wrecked planes and burned out tanks from the South Pole to the steppes of Russia. . . . We get smugger all the time. We call forces of destruction and speed, the March of Progress. . . ."

"Born in the States, sir?" I said feebly after a pause.

"Born there, corporal, but probably sha'n't die there. I had ideas of aristocracy without class, of brotherhood without familiarity and sentimentality. And I studied and I read and I admired nature and art. And I said what a piece of work is man, and I believed it. But it looks as though individuality is going out forever. Yet the propaganda assures me that a new age is at hand."

132

"It's the turning point in history, sir, for the little man. . . ."

I murmured this, for it was something I'd read that morning in *Stars and Stripes, Mediterranean*.

"The fallacy of the machine and the mob, corporal. If the murder gets over, everything will then be geared to the lowest common denominator, as it is in the American public schools. The queer, the beautiful, the gentle, and the wondering will all go down before a race of healthy baboons with football letters on their sweaters. . . . I was a letter man at Yale. . . . And the end of the world will come as a tittering anticlimax, because we're going to shut ourselves out from the stream of truth, and drown in pettiness and small talk."

"You fear the little man, sir?"

"The term little man is a phrase of self-pity. Faugh, corporal. . . ."

I remember that I excused myself from the second lieutenant of the engineers and went out of the Aletti into the streets of Algiers. I looked back at him as I turned out the door, bumping into a colonel. I remember thinking with an ache of pity and laughter that this was the last time the young lieutenant would speak. For no one man can put his hands up to stop a locomotive. . . .

FIFTH PORTRAIT

Momma

MOMMA always lay a while in her bed when she awoke. Poppa was up four hours earlier and went out into the streets of Naples for a walk, to buy *Risorgimento* and to drink his caffè espresso. He said it made him nervous to lie beside her because she cooed to herself as she slept.

That love which Poppa no longer desired of her Momma showered on the clientele of her bar. One reason she cooed in her sleep was that she was one of the richest women in Naples. She could afford to buy black-market food at two thousand lire a day. She ate better than the Americans. She had furs and lovely dresses and patent leather pumps which even the countesses in the Vomero couldn't afford. Momma had come from a poor family in Milan, but she'd made herself into one of the great ladies of Naples. And the merchants of Naples, when they sent her monthly bills, instead of writing signora before her name, wrote N.D., standing for nobil donna.

As the churches of Naples struck noon, Momma got out of her bed. She was wearing a lace nightie brought her from Cairo by an American flier. Momma knew that the flier had made money on the deal, but no other woman in Naples had one like it. In the old days she'd have driven Poppa mad with this lace nightie. But now he simply crawled in beside her, felt the sheer stuff, and clucked his tongue in disapproval. Poppa was first and last a Neapolitan. Even in the early days of their marriage he'd never grasped the fineness of Momma's grain. But she was beyond such bitterness now. She loved the world, and the world returned her love in her bar in the Galleria Umberto.

Beneath a colored picture of the Madonna of Pompeii, flanked by two tapers and a pot of pinks, Momma said her morning prayers. She thanked the Virgin for saving her during the bombardments of Naples. But the Virgin hadn't spared that lovely appartamento in Piazza Garibaldi. And Momma prayed for all the sweet boys who came to her bar, that they might soon be returned to their families—but not too soon, for Momma loved their company. And she prayed also for the future of poor Italy, that the line up by Florence might soon be smashed by the American Fifth Army. And she prayed that Il Duce and his mistress Claretta Petacci might see the error of their ways. Finally Momma prayed that all the world might be as prosperous and happy as she herself was.

With the bombing of her apartment in Piazza Garibaldi in March, 1943, Momma'd been able to salvage only her frigidaire. Everything else had been destroyed —the lovely linens she'd brought Poppa with her dowry from Milan, her fragile plate, her genteel furniture. Only the frigidaire was to be found among the rubble pert and smiling as a bomb shelter. Momma'd wept the whole day; then she and Poppa had moved into a dreary set of rooms on the third floor of the Galleria Umberto. Momma'd got

134

the rooms cleaned, set the frigidaire in the kitchen, and bought secondhand furniture by cautious shopping in Piazza Dante. But her heart as a homemaker had died in the ruins of that appartamento to which Poppa had brought her as a bride.

She lived now only for her bar and for the Allied soldiers who came there every night except Sunday. In fact Momma was only treading water all day long until 1630 hours, at which time the provost marshal of Naples allowed her to open her bar. At 1930 MP's came to make sure it was closed. Three hours. Yet in those three hours Momma lived more than most folks do in twenty-four.

She'd opened her bar the night after Naples fell to the Allies, in October, 1943. Some American of the 34th Division had christened her Momma, and the name stuck. And because Momma had an instinctive knack for entertaining people, her bar was the most celebrated in Naples. Indeed a Kiwi had once told her that it was famous all over the world, that everyone in the Allied armies told everyone else about it. Momma rejoiced. Her only selfish desire was to be renowned as a great hostess. She was happy that she made money in her bar, but that wasn't her be-and-end-all. She knew that she was going down in history with Lili Marlene and the Mademoiselle of Armentières—though for a different reason.

Momma brushed her teeth with American dentifrice while the water ran into her tub. She studied her hair in the mirror. For ten years she'd been hennaing it. But she was too honest to go on kidding the world. She was forty-six. In the face of that sacred title, Momma, it seemed to her sacrilegious to sit every night behind her cash register with crimson hair glowing in the lights. So she'd stopped using the rinse. Now her hair was in that transitional stage, with gray and white and henna streaked through it. But the momentary ugliness of her hair was worth her title. At closing time in her bar, some of her boys, a bit brilli, would cry on her shoulder and tell her that she looked just like some elderly lady in Arkansas or Lyon or North Wales or the Transvaal or Sydney. Then she'd pat their hands and say:

"Ah, mio caro! Se fosse qui la Sua mamma! . . ."

She'd never been able to learn English, though she understood nearly everything that was said to her in it.

135

Momma climbed into the tub after she'd sprinkled in some salts a merchant seaman had brought her from New York. Her body was getting a little chunky, but she tried her best to keep it trim, the way a Momma's should be. At first she'd worn a pince-nez until Pappa had told her she looked like a Sicilian carthorse with blinders. So she had reverted to her gold-rimmed spectacles. She doted on American black market steaks, her pasta asciutta, her risotti, and her peperoni. She knew that a Momma mustn't be skinny either.

She dressed herself in black silk and laid out a quaint straw hat on which a stuffed bird sprawled eating cherries. She opened her drawerful of silk stockings. You could count on the fingers of one hand the women in Naples of August, 1944, who owned sik stockings—were they prostitutes on the Toledo or marchese in villas at Bagnoli. But Momma had em; she averaged a pair a week from her American admirers. Momma considered herself one of the luckiest ladies in the world. She knew that no woman gets presents for nothing.

Finally dressed and fragrant and cool in spite of the furnace that was Naples in August, 1944, Momma took up her purse and looked around the apartment before locking it. She checked the ice in the frigidaire. Sometimes, after she was compelled to close her bar, she invited her favorite boys up for extra drinks. She didn't charge for this hospitality.

She walked through the Galleria Umberto. At this hour it was empty of Neapolitans because of the heat. But the Allied soldiery was already out in full force. The bars weren't open, so they just loitered against the walls reading their *Stars and Stripe*s or whistling at the signorine. A few waved to Momma, and she bowed to them. Then she went onto the Toledo, which Il Duce had vulgarized into Via Roma. Here she clutched her bag more tightly. Like anybody else born in Milan, she had no use for Neapolitans or Sicilians. They thought the world owed them a living, so they preyed on one another with a malicious vitality, like monkeys removing one another's fleas. And now that the Allies were in Naples, the Neapolitans were united in milking them. Momma knew that the Neapolitans hated her because she was rich and because she refused to speak their dialect. She walked through them all with her head in the air, clutching her

136

purse. Some who knew her called out vulgar names in dialect and cracks about Napoli Milionaria, but she paid them no attention.

She and Poppa usually lunched together at a black market restaurant on Via Chiaia, patronized by Americans and those few Italians who could afford the price of a meal there. Today Poppa was out campaigning for public office at the Municipio, so Momma ate alone at her special table. Sometimes she suspected that Poppa had a mistress. But then he wouldn't stand a chance at snapping up anything really good, what with all the Allies in Naples.

The treatment Momma got at this restaurant was in a class by itself. Naturally the Americans got fawned on, but then they didn't know what the waiters said about them in the kitchen. Whereas Momma, as an Italian who'd made a success in the hardiest times Naples had ever known, always got a welcome as though she were Queen Margherita. There were flowers on her table and special wines rustled up from the cellar, although the Allies got watered vino ordinario. And when Momma entered, the orchestra stopped playing American jazz, picked up their violins, and did her favorite tune, "Mazzolin di Fiori." Momma tapped her chin with her white glove and hummed appreciatively.

While she picked at her whitefish and sipped her white wine and peeped around the restaurant from under the shadow of the red bird that forever ate cherries on her hat, Momma observed an American sergeant wrestling with an American black market steak. He was quite drunk, and to Momma, who knew all the symptoms so well, he seemed ready to cry. She debated inviting him to her table and treating him to his lunch. But he gave her the I-hate-Italians scowl, so she thought better of it. He wasn't the sort who came to her bar anyhow. Momma was basically shy, except with people she thought needed affection. Then she'd open up like all the great hostesses of the world. However, she did take out of her purse a little pasteboard card advertising her bar. She sent it by a waiter over to the sergeant, plus a bottle of Chianti. He scowled at her again, and Momma decided basta, she'd gone more than halfway. Then he tore up her card and began to guzzle her wine.

She finished her lunch and smoked a cigarette. There

137

seemed to be a rope about her neck pulled taut by all the evil fingers of the world. She wanted to go somewhere and have a good cry. She needed a friend. Poppa had never been close to her since, in the first year of their marriage, he discovered that she wasn't going to be fertile, like all the other women of Italy. Momma had conceived just once. In her Fallopian tubes. After the medico had curetted her out and she'd all but died, he'd told her she could never have a child of her own. And Poppa in disgust had taken to politics and reading the papers. Momma'd only begun to love again since the night in October, 1943, when she'd opened her bar in the Galleria Umberto. . . .

She arose from table and drew on her white gloves. As she walked to the door, she saw herself pass by in the gilded mirror, a dumpy figure holding in its chin, a scuddling straw hat under a bird chewing cherries. She knew that if she didn't get outside soon, she'd bawl right there in front of the waiters, and the drama she'd built up of a great lady would collapse forever. On Via Chiaia she debated what movie she'd go to. Since she went every afternoon, she'd seen them all. A few American films were beginning to dribble into Naples, and Momma'd enjoyed Greer Garson or Ginger Rogers with an Italian sound track. Yet movies bored her unless there was lots of music and color. The truth was that she went every afternoon because she'd nothing else to do; she was just killing time till the hour to open her bar. She decided on the Cinema Regina Elena off Via Santa Brigida.

She found a seat three-quarters of the way back from the screen, put on her glasses, and watched the show. It was an Italian film made in Rome on a budget of a few thousand lire. Momma was used to the tempo of American movies, so she found herself nodding. There wasn't even anything worth crying over. She eased her feet out of their patent leather pumps, cursed the pinching of her girdle, and settled down. Sometimes she drew a peppermint patty out of her bag and sucked it thoughtfully. Every half-hour the lights came up for an intervallo; the windows were opened, and people came in or out or changed their seats for various reasons. Momma'd have liked an Allied soldier to be sitting beside her. But to these the cinemas of Naples were off limits because of

138

the danger of typhus and because of certain nuisances they'd committed in the dark just after the city fell. During the intervalli Momma stayed in her seat and smoked a cigarette. She wasn't going to force her feet back into her pumps.

The Italian film went on and on; Momma fell asleep and dreamed in the moldy dark. Her dreams were always the same, of the boys who came to her bar. There was a heterogeneous quality about them. They had an air of being tremendously wise, older than the human race. They understood one another, as though from France and New Zealand and America they all had membership cards in some occult freemasonry. And they had a refinement of manner, an intuitive appreciation of her as a woman. Their conversation was flashing, bitter, and lucid. More than other men they laughed much together, laughing at life itself perhaps. Momma'd never seen anything like her boys. Some were extraordinarily handsome, but not as other men were handsome. They had an acuteness in their eyes and a predatory richness of the mouth as though they'd bitten into a pomegranate. Momma dreamed that she was queen of some gay exclusive club.

She awoke and glanced at her watch. It was time to go. She'd seen almost nothing of the film. But she didn't care. She felt more rested than she did by Poppa's side. A silver hammer in her heart kept tapping out that in fifteen minutes more her life for the day would begin. She had the yearning hectic panic of a child going to a show. She shot her feet into her pumps. As the lights came up for the secondo tempo Momma left the theater. She looked a little disdainfully at the audience, contrasting it with what she'd shortly be seeing. Peaked Neapolitan girls on the afternoon of their giorno di festa, holding tightly to the arms of their fidanzati wearing GI undershirts; sailors of the Regia Marina and the Squadra Navale in their patched blue and whites; housewives from the vichi and the off-limits areas who'd come in with a houseful of children to peer at the screen and lose themselves in its shadowy life.

Her patent leather pumps hurt Momma's feet, but she sprinted up Santa Brigida. She turned left at Via Giuseppe Verdi. Once in the Galleria Momma all but flew. She wondered if she looked spruce, if her hat was chic.

The Galleria was milling and humming, for all the bars opened within a few seconds of one another, just as clocks stagger their striking the hour throughout a great city. Momma had a presentiment that today was going to be especially glamorous.

The 1630 shift of troie were coming into the arcade with the promptness of factory girls. From now until curfew time the Galleria would be a concentrated fever of bargaining and merchandising peculiar to Naples in August, 1944.

The rolling steel shutters of Momma's bar were already up. Gaetano was polishing the mirrors. He greeted Momma and went back to thinking about his wife and thirteen children and how it wasn't fair that a man who'd never signed the Fascist tessera should live like a dog under the Allies Vincenzo was wearing a spotted apron, so Momma lashed him with her tongue and forced him into the gabinetto to put on a fresh ore. She stitched them up herself out of American potato bags. Momma also inspected the glassware, the taps on the wine casks, the alignment of the bottles. She was kilometers ahead of the sanitation standards set by the PBS surgeon and the provost marshal.

She seated herself behind the cassa, unlocked the cash drawer, and counted her soldi. At this moment the old feeling of ecstasy returned. For Momma loved her bar: the mirrors in which everyone could watch everyone else, the shining Carrara marble, the urns for making caffè espresso. Behind her on the mirror she'd fastened a price list. She offered excellent white wine, vermouth, and cherry brandy. She hoped soon to be licensed to sell gin and cognac, which were what the Allies really wanted. When stronger liquors were available, the tone of her place would go sky-high, along with the moods of her clientele.

No one had yet turned up. Momma knew with racecourse certainty the exact order in which her habitués came. Her patrons were of three types: some came only to look, some with a thinly veiled purpose of meeting someone else, some just happened in.

A shadow cut the fierce light of the Galleria bouncing around the mirrors. It was Poppa treading wearily and carrying his straw hat. Momma flinched. She had no de-

140

sire to see Poppa now. If he addressed her in dialect, she'd refuse to answer. He had rings under his eyes, and through his brown teeth came the perfume of onions. Momma told him that there was half a chicken waiting in the frigidaire. But he seemed to want to talk. Momma got as peeved as though someone tried to explain a movie to her. So Poppa, after a few more attempts to talk, put on his straw hat and went out. But he called back to her from the entrance:

"Attenzione, cara. . . ."

"Perchè?" Momma cried, but he was gone.

Nettled and distracted, she settled herself behind the cash register and folded her hands. Where *were* they? All behind schedule tonight. She began to wonder if some of the other bar owners had sabotaged her by passing around the rumor that she was selling methyl alcohol such as would cause blindness.

The husky figure of a major entered the bar. Momma smelled a rat because this major was wearing the crossed pistols of an MP officer. On his left shoulder he wore the inverted chamber pot with the inset blue star, symbolizing the Peninsular Base Section. The major set his jaw like one asking for trouble. He ran his hands through some of the wineglasses and blew on the wine spigots for dust.

"Ees clean the glass, the wine, everything!" Momma cried cheerily. "Bar molto buono, molto pulito. . . ."

The major advanced upon her. She was beginning to tremble behind her desk. He walked with the burly tread of one accustomed to cuff and kick. Momma remembered that some of the Germans, when they'd been in Naples, had walked like that.

"Lissen to me, signorina," the major said, dropping a porky hand on her desk.

"Signora, scusi," said Momma with dignity.

"I don't give a damn one way or the other," the major said. "But don't try an play dumb with me, see, paesan?"

"Ees molto buono my bar," Momma twittered, offering the major a cigarette.

Vincenzo and Gaetano were watching the proceedings like cats.

"Molto buono, my eye. You're getting away with murder in this joint. . . . Now you can just take your choice.

141

Either you get rid of most of the people who come here, or we'll put you off limits. And you know we damn well can, don't you?"

Momma quailed as she lit the major's cigarette. The words "off limits" were understood by any Neapolitan who wanted to keep his shop open. Nothing could withstand the MP's closing a place, unless you were friendly with some colonel of PBS.

"You know as well as I do," said the major. "An old doll like yourself ain't as dumb as she looks. We don't want any more Eyeties comin in here to mix with the soldiers. Do I make myself clear? And you gotta refuse to serve some of the other characters. . . . Don't come whinin around that you ain't been warned."

Momma motioned to Vincenzo and Gaetano to bring out a glass of that fine cognac from which she gave her favorites shots after closing time. It was set at the major's elbow. He drank it off, glaring at her the while, set down the glass with a click, and left.

"Capeesh?" he cried as he belched like a balloon out into the sunlight of the Galleria.

Momma couldn't decide what grudge the MP's had against her. There had been occasional fights in her bar, yet the other bars of Naples had even more of them. Her soldiers were gentle. All she was trying to do was run a clean bar where people could gather with other congenial people. Her crowd had something that other groups hadn't. Momma's boys had an awareness of having been born alone and sequestered by some deep difference from other men. For this she loved them. And Momma knew something of those four freedoms the Allies were forever preaching. She believed that a minority should be let alone. . . .

In came the Desert Rat. He took off his black beret and pushed a hand through his rich inky hair. He said good evening to Momma and bought his quota of six chits for double white wines. It would take him three hours to drink these. He was always the first to arrive and the last to leave. He never spoke to a soul. He was the handsomest and silentest boy Momma'd ever seen. Why did he come at all? His manners were so perfect and soft that at a greeting from another, he'd reply and recede into himself. Momma wondered if at Tobruk or El Alamein someone in the desert night had cut his soul

142

to pieces. He'd loved once—perfectly—someone, some-where. Momma would cheerfully have slain whoever had hurt him so.

The face of the Desert Rat was an oval of light brown. His short-sleeved shirt showed the cleft in his neck just above the hair of his chest. He wore the tightest and shortest pair of shorts he could get into, and he leaned lost and dreaming against the bar with his ankles scraping one another in their low socks and canvas gaiters. Those legs were part of the poetry of the Desert Rat for Momma—the long firm legs of Germans, but tanned and covered from thigh to calf with thick soft hair. For three hours this English boy would stand in Momma's bar, doped and dozing in maddening relaxation and grace from the white wine.

Momma tore six chits out of the cash register and gave the Desert Rat four lire back out of his one hundred. Tonight she went so far as to pat his wrist, a thing she'd been longing to do for months.

"Eees warm tonight, no?"

"Oh very, madam," the Desert Rat said.

It was the first time she'd seen his smile. And Momma suddenly saw him in someone's arms by moonlight in the Egyptian desert, in the midst of that love which had sliced the boy's heart in two. . . . He left her and went to the bar. In the next three hours it was usually at him that Momma'd look when she wasn't making change. She saw him from all perspectives in the mirrors, all the loveliness of his majestic body.

Next to arrive was a Negro second lieutenant of the American quartermaster corps. Momma smiled to her-self as the Negro made an entrance. He seemed to have the idea he was stepping onto some lighted stage. He moved his hips ever so slightly and carried his pink-insided hands tightly against his thighs. For some dra-matic reason he wore combat boots, though Momma knew he'd never been farther north than the docks of Naples.

"Hulllllo, darling," he said to Momma, kissing her fin-gers. He had a suave overeducated voice. "You look simpppply wonderful tonight. Who does your hats? Queen Mary? . . . Uh-huh, uh-huh, uh-huh. . . ."

Then he stationed himself at the bar quite close to the Desert Rat. They looked at each other for a swift ap-

143

praising instant. Then the Negro lieutenant began to talk a blue streak at the Desert Rat.

"It's going to be brilliant here tonight, absolutely brrrrilliant. I feel it way down inside. . . . My aunt, you know, is a social worker in Richmond, Virginia. But do you think I'm ever going back there? No, indeed, baby. I found a home in Italy, where the human plant can't help but thrive. I like the Italians, you know. They're like me, refined animals, which of course doesn't bar the utmost in subtlety and human development. . . . They talk about French love. . . . Well, the Italians know all the French do, and have a tenderness besides. . . . My God, why doesn't everybody just live for love? That's all there is, baby. And out of bed you have to be simply brilllllliant. . . ."

Momma sometimes pondered to herself the reason for the wild rhetoric talk by some of the people who came to her bar. It wasn't like Italian rhetoric, which makes good Italian conversation a sort of shimmering badminton. At Momma's most of her customers talked like literate salesmen who cunningly invited you out to dinner—all the time you knew that they were selling something, but their propaganda was sparkling and insidious. At Momma's there were people who talked constantly for the whole three hours. There were others who simply listened to the talkers, smiling and accepting, as though they'd tacitly agreed to play audience. And Momma could tell the precise time in her bar by the level of the noise, by the speed with which the words shot through the air like molten needles, by the ever mounting bubbles of laughter and derision. Under this conversation Momma sensed a vacuum of pain as though her guests jabbered at one another to get their minds off themselves, to convince themselves of the reality of something or other.

There now arrived the only two Momma didn't rejoice to see, two British sergeants wearing shorts draped like an old maid's flannels. They were almost twins, had peaked noses and spectacles that caused them to peer at everyone as though they were having difficulty in threading a needle from their rocking chairs. Momma wished they wouldn't stand so close to her desk, blocking her view. But stand there they did until the bar closed. Their conversation was a series of laments and groans

144

and criticisms of everyone else present. They called this
dishing the joint. Momma thought that they came to her
bar because they couldn't stay away. They were disdainful and envious and balefully curious all at the same
time. They reminded her of old women who take out
their false teeth and contemplate their photograph of
forty years ago. These sergeants bought some chits, took
off their berets, and primped a little in the mirror behind
Momma.

"Esther, my coiffure! Used to be so thick and lus-
trous. . . . We're not getting any younger, are we? We'll
have to start paying for it soon. Shall we live together
and take in tatting?"

And the other sergeant said, giving himself a finger
wave:

"Well, I've read that the end of all this is exhaustion
and ennui. As we've agreed steen times before, Magda,
the problem is bottomless, simply bottomless. No one but
ourselves understands it, or is even interested. You put
your hand into a cleft tree to your own peril, Magda.
When you take out the wedge, the tree snaps together
and breaks your hand. . . . And you cry your eyes out
at night, but it doesn't do any good. . . . It keeps coming
back on you because it's in you. Even though you don't
get any satisfaction, you go back to it like a dog to
his vomit. . . . That's what it is, Magda, vomit. Why kid
ourselves and talk of love? Love is a constructive force.
. . . We only want to destroy ourselves in others because
we hate ourselves. . . ."

At 1700 hours Rhoda appeared after she'd had evening
chow at the WAC-ery. Rhoda was the only woman who
came to Momma's bar. No one ever spoke to Rhoda,
who did her drinking standing at the far end of the counter, reading a thick book. She always made it a point to
show Momma what she was reading. Rhoda worried
about the state of the world. She studied theories of leisure classes and patterns behind governments.

"I'm not good for much of anything," Rhoda once said,
"except to talk up a storm."

To Momma's Italian ear Rhoda had a voice like a
baritone; everything she said carried about a kilometer.

"What am I?" Rhoda said once. "The reincarnation of
L'Aiglon."

It seemed to Momma that Rhoda was happy in her
145

WAC uniform—the neat tie, the coat, the stripes on the sleeve, the skirt that didn't call attention to the fact that it was a skirt. Under her overseas cap Rhoda wore an exceptional hairdo. It was something like the pageboy bob of twenty years ago cut still more boyishly. And under this cropped poll were Rhoda's stark face, thin lips, weasel eyes. Rhoda looked as though she were lying in ambush for something. She bought a slew of tickets from Momma and went to her accustomed place, reading and drinking. She turned the pages by moistening her forefinger and looking quickly at the other persons in the bar.

Rhoda was the only American girl whom Momma knew well, but she was a symbol. Momma had a theory that romantic love was on the wane in America because if all the women were like Rhoda, American girls were mighty emancipated and intellectual. Since Rhoda was so cool and unfeminine, Momma foresaw a day in the United States when all the old graceful concepts of love would have perished. The women would have brought it on themselves by insisting on equality with the men. To Momma, thinking of her girlhood in Milan, this wasn't an inviting picture. . . .

"Why don't signorine come here?" Rhoda asked authoritatively of Momma. "Intellectual Italian women, I mean. I'd spread the gospel to them. I'm the best little proselytizer in the world. I'd make them socially conscious. We'd read the *Nation* and John Dos Passos. I might even pass out copies of *Consumers' Research* to help Italian girls buy wisely."

Momma smiled. She knew quite well that if Signorine started coming to her bar, most of her patrons would go away. It was an easy matter to get a signorina anywhere else in the Galleria Umberto or on the Toledo. Momma had indeed been ill at ease when Rhoda had first appeared, but the boys had accepted Rhoda while ignoring her. And so long as there was harmony, Momma didn't care who came to her bar. . . .

"Oh this place of yours," Rhoda boomed with a thick shiver. "It's positively electric here, Momma. I get so much thinking and reading done in this stimulating atmosphere. . . . Just like a salon."

The two British sergeants eyed Rhoda. Momma'd been
146

expecting them to accost one another for the past week. And tonight the bubble was going to burst.

"We've been asking one another why you come here," the sergeant called Esther said. "You must have a Saint Francis of Assisi complex. Or else you're a Messalina. . . . If you want to give us a good laugh, why don't you bring one of your Warm Sisters with you and make a gruesome twosome? You shouldn't come here alone, darling. Momma's bar is like nature, which abhors vacuums and solitary people."

"I'm not answerable to the likes of you," Rhoda roared back, bristling with delight. "But I will say I've always sought out milieux that vibrate in tune with me. . . . So you two just get back to your knitting. Just because you two are jaded and joaded, that's no sign I should be too."

"Magda, she's a tigress," the other British sergeant said, "but a veritable tigress. We must have her to our next Caserta party."

"Don't think I don't know those parties," Rhoda rumbled. "The height of sterility. Everybody sits around tearing everybody else to pieces, thinking, my God, ain't we brilliant. Everybody gets stinking drunk. Then somebody makes an entrance down the stairs in ostrich feathers and a boa. . . . No, thank you, my pretty chicks."

"Well, get you, Mabel," the first British sergeant tittered.

Momma cleared her throat. She hated the turn things were taking by her cash desk. It was as though the three were armed with talons, raking at one another's faces.

"We understand one another all too well, don't we?" Rhoda said triumphantly. "I pity you two from the bottom of my swelling heart. If you had a little more of what I have, or I had a little more of what you have, what beautiful music we could make . . . a trio. . . ."

"Darling, I see you in London," the second sergeant said. "A sensation. But you aren't quite Bankhead, darling. But you are happy in the WAC's, aren't you, dear? Your postwar plans are to run a smart little night club . . . wearing a white tuxedo . . . but darling, you just haven't the figger for it."

"It's no use trying to scratch my eyes out," Rhoda rumbled in her open diapason. "I have a perfect armorplating against elderly queans."

"Plesa," Momma murmured, clearing her throat again, "plesa. . . ."

In her bar things moved by fits and starts. Incidents in the course of three hours followed some secret natural rhythm of fission and quiescence, like earthquakes and Vesuvio. Each time the climaxes grew fuller. This first was only a ripple to what she knew would happen later.

Rhoda and the two British sergeants glared at one another. She reopened her thick book and retreated into it like an elephant hulking off into the jungle. The two sergeants put arms about each other's waists and executed a little congratulatory dance.

After the first incident the Desert Rat raised his fine dark head, looked into the mirror, and ordered another white wine. The Negro second lieutenant stopped his monologue and called out:

"Everyone's still wearing their veil . . . but wait. . . ."

An Italian contingent always came to Momma's on schedule. They entered with the furtive gaiety of those who know they aren't wanted, but have set their hearts on coming anyhow. They wore shorts and sandals and whimsical little coats which they carried like wraps around their shoulders, neglecting to put their arms into the sleeves. Momma knew that her Allied clientele didn't care for them. And besides they never drank more than two glasses apiece, if they drank that much. They just sat around and mimicked one another and sniggered and looked hard at the Allied soldiery. Each evening they had a fresh set of photos and letters to show one another. Momma thought of nothing so much as a bevy of Milan shopgirls having a reunion after the day's work. She knew them all so well. The Italians treated Momma with a skeptical deference, as though to say, Well, here we are again, dearie; your bar is in the public domain; so what are you going to do with us if we don't make a nuisance of ourselves?

There was Armando, who worked in a drygoods store. He was led in by his shepherd dog on a leather thong. This dog was Armando's lure for introduction to many people. He had tight curls like a Greek statue's, a long brown face, and an air of distinction learned from the films. He wore powder-blue shorts. It was Armando who translated all his little friends' English letters for them.

There was Vittorio, with the blue eyes of a doll and

gorgeous clothes such as Momma'd seen on young in-gegneri in the old days in Milan. Vittorio worked as a typist at Navy House on Via Caracciolo. He worked so well and conscientiously that the British gave him soap and food rations. Sunday afternoons he walked by the aquarium with an English ensign who murmured in his ear. Vittorio had arrogance and bitterness. He was the leader of the others. All evening long at Momma's he lectured on literature and life and the sad fate of hand-some young Neapolitans in Naples of August, 1944. In Momma's hearing he said that he'd continue his present career till he was thirty. Then he'd marry a contessa and retire to her villa at Amalfi.

There was Enzo, who'd been a carabiniere directing traffic until the Allies had liberated Naples. Now Enzo led the life of a gaga, strolling the town in a T-shirt, in-viting his friends to coffee in the afternoon, and sing-ing at dusk in dark corners. Momma thought Enzo the apogee of brutal refinement. Over his shorts he wore shirts of scented silk or pongee. Under these the muscles of his back shimmered like salmon. The nostrils in his al-most black face showed like pits, flaring with his breath-ing.

There was also a tiny sergente maggiore of the Italian Army. He held himself off from the rest, though he al-ways came in with them. He used them as air-umbrella protection for his own debarking operations. The name of this sergente maggiore was Giulio. His eyes darted warily about, and once in a while he'd call out something in a barking voice, to show that he was accustomed to command. He insisted on wearing his smart fascist peaked cap, the visor of which he would nervously tug when he got an unexpected answer.

The last Italian to arrive at Momma's was the only one she respected. He was a count, but he permitted himself to be known only as Gianni. Besides his title he had a spacious apartment in the Vomero. Momma respected his rank, and she hoped some day to be presented to his mother the countess. Momma liked Gianni as a person too. He was always dressed in black, with a white stiff collar and a black knitted tie. His black eyes smoldered with a remote nostalgia. For some months now he'd come to Momma's, drunk a little, and gone away. But tonight he seemed purposeful. He agreed Momma with a tender

149

wretchedness. Momma knew his disease. He was a Neapolitan conte, dying of love. Gianni avoided the other Italians, who had perched themselves on a counter at the rear of the bar, and went straight up to the Desert Rat. Momma leaned over her cash desk and watched with popping eyes.

"May I speak to you, sir?" Gianni said to the Desert Rat.

His English was as slow and exquisite as that melancholy that lay over him like a cloud.

"Speak up, chum," the Desert Rat said in his almost inaudible voice.

"Do you like me a little, sir?"

The Desert Rat didn't answer, but his tall body stiffened.

"I had a friend once," Gianni said, almost crying. "He was a German officer. He taught me German, you see. He was kind to me. And I think I was kind to him. I think I am a good person, sir. I am a rich count, but of course to you that does not import. . . . I seek nothing from you, sir . . . like the others. . . . You look so much like the German officer. I was happy with him. He said he was happy with me. . . . Would you like sometimes to come to my house in the Vomero, sir?"

The two British sergeants set up a screaming like parrots. Gianni fled. Momma put her hand to her heart, which had given one vast jump. The Desert Rat quietly put down his wineglass. He took the two British sergeants and knocked their heads together. Then he ran out through the bar. Momma watched him stand outside, peering up and down the Galleria and shielding his eyes against the sun. After a while he returned to his place and fell into his old reverie. He seemed as stirred and angry as a true and passionate boy.

The two British sergeants were shrieking and sobbing and looking at their reddened faces in the mirror. Then they repaired to the gabinetto. Momma could hear them inside splashing water on their faces and gibbering like chickens being bathed by a hen.

Rhoda looked over her book at the silent Desert Rat. The second incident rolled through the bar like the aftertones of a bell. Momma just held onto her cash register and prayed, for she knew that this was going to be an evening. The Negro second lieutenant began to sing

150

something about "Strange Fruit." The Italians foot-
noted the incident to one another. Momma's bar wasn't
nearly full yet, but it was buzzing like a bomb.

Presently the two British sergeants swept out of the
gabinetto, their faces swollen and their eyes flushed from
weeping. They looked like hawks for someone to prey on.
Enzo stepped easily up to them, placed a hand on his
hip, and extended his powerful jeweled hand:

"Buona sera, ragazze."

"You go straight to hell!" the first British sergeant
screeched. "Why do you come here at all, you sordid
little tramps in your dirty old finery? Do you think we
feel sorry for you? Go on Via Roma and peddle your
stuff and stop trying to act like trade. . . . We see through
you, two shilling belles. All of you get out, do you hear?
Nobody here wants anything you've got. The Allies are
quite self-sufficient, thank you. We did all right before
Naples fell. . . . Why, the nerve of you wop queans!
Glamor!? Why, you've all got as much allure as Gracie
Fields in drag. . . . Go find some drunken Yank along
the port. . . . But get the hell out of here!"

The Italians replied to the sally of the British sergeants in their own indirect but effective way. Momma
decided that the Italians were more deeply rooted in
life, that they accepted themselves. For the Italian contingent merely sent up a merry carol of laughter. If they'd
had fans, they'd have retreated behind them. This laughter hadn't a hollow ring. It was based on the assumption
that anything in life can be laughed out of existence.
Momma had never admired the Italian element in her
bar. Now she did. They shook with the silveriest laughter, lolling over one another like cats at play. Their
limbs gleamed in their shorts. Even the tiny sergente
maggiore joined in the badinage. And the two British
sergeants stepped back by Momma's cash desk and resumed their jeremiad.

"What will become of us, Esther? When we were
young, we could laugh off the whole business. You and I
both know that's what camping is. It's a Greek mask to
hide the fact that our souls are being castrated and
drawn and quartered with each fresh affair. What started
as a seduction at twelve goes on till we're senile old aunt-
ies, doing it just as a reflex action. . . ."

"And we're at the menopause now, Magda. . . . O God,

if some hormone would just shrivel up in me and leave me in peace! I hate the thought of making a fool of myself when I turn forty: I'll see something gorgeous walking down Piccadilly and I'll make a pass and all England will read of my trial at the Old Bailey. . . . Do you think we would have been happier in Athens, Magda?"

"Esther, let's face facts. You can't argue yourself out of your own time and dimension. You and I don't look like the Greeks and we don't think like them. We were born in England under a late Victorian morality, and so we'll die. . . . The end is the same anyhow, Greek or English. Don't you see, Esther? We've spent our youth looking for something that doesn't really exist. Therefore none of us is ever at peace with herself. All bitchery adds up to an attempt to get away from yourself by playing a variety of poses, each one more gruesome and leering than the last. . . . I'm sick to death of it, Esther. I can think of more reasons for not having been born than I can for living. . . . Is there perhaps some nobility stirring in my bones?"

"Then is there no solution, Magda?" the second British sergeant asked wistfully.

He cast his eyes about the bar like a novice about to take the veil.

"Millions, Esther. But rarely in the thing itself. That's what tantalizes us all. We play with the thing till it makes of us what we swear we'll never become, cold-blooded sex machines, dead to love. There are so many ways of sublimating, Esther. . . . But are they truly satisfying either? For some hours I've known, though they'll never come again, I'd cheerfully pass all eternity in hell."

"And I too, Magda. That's the hell of it. We all have known moments, days, weeks that were perfect."

"All part of the baggage of deceit, Esther. God lets us have those moments the way you'd give poisoned candy to a child. And we look back on those wonderful nights with far fiercer resentment than an old lady counting the medals of her dead son."

"But we've had them, Magda; we've had them. No one can take them away from us."

The two British sergeants lapsed into silence, for which Momma was grateful. Their conversation was a long swish of hissing s's and flying eyebrows. They began to scratch their chevrons in a troubled and preoccupied way,

152

and their faces fell into the same sort of introspective emptiness that Momma'd observed on old actresses sitting alone in a café. There was a lost air about them that made her prefer not to look at them, as though the devil had put her a riddle admitting of no solution, and a forfeit any way she answered it.

It was 1830 hours in Momma's bar, the time of the breathing spell. She was quite aware that, gathered under her roof and drinking her white wine and vermouth, there was a great deal of energy that didn't quite know how to spend itself. And since there's some rhythm in life, in bars, and in war, everybody at once stopped talking and ordered fresh drinks. She could see them all looking at their wrist watches and telling themselves: I have another hour to go—what will it bring me?

Momma's sixth sense told her there was trouble brewing. A group of soldiers and sailors entered her bar. From the way they shot around their half-closed eyes she knew that this wasn't the place for them. They had an easiness and a superiority about them as though they were looking for trouble with infinite condescension. Cigars lolled from their mouths.

"Gracious," the Negro second lieutenant said, "men!"

"Look, Esther," said the first of the British sergeants, "look at the essence of our sorrow. . . . What we seek and can never have. . . . And each side hates the other. The twain never meet except in case of necessity. And they part with tension on both sides."

For there were two American parachutists who lounged insolently, taking up more cubic space than they should have. And with them were two drunken American sailors, singing and holding one another up. Momma now wished that Poppa were here to order this foursome out summarily, under threat of the MP's. Vincenzo and Gaetano were no help at all in such circumstances. Then what she feared happened. Someone of her regular clientele let up a soft scream like a pigeon being strangled. At once a parachutist stiffened, flipped a wrist, and bawled:

"Oh saaaay, Nellie!"

This was the moment the Italians had been waiting for. They picked themselves off the flat-topped counter where they'd been idling and padded toward the four newcomers. They were cajoling and tender and satiric and gay. They

153

lit cigarettes for the parachutists and the sailors, and took some themselves. It became a swirling ballet of hands and light and rippling voices and the thickened accents of the sailors and the parachutists.

"Jesus, baby, those bedroom eyes!" someone said to Vittorio.

"I hateya and I loveya, ya beast," one of the sailors said.

"Coo, it teases me right out of my mind," one of the British sergeants said. "So simple and complex. Masculine and feminine. All gradations and all degrees and all nuances."

"The basis of life and love and cruelty and death," said the other British sergeant, looking as though he would faint. "And in the long run, Magda, who is master and who mistress?"

From a tension that was surely building up, Momma was distracted by the appearance of an assorted horde. In the final hour of the evening her bar filled until there were forty wedged in, six to eight deep from the mirrors to the bar. Her eyes had a mad skipping time to follow all that went on. It was like trying to watch a circus with a thousand shows simultaneous in as many rings.

First came an Aussie in a fedora hat, to which his invention had added flowers and feathers. Tonight he was more than usually drunk. He slunk in with the slow detachment of a mannequin modeling clothes. He waved a lace handkerchief at all:

"Oh my pets, my pets! Your mother's awfully late tonight, but she'll try and make it up to you!"

"Ella's out of this world," someone said. "She's brilliant, brilliant."

A glazed look came over the sailors' eyes like snakes asleep. Ella the Aussie kissed their hands and bustled off while they were still collecting themselves.

"Don't call *me* your sister!" Ella shrieked, waving at his public while buying chits from Momma. He kissed Momma on both her cheeks, leaving a stench of alcohol and perfume.

There was a rich hollow thud. Momma at first feared that someone had planted a fist on someone else's chin. But it was only Rhoda, the WAC corporal, closing her book. That evening she read no further. It was getting too crowded in there even to turn pages.

154

Next to appear at Momma's was a British marine, sullen in his red and black, with a hulking beret. Momma knew he was a boxer, but not the sort who made trouble. He'd a red slim face, pock-marked and dour; the muscles in his calves stood out like knots. While drinking he teetered up and down on his toes and was a master at engineering newcomers into conversation. He observed everyone with a cool devotion. Often he'd invited Momma to his bouts at the Teatro delle Palme, but she hadn't gone because she couldn't bear to see him beating and being beaten in the ring. This British marine was on the most basic and genial terms with himself and the world.

Next came a plump South African lance corporal with red pips, and a Grenadier Guardsman, tall and reserved and mustached. The South African lance corporal was a favorite of Momma's because he made so much of her. She knew he didn't mean a word of it, but the whole ceremony was so much fun to her.

"Old girl, I've finally got married," said the plump lance corporal, presenting her to the Grenadier Guardsman, who looked terrified and bulwarky at the same time. "This is Bert. You'll love Bert. He saved my life in Tunisia. And he understands me. So he's not as stupid as he looks. And his devotion, darling! Coo! Just like a Saint Bernard Bert is. He knows how to cook, you know. . . . Bert's essence is in his mustaches. The traditionalism, the stolidity, and the stupidity of the British people produced those mustaches of Bert's."

Momma was in such a whirl of happiness that she gave the guardsman a chit for a drink on the house. Meanwhile the South African lance corporal whirled about the bar, burbling to everyone and formally announcing his marriage to Bert.

Momma was beginning to believe that she wasn't going to have any trouble from the parachutists and the sailors. They and the Italians were lazily drinking and mooing at one another. Momma tried to spell out for herself some theory of good and evil, but the older she got and the more she saw, the less clear cut the boundaries became to her. She could only conclude that these boys who drank at her bar were exceptional human beings. The masculine and the feminine weren't nicely divided in Momma's mind as they are to a biologist. They overlapped and blurred in life. This trait was what kept life and Momma's bar from being black and white. If everything were so clear cut, there'd be nothing to learn after the age of six and arithmetic.

Among the later comers to Momma's were certain persons from the port battalion that sweated loading and unloading ships in the Bay of Naples. They turned up in her bar in the Galleria Umberto as soon as the afternoon shift got off, just as the truck drivers make a beeline for coffee and doughnuts. They usually came with fatigues damp with their sweat, with green-visored caps askew on their knotted hair. Because they were out of uniform Momma feared trouble with the MP's. But some of these port battalion GI's were Momma's favorites since they brought her many odds and ends they'd taken from the holds of Liberty ships: tidbits destined for generals' villas and the like. They knew Momma's nature as a curio collector of things and people.

There was Eddie, an American corporal. Momma loved Eddie the way she'd love a child of her own who was born not quite all there. Eddie'd been a garage mechanic in Vermont. He squirmed with that twisted tenderness often acquired by people who spend their lives lying under motors and having axle grease drip on them. Eddie had misty lonely eyes; his mouth was that of one who has never made the transition out of babyhood. His red hair yielded to no comb, and there was always a thick mechanical residue under his fingernails, which Momma sometimes cleaned herself. Eddie was drunk on duty and off. As he bought his chits, he leaned over Momma and patted her clumsily on her hair.

"Come stai, figlio mio?" Momma asked.

"Bene, bene, Momma," he replied.

Eddie would caress people in a soft frightened way and then run his tongue over his lips. After he'd got good and tight, he'd go through the crowded bar playing games, pulling neckties, snapping belt buckles, and thrusting his knee between people's legs. He was like a little dog that has got mixed up in society and desires to find a master.

Then there was a supply sergeant of the port battalion, with his vulture face. His every movement seemed to Momma a raucous suppression of some deeper inferiority sense. He talked constantly like a supply catalogue,

156

reeling off lists of things in his warehouse for the potent music of their names. Then he would shoot out his jaw and the blood would capillate into his eyes. Momma got him rooms around Naples with spinster acquaintances of hers. He stayed in these rooms on his one night off a week. This sergeant loved to sally into off-limits areas and wet-smelling vichi.

"Color and glamour," the sergeant said, "all there is to life, baby. . . ."

Eddie meanwhile had drunk three glasses of vermouth and came and stood by Momma, slipping cakes of soap into her hand behind the cash desk.

"Jees, I tink I got da scabies, Momma . . ."

The last delegate from the port battalion was one of its tech sergeants named Wilbur. He treated Momma like a serving girl and spent his time going over everyone with his eyes. Wilbur should have been born a lynx, for he draped his length over any available area with a slow rehearsed lewdness. Tonight he was growing a mustache, but it didn't camouflage his violet eyes that glowed like amethysts in his face. Momma could never get him to look her in the eyes. He simply drawled at everyone, and all the things he said lay around in gluey pools like melted lavender sherbet.

"Bonsoir, ducks," Wilbur said to the two British sergeants. "When is all this blah going to end? Because it is blah, and nobody knows it better than you. . . . Done any one nice lately? What a town to cruise this is. All the belles in the States would give their eye-teeth to be in Naples tonight. And when they saw all there is here, they'd be so confused they wouldn't know what to do with it. . . . Can you imagine the smell of their breaths? . . . Blah, that's all it is."

Two of Momma's more distinguished patrons now entered from the Galleria. They did it every evening, but every evening a little hush fell over the drinkers. They came in a little flushed, as though they'd been surprised in a closet. Perhaps the momentary pall proceeded from a certain awe at their rank, or at their temerity in coming at all. For by now the party was well under way, susceptible to that hiatus in levels of euphoria when people come late to a group that is already from alcohol in a state of dubious social cohesion. One was a pasty-faced major of the American medical corps who gave Momma a free physical examination every month and got his dentist friends to clean her teeth gratis. The major's breath always boiled in an asthmatic fashion, as though he were in the last stages of love-making. With him was his crony, a not so young second lieutenant who'd been commissioned for valor in combat at Cassino. The major and the lieutenant both wore gold wedding bands on their fingers. Momma gathered that they preferred not to discuss their wives, since these little women were four thousand miles away.

"Poor pickins tonight," said the major to the lieutenant.

"I don't waste any time any more," the lieutenant grunted, paying for his chits. "I just say do you and push'em into a dark corner. . . . Piss on all introductions and flourishes. . . . Who started this war anyhow? Not me, buddy. . . ."

Momma looked at the half-bald head of the lieutenant under the crazy angle of his cap. She knew that he'd been most heroic in battle—that was how he'd got his commission. There was strife in his low grating voice. Once he'd told her of last winter in battle of an Italian boy sewing by moonlight in the arch of a bombed house near Formia:

"I was drinking vino with my GI's. . . . And he just sits there looking at me. Fifteen, he said he was . . . white skin. I remember his eyes over his needle. . . . I wonder where he is now."

As the lieutenant fumbled to pay her for their chits, a woman's picture fell on Momma's counter out of his pocket:

"Ees your wife in Stati Uniti?" Momma said, trying to turn the glossy print over.

He covered it from her gaze with a hand pocked with sand-fly bites and umber with cigarette stains. His eyes were close to hers, yellow and protruding.

"Never mind that, Momma," he said, restoring the picture to his pocket.

Momma knew that the bravest and coolest entered her bar alone. They entered with a curt functionalism that informed everyone that hadn't come just to drink or to watch or to brood. Still others came in specious twosomes, talked together a little, and spent most of the time ignoring one another and looking into the mirrors in
158

a sort of reconnoitering restlessness. And a few came in groups of twos and threes for protection. When Momma's bar was full, it was like a peacock's tail because she could see nothing but eyes through the cigarette smoke. Restless and unsocketed eyes that wheeled all around, wholly taken up in the business of looking and calculating. Eyes of every color. Momma's bar when crowded was a goldfish bowl swimming with retinas and irises in motion.

Next there came two French lieutenants and two French sailors. The sailors were ubriachi and the lieutenants were icily sober. In the two French officers Momma'd always noted an excellence in the little braided pips through their shoulder loops, their American khaki shirts, and their tailored shorts. Their conversation played over the heads of their sailors with a silvery irony. Momma understood their tongue decently enough, that perfect language which gave all their remarks a literary quality beyond even the intelligence of the speakers.

"Ainsi je noie toute mon angoisse," said the first French officer.

"C'est ma femme qui m'incite à de telles folies," said the other.

"Tilimbom," the drunken sailors said, clapping the pompons on their caps.

The French officers had a jeep which they parked at the steps of the Galleria. When Momma closed her bar, she knew that they whisked into this jeep an assorted and sparkling company and drove to the top of Naples to admire the August moonlight. Momma wondered if the ripple of their epigrams and refinements ceased even when they were making love.

"C'est une manie, Pierre."

"Bon appétit, André."

Momma had less than half an hour till closing time. Her bar, into which people now must wedge themselves, was swimming in smoke and a terrific tempo of talk and innuendo. Under its surface there was a force of madness and a laughter of gods about to burst. Momma put her hand to her throat and swallowed hard in the strangling ecstasy of one dropping down an elevator shaft. For this was the time she loved best of her three hours: a presentiment of infinite possibilities, of hectic enchantments, of the fleeting moment that never could be

159

again because it was too preposterous and frantic and keyed up.

The Desert Rat was finishing his fifth white wine in his prison of detachment and musing. Ella the Aussie was being removed by Gaetano and Vincenzo from the top of the bar, where he was executing a cancan. Rhoda was booming out a quotation from Spengler. The Negro second lieutenant was examining his nail polish. Eddie had put his arms around one of the French officers, talking about parlayvoo-fransay. And the two British sergeants reared up like Savonarolas.

"I'm asking you, Esther, to take a good look at all these mad people. For they are mad. And consider the subtle thread that brings them all together here. Not so subtle as that either, Esther, since their personalities are so deeply rooted in it. What an odd force to unite so many varied personalities! Something they all want . . . and when they've had it, their reactions will be different. Some will feel themselves defiled. Others will want another try at it. Others will feel that they haven't found what they were looking for and will be back here tomorrow night."

"Does either of us know what these people are looking for, Magda?" the second sergeant asked with thickened tongue.

"Don't be dull, Esther. They're all looking for perfection . . . and perfection is a love of death, if you face the issue squarely. That's the reason why these people live so hysterically. Since the desire to live, in its truest sense of reproducing, isn't in them, they live for the moment more passionately than most. That makes them brazen and shortsighted. . . . In this life, Esther, when you find perfection, you either die on the spot in orgasm, or else you don't know what to do with it. . . . These people are the embodiment of the tragic principle of life. They contain tragedy as surely as a taut string contains a musical note. They're the race's own question mark on its value to survive."

"Is there any hope for them, Magda?" the second sergeant whimpered, wiping a mist from his glasses.

"In the exact measure that they believe in themselves, Esther. Depending on how they control their centripetal desires. Some hold back in their minds and distrust what they're doing. In them are the seeds of schizophrenia and

160

destruction. Others give themselves wholly up to their impulses with a dizziness and comic sense that are revolting to the more serious ones. . . . Lastly there's a group which sees that they can profit by everything in this world. These are the sane. The Orientals are wiser in these matters than we or Queen Victoria. No phase of human life is evil in itself, provided the whole doesn't grow static or subservient to the part. . . . But beware, Esther, of the bright psychiatrists who try to demarcate clearly the normal from the abnormal. In the Middle Ages people suffered themselves to be burnt as witches because it gave them such satisfaction to keep up their act. It was just a harmless expression of their ego. And children allow themselves to be pinked by hot stoves just to get a little sympathy out of their parents."

"What does God think of all this, Magda?" mourned the second sergeant.

"Thank Him, if He exists, that we don't know. . . . A new morality may come into existence in our time, Esther. That's one of the few facts that thrills me, old bitch that I am. Some distinction may be made between public and private sins, between economic and ethical issues. In 1944 you find the most incredible intermingling, a porridge of the old and the new, of superstition and enlightenment. How can we speak of sin when thousands are cremated in German furnaces, when it isn't wrong to make a million pounds, but a crime to steal a loaf of bread? Perhaps some new code may come out of all this . . . I hope so."

"And if not?"

"Why then," the first British sergeant said in drunken triumph, "we shall have a chaos far worse than in Momma's bar this evening. This is merely a polite kind of anarchy, Esther. These people are expressing a desire disapproved of by society. But in relation to the world of 1944, this is just a bunch of gay people letting down their back hair. . . . We mustn't go mad over details, Esther. Big issues are much more important. It is they which should drive us insane if we must be driven at all. . . . All I say is, some compromise must and will be reached. . . . Esther, I'm stinko."

Momma watched the two British sergeants embrace each other with an acid tenderness. Then they slid to the floor unconscious, in a welter of battle dress and chevrons and spectacles. They lay with their eyes closed in the quiet bliss of two spinsters who have fought out their differences at whist, falling asleep over the rubber. And it was typical of Momma's at this time of the evening that no one paid any attention to the collapse, just pushed and wedged in closer to give the corpses room.

The talk was now at its full tide of animation, like a river ravenous to reach the sea, yet a little apprehensive to lose its identity in that amorphous mass which ends everything. Momma knew the secret of an evening's drinking, that life grows sweeter as the sun sets and one gets tighter. If only drinkers knew how to hold their sights on that yellow target bobbing on their horizons! For Momma understood the drunkenness of the Nordic better than most Italians did. They drank out of impatience with details, with personalities that were centrifugal, with a certain feminine desire to have a crutch for the spirit, with a certain sluggishness of their metabolism. Momma thought it weak of them to drink, but it was a weakness as amiable as modesty, courtesy, or the desire to live at all when the odds were against them.

In a delirium Momma leaned over her cash desk and strained her ear at the hurtling shafts of talk:

"How can you possibly like actors? Every goddam one of them is constantly playing a part. Off the stage . . ."

"I am essentially an aristocrat. People must come to me. But I'm by no means passive . . ."

"My aunt, a refined colored woman, brought me up most circumspectly. I come from a long line of missionaries. So don't think I don't spread the good word among the Gentiles . . ."

"I don't know why our sort is always in the best jobs and the smartest . . ."

"First time for me, ye see. I'm not the lowered-eyelash kind . . ."

"So I told this Nellie to go peddle her fish somewhere else. And she did . . ."

"Do you remember loathing your father and doting on your teachers? . . . You didn't? . . ."

". . . not responsible for anything I do tonight . . ."

"Il ny a rien au monde comme deux personnes qui s'aiment . . ."

"Every time I think this is the real thing, the bottom

162

falls right out from under me. Here I go again . . ."

". . . un vero appassionato di quelle cose misteri-
ose . . ."

"I could be faithful all night long . . ."

"Ciao, cara . . ."

"In the Pincio Gardens all I saw was flesh flesh
flesh . . ."

"Sometime we'll read the *Phaedo* together. Then you'll
see what I mean . . ."

"There's somethin in ya eyes. I dunno, I just know when
I'm happy . . ."

"Let's you and me stop beating around the bush . . ."

"Don't you feel you have to be elegant with me,
Bella, cause your tiara's slippin over one ear . . ."

"For Chrissakes, what in hell do ya take me for? . . ."

"They're all suckin for a bruise . . . or somethin
else . . ."

". . . am frankly revolted with the spectacle of human
beings with their bobbie pins flying all over the place . . ."

"And when they expect you to pay them for it . . ."

"Pussunally I tink da Eyetalians is a hunnert years behind da times . . ."

"Why do I wear a tie? Just to be different, that's
why . . ."

". . . simply no idea of the effect of Mozart coming
over a loudspeaker at the edge of the desert. The Krauts
simply lovedddd ittt! . . ."

"In a society predominantly militaristic . . ."

"Ciao, cara . . ."

"I looked at you earlier . . . but I didn't dare
think . . ."

A sudden silence descended on Momma's bar. There
was a movement of many bodies giving way to make
space. She now knew exactly what time it was and who
had come. It was Captain Joe and the young Florentine. This was the climax of every evening. Captain Joe
stalked cool and somber in his tank boots, a green
bandanna tucked round his neck in the negligence of
magnificence. He had gold hair which caught the light
like bees shuttling at high noon. He had a hard intense
sunburned face that smoldered like a monk in a Spanish
painting. Momma knew that he was a perfect law unto
himself, though gentle and courteous with all. He came
only in company of the young Florentine, whose eyes

163

never left his face. The captain smiled with amusement and understanding at all, but he spoke only to his friend. Their faces complemented one another as a spoon shapes what it holds. The Forentine had dark thoughtful eyes and olive skin. He seemed wholly selfless. He and Captain Joe shared a delight and a comprehension that couldn't be heard. But they gave out a peace, a wild tranquillity.

"Buona sera a Lei," said Captain Joe to Momma. "You keep a great circus at Naples, signora. And the miraculous thing about you is that you don't need the whip of a ringmaster. . . . You and I and Orlando are the last of a vanishing tribe. We live in the sunshine of our own nobility. A perilous charge in these days. I wonder if our time will ever come again. We give because we have to. And others try to draw us into their own common mold, reading their own defects into our virtues."

Momma signaled to Vincenzo and Gaetano to shut down the rolling steel shutter. It was closing time. Captain Joe lit her cigarette.

"Happiness," Captain Joe said, "is a compromise, signora, between being what you are and not hurting others. . . . We smile, Orlando and I. . . . Genius knows its own weaknesses and hammers them into jewels. All our triumphs come from within. We've never learned to weep . . ."

A shout, a thud, and screams tore the air.

"Ya will, willya!" a drunken voice roared, hoarse with murder. Fists began to fly and people retreated against the walls. There was kicking and petitioning and cursing. The Desert Rat roused from his torpor and leaped in to defend the fallen. In the narrow bar persons swirled back and forth in a millrace. There were bloody noses and snapping joints. And when Momma saw the MP's break in from the Galleria, flailing their night sticks, she knew that the time had come for her to faint. So almost effortlessly she fell out and across her cash desk. She'd been practicing mentally all evening long.

FIFTH PROMENADE

(Algiers)

I REMEMBER that along the harbor of Algiers there's a sea wall. It dams the city up on the side of the hill lest it slide into the sea. In daylight I used to walk along this wall back of the Hôtel Aletti. There were Ayrab cameramen who took pictures that came out in reverse on gray sensitized paper. These photos made me look as though I'd happened before 1865, in a sad light such as surrounded Mr. Lincoln. And alongside the box camera on clothespins there were suspended pictures the Ayrab was especially proud of: a French family on Sunday afternoon, sailors with their arms around girls, and GI's peering out of an evil mist, with their shirts open and flowers in their buttonholes. Then I knew that they were drunk, with that same sharp exhibitionism of convict photos or those taken in penny acades under cruel lighting, so that all subjects look depraved and pimply.

I remember how men overseas in Algeria in 1944 tended to gather round the water front, as though by going near water they were challenging the barrier that kept them from home. They'd hang over the concrete balustrade and glare at the water and at the hospital ships and at the barrage balloons. They were people who stood on the edge of the moon, looking longingly at the earth. And all along this sea wall were sentry posts of antiaircraft installations. Back of these, thousands of soldiers peered out to sea or into the heavens. The British in their shorts rubbed themselves against the cement and murmured to one another:

"Choom, I'm browned off. Are you?"

I remember how they talked of Africa and Africa and Africa, of how they'd been in the bloody place for four years, and would they ever get back to Blighty. Nor were the Americans any the less on the griping, except that it was more focused—against officers and against food and against what the folks in America were doing. The Americans and the British rarely liked one another.

The limeys thought we had too many PX's and cinemas where they couldn't go, and too good rations and all the wimmin. And we thought that their battle dress smelled musty, and that what with the radio there was no excuse for so many accents and dialects as they spoke. Neither understood the other, or tried to. But we shared places with them along the Mediterranean at Alger. Their shorts hitched high as they leaned over the wall, pointing out things in the harbor. And our pants tightened over our buttocks as we pressed ourselves against the concrete, observing the shipping riding at anchor. There's a torture in ports when one is landbound. Along this gauntlet of men reaching out to sea and wishing they weren't there the French families of Alger used to take their Sunday walks. I thought it wasn't fair for them to be so natural and at home in a foreign land. Also there used to be ladies who got whistled at, and French officers on leave, and little Ayrabs trying to turn a franc. For the money in North Africa was like tinted toilet paper with murals on it. It was so dirty I couldn't be convinced of its value. It was printed in Philadelphia, however.

I remember that in the evening the press around the harbor got thicker. Then the wall was lined with uniformed men standing elbow to elbow, as though they were in a firing squad. The moon showed their faces or their backs. There was a ripple of talk like the afterswish of a wave. But most just stared. Their eyes were points like a battalion of waiting cats in single file. There was a mute panic in them. At one cry they'd have pushed down the wall and tumbled into the Mediterranean.

"I should thrill to be in Algiers, I suppose. But in wartime nothing gives you any satisfaction, does it? You do all sorts of things and find that it's like sucking dried fruit. You thought you wanted it from the outside, but inside there's nothing but ashes."

"The MP's let me into the Kasbah this afternoon. I went to a house and persuaded the Fatima to let me take pictures of her, bollocky. Such exposures too. I'm squeezing this and I'm squeezing that of her anatomy. She just loved to be photographed . . . for a price. So now I have my own French pictures. But much clearer than those they peddle on the streets back home. I'm having copies struck off for all my boys."

By moonlight too I remember the mustaches of the old French gentlemen who used to talk to me and bum cigarettes. I'd lift them up on the wall beside me. In their quavering voices they'd speak of Pétain and De Gaulle and Paris before 1940. They hated the Germans as a father hates the man who has ravished his daughter. Shaking palsied hands in the moonlight, they'd vow that France would rise again. Only my country wasn't helping her enough.

"What in God's name do you want, monsewer? We have our own war to win, you know."

"Frogs, frogs, frogs. First and last and always frogs. They kicked us in the pants in 1919 and they'll do it again. Mark my words. That goddam little teakettle still thinks she's in the eighteenth century. You may talk of the perfection of their culture and the polish of their language. But you must consider too their penury and their bigotry for anything that isn't France. And her squat little men with the braided caps were caught snoring in 1940. France had graft and filth within her . . . and that disease has sapped all the frogs."

I remember how some nights I'd walk up from the sea wall through a little park into the Place de l'Opéra. I'd climb a flight of stairs into that intimate theater. I heard *Tosca* and the *Barber of Seville* in French. There was also the *Desert Song* with asides in English to please the Americans. I heard opera in a warm frenzy because I could drink white wine between the acts. The orchestra was thirty. The singers looked better than they sang. In the intermissions the white wine tempted me to slide down the Lon Chaney staircase and mistily eye the people there: chic women of Alger fanning themselves in the heat, French naval officers, British holding receptions in bad French. I soon discovered that the Opéra of Alger was a great meeting place, classier than the parks or the sea wall. For to the opera came coiffured ladies whose husbands had died in France or in Tunisia.

"Geez, what a dainty little auditorium! Like Liederkranz Hall."

"What the hell is all this movement that goes in theaters? I came to see the show even if they didn't. Why don't they have some consideration for others? I didn't come to be stared at."

167

"And those ushers that make ya stand in line till they get around to showin ya to ya seat. They just want my tip."

"Of course, of course, butch. You're beginning to see into the parasitical life of Europe."

"And while we're on the subject, it burns me to haveta shell out five francs to some old doll every time I take a notion to relieve myself in the little boys' room. What's she there for, to see that I don't spill it all over myself?"

Or I remember how some nights I used to climb the interminable stairs to the Salle Pierre Bordes for concerts. There the Orchestra Symphonique gave a concert of modern English music. All the French walked out when they heard Vaughn Williams and Arnold Bax and Delius. And there too Lélie Gousseau used to play the piano. I'd sit and watch the somber trance in which she floated onto the stage of the Salle Pierre Bordes. She played Ravel with a rush of silver. Lélie Gousseau never seemed to me to be fully awake. But she was something miraculous and noble. She leaned over the keyboard and stopped breathing while she played.

"Ya see how that babe plays the pianer? Ya know what she needs, don't ya?"

"Ah, can it. Every time I try to get kultchah, ya open ya trap and talk like ya was at a stag party."

At one of her concerts a Negro corporal started a ballet on the stage behind her. She simply lifted her hands off the keys and laughed without a sound till the drunk had been removed by two French janitors. Then I was sure that Lélie Gousseau was a great artist.

I remember that in Algiers, because I had too much time to think and because the Mediterranean lay in front of me like a soft yet cynical mirror of time, I began to ponder on variety and difference. I lost something, because I became other people by thinking about them. For better or for worse I think I annihilated myself at this time.

"Just wait," said the pfc with the horn-rimmed glasses, "everything we know is going to be swept under."

"But sex is here to stay," the mess sergeant said, chewing on a toothpick.

"I didn't say it wasn't," the pfc said. "But so many things are coming into your life that you can't imagine.

Imagine a world in which there's a flatter plane of possible experience, in which the levels of poetry and prose come closer together than they ever have before. There's too much difference between the people of the world, yet surprisingly little variety. . . . . What sort of world do you want, anyway? A world in which no one speaks to anyone else, like the people in a New York apartment?"

"If ya'd take off ya glasses," the mess sergeant said, "and look at the world insteada books . . ."

"Well, that's my tragedy," the pfc said. "I'm steeped in the past. I'm not yet convinced that the break with the past is going to be complete. . . . I hope not, anyhow."

I remember the tiny dark Ayrab kids with brilliant eyes who shined shoes in front of the Red Cross. What was the difference between them and me, except that they were Ayrabs? They were so much smarter than I, but they hadn't been born in Detroit. They had the same mouths as I; they loved American chewing gum. But they lived in a world where people didn't even pretend to have ideals. Consequently they lived in a world realer than my own. And I wondered who was equal to the world in 1944, who was capable of seeing and understanding everything. Why wasn't I a prostitute? or a French child begging? or a Foreign Legionnaire with scars instead of milky skin? Why was I alive at all? How had I possibly managed to live?

"You won't go mad," the pfc said laughing. "You're attempting to be great in the old patterns. You have the disease of empathy. You try to enter into the minds of others. Perhaps you do."

"When I see an Ayrab child watching the chocolate bar in my hand, something tears at me."

"It should. You're arriving at the focus of the modern world. People are killing one another right and left. The newspapers don't say why. It's very simple. There's an unfair distribution of the world's goods. . . . We're heading either for world socialism or complete destruction."

"You mean I'm not crazy when I feel like crying all the time?"

"You're hopelessly sane. Most people have to go to the movies to bawl. A few do it over the life they see around them. . . . The only advancement made by the human race is because some guy discovered pity. He found out that everyone was really quite like himself, with unimportant differences. We all must die alone. And we start

169

dying with our birth. And a thousand years from now we'll all look equally silly: the movie star, the Ayrab whore, the financier, and the hustler. . . . If only we could publicly acknowledge our silliness for the few years that we are alive, we could then pool whatever dignity we possess. Then life would be worth living for all, instead of for the few."

I remember that in Alger, through too much thinking, I did something I never used to do in the States. I'd leave the boys and go into the city by myself. Perhaps it was because I was getting to know them too well. When you live only with men, something in you revolts after a while. Men by themselves are sterile; they tend to become brutal and onetrack. Night after night the same jokes keep popping up, the same crap games, the same vocabulary, the same weary comedy. So everyone in a group of men grows to hate the others with affection, as people do after a long marriage in which they've had no children to distract them from themselves.

To this day I don't know what I was looking for in the dark streets of Algiers. But I was alone; I heard my blood softly boiling. My brain was going like a stove. I started again to justify my own life. Why had I been born? Was there some scheme from which I wasn't distracting, some harmony that I was smashing? In those evenings whatever God I believed in receded from me like a comet. I found myself walking in a world in which I was an alien. I'd just come out of the womb, but there was no mother to take me by the hand.

Often around midnight in a glacial fever of horror and loneliness I thought I hated everyone in the world, which had thrust me into exile. And all the cordialities that men pay to one another seemed to me only a polite uproar to drown the rattle of death. All men, I came near deciding, were secretly enemies. I'd wonder what would happen to three men who found themselvse alone at the end of the world. Would they kill one another? Society therefore simply a charade to ease the torture of life? Were we all more divided than we were united? At such times I'd lay my head on the concrete wall along the Mediterranean. I wanted to cry, but nothing came except some dry hiccoughs. You're a monster and a misanthrope, I'd tell myself. . . .

170

I remember that one night in June, 1944, I was walking in the garden leading from the Place de l'Opéra to the port of Alger. It was near midnight. The lights flickered yellowly through the trees. Sometimes an Ayrab working at the port would stumble past and cadge a cigarette. Little old men muttering to themselves made their way home. I thought of my tent at Maison Blanche. I wasn't sorry for myself, but I felt passionately displaced, a body already buried alive. I chattered in my bones with a paraoxysm of anguish. I put my hands tightly against the suntans on my back and called out to the leaves and the moon and the sky:

"O my God, my God! . . ."

I was still sane enough to laugh after my outcry because something in a safe corner of my brain said I was acting like a Shakespearean ham. But all the same I was alone, and for the moment out of my mind. I heard a noise behind me and turned to look, with my cry still dribbling on my lips.

Behind me was a Frenchman of Algiers, not a man, not a boy. Under the twittering uncertain French bulbs his face was like a hawk's in repose. He was wearing shorts and a torn faded blue shirt that was open in the June heat. Under his arm he had a sheaf of typewritten papers.

"Qu'est-ce que tu as, Yank? Nous autres Français, nous connaissons bien la mélancholie."

I felt compelled, like a little child, to give him my arm. He took it naturally.

"Je suis écrivain," he said, flourishing his manuscripts with a smile bitter and consoling.

And I knew he'd been farther down than I'd ever yet known. He talked of Rimbaud and Verlaine and Debussy. His voice was all around me in a stream of cool elegance. He told me he'd been born in Rio, but had sought out Paris:

"Parce que c'est là, tu vois, ma patrie spirituelle. . . ."

His room smelled of the linen on his cot and a dish of fruit on his night table and the leather of his books. These were his only riches. He poured me a glass of sweet yellow wine. I sat in his one chair while he read me verses out of his few books. He made shooting gestures of delight with his hands, often looking at me to see whether I was following him. Evidently he desired to know how good an audience I was. Sometimes he reached

171

over and took a cigarette out of my breast pocket. He
knew some magic of disenchantment and exorcism. He
told me that I was still young, and that all was vanity.
But not yet. He said that men had wept before I was
ever born. . . .

SIXTH PORTRAIT

The Leaf

SOMETHING kept telling him that the war of 1918 hadn't
been the last. He'd enough of the Virginia gentleman in
him to know that men always have fought and always
will fight over women or more abstract ideals. And he'd
a degree from a southern university which had incul-
cated on him a certain esprit de corps. He decided to get
himself a reserve commission. So he wrote to the adjutant
general in Washington, went to camp each summer, and
before he knew it he was a second lieutenant. He wore
his uniform on state occasions: at the Rotary Club, at
the Elks', at the Masons'. At their luncheons they called
him captain or colonel with a certain manly affection.
They spoke of him as a young man with an eye to the
future of his country and of himself.

He spent his time in his laboratory at Roanoke. He
was a petroleum engineer. By nature he was a dreamer.
He thought of himself as a catalyst of the aristocracy of
the Old South who'd somehow made the conversion to
the world of 1930. He never spoke of the Civil War because he liked to assert huffily that he lived very much
in the present. And he'd married a dreamer too. She
was a belle of Roanoke, belonged to the DAR and the
Methodist Church. She wrote poetry with the rapt efficiency in which most women cook. And when no editor
took her verses, which fluttered and sighed like herself,
she published them herself. Though she had no children,
each year she Brought Out a slim lavender or ocher or
mauve book containing her thoughts on love, flowers,
and life. She said that she loved life with a fierceness
known only to the elect. She'd married him because great
loves, unlike butterflies, can be pinned down.

172

Yet they saw little of each other in their Roanoke apartment. She wrote her poems and read them at women's clubs, where she was applauded by wrenlike elderly ladies who then drank iced tea and champed on shortcake. He in his laboratory brooded on the possibilities of gasoline. Sometimes he forgot to take any food for a whole day, and she was too preoccupied with what she called her muse to bring him anything.

"Ours is the ideal love," she'd say with a towel round her head in the steaming Virginia summers. "Few men or women have had a relationship as spiritual as ours."

Or sometimes when a visiting business associate was about to slide under the table from bourbon, he'd read him excerpts from his wife's poetry.

"Has she any children?" the business associate would say.

In 1941 his hour struck. He was already a captain in the reserve of the Army of the United States. This, he told himself, was no small potatoes. With the passage of selective service he found himself ordered to active duty to a new infantry camp in South Carolina. So he had all his uniforms dry-cleaned. And he polished his jewels, as he called his brass, with a blitzcloth. On his final night at home they gave the nigress the evening off and went out to dinner. It was the first time they'd appeared together in public in five years. They'd had few friends. Lucinda'd been busy with her poetry. And he— well, a petroleum engineer is like a priest.

Lucinda sat across from him over her lobster salad and iced coffee. Her eyes were crinkling, for she had a splitting headache. Bravely she rolled her gentian eyes in torment:

"I should have stood in bed tonight. I'm doing it for you, lovey. Who knows how often we'll see each other during this frightful emergency? . . . As I wrote today in blank verse, Europe has again invaded us. . . . We Americans try to lead decent lives on our own continent, and those Europeans always manage to suck us in. I see now why our ancestors left Europe. She's rotten through and through. . . . Perhaps it would be better if she were destroyed utterly."

"Or perhaps we should send the goddam nigras there," he said laughing.

Since tomorrow he was going on active duty, he was

173

now permitting himself a modicum of profanity. After all, he was going to have to emerge from the cloister of his laboratory and deal with men from every state in the Union. He looked down at the crossed rifles on his dinner jacket, seeing himself shouting at his company. Yes, he'd have a company, his very own. He thought long about that company. He'd already planned the precision of his whole organization. He saw an order emanating from himself and passing down Through Channels and being put into effect with clarity of detail and economy of effort.

He was silent over the strawberry shortcake. He and Lucinda never spoke much except about her poetry. That was the excellence of their marriage, that neither needed to say much. Since they both had the temperaments of dreamers, the essential thing was that they shouldn't get in each other's hair, or dreams. Now a sheet of silence hung between them like plate glass. He broke it.

"If you like, I could take an apartment for you near camp. It's not fair that you should hang around Roanoke like a goddam grass widow."

Lucinda held up her little cramped hand on which the solitaire glittered like a hag's eye:

"Lovey, don't. You'll make my migraine worse. It's caused by your leaving me. Please don't make me suffer any more than I'm doing, lovey. . . . I'd go mad in the red sand of South Carolina. I need green grass and the fluting of the birds of Virginia. . . . Besides there's my 'Ode on Thomas Jefferson.' Outside this state, I'd lose all feeling for the mood. . . . I'm an honest artist, lovey. I write only what I see and what I feel, not what the public wants. That's why my books are so sad and solitary. . . . And in South Carolina I couldn't recapture what I feel right now in Virginia. . . . Perhaps around Christmas I might be down. But right now there's something in me that says No. . . . Lovey, don't urge me. You know what my soul is like . . . a bird at dusk. . . ."

So he put out his hand and stroked her wrist. He'd never been much of a caresser; possibly his mind was a trifle chilly. He remembered how in college the boys would run after spirits and nigresses, while he'd sit in his room and read. Lucinda withdrew her hand and poked at the swilled whipped cream on her plate.

174

"Oh lovey," she said, "I thank you for our love. There's something perfect between us. Because it's not . . . passionate . . . it can never burn itself out."

"Lucinda," he said, "your name is you. . . ."

It was the wildest transport of fantasy he'd ever permitted himself. And after a while she said she was cold and her headache worse. He got her wraps. At the house before going to her room she kissed him on the corner of his mouth.

"You'll be gone when I get up in the morning," she said. "And I wonder if you know how sometimes I wish I could be the sort of wifey who could get up and cook your breakfast and do all those little things that wifeys do. . . . But I can't, lovey. When a woman sets out to write poetry, she sacrifices most of herself . . . for a higher good. Sappho knew it. So did Elizabeth Barrett Browning."

"Goddam it, hush," he said gallantly. "I'd rather you gave me a ticket to immortality than slave over a hot stove. Any wife can do that."

"I swore," she said, making a gesture of weary renunciation in the dim hallway among the antiques, "that I'd never marry. But you dissuaded me, lovey. And I've never regretted it. For I've had you and my art too. . . ."

When he left in the morning he found a manuscript lying on the top of his visored cap. It was dedicated to his initials:

> For you, my love,
> Through all the bridegroom spontaneity,
> Through all your e'er-retreating suave compassion,
> A thrill immutable
> Sustains me like a wing of eider.
> And I know
> That I shall never faint or feel forlorn
> As long as you, my love,
> Return to me like snow, like spring, like birds.
> The seasons' secret
> Turns in me as the earth remembers time,
> Remembering and wanting and desiring:
> These are the solitary sins of wives,
> And I am scarlet with them,
> Vermilion with my love for you, my love.

He read this lovely thing through in the chill dead light of the dawn in the streets of Roanoke. He had a vague impulse that he should seek Lucinda out in her bed and smother her with kisses. But then he reconsidered and went to his train.

Captain Motes arrived at the infantry camp in South Carolina. He came with just a smidgin of fanfare. He knew that it was all very well to slip into your place like a late guest. But this was different. He was a captain in the Army of the United States, and he desired to make his position plain, without goading anybody. Consequently he determined a little more attention than civilians were getting. And he got it on the train because officers' uniforms were still virtually unknown. His tactical intuition told him that soon America was going to war. Americans must accustom themselves to the idea of the army officer. Consequently he sat haughtily in his parlor car and answered in considerable detail the questions of anxious old ladies. He made dark prophecies of what their grandchildren might have to go through in the next few years.

At the station he was slightly autocratic with the nigra porters. Arriving at five-thirty in the morning, he spent half an hour calling goddam over the telephone wires till he got some action. Rancid from their sleep, a group of drowsy nigras turned up in dungarees. They fumbled around with his baggage, heavy with his impedimenta and Lucinda's poems.

"Goddam it, get a move on," Captain Motes called. "Are you still waiting for John Brown?"

"Yassuh," the nigras said in chorus.

At the gate of the camp a sentinel stopped his taxi and saluted. It was the first time he'd been saluted outside of summer camp. He knew that soon, all over America, young men would be saluting him on every street in every town. He'd got in early. Soon he'd be Major Motes, and then Lieutenant Colonel Motes, and then. . . .

The dawn in South Carolina is a red and sullen thing. First the trees stand out like corpses with splayed arms. Then the captain saw the rocks resting on the hillsides, the hardness of the sky, and the burnish of the air.

While waiting for headquarters to open, he took his breakfast at the PX. He hadn't a stomach for coffee,

176

but he did take some tomato juice, several glasses of milk, and a piece of toast.

"Guess it's not often that you see an officer here, eh?" he said cheerily to the waitress.

"No suh," she squeaked. "An dey ain't supposed to come here at all at all. Ah hates officers. Tinks dere rears doesn't stink like other folkses' does. When dese American men gits a piece of brass on dere shoulders, dey tinks dey's Mussolini. No suh, ah done want no truck widdem, ah don't."

"Well, there are officers and officers," Captain Motes said, laughing indulgently.

"Dere shouldn't be any officers at all," the nigra waitress said, furrowing her mouth and mopping the other tables. "When you gits an army, you gits to killin fore ya knows it. An killing makes trouble to Americans. Dey ain't used to it, cept on a small scale like in lynchins. An when you makes some better dan udders, you is askin for a bruise."

"Wishful thinking," Captain Motes answered, leaving her a nickel tip. "There have always been wars and there always will be wars. And there will always be officers and enlisted men."

"Dere's wars," said the nigress, retreating and waving an umber arm, "cause a few men wants 'em. An ah sees yo is one of dose men. . . . Goomawnin to yo, capting."

At post headquarters he went through the formality of saluting the adjutant, even though this officer was only a first lieutenant. Captain Motes enjoyed the games of the army. After his salute he stood alertly at attention in the ideal position of the officer, according to the *Officers' Guide*. The adjutant had a Vermont twang and the businesslike air of one whose inner life is at loose ends.

"Captain Motes, we are somewhat embarrassed. . . . You're a Virginia man. . . . May I ask whether you have all the prejudices and double standards of Virginia men? I have never yet met one who realized he was living after the year 1861, either in respect to the Great Rebellion or in his relations with women."

"Goddam it, sir," cried Captain Motes, keeping his hands tight against the seam of his trousers, "we're all together in the service of our country. I was ordered to active duty, sir, not to fight Mr. Lincoln's war all over

177

again. You think that all we southerners are on the aggressive against you . . ."

"You reassure me, captain," the adjutant said, uncramping his Vermont fingers. "The fact is, a captain is a difficult rank to fit into an infantry replacement training center. . . . You're neither a second nor a first lieutenant, with whom we could do something. . . . Thus I must inform you that the verbal orders of the commanding general are for you to command D Company of the 50th Battalion. This is an all-Negro outfit. Report to regimental headquarters for your billet. Good morning, Captain Motes."

For more than a year he was company commander to one hundred and fifty nigras. Since they had a thirteen-week training cycle, he saw the same black faces for three months. He saw the same black mess sergeant who kept thick steaks for him in the icebox of the mess. Cycle after cycle he saw the same black first sergeant who'd gone to Harvard and wrote sonnets. Cycle after cycle he saw the same black supply sergeant who whisked GI equipment into town and sold it through the nigress with whom he shacked.

"These goddam nigras will drive me mad," Captain Motes said to himself as he played solitaire in the bachelor officers' quarters.

Gradually therefore he evolved a policy whereby the nigras shouldn't drive him mad. He knew that the War Department vacillated on the nigra issue. On one hand every privilege was given them, but on the other their segregation was complete. Captain Motes, from under his campaign hat with the oak leaves, standing rigid and tense in his leggins, watched his nigras fire on the range, run the obstacle course, take their short-arm inspections. He shook his head over MP reports on their Saturday nights in town. He cut out all passes. He smelled the musk of their bodies as they forgot to stand at attention before his desk in the orderly room. Their venereal rate was the highest in camp. He tried court-martialing for every case of venereal disease until the commanding general heard of it. Finally he no longer dealt with his men personally. From his orderly room, himself unseen, came a vise of control and discipline. On Sunday afternoons he had his men, wearing full field packs, out washing their barracks windows.

Pearl Harbor came and went. Every month Captain Motes put in for a transfer away from his nigras. He was always refused. His invisible regimentation froze his nigras and their officers. They became machines. Captain Motes said that, now America had declared war, this was the way it should be. He'd sacrificed friends and the good will of his men for results. He was always by himself, playing solitaire or charting graphs of training cycles.

In the Louisiana maneuvers Captain Motes's nigras were captured to the last man while storming Hill Fifty-eight.

"Captain," a brigadier general said, "you have done a beautiful job in killing all combat initiative in your men. I hereby hand you the booby prize as an infantry company officer."

In the summer of 1942 Captain Motes was relieved of his nigras. Summoned by the adjutant, he found the Vermonter, still a first lieutenant, crinkling typewritten onionskin in his hands.

"Captain," the twang clattered, "the War Department wants you. Remember us when you go to Washington. Think of us poor foot soldiers. Yours is the fate of all those too good for the infantry. . . . You're going into military intelligence. You seem to have some recherché talent that the rest of us lack. Or perhaps you know your congressman too well? . . . At any rate here are your orders, and Godspeed to you. . . . I have a feeling you won't die in this war, captain."

"Goddam it, sir," Captain Motes said, "we can do no more than obey our orders, can we?"

"Some orders," said the lieutenant, returning the salute, "are easier to take than others."

Captain Motes was sent to Camp Ritchie to learn prisoner-of-war interrogation. On the way up he wondered how he'd ever learn German. But then any Kraut knew German. So for days at Ritchie he fought from dummy house to dummy house. When those playing the part of prisoners allowed themselves to be interrogated, he'd listen to the hiss and sputter of their German, and his face would ease into an understanding smile. At every ja he'd nod his head. Colonels often came to Ritchie from

Washington to look at the school, for it was a pet of the War Department. Then Captain Motes would take it upon himself to explain what was going on to these visiting dignitaries. He kept on the lookout to buttonhole inspecting parties. The other student officers were all too busy practicing hiccoughing in German at one another.

Such and other things he told Lucinda. Occasionally he could get up to see her in Roanoke. Spreading his hands on the oilcloth in their antique kitchen, he'd hint of task forces, of combat teams. His strategic sense told him that there must be an invasion of North Africa to start taking the Mediterranean away from the Axis. Ripples of horror spread over Lucinda's face. It was the first time he'd ever really been eloquent with her. He bought an illuminated globe for their library and a supply of colored ribbons and thumbtacks so that she could plot every phrase of the coming American struggle in Europe. She began reading *War and Peace* and wrote a poem beginning:

Men who run forth to die
From the Mississippi, from Iowa, from Nohwata
    Oklahoma . . .

It was published in a Roanoke evening newspaper. The ladies' clubs said that she would be the Winifred M. Letts of this war.

"If I should die someplace in Europe," Captain Motes said. Lucinda covered her temples with her hands.

"Goddam it, darling," he resumed, "how strange life is . . . all my life I've had something unsatisfied in the back of my brain."

"Don't," she breathed, looking at him through her fingers, "don't, lovey. We play with greatness to our own peril. It's such a perilous thing. We mature so slowly, keeping within ourselves the kernel of our own time sense. And suddenly it bursts on the world. . . ."

Her fecundity in these days was such that she wrote and wrote, standing at her black walnut antique writing desk. She would have fainted if Hattie the nigress hadn't occasionally brought her a tray with sandwiches and fruit juice.

In October, 1942, Captain Motes was alerted for overseas movement. Washington was whirling softly and pregnantly. People ducked in and out of the Mayflower and the Willard. Briefcases tossed through the streets like flat somber Japanese lanterns.

And Captain Motes got a company of one hundred men. Daily he went with them on the range, insisting on their firing all the weapons in the training manuals. There kept recurring in his vocabulary phrases such as D-Day and Cut to Pieces. He scurried around tight-lipped and absent, forgetting to speak to old acquaintances.

One night, though they were alerted for staging, he slipped under the barbed wire and met Lucinda at Hampton Roads. It was forbidden to hold any communication from the port of embarkation, but Captain Motes knew that as an intelligence officer he could trust himself. Lucinda wept when he told her they were sailing the following morning. He told too the number of ships in the convoy. He guessed also that they'd land on the northwest coast of Africa.

"We must rig up a code, lovey," she said panting, "so I'll always know just where you are. And all the other pieces of information a wifey needs for her peace of mind."

"Not necessary," he answered smiling and patting her hand.

He looked around the restaurant with a hideous penetration, then took something with a wooden handle on it out of his pocket.

"Mercy, lovey! What's that, a grenade?"

"A base censor stamp. With this on the envelope I can write you every goddam thing that happens. . . . And . . . if I shouldn't come back, remember me as I am tonight . . . and if I have ever hurt you . . ."

She laid her head on the tablecloth and streaked it with the rivers from her eyes. Captain Motes kissed her on the hair and raced out into the night. That was the way he desired to remember Lucinda in the pelting of bullets and the screaming and battle fury of maddened and dying men.

On 7 November 1942, the great armada bobbed uncertainly. Word passed that they were off the coast of Africa.

"This is it, kids," was the word that flicked from mouth to mouth like a tight bit.

Captain Motes spent all his time with his men, though it was difficult to brake himself down to their tempo, which seemed maddeningly inert. They chewed gum and shot craps. He encouraged them and cracked jokes at them. He called up his store of warlike stories, even going back to Julius Caesar.

"One of the great moments in the history of the world! Goddam it, men, *look* at me!"

Whereas the other officers on his ship seemed idiotically calm, like men playing in the shadow of doom. This was the way it had been at Pearl Harbor, Captain Motes told himself, pitying them their complacency.

"Captain," one officer drawled, "you're purple. How's your blood pressure?"

"Fine, fine, goddam it to hell!" he screamed and raced about the deck with his field glasses.

Before dawn on 8 November 1942, a fearful roaring set up. The convoy began to move in toward the murky outlines of Africa. The sky vibrated with lights and tracers. The navy opened up on Casablanca and Fedhala. Captain Motes, sleeping clothed and in his leggins, rushed to hearten and exhort his troops. Poor lads, this was the last of life for many of them.

But nothing happened. Captain Motes raced over the decks shouting that someone had blundered, that they should all be on shore by this time. Then through the hell of firing and smoke a voice roared through the speakers on the bridge:

"Put on ya helmet or go below. We ain't landin' for a week yet. What the hell do ya think ya are, assault troops?"

One week after the Casablanca landings, after lying offshore several miles, Captain Motes's ship entered the harbor and leisurely unloaded. But that week he spent tossing in the slow swells of the gray Atlantic and listening to the firing ashore was the most tantalizing the captain had spent in his life. He began to accuse his company of malingering and cowardice when he detected signs of relief that they hadn't been in on the landing operations. He heard news from the shore that casualties had been heavier than expected because the French and the French Navy hadn't been quite so co-operative as everyone had counted on. He heard of legs floating off Oran. He heard of American dead at Fedhala, of

182

French sniping from the windows in the Place de France in Casa. He heard how Ayrabs went from side to side selling information and perpetrating ghoulish atrocities on dead American engineers. He heard of General Patton making his bed in the Villa Miramar after the German armistice delegation had fled into the torchy night with their mistresses and their nightshirts. He heard how the entire 3rd Division was bivouacked on the Fedhala golf course. Captain Motes scrambled fretfully about the vessel, shuttling between the navy gun crews and American officers waiting to go ashore.

"Fine scrap, fine scrap . . . and we *would* have to miss it. I was itching for the real thing. . . . Well, they goddam won't do me out of it a second time."

On 16 November 1942, he entered Casa with his company. They marched tranquilly off the ship. There was little to show that only eight days ago Americans had been killed here—a little wreckage in the harbor. The Ayrabs were already well versed in the Americanese of cigarettes, bonbons, and chewing gum. The French on the streets were lean and leering, just as he'd expected them to be from books. Captain Motes knew at sight that he'd never trust the French. And as for learning their language, that would be like apprenticing himself as a quisling to the Vichy government. His eyes narrowed under his helmet as he marched along, tearing at the strap of his carbine. Under his armpit a tiny revolver nestled. He was ready for anything. The privilege of entering Casa on D-Day had been denied him. But he'd make up for it.

The Atlantic Base Section was already in operation. Its function was supply. Choice hotels and villas had been requisitioned from Casablanca to Fez. There were already messes and clubs throughout French Morocco. Some officers of the base section had already chosen their mistresses and had settled down to the luxurious drudgery of rear area life, where they expected to vegetate for years.

Captain Motes got a room at the Hôtel Majestique. It had a floor of Moroccan tile with cabalistic symbols, a chamber pot, and a closet. The bed smelled like the Ayrabs. To clean his room he'd a Fatima with blue stars on her cheeks. She giggled and filliped her small breasts. She wore an American mattress cover and clinking jew-

183

elry. He gave her cigarettes to stay out of his room while he was in it, for she stank like goat's milk. After he'd unpacked his bedding roll and hung up his carbine and helmet in a military and sinister manner, he sat down to write a letter to Lucinda.

Somewhere in North Africa
9 November 1942

My Darling,

The headlines will have told you exactly where I am. I'm lying under my shelterhalf as I write this. In the distance I can still hear the firing. It sounds like fat popping in a frying pan. Darling, I've been through an indescribable twenty-four hours. With your lovely poet's mind you can intuit the horror of it all. I'll spare you the details. Suffice it to say that they gave us hell.

I haven't suffered so much myself. I'm still in one piece. What got me was to see those lovely fellows in my company fall bubbling into the ocean or drop soundlessly in their tracks as I led them up the beach. I'm writing to you first, my darling. After that I have a long string of letters to get off to the families of my poor devils.

Lucinda, I know what death means now. I noticed some white hairs in my beard as I was shaving out of my helmet this morning. But this is war, and I hope the American people wise up to the fact—but fast. I'm living in a grove where the rain never stops falling. The mud of North Africa is like melted chocolate ice cream.

A sentinel has just passed. Perhaps he too is thinking of his wife. The image of you is constantly before me. Keep sweet. . . .

Captain Motes read his letter over several times. Then he filled his washbowl and put the sheet of paper into it. He swooshed his letter quickly around in the water, then let the blurred letters dry. He sealed it in its envelope. On the lower left-hand corner he affixed the base censor's stamp he'd brought overseas with him. He didn't know whether a base censorship detachment had yet been set up in Casa; but if it had, that stamp would let his letter go through unopened.

Next morning Captain Motes, wearing leggins and side arms, reported to the Shell Building on Boulevard de la Gare. It was the headquarters of the Atlantic Base Section. He went at once to a certain office, the location of which he'd demanded of the MP. This was the most ornate

184

and inaccessible of all the offices. At the desk was the captain who was aide to the commanding general. This aide sounded off, out of an easy familiarity with the great:

"Don't be a goon, captain. You simply can not see the general. He's still setting up ABS. The fighting stopped in Casablanca only last week. He's a very busy man, the general . . ."

"I'm afraid you don't understand, sir," said Captain Motes with a mellow laugh. "I am . . . keep this under your hat . . . an intelligence officer . . ."

"A dime a dozen, captain," the aide beamed, picking up a phone. "There were scads of em running around and asking stupid questions on the beach under fire. . . . He hates em. Now they're coming out of their holes and askin for cushy jobs. Come back in a month, captain . . ."

"I advise you to let me see the general," Captain Motes said, raising his voice to underline his intentions.

Then a short fierce man with a star on his collar stormed out of the inner sanctum. His white eyebrows met over his nose. His mouth was a cold dash of red on his face. Captain Motes snapped to attention.

"For Chrissake step inside," the general bawled. "Stop rubbing your hands together and talk to me as man to man. . . . I suppose they flew you over from Washington. That's the way the hellish thing always operates. No replacements or no prophylactics or glare goggles, but they're forever flying in intelligence officers and the CID to check up on me. . . . I knew they'd put the hooks to me because I haven't had time yet to take care of the security angle. What for Chrissakes do they think a war is in Washington? Cutting up letters?"

The little old man ran round his desk like a terrier trying to remember where he's buried a bone. Back of his desk was an American flag drooping from an ebony pole, the perch of a golden eagle. Captain Motes hesitated, prodding his dubbined toe into the rich nap of the rug.

"I won't lie to the general," he said softly, returning to the position of attention. "Washington is . . . well, disappointed at the intelligence setup here. No BCD. No traveler censorship at the airport. As they understand it, and the general does too, a base section must do all the brainwork for our fighting men . . ."

185

"Close your yap," the general screamed, running in the opposite direction. "I suppose this means I'll never get my second star."

"There was talk in Washington," Captain Motes said, discreetly lowering his voice, "of the fine work the general is doing here. . . . One man can't think of everything, sir."

"Very well! . . . Shut up and listen to me, and stop rubbing your hands. I'm giving you a direct order. VOCG. The stencils will be cut this afternoon. . . . It is my desire that you take charge of all censorship in the Atlantic Base Section. . . . Are you listening? I don't want to be bothered ever again with any of this damn G-2 nonsense, do you hear, captain? I delegate it all to you. Read all the letters you please. But I don't ever want to see your face again unless I send for you. Now get the hell out of my office."

Captain Motes saluted and wheeled into the streets of Casablanca.

So as the North African Theater of Operations became the ominous and murky name NATOUSA, Captain Motes became postal censor of this area, which some thought was an Ayrab city which they sought in vain on the maps of Morocco and Algeria. The importance of the work of censorship made Captain Motes secretive and distrustful. He was jealous of the weight of his own mission. He thought of himself as uneasy and as friendless as a king. After office hours he tended to spend all his time in his hotel room, dreaming up ways to extend his censorship empire. Eventually, as the war came onto the continent of Europe, he saw himself as chief theater censor with offices in each new fallen city. And as Hollywood magnates acquire the feeling that they control the emotions of the world, so did Captain Motes grow aware that he wielded a baton over the thoughts of all the soldiers and officers in North Africa.

He became more nervous. His walk developed a sidelong twitch that was almost a swish. He smoked more because he couldn't take to cognac and Casablancaises the way all the others seemed to. His head was too full of military secrets and classified material for him to trust himself to relax. If he drank or made love, he'd babble of recondite things. His hair was growing gray. He never

186

told Lucinda exactly what he was doing, even though he had the privilege of sending his letters out of the theater with his special stamp affixed. He discouraged his officers' leaving the city where they worked, for he had a dread of intelligence officers' getting together and hashing over what they knew. Finally he decreed that all officers working together should mess and live together in the same billets.

"Captain," said one of his examiners, "isn't it hell enough to have to read mail all day long side by side with sixty other officers at the same table? Do I have to look at their ugly faces for twenty-four hours on end?"

"This is war," Captain Motes answered, lighting a cigarette from the butt of the last. "People in Tunisia are living in the same foxholes month after month. Goddam it, you're better off than most of the people in the States."

"Are you threatening me with the front? It would be heaven besides sitting on my arse for eight hours a day and going blind over trying to decipher what an illiterate Negro writes to his ex-shackjob back in Georgia. . . . Smiles. . . . Ha-ha, baby. . . . Letter writing is no longer a fine art, captain. . . . I'm bucking for a section eight."

"You were commissioned in military intelligence," Captain Motes replied, toying with Lucinda's picture. "Do you wish to resign your rank?"

"I'm going rapidly mad," the lieutenant said.

"If you think you are, it's a sure sign you're not. . . . Take the afternoon off and go to the movies."

Captain Motes heard that his officers were using the unit's trucks for week-end trips to Fez and Rabat. He ordered the practice to cease at once. What would the taxpayers say if they knew that the gasoline they were doing without was being used for pleasure jaunts? He took none himself. He even begrudged himself his personal jeep. He looked with a bloodshot eye on the time his officers spent with the girls of Casablanca, talking French, which he couldn't understand. God only knew what military secrets they might be revealing to these girls. One day he made a speech to all his command as they sat under the rows of strung lights at the long tables laden with mail. They peered at him from under their eyeshades:

"We must not forget, men, that a short time ago these
187

French were entertaining the Germans. They shot at our boys when they landed here. . . . I'm putting this to you as American commissioned officers. Do you think it . . . prudent to . . . fraternize with these French? . . . I am not forbidding it, gentlemen. I merely suggest that you think it over. On whose side are you fighting? These North African French are simply milking you for all they can get."

"But the captain knows no French," a voice spoke up. "A lot of us do, and enjoy talking the language."

"That's beside the point. Neither do I know Japanese. I simply would think twice about handing over my PX rations and my health to some woman who doesn't even pay me the compliment of learning my language. God only knows what's going on in the back of a frog's head."

"I resent that!" another voice cried. "The French are our allies."

"Well, think it over, gentlemen," Captain Motes said. "Think it over. . . . Remember that you're in Africa to help win a war."

After this uneasy session Captain Motes rarely addressed his commands directly. He knew their hostility. He arranged that the base post office should send him all his officers' mail. He read it and censored it in his hotel room each evening. A leader must know how far he can trust his subordinates. Many evenings at his desk his cheeks scorched at what was said about him in V-mails. But now he had an exact index of whom he could trust of his officers and how far. From the letters of a plump sturdy lieutenant he chose his executive officer.

Lieutenant Frank was a cavalry sergeant of the regular army, paunchy, bluff, and, he said, straightshooting. He'd come up the hard way, so he had no use for an army of conscripts and pale civilians commissioned after ninety days at officer candidate school. Lieutenant Frank entered rooms like a steam roller, never knocking, but kicking doors open. Oaths dropped liberally from his lips. He said that men must be sworn at to get things done.

"Them goddam letter openers," he would cry. "A buncha ninnies. Commissioned schoolteachers. . . . Ya too kind with em, captain. I treat em like an old first sergeant, and they think morea me. Throw the book at em when they step outa line. It's the only language they'll understand."

"But they're commissioned officers in the United States Army."

"Ah, crud. They'll do as they're tole. They're in the army, ain't they? They'll take their orders just like you an me."

Lieutenant Frank sometimes nudged his commanding officer to bring home the point of his remarks. Captain Motes smiled fastidiously. But under the influence of Lieutenant Frank a new regimen was adopted in all the base censorship detachments of North Africa. The ten-minute break for each hour was abolished. Examiners were permitted one fifteen-minute interval in the morning, one in the afternoon. A time clock was set up at the entrance of each examination room. Each officer must punch his ticket as he entered and left work. There was no going to the latrine without permission of the front office. In order to step up the number of letters that each officer read, no talking or whispering was permitted at the examination tables. Officers late to their office hours were restricted to quarters for the weekend and given a punishment OD. Captain Motes told his officers through the mouth of Lieutenant Frank that they must not forget they were still in the army; there was danger of hemorrhoids and potbellies from too much sitting.

Sometimes, sitting till after midnight in his hotel room and hearing the buzz of Casablanca fade out till there was only the moaning of the sea, Captain Motes found it necessary to condemn letters that his officers had written home. He read them all now every night. For they bitched to their wives and friends about the work and about himself. He was hurt and astonished to see how indiscreetly intelligence officers wrote. He suspected that the constant handling of classified matter had blunted their sensitivity to security measures. One officer wrote to his girl:

A commissioned officer in the United States Army! Why, with this introverted bastard who's our CO, I had more prestige and privilege as a Pfc! I think that nothing worse can happen in this outfit, and it always does. . . .

Captain Motes didn't speak directly to the officer who wrote this letter. He simply had him transferred to the Oran office, with orders that he be employed on the ta-

189

ble where all day long packages were opened, censored, and tied up again. Work for grocery clerks, but done by men with bars.

Often in the mornings he'd stand in front of the plate-glass screen that shut off the front office from the room where the mail was examined. He'd observe the examiners at their work, how many were reading *Stars and Stripes* or magazines on the government's time, how many were writing V-mails, how many were staring into space. As a result of this reconnoitering a new order came out, signed by Lieutenant Frank as executive officer. This order stated that each officer must read two hundred ordinary letters or five hundred V-mails in one working day. Those who fell below their quota would report for evening duty. But because Captain Motes had observed how pale and weary his examiners had grown under the screaming nitrogen reading lamps, he prescribed one hour of close-order drill for all officers after work was done in the afternoon, to be taken in the open sunlight. The order ended rationally and sweetly:

"We are all officers and owe it to ourselves and our country to keep in A-1 physical condition."

As he was about to leave the front office that evening, Captain Motes had a visit from one of his letter openers, the red-headed Lieutenant Almeranti, who'd been yanked out of the armored force into censorship. Captain Motes knew him only from the beetling and whining letters he wrote home. Lieutenant Almeranti's red eyebrows were bouncing like springs. He leaned with both hands on Captain Motes's desk.

"Don't you believe in standing at attention before your commanding officer?"

"I'm not an enlisted man. And I'm tired of playing soldier around here. . . . You're demoralizing all of us by treating us like prisoners of war. You've made a sweat-shop of this detachment and then you turn around and pretend you're GI. You're not. You're the warden of a reform school. . . . Captain, I want a transfer. . . . Are you trying to drive us all crazy? Have you ever sat and tried to read mail for eight hours? After a while your head starts to whirl and all you can think about is the war and your home and your wife . . ."

190

"It *is* a difficult task," Captain Motes said smoothly. "As your commanding officer, no one is more aware of your complaints than I. . . . As I wrote my wife only last night, there are many unsung heroes in the rear echelons. At the front they face danger. Here we die of boredom. . . . Did I ever tell you about my wife? She's something of a writer. This is her latest book of verse, Lieutenant . . . ?"

"Can't you even remember my name? . . . Listen, captain. I want to pull out of this censorship shit. I was trained for the armored force. I'm willing to go into combat. . . . It's this negative work, day after day after day, that gets me. . . . I want some action. I'll risk my life rather than my reason. . . . But I won't sit out the war on my tail snipping Casablanca off the dateline of letters."

"Don't undervalue yourself," Captain Motes said, lighting another cigarette. "You're an expert, and censorship is a very restricted field. Don't imagine that every officer in the army is capable of doing what you're doing."

"That's all very fine," Lieutenant Almeranti said, tossing his lion's mane, "but I still wish to get transferred out of your outfit."

"Then have the sergeant major type you up a transfer."

"What good will that do if you only write disapproved on it? . . . Listen, captain. I know G-2 policy inside out. They hold onto their personnel like bulldogs so they can have big commands and get promotions . . . by our sweat. . . . I want your permission to go over your head for this transfer."

"You have it," Captain Motes said with weary sweetness. "Tomorrow I'm giving you an hour off from work to go to the Shell Building and see the A C of S G-2 yourself."

"This is almost too good to be true," Lieutenant Almeranti said.

He saluted and left the front office.

When the Lieutenant had gone, Captain Motes thought and smoked three cigarettes. Then he put out his hand for his field phone. He knew that the assistant chief of staff G-2 for ABS stayed late in his office in the Shell Building. There he drank, played solitaire, wrote poetry for *Stars and Stripes,* and made love to his French secretary. So Captain Motes dialed, hoping to find this colonel in. He was.

"Colonel? Evening. . . . Motes speaking, sir. . . . How are tricks? Long time no see. . . . Well, fancy that, sir. . . . Sir, I have a problem, and a man of your experience should be able to see right to the bottom of it. Are you listening, colonel? I'll only take a moment of your time, sir. . . ."

Then over the phone, dropping his voice as though the wires were tapped, Captain Motes told the tale of a certain officer of his who wished to leave his outfit. Of how the man was incompetent and unworthy of his commission. Of how this officer should not be permitted to go to another outfit, where he might irreparably sabotage the war effort of the United States. Of how at present he was doing a minimum of harm by reading letters, which after all was a job for a deadhead. How Captain Motes hoped by his influence to rehabilitate this officer and make him again into a real man. Of how this officer was often drunk and scandalous in public. Of how this officer in question would probably come in to see the colonel tomorrow with a pack of alarmist lies. . . .

When he'd finished telephoning, Captain Motes sighed over the perfidy of the world, donned his field jacket, and went out into the sunset on the Boulevard de la Gare. He messed at the Roi de la Bière. As he sat down to his soup of C-ration, a young lieutenant in the seat opposite rose until he'd taken his chair. This pleased Captain Motes. Deference to rank was rarely observed in officers' messes outside the United States. Then he realized he'd seen the young lieutenant that very morning, one of five fresh replacements to his own detachment of censors. As he dabbed at his mouth with his napkin, he looked the young lieutenant over: the brown face, the thick oiled mustache, the huge eyes of beasties peering out of copses (Lucinda's phrase).

"Just call me Stuki," the lieutenant said.

His teeth seemed of vanilla.

"Well, of course there are certain formalities to be observed," said Captain Motes amiably. "Unless I'm mistaken, I'm your new commanding officer."

"I know it. . . . Pleased ta meetcha, I'm sure. . . . And can I say somethin, captain? I felt sorta bad this mornin when ya didn't come over an shake me by the hand. . . . A fella sort likes to meet up with his CO when he reports to a new assignment."

"Of course; of course. . . . I was very busy . . . but I made a note on my desk calendar to call you in first thing tomorrow morning."

"The boys tole me," Stuki said, sailing languorously into his meat loaf, "that ya never have anything to do with em. . . . That's what they said. . . . But when I sawya in ya office, I said to myself, That's a soldier. Regular army maybe. The kind of guy that knows he has a job to do an no nonsense. That's the kinda guy I like to take orders from. Also (he leaned forward, twitching his mustache daintily) I thought to myself that guys that talk that way about their own CO must be yella rats."

"They *are* difficult men to deal with," Captain Motes conceded.

"I hope ya don't mind me talking to ya in this frank manner," Stuki said, a warm glaze crinkling his eyes. "But I like ta put my cards on the table, captain. I came into this man's army to do a job and take orders. . . . Willya shake hands with me, captain?"

Captain Motes was ignited from within by a strange flaring of hope and joy. He'd been lonely. Yet he must be on his guard. He'd got so used to living in himself, to trusting no one, that any kind little remark lit him up inside. But he put out his hand across the catsup bottles and pressed Stuki's. Into his own slid a warm and slightly moist hand like a bird into her nest. Stuki held on to the captain's hand with varying pressures and affections.

"Gee, thanks," Stuki said, his mustache in repose like a setting hen. "Now I feel better. . . . Ya'll never know how I felt this mornin comin into ya outfit. Seemed like nobody wanted me, treated me like I had mental BO. . . . An I take a bath every night. . . . They just sat an looked at me and kept sayin, You'll be sorry! . . . The resta the time they tore you apart."

"They hate me. I try to be impartial and end by pleasing no one."

"So there ya are," Stuki sighed. "That's life for ya. . . . But when I heard the way they talked about ya, I knew they was a bunch of stinkers."

"Perhaps you can help me to understand them better," said Captain Motes.

As the meal advanced, so did their intimacy. They seemed to have known one another a long time. By the pineapple, it was clear to Captain Motes that Stuki had conceived a doglike devotion to him. A rocket of inspiration went off in Captain Motes's head. In spite of the difference in their ranks, he invited Stuki to share his hotel room.

With Stuki he began a new sort of life, centered around a freedom and devotion he'd never before known. Stuki took care of everything: sending out laundry, tipping the Fatima who cleaned the room, even writing the captain's letters for him. By May, 1943, when spring came to Casa with a smell of jasmine and dung in bittersweet layers, Stuki would lie nude under his mosquito netting and listen while Captain Motes read aloud from Lucinda's poetry. Stuki's body was black and sheathed in glossy fur. He'd squirm and groan with pleasure at Lucinda's love poems. Or during her sonnets on renunciation Stuki would lie motionless, his cigarette a glowing dot of red, his mustache placid as a half-moon.

"Gee, she sends me. Ya wife's a great poet. One of these days I'm gonna meet her. Da ya think she'll like me? Da ya think she'll adopt me inta the family?"

Captain Motes got so he couldn't bear to spend time away from Stuki. The relationship between them was perfect: Stuki never overstepped the boundary between their ranks; there was a subtle deference in everything he said to Captain Motes, though he called him simply *you* when they weren't in public. Eventually, to have his lieutenant always with him, Captain Motes ordered that Stuki be taken off the examination table. Another desk was put in the captain's glass front office, and the position of supply officer was created for him. That night in their room Stuki got drunk on Casablanca rum and began to cry:

"Gee, thanks for takin me off that table of letter openers. . . . Ya know what they call me? . . . Brown-nose. . . . They said that no second lieutenant should be the roommate of his commanding officer . . . If it's gonna cause ya so much embarrassment, I'll move out."

"Goddam it," Captain Motes cried nobly, "I won't hear of it."

In the spring of 1943 his nerves were stringy. Stuki could deal with that too. The captain would lie belly down

194

on his bed, and Stuki would massage his spinal column. His body would go slack all over as those powerful moist fingers tugged at his nerves, and he'd fall into a swoon-like sleep. He'd awake at dawn next morning to find that Stuki'd undressed him and had put up his mosquito netting. And by the rising sun Captain Motes would look over into the other bed and see that dark face snoring soundlessly up at the ceiling, the mustache furled like wings over the half-open mouth. And Captain Motes's letters to his wife were full of Stuki. One day Lucinda wrote back in a V-mail:

"And who, pray, is this Stuki? I suspect you have an Arab mistress. . . ."

On week ends he and Stuki would take the jeep and drive out to Fedhala for golf, or to Rabat to a black market restaurant for spicy lobsters and wine. Or they'd go swimming by Villa Moss. Stuki would lie in the sun till his skin got like teak.

Stuki went to the Sixth General Hospital for a three days' reaming because he got piles from too much desk work. Captain Motes felt lost in his office and in his room. Each night he visited his roommate in the Sixth General, bringing fruit and flowers.

"Ya shouldn't do all this for me. Ya mustn't put ya-self out this way. Ya too good."

Meanwhile Captain Motes did some manipulating and some furious talking to the assistant chief of staff G-2. So when Stuki limped out of the hospital, the captain was waiting for him in the jeep, looking secretive. He drove Stuki out to look at the sea at Fedhala. He took the gold bar off Stuki's collar and pinned on a silver one. Stuki looked down; his chest began to quiver:

"Oh ya shouldn'ta, ya shouldn'ta, chief. . . . Now they'll hate me all the more. . . . I have ta *live* among them vultures and hyenas."

After Stuki's promotion the situation in the front office got involved. Lieutenant Frank sat at his desk and glowered at Stuki's new silver bar. Lieutenant Frank's paunch was growing heavier; his rear end had a spread like an ashcan dropped from a top story. He had a Casablancaise mistress and smoked two PX rations of thick dark cigars. But he wasn't happy. He mumbled to himself about the length of time he'd been in grade, and how doing your job in the army really didn't pay off. He glared at Captain Motes out of the fat around his little eyes, and he stared at Stuki, who bridled a dozen times a morning, flickered his mustache like a squirrel and twittered:

"Fressssssh! Whaddya lookin at? Didja bang yaself silly all las night?"

The strain in the front office was palpable even to the files of officers sitting out in the examination room under the harsh lights, reading their mail or talking up their whispering campaign. Their eyes in their black glasses or horn-rimmed spectacles would pierce the glass partition, where they could see the uneven and unequal triangle of Captain Motes, Stuki, and Lieutenant Frank peering at one another. Captain Motes at first thought it might be necessary to transfer his executive officer to Oran or Algiers. But then, who but Lieutenant Frank was capable of talking to the men and striking the fear of God into them?

"Fressssssh!" Stuki said again. "Nervous in the service? Why don'tcha go out for a nice long walk?"

Lieutenant Frank strode into the examination room. They could hear his voice and see his broad rear in pink pants. He was lecturing the officers on military courtesy. Someone had passed him in the streets of Casa without saluting. There was a swish and a hiss. Into the open door of the front office hurled a censor's exacto knife. It gibbered in the cork wall behind Captain Motes's head like a movie dagger. Simultaneously there was bedlam in the examination room. Stuki and Captain Motes ran out to the examination tables. The officers had left their work and were standing in a numb knot around Lieutenant Almeranti, who was winding up to let fly another exacto knife. He was chuckling to himself:

"Incest, kids, incest. . . ."

Then Lieutenant Almeranti took a pile of unread V-mails and tore them to pieces. He was ripping to shreds letters written by officers and GI's of the army in Africa. The pupils of his eyes were popping like eggs, his forehead was glistening with sweat.

"Stop him, someone," Captain Motes hollered. "This is a court-martial offense."

He took several steps forward, and Lieutenant Almeranti smashed the rest of the stack of mail into his face. The censors peered at the scene with dull absorption, like moronic children.

196

"Censorship!" Lieutenant Almeranti chortled. "I'll censor all! I'll G-2 you! . . . There ain't no promotions this side of the ocean."

"Put down that knife, ya fool!" Stuki shrieked.

Lieutenant Almeranti bore down again on Captain Motes. His arms were swinging, his eyes bloody and spinning.

"And this, kids, is our chief base censor . . ."

Stuki leaped through the air. Captain Motes saw the blur of his rush and Stuki's mustache grim and taut. There was a smell of cologne. Lieutenant Almeranti went down under Stuki in a litter of torn V-mails and ruptured envelopes. He went rigid, his eyeballs rolled up, he had a quick sighing paroxysm, and passed out. Now Lieutenant Frank became the man of action. He champed on his cigar, called out orders in his beefy voice, and stamped to the phone for a psychiatrist and ambulance from the Sixth General Hospital.

"Go right on with ya readin, boys," Stuki said, picking himself off the floor and mopping his face with a fragrant yellow handkerchief.

But there was little work done that morning. The examiners sat at their tables and smoked and muttered. It seemed that Lieutenant Almeranti had gone nuttier than a fruitcake and would be sent back to the States. Lieutenant Frank made two speeches, telling them they could all hope to end up like Almeranti if they didn't settle down:

"Why don'tcha act like officers insteada the wimmin's garment union?"

"Send em all back to their billets for the day, huh, chief?" Stuki said.

"I won't coddle them!" Captain Motes shouted, pacing the front office. "We have our quota of mail for each day. They'll read it, goddam it, they'll read it."

He'd decided however to fly to Algiers that evening to investigate censorship procedures at Allied Force headquarters. He told Stuki to pack two bags and meet him at Cazes airport. They heard the voice of Liteutenant Frank still haranguing the frightened examiners:

"Oh ya don't believe me? I can court-martial each an every one a yez an have ya returned to the ZI in the permanent grade of private. . . . Ya don't believe me?"

On their second day in Algiers they had a phone call

from Lieutenant Frank, shouting over the wires as though he desired to make himself heard all the way from Casablanca:

"Ya, ya heard me right. . . . The inspector general's here givin ya entire outfit the shakedown. . . . No, it ain't a routine inspection. All ya goddam officers petitioned for him to come here. . . . Ya, that's right. Right now he's sittin at the desk in ya office. Every officer and GI of ya command is standing in line, waiting his turn to cry on the IG's shoulder. . . . Some of them has written out complaints a mile long. Half the officers tole me ta my face that the least you could expect after the IG gets through with ya is Leavenworth. . . ."

That evening in his Algiers billet, thinking of what the inspector general must be doing in his office in Casa, Captain Motes had one of his nervous fits. As the moonlight tittered in, he lay under his mosquito netting. His teeth began to click and his eyes to roll. He gave out small moans and gasps like a woman in love. Cramps gathered in the calves of his legs. He felt his fists clenching at his sides. It seemed to him he'd never known such indefinable terror, with all the frightful things of this world and the next gathering in the dusk to spring upon him. Stuki jumped out of his bed and was at his side in a flowered kimono.

"Whassamatta, chief?"

"My God, they're crucifying me in Casa," the captain murmured, cushioning his forehead.

"They're filthy sneakin dogs. Don't pay no heed to em. . . . Ya'll come out on top."

And Stuki's moist hard hands commenced working at the captain's spine. And Stuki's voice dropped to the liquid caressing whimper that it adopted on such occasions:

"Ya hear me, chief? Ya much too good for the whole dam lot of em. . . . Lissen ta me, chief. Ya all right? . . . We'll lick em together, you an me."

After a while the spasms faded and the horrors paled. Captain Motes fell asleep. The last thing he remembered was hands, kind hands that knew him as well as a mold informs a piece of clay to its own image.

On the following morning he and Stuki called on the chief of staff G-2, AFHQ, in the Saint George Hotel. He was a cheery colonel who before the war had owned a grocery store in Chicago. Now with a brigadier general and a British and American staff he ran most of the intelligence operations in the North African theater. His shirt breast was plaqued with ribbons. On his collar was the star of the general staff corps. He had the red and seamy face of one accustomed to attend midnight sessions of plotters and planners. He shook hands with Captain Motes and Stuki, who surprised him doing a crossword puzzle.

"Well, well, well! Surprise, surprise, surprise! . . . Didn't know you were in Algiers. . . . We call you our country cousins from Casa. How's every little thing? Just step in to my inner office. . . . Got a little treat for you."

The colonel's inner office was four walls covered with enameled maps. All the maps were stamped SECRET in red block letters at top and bottom. They were planted with hedges of thumbtacks from which streamed ribbons of pastel silk. On the colonel's desk was a herd of camels of graduated sizes walking along the glass in safari file.

"This office," said the colonel clearing his throat, "well, you might almost call it the brain of all NATO-USA."

"Gee, sir," Stuki said, fingering a map stamped MOST SECRET EQUALS BRITISH SECRET, "sorta makes a guy stop and think, don't it?"

"I'd advise you not to try to take secret photographs of those maps, lieutenant," the colonel said loudly.

"He's my most trusted officer," Captain Motes said timidly.

"I know, I know," the colonel said, leading them away from the maps and slapping their backs. "But we in military intelligence can't even afford to trust one another, can we, ha-ha. . . . You know how it is, boys. . . . My God, when I think of how much I know, I'm almost afraid to chugalug a drink or go out with a pretty little French girl, ha-ha. . . . Sometimes I wake up at night with a cold shiver and think of how much there is in this old skull of mine, ha-ha."

"Ya wouldn't be wearin that eagle if ya weren't capable of ya job, sir," Stuki said.

"Well, thank you, ha-ha, thank you," the colonel boomed, bending over his desk drawer. "And now, Captain Motes, if you'll be so good as to take off your insignia . . ."

Captain Motes felt his heart dive from some trapeze. But he reached up and fumbled with his collar, tearing loose his silver tracks. The colonel took something out of his desk drawer and approached him. He opened his palm to display a chaste gold leaf, which he then with his own hands fastened to the collar tab from which the former insignia had been tremulously torn away.

"*Major Motes!* Military intelligence takes care of its own. For a long time our office has been watching your operations down Casablanca way. We lamented that we couldn't do more for you. . . . But like all great and honest men, you can now reap more than the inner reward, satisfying as that may be, ha-ha. . . . If I was French I'd kiss you on both cheeks. . . . You are the father of censorship in North Africa. And what a bouncing healthy baby it is, ha-ha. . . . Congratulations, Major Motes."

Major Motes saw the whole vaulted office, its maps and indirect lighting, whirling like a pinwheel before his eyes. People streamed in from the other offices to shake his hand. British colonels in their shorts and pipes and scarves pressed his hand and called him Old Man. Stuki stood beside the new major like a hostess, murmuring his name to the queue of officers. Stuki even linked his arm with Major Motes's, who was so moved he could scarcely stand. Then there was a shrill yap of attention. There entered goutily an elderly British brigadier, carrying in both hands a small medal hanging from a broad violet ribbon. This he suspended round Major Motes's neck, all the while burring away like a sewing machine:

"His Majesty, the King of England is pleased to acknowledge Major Motes's services to military censorship. . . . Stout fellow. . . ."

That evening Allied Force G-2 gave a party for Major Motes. It began on the beach at Ain-Taya. Colonels, majors, and captains all went swimming in the mellow surf of the Mediterranean. Stuki's was the lowest rank there, but the major kept his assistant always with him and presented him to all, beaming:

"This, gentlemen, is the backbone of censorship in Casa. I have a hundred other officers like him. But he's the cream."

200

And Stuki, shy at first, gradually sallied forth with a good word to this colonel or that major. Major Motes was surprised to find that Stuki knew all their names, and in exactly what branch of G-2 they were: maps, photo reconnaissance, documents, liaison, topography, code and cipher. Stuki's mustache was foam-flecked from the salt water. After a few drinks he'd chase a major on the beach or crack a joke with a captain from the I and E office.

Major Motes was slightly worried when he saw how alcoholic the party was going to be. Tonight he'd have to let himself go a bit. After all, it was his promotion party. He'd dispatch Stuki to pour every other glass out in the sand. In the clubhouse at Ain-Taya a keg of American beer was broached. It burst its staves, and one of the British majors lay down in the foamy flood on the tile floor and did the breast stroke.

"Oh that type!" the British chortled.

"Character!" howled the American officers.

The dinner was a relay affair, with one course served at each colonel's villa around the hills of Algiers. The party would pile into jeeps and staff cars and screech through the streets from one villa to the next. They'd have soup in Maison Carrée and steak in Maison Blanche. Major Motes was a little envious, for he now knew that Casa was pretty small potatoes compared to the way The Boys lived at AFHQ. All officers of field grade had villas. In each the major noted the presence of a lovely Algérienne as hostess.

The last course of dinner ended at 2200 hours. All the officers were in high spirits. They decided to round out the evening at the Center District Club of the Mediterranean Base Section, three blocks from the Aletti Hotel, near Algiers Harbor. Jeeps and staff and command cars tore through the blacked-out streets of Algiers, screaming at the French to get the hell off the roads. Captains and majors and colonels yelled good fellowship at one another like kids on an outing. Occasionally (just for sport) two jeeps would drive parallel till they were abreast. Then they'd lock wheels. Just kids at heart.

"I think I'm going to be sick," Major Motes said into Stuki's ear.

"Now just ya hold on, chief. It's all in ya imagination.

. . . An say, ain't this fun? . . . We gotta leave that stinky Casa, huh? We gotta move here an get in with these big-time operators."

The Center District Club was low and cool, hung with green and ocher chintzes. Service was by Italian prisoners of war in white linen coats. These stood behind the bar leaning on their elbows, their eyes misty with nostalgia. Seeing the P/W, Major Motes revived from his rum dizziness and said impressively to a small circle:

"Goddam it now, boys. Look at those goddam Dagos. Feeling sorry for themselves, as usual. . . . Don't they like American rations? A few months ago they were killing our boys in Tunisia . . ."

A Negro band blared up. An elderly lieutenant colonel of the party lurched to his feet and cried whoopee. He grabbed the prettiest and youngest of the P/W waiters and pushed him into a tango over the floor among sparring junior officers and nurses and the girls of Algiers. From the club's doorway came an MP to break up the clinch of the colonel and the Italian, who had begun to cry.

Stuki left Major Motes's side and went to talk with the Italian bartenders. His mustache quivered with joy as his Italian poured out. Soon he came back to tell the major that their names were Otello and Enzo and Gabriele, and how he'd upbraided them for declaring war on us, how he'd taunted them for Mussolini and for betting on the wrong horse. In short Stuki'd told those wops a thing or two. Presently the prisoners of war began to blubber and bawl as they drew the beer and rum. This brought out the sergeant and the officer in charge of the club, who yelled and waved threats at their help.

"Call a strike, Ginsoes!" Stuki railed at them, his mustaches quivering with passion. "I dare ya! Call a strike."

The G-2 section roosted on the edge of the dance floor. British and American mingled. Drinks kept coming and coming, the strongest sweetest rum, schooners of beer, tall emerald Tom Collinses. Major Motes's stomach was squeezing like an accordion. So he sat where he could pour most of these libations into the base of the potted palm behind him. Toward midnight the Negro band got hotter and hotter. The girls of Algiers in the scented gloom of the dance floor lay across officers' laps and

202

submitted to long laughing embraces while their escorts' hands tore at the straps of their gowns.

"Ya livin, kids!" Stuki screamed over the brass and drums.

Then a captain arose from his cane-bottomed chair and bounced it off the chintz-arrased wall.

"Christ, but this place is dull! I want action."

So the party repaired to their jeeps and staff cars. They formed a drunken convoy and tore through the town of Agliers, where only thimbles of light showed through the trees on Rue Michelet. Then even these tiny landmarks flickered out. Sirens began to shriek all over Algiers. The convoy screeched to a stop. Two jeeps telescoped. All the officers wove or were carried out of their vehicles to the side of the road, where they threw themselves down on their faces in a culvert.

"Bes thing in an air raid is a woman!" someone shouted with his mouth against the dirt. "Where is she? Beaucoup women, beaucoup dive bombers!"

But no planes came over Algiers that night.

Major Motes and Stuki landed at Cazes airfield and took the ATC bus into Casblanca. They had hangovers. It was the middle of the morning. The domes and finger-slim white apartment houses of the city glowed like solid geometry alive.

"Ya got a ordeal aheada ya, chief," Stuki mumbled.

Lieutenant Frank was waiting at the office with a clipped-together file of typewritten paper. He chomped on his cigar and twisted at the embossed belt about his paunch. His pink pants had a stain over his left cheek. In the examination room Major Motes saw that the examiners were bent over their *Stars and Stripes*. There was peace with them. Nevertheless he called out a bright good morning. They glanced up, and, noting the new gold leaf on his collar, blanched and blinked. He heard them whispering chaotically to one another as he took the document from Lieutenant Frank's mottled hand and went behind the glass partition of the front office to scan it. He had to keep from trembling at his desk, for he knew that every eye was upon him. For the first time he cursed the glass wall of the front office that made him as vulnerable as a floodlighted thief.

The report of the inspector general was a lengthy and detailed document. Before he settled down to reading it, he leafed through it for a skimming, lighting a cigarette with shaking all-thumbs and moistening the tip of his forefinger. He observed that nearly every officer and GI of his detachment had registered a complaint against him. It was all there in stenographic fullness. He had the sixth carbon.

Major Motes took an hour to read the report. He pored over it in a concentration of horror, just as a hypochondriac notes the symptoms of a disease in an encyclopedia and compares them with his own.

His officers had complained to the IG that they enjoyed none of the prestige or authority of their commissions. Some mentioned having been humiliated by Lieutenant Frank in the presence of enlisted men. All agreed that the process of censoring mail had been reduced to a frightful and unnecessary drudgery. One used the expression that they were worse off than slaveys at sewing machines in a sweatshop. In the depositions of the officers there recurred the phrase Unholy Three, meaning Major Motes, Stuki, and Lieutenant Frank. They were also called the Inner Circle. Others averred that the outfit was run in a style befitting a reform school for girls, with flagrant abuses occurring under a façade of being GI. There were protests against the freezing of transportation, whereas the Unholy Three used jeeps and trucks at their own sweet pleasure. Officers swore that they weren't allowed to entertain ladies in their billets, but that Lieutenant Frank violated the order continually and with impunity.

The GI's of the outfit had told the IG that they never knew where they stood with the officers. The sergeant major said that Captain Motes never looked him in the eyes when he gave him an order. Other GI's said that some officers had drunk with them and played golf with them at Fedhala, while other officers would press court-martial charges without provocation. But the focus of all the pissing and moaning was that Captain Motes was a spineless commanding officer, that the disunity and confusion and cruelty of the detachment all stemmed from him, that he gave his orders through his mouthpiece, as though he himself were afraid and unsure.

Major Motes began to exude an icy sweat when he got to the recommendations of the inspector general. There
204

were three. That officers should not be forced to live so close together when off duty. That stricter demarcation be made between the treatment of officers and enlisted men. That Captain Motes establish sound policies of leadership or else be removed from command of his detachments.

He rose from his desk, made a giant effort to master the quaking of his nerves, and rushed out into the examination room with the IG report in his hand. There he summarily had an officers' call. He read to all his examiners the report of the inspector general even to the recommendations, not sparing himself. When he'd read the last sentence, with its implication of his being removed from command for incompetence, he laid his face in his hands and wept noisily.

"Gentlemen, forgive me. . . . All I can say is that if we have had dirty linen in this detachment, we should have aired it together . . . but in privacy."

He continued to sob snortingly for a full minute. Then a round of applause rippled through the examination room, and one officer got to his feet and called:

"Major, you're a man's man. We'll stand by you."

"Let's wipe the slate clean and start anew," Major Motes sniffled, diving for his handkerchief.

"Let bygones be bygones;" a roar went up through the room.

The entire detachment entrained for Algiers.

On the three-day train ride Major Motes busied himself creating new titles for almost all his officers. This one would be mess officer, this one soldier voting officer, another in charge of special service, another PX officer, another war bond officer. Major Motes rushed from car to car, personally distributing special orders and designations and citations he'd had the sergeant major type up. Thus with all the officers becoming something in their own eyes, the trip was made in a gala and phoenix spirit.

He spoke much of the advance detail of specially trusted officers he'd dispatched in trucks to Algiers to set up housekeeping. Yet when they detrained at Maison Blanche at the depot where they were to live, it was discovered that the advance detail hadn't yet arrived. But Lieutenant Frank did some shouting and cigar chewing, and at last the dirty weary frayed detachment was permitted to partake of Spam in an abandoned mess after a nigra band had finished its chow.

For himself and Stuki he chose a pyramidal tent at the head of a blocked row close to the latrines. On the sand in front of it was an attempt at a lawn, colored pebbles and flowers plotted out by the Italian P/W who were their orderlies.

Next morning Major Motes was awakened at 1000 hours by a full colonel standing over him and prodding him.

"Stand at attention. Who the hell are you?"

Major Motes scrambled out of his cot in his flowered pajamas.

"You're in charge of that censorship gang that moved in yesterday? In the future you and all your detachment will stand reveille, like everyone else in this depot. We're all in the army here."

"But we're a separate intelligence outfit. We're simply billeted here for the convenience of AFHQ . . ."

"You heard me," the colonel yelled. "I am in command of this depot. As long as you and your letter openers live in these tents, you'll abide by my orders. . . ."

Major Motes spent much of his time at AFHQ offices in Algiers. He carried in his briefcase samples of comment sheets, which are extracts of violations found in troop mail. He was like a peddler going from door to door. He had a theory that military censorship still hadn't the importance it deserved. By persistence he soon made his organization well known. Shortly afterwards, at his own request, there was transferred to his detachment one of the bright young men of AFHQ. This young officer told Major Motes that he could never forgive the war for interrupting his doctor's dissertation in Erse philology.

Lieutenant Mayberry sought out Major Motes every night. He was a short boyish second lieutenant with thin blond hair and an incisive baritone. He always carried with him Fowler's *Modern English Usage*. Before long Major Motes said to himself that Lieutenant Mayberry was the most cultivated and disciplined mind he'd even known. Each night he'd root out the major and Stuki where they sat working late in their office, entering the Boyle hut after a businesslike knock. He'd take off his field jacket and set down his Blue Book.

206

"I'm afraid, lieutenant," said Stuki languidly, "that we ain't good enough for ya here. We don't know much about readin and writin."

"Do you mind leaving us alone? I have some business with your commanding officer."

Lieutenant Mayberry had a way with Stuki as though he weren't even in the room.

"Who the hell ya talkin to?" Stuki shrilled. "I know more about postal censorship than you do. . . . So ya better be nice to me. . . . Besides I think ya pretty fressssssssh bargin in here this way. . . . Nobody asked for your advice."

"I appeal to you, sir," Lieutenant Mayberry cried to Major Motes with a Shakespearean gesture of outraged sensibility. "This is a confidential matter I wish to discuss with you."

So Stuki left the Boyle hut, his mustache working and his brown eyes sparking.

"That fellow should change his hair oil," Lieutenant Mayberry said. "I speak of him so frankly with you, sir, because I know that in your heart of hearts you size him up the way I do . . . he's a *creature.*"

"He means well," Major Motes said quickly.

"Takes more than good intentions to win a war, as you and I know well, sir. . . . That fellow is what I'd call a greaser. . . . Frankly, sir, do you trust Italo-Americans of the first generation? Cloak and dagger, that's all they are. . . . But why am I telling you these things? Perhaps I lecture a little bit too much. . . . I've just come from working with inferior minds. I've got into the habit of underscoring everything I say. . . . Sir, I was delighted to be transferred to your command. I was getting sick of the intellectual stagnation of Algiers. Fed up with it. . . . Sir, I desire to place at your disposal certain talents which have so far been wasted. . . . Special skills suffer in the army, don't they? You, sir, should know . . . for you are a specialist."

"Thank you," Major Motes said.

"Don't thank me for facts, sir. I don't underestimate myself. And I speak thus frankly to you because I've known you and heard of you as a man who lives by plain dealing. . . . I don't pay oily compliments, sir. My semantic training has taught me the value of language.

Oh sir, the waste that goes on in meanings in this modern world! . . . With your permission. . . ."

Lieutenant Mayberry brought a folding metal chair to the desk and seated himself next to the major under the green-hooded white light. Major Motes studied the thinning yellow hair, the tuft of yellow mustache, the slashed line of the mouth. The forehead was etched out in pool-like hollows, the pale blue eyes were hooded with thought. Lieutenant Mayberry opened a folder full of diagrams and figures.

"Major, sir, in justice I must tell you that I know all about your unfortunate . . . incident in Casablanca. . . . I read all the files. And I said to myself, there's a man being done to death. A modern Acteon. . . . My heart bled for you, sir."

"The . . . incident . . . has all blown over," Major Motes said, making a vague pass at the air.

"Thank God justice has been done," Lieutenant Mayberry murmured, devoutly lifting his eyes into the dark beyond the shaded light. His white hand moved over the figured sheets, which were full of lines and arrows and labeled boxes. There were also sheets of graph paper and canals in particolored crayon.

"Now sir, work of your kind is enormously important to the Allied war effort. . . . But because censorship is essentially negative in action and results, it needs advertising and pictorial aids to keep it before the eyes and in the consciousness of the bigwigs in Algiers. Pardon the vulgarism. . . . Otherwise your valuable work gets lost in the shuffle of more voluble intelligence agencies."

"I see what you mean," Major Motes said, warming, and eying the patchwork quilt of graphs.

"Of course you do, sir; of course you do. . . . Now, do you get out a mimeographed monthly report? Are you making the fullest possible use of charts and figures as visual aids? . . . Think for example of the stunning effect on some stuffy brigadier general of a huge colored sketch on oilcloth, showing the ratio of V-mail read in relation to the number of ordinary letters, with legends and percentiles of the types of censorship violations. . . . Then you will of course forward carbons of your comment sheets to all user agencies. . . . Do you have punch head-lines to attract the weary and wandering eye? . . . Do you make appropriate use of underscoring and italics in

208

order to—shall we say—*slant* the material? Do you
quote only sections that are pertinent? . . . And have you
arresting-looking buckslips to be returned from the offices
concerned, showing what action has been taken, or
whether they've simply thrown your precious submissions
into the wastebaskets? . . ."

As Lieutenant Mayberry talked, vistas fell open to
Major Motes's eyes. He saw that to this hour he hadn't
even tapped the potentialities of censorship. It was one of
the most vital of all America's secret weapons. The two
men shook hands after a three-hour discussion. Major
Motes was exhausted and thrilled by the controlled violence of Lieutenant Mayberry's mind, by the clarity and
ruthlessness of his new young officer's thinking.

The following morning a desk was set up in the front
office for Lieutenant Mayberry. Over his head was suspended a sign, lettered by an Italian P/W: REPORTS,
RETURNS, AND STATISTICAL DIVISION. Stuki sat at his own
field desk and glared and purred rawly. And all day long
every error in Stuki's grammar was pounced on by Lieutenant Mayberry, with Fowler's book open to be cited as
the authority. To all this Major Motes listened with pride
and avidity. One day he gave Lieutenant Mayberry authority to wear his Phi Beta Kappa key on his watch
chain. He'd got into the habit of reading aloud his
V-mails to his new section chief, who'd make slight emen-
dations in their style.

"You write a fine prose, sir. . . . But do read a little
more Macaulay."

It took less than a week for Lieutenant Mayberry to
work drastic changes in the front office. He undertook
first the rehabilitation of the enlisted clerks of the detachment. In his evenings (he never went to Algiers for amusement or distraction) he gave French lessons to several
corporals from Baltimore, bending his blond mustache
over them as they squirmed and parsed under the brilliant
shaded lights. Then he made them read François Villon,
saying that it would help them with their Algerian loves.
Nor did the first sergeant or the sergeant major escape
him. He waged a cultural war on them. First he made
them feel ridiculous and loutish by working up a comedy
campaign against them every time they took out their
comic books from under their typewriters. In two weeks
he'd reduced them to such despair that they were spelling
209

out Thomas Mann and puzzling over Lieutenant Mayberry's favorite poem, a line of which was always on his lips: "I have been faithful to thee, Cynara, in my fashion. . . ." He told the whole GI office force that than this poem there was nothing more magic or golden in all literature; it was better than Joyce Kilmer or Henry Wadsworth Longfellow.

Lieutenant Mayberry said that the modern American language was falling apart from lack of discipline or surface tension. Therefore as an antidote he insisted on a Victorian tautness and periodicity in all the prose emanating from his office.

He organized a glee club for the officers and enlisted men of the detachment. Major Motes, observing that, while they sang, his command had the first unity of its army career, made attendance at glee club rehearsals compulsory to all. On nights when Lieutenant Mayberry bullied his choir through nigra spirituals in an abandoned mess hall, nobody got a pass to Algiers.

But the noblest achievements were wrought at month's end in the monthly censorship report that went to AFHQ. When this was in the mill, starting with the twenty-seventh of each month, Lieutenant Mayberry would shut himself in the office till midnight and be unapproachable. It was miraculous what he could do with the detachment's figures, which, unvarnished, were simply a list of the number of V-mails and ordinary letters read each month, violations of military security, and recommendations of new ground rules for postal censorship. What went to G-2 in Algiers was a ten-page mimeographed brochure accompanied by graphs, charts, arrows, slots of different altitudes and colors. And the history of the censorship detachment for each thirty days was set forth in gorgeous army-ese, with paragraphs commencing with such stately tidbits as:

"Attention is directed to a chain of malfeasances by . . ."

"It is felt that such directives would irreparably condone . . ."

Major Motes had never been so happy or important or aware of his contribution to the war effort. He had frequent meetings with his officers in which he lashed them on to new heights of work and achievement. Officers who read fewer than five hundred letters a day were

210

excoriated in Mayberry prose on the bulletin boards. The examination of mail reached such velocity that a wit remarked that the turning over of letters on the examination tables created a breeze which blew planes backwards at Maison Blanche airport.

In his executive ecstasy Major Motes created still more posts for his officers. Nothing now was too good for them. He gave Lieutenant Mayberry a jeep all his own, which that officer christened under its windshield CYNARA in letters of Caslon style several inches high. Major Motes designated a club officer to open a little bar in an empty tent. He named an assistant recreational officer to preview all films to be shown to the detachment. There was only one fly now in the ointment: it was still difficult to get promotions for his officers in relation to their just deserts. Reading their mail in the evenings, he noticed a rising tendency to bitch about promotions. Requests for transfer again mounted and had to cool off in his top desk drawer.

One day Major Motes asked the A C of S G-2 to come and address his examiners. The colonel turned up and talked for an hour in a masterful yet cajoling way. He scolded and railed and wept and tore at his iron-gray hair, saying how he himself would like very much to be a brigadier general, but how he too was making a sacrifice. And in a roaring peroration the colonel told the officers that there were richer rewards in the army than the outward one of changing the brass on their collars. He concluded:

"Ah, gentlemen, gentlemen! When your babies cluster around your knee and ask, Daddy, what did you do to help win the war? you can bow your heads without shame and say, Son, I had the hardest job of all. I was in the intelligence service of the Army of the United States. . . ."

In May, 1944, pressure was put on AFHQ by Washington. It was felt that there were in North Africa altogether too many officers and enlisted men hanging around the base sections with nothing to do but keep meaningless office hours, put their feet on their desks, and read *Stars and Stripes*. Many of these malingerers, Washington hinted, could very well be sent to the Italian front as infantry replacements. The general officers of AFHQ went into a panic. Hadn't they figured on huge commands

211

simply to take up the slack, on the principle that a team must have many substitutes on the bench? But the reckoning came to AFHQ, in the persons of inspecting generals flown to Algiers from the Pentagon. They represented the War Manpower Commission, and they came with the conviction already implanted in them that work in the Algiers area could be realized with a cut of one-third of the personnel.

When Major Motes got a phone call that a brigadier general of WMC would visit his detachment that afternoon, he held a conference in the front office. Present were Stuki, Lieutenant Frank, and Lieutenant Mayberry.

"Goddam it, what am I going to do?" Major Motes screamed in executive anguish. "They'll cut half the detachment. I simply can't get along on a skeleton office force. You all know how vital our work is. . . ."

There was some hasty whispering and planning. Shortly afterwards Lieutenant Frank stalked out into the examination room, bit his cigar, called for the officers' attention, and said in a curdling voice:

"News item: They're hard up in Italy for infantry replacements. If they don't find those replacements damn quick, they're gonna start pickin em outa the hat. Here for instance. . . . Those of ya who wish to volunteer for combat kindly step into the front office after this meetin is over. . . . Ya'll get six week's training an then be sent to the Eyetalian front. . . . After all we gotta take Rome, ain't we? . . . An I know that some a ya feel ya could make a more important contribution than ya been makin. . . . Like leadin a platoon inta a chatterin machinegun nest. . . ."

Almost immediately a fat looie tottered into the front office. He dragged Major Motes into one of the shed latrines. He gibbered and sobbed:

"Major, lissen . . . I never caused ya no trouble, did I, now? . . . An there's sonsabitches out in that room ud cut ya throat. . . . Single guys. Now I gotta wife an two kids I ain't never seen. . . . I wanna go back to em in one piece, see? . . . Ya wouldn't, ya couldn't . . ."

"I understand, I understand, goddam it," Major Motes said hoarsely, wringing the officer's hand.

And after noon chow there turned up a brigadier general from the War Manpower Commission in an olive-drab staff car, with a pretty WAC sergeant for a secretary and

212

a covey of aides with clipboards. Meanwhile Lieutenant Mayberry and Stuki were busy in the examination room. They dumped all the mailbags on the reading tables, so that each examiner, when he returned from lunch, would find himself surrounded with sufficient mail to censor for the next month. They piled the mail on three sides of each examiner's field desk. When they'd finished, each desk looked like a machine-gun emplacement.

While this was going according to instructions, the general was standing in the front office, haranguing Major Motes and Lieutenant Frank, who'd offered him a fine chunky cigar.

"We're convinced back in the Pentagon," said the general, nibbling at the tip of the cigar, "that something funny is going on over here. We believe that many overseas headquarters are something of a war crime in themselves. They tend to get bigger and bigger, like a snowball. . . . While on the Italian front there's a critical shortage of infantrymen. We suspect that Allied Force Headquarters is ridiculously overstaffed."

"Well, sir, I know only my own outfit," Major Motes said meekly. "A good commanding officer must stay at home and tend to his own washing."

"There must be some of your personnel you feel you can get rid of," the general roared.

"Will the general look at my poor clerks?" the major moaned, gesturing at rows of corporals who were beating the life out of their typewriters. "Sir, a good officer thinks of his GI's first. . . . And these poor joes, sir, I haven't been able to give them an Algiers pass this week. . . . They have to work nights . . . beg to, poor devils. . . . And I've got three officers in the hospital, sir . . . nervous breakdowns . . . overwork."

"Let me see the room where the mail is read," said the general.

"Let me impress upon the general that everything he's about to see is strictly confidential. . . . Examination of personal mail is the privilege and the responsibility of the cream of American commissioned officers."

The general blew out a tuberose of cigar smoke. The major stepped aside to let him pass into the examination room. Here there was the silence of a library. The head of each examiner could barely be seen over the top of the litter of letters that Stuki and Lieutenant Mayberry had

213

piled on the field desks. It looked like Christmas Eve in a post office.

"O my God!" the general said softly. "Don't envy those poor fellows. Read read read . . . is this a normal day for them, major?"

"Quite normal, sir. . . . Perhaps when the general goes back to Washington, he may remember to mention in his report officers he saw who never make the headlines or the Purple Heart, but who just as surely were giving their eyes in the service of their country."

The brigadier general later left, muttering apologetically that Major Motes did indeed need a larger staff, and that he himself would personally see what could be done. Lieutenant Frank told the examiners that they might take the rest of the afternoon off:

"But don't go tattlin' to ya little friends in Algiers about what happened here this afternoon . . . if ya wise. . . . That general wanted to send ya all to the Eyetalian front and replace ya with WAC's. . . . Not that they couldn't do a better job. . . ."

Major Motes's triumph of the day was complete when Algiers phoned at 1600 hours to state that Lieutenant Mayberry was now a first lieutenant and Lieutenant Frank a captain. Out of his secret drawer Lieutenant Frank fished a set of silver tracks and pinned them on himself.

"Seventeen months of sweatin!" he bellowed. "An I got gold leaves bought too."

"I have no silver bars," Lieutenant Mayberry murmured piteously to himself. "I didn't come overseas expecting to be promoted."

"Well, I ain't got no extras to giveya," Stuki said, yellow under his tan.

Like a bridegroom bull Captain Frank hurtled around the front office:

"So they called me a permanent first, hey?"

He then ripped the old silver bars off his cap and off his field jacket and threw them like deadly little brooches with the pins open at Lieutenant Mayberry, who caught them humbly, his eyes shining thankfulness, his blond mustache rampant.

"Take em take em take em. . . . Ya can shove em up if ya like. . . ."

Major Motes wasn't a great one for wasting the pay

214

of the army, but his Virginia sense told him that tonight was the unavoidable occasion for a party. Promotion parties are simply de rigueur to old soldiers. So he invited Stuki, First Lieutenant Mayberry, and Captain Frank to be his guests for the evening. They got into his jeep with festive solemnity and headed for Algiers. Even as he drove, Major Motes was aware that Stuki was brooding because he hadn't been promoted too.

"A few more months yet," he said cheerily in Stuki's ear, laying his hand consolingly on his roommate's arm.

"Few more months, balls," Stuki said with feeling.

At first Major Motes wondered whether he could get away with taking them all to the TAM mess, paying five francs for each, and throwing in two bottles of white wine. But as they descended into Algiers where in the blue water the hospital ships were falling and heaving under the barrage balloons, he knew he couldn't get away with that for a promotion party. So he took them to a black market restaurant off Rue d'Isly, where for two thousand francs they got a peasant soup, eggs, a thin steak, a salad, pastry baked without sugar, and wine.

"Kinda expensive, these promotion parties," Stuki leered. "Betcha glad they don't come around too often, huh, chief?"

Then they picked up in the jeep Captain Frank's Algiers mistress, a huge and vociferous French girl with hair under her arms. When she saw her lover's new insignia, she screamed and ran her tongue over his thick purple lips. The final touch in Major Motes's hospitality was an invitation to the Center District Club for drinks. He himself got nervous and broody as usual with alcohol. But he pretended for the occasion's sake that he was having mad fun, even to nudging the mistress once, for which she goosed him feelingly and invited him up some evening when her capitaine couldn't come. Then all except Major Motes got drunk on P/W gin. Captain Frank believed himself Napoleon, putting his cap on sidewise and sticking a hand inside his meaty chest. Lieutenant Mayberry lectured on the English language as distinct from Americanese. And Stuki just drank and drank till the tears dribbled off his mustache into his gin. At midnight he announced he was going out into the streets of Algiers to cruise up a little heavy lovin.

215

On Saturday morning 31 July 1944, Major Motes first saw the city of Naples checkered in the sunlight. Over the bay rode the smell of all the world's garbage.

"My ole man started out from this burg," Stuki said. "His ole man put him on a boat when he was eleven. Told him to shift for himself, he didn't never wanna see his puss again. . . . Now I'm comin back to Napoli. I'll show em they couldn't treat my ole man the way they did."

"All your relatives' houses will be off limits anyhow," Lieutenant Mayberry said. "So you'll be spared the trouble of a courtesy call on them. . . . I smell that pasta and hair oil already."

It took six hours to unload the ship. It was late afternoon when they and their baggage rattled out of the barbed wire round the port. Major Motes appraised the ruin around Naples Harbor.

"Goddam it," he cried exulting. "See what happens to people who declare war on Uncle Sam?"

Lieutenant Mayberry wondered aloud:

"I wonder how many greasers are still lying under that rubble? . . . Well, Italy always was overpopulated. Musso sends the birth rate up, so we choose our own means of bringing it down."

"That's what they get for kickin my ole man out," Stuki said, tweaking his mustache in approbation. "So now I'll stamp all over their ole ruins. . . . My ole man says Italy always did have too many monuments."

Captain Frank looked at the carts picking through the narrow streets.

"So I left my baby doll in Algiers for this. . . . Well, guess there'll be choicer pickins here, though."

When Major Motes first saw it at the end of July, 1944, Naples was a steaming and shattering anthill committed to some furious project. Besides the Neapolitans, the streets were mad with Allied soldiers. He felt already faint from the heat. They drove to the palazzo where their offices were to be set up. It was a huge block of stone and balconies that had once housed offices and German companies. On its four floors room after room yearned out emptily, echoing rooms with painted plaster and nothing else but rubble in them.

He and his party climbed to the roof of the palazzo, which was a flat square of gravel girdled with a railing.

216

They could see the shrill blue of the Bay of Naples. To their rear was a column and a heap of plaster shag from which flowers were already poking out their heads like war orphans. To their right was a church where the bombs had ripped away half the wall; they saw the statues and the benches and the organpipes and the tattered winy draperies that once sheathed the arches. To their left was the turn of an alley from which rose the steam of urine vaporizing in the sun. Here stood a queue of GI's waiting at the entrance to a house. Girls peeped out from its tiny balconies on the second floor; screaming children were hawking the charms to be bought upstairs. In and out of this house the GI's were in constant motion. They'd posted watches against the coming of MP's. Captain Frank watched this shifting line with interest. Finally he leaned his paunch in its pink trousers over the railing of the roof terrace and hooted paternally at the GI's.

"Oooh you VD!"

Lieutenant Mayberry looked out over the housetops, heavy with his sense of history and of time:

"That's the Italy of the guidebooks and paintings for you: a cat house next door to a church."

"It stinks," Stuki said, holding his nose over his mustache. "I see why my ole man never came back to it."

"I feel," the major said, "that our organization is going into a new and brilliant phase here in Naples. . . . I want you all to share my triumphs."

Early in August, 1944, Major Motes's palazzo opened for business. He'd made it the headquarters for most of the censorship in meridian Italy. He'd screened out hordes of Italian civilians who desired to work for the Allies at twenty-one hundred lire a week: refugees from Trieste, penniless students of the University of Naples, pale Jews who'd hidden from pillar to post in Italy. And Major Motes got them all seated at long examination tables in hushed rooms under hard lights. He locked the massive wooden doors on them and labeled the entrances with secret designations. Inside these inquisitorial rooms the furren examiners unfolded the long green sheets of the provost marshal general and read:

"Carissima mamma, io sto bene, e così spero di te e dell'intera famiglia . . ."

"Was ich auch von dir hoffe . . ."

those twenty-four lines which Italian and German P/W
wrote their families each week by permission of the
Geneva Convention. These furren examiners brought
their lunches to work wrapped in old copies of
Risorgimento: black bread and cheese. Soon they petitioned for American rations to be served as the noon
meal, since they were now in the employ of the United
States Army.

"Those Ginsoes expect us to serve em a lunch!" Stuki
cried.

"The only logical position for a greaser," Lieutenant
Mayberry said, "is under a wolf, sucking her teats like
Romulus and Remus."

"They're like nigras and must be kept in their place,"
Major Motes said.

But since so many of the Italians fainted away at their
work under the hard lights in the airless examination
rooms, he promised to try for a GI food issue. To himself, however, he declared that he'd never lift a finger to
help feed a people which had declared war on the United
States and which had been the turncoat traitors of Europe
throughout their history. More Italians fainted while censoring the mail, and more were hired to take their places:
dottori and professori and geometri and ragionieri and
studenti. Next it was arranged that the Italians and the
American officers should dine and be released at different
hours in order that they should never meet to make
friends or compare notes on the winding staircase of the
palazzo. And often in the afternoons Major Motes would
stand in the cortile of the palazzo to watch his workers
streaming out when the bell set them free. The Italians
walked arm in arm or skidded along in sandals and
shorts carrying their umbrellas. The American officers
looked like moles coming from underground and rubbing
the itching of their eyes. Major Motes got to feel like
Henry Ford watching his plants empty at the changeover
of a shift.

By trips to Caserta and crying on colonels' desks and
pleading with section chiefs, Major Motes got Stuki and
Lieutenant Mayberry promoted to captaincies. Mayberry
said his own cap would get too small if the major didn't
stop being so kind. And Stuki in his shining double bars

218

presided over rooms of gray brooding Italians reading P/W mail. One examination room opened into the next. From his high rostrum Stuki looked like a master in study hall tyrannizing over the bowed heads, the thick lenses of the spectacles, the shabby dandruffed shoulders. He sat all day long on this dais screaming exhortations at his slaves, lecturing on Italy's political perfidy, or tapping with the eraser of his pencil while he scribbled V-mails to his Mom informing her that he'd at last got to be a pezzo grosso in the city they kicked Pop out of. Stuki loved to fire Neapolitans for the slightest laxness in their duties. If they asked for half an hour off to go to the questura to bail out their sisters on charges of prostitution, he fired them for goldbricking. If they fainted from hunger at their work, he gave them the sack for shirking their duty to the United States, which had liberated them.

"Perchè avete buttato fuori mio Papa, eh?" he would cry.

Considering the huge office force under his control, Major Motes rejoiced that there were so few incidents. One afternoon on the second floor some Austrian refugees beat up an Italian Jew who was reading P/W mail in German. Major Motes arrived on the scene with his interpreter, the sergeant major, and two MP's from the questura. All the offenders were fired and jailed for investigation and trial by AMG in the Provincia Building.

"More screening, that's the answer," Major Motes told higher headquarters at AFHQ in Caserta.

"What a comedy," Captain Mayberry said, looking up from his charts and reports. "A year ago the Italians were at war with us. Now they're reading the mail of their own prisoners of war. . . . What an obscene comedy."

"The whole war is obscene, goddam it," Major Motes said. "All Europe and its parasitic population are obscene . . . like the nigras. . . ."

On the ground floor of the palazzo Major Motes established a mess hall for the American personnel, a barber shop, and a glassed-in booth where an armed guard sat and frisked all the furren help when they came to work in the morning and left in the evening. At noon the Neapolitans pressed their noses against the screen door of the mess and watched everything the Americans lifted to their mouths. Some of them wept when they saw half-eaten dishes dumped into GI cans.

"Set up garbage pails in the cortile!" Stuki railed. "Let em dive for the food we waste! That oughta nourish the bastards!"

When he wasn't necking the panties off the signorina in his office, Captain Frank amused himself with a game against the Neapolitans on the sidewalk below his window. He'd stand smoking his cigar and holding a pail of water. Every Neapolitan who relieved himself against the wall below this window got a bucket of water dumped on his head. Major Motes wrote Lucinda that ha-ha, they were teaching the Neapolitans a little practical sanitation.

Major Motes was the first at the door of the palazzo in the morning. Some evenings he stayed till midnight. There wasn't a place in the palazzo where his quick step mightn't be heard at any moment. He'd peer with pride at his jeeps and trucks in their rows in the innter cortile, at the mailbags ferried in and out of the great double-gated portone. And he observed the stream of Italians and American officers swarming up and down the staircase, which he called Jacob's Ladder in a V-mail to Lucinda. In the daylight hours there was always in his palazzo a combination hum and silence, a clatter of typewriters and that air of concentration and mystery befitting the intelligence service of the United States. He pardoned himself his pride. All this had been his dream. He alone had realized it.

As one of the leading cenorship officers in the Mediterranean theater he was invited to visit the front, attached to the 34th Division. It would mean a month's absence from Naples and his clockwork command, but he left Stuki and Captain Frank in charge. He spent a week rubbing dubbin into his combat boots and having officers' calls in which he told them how lucky they were to be in the security of Naples. But at the last moment his orders were canceled because Caserta said that the Arno front was far too risky and his own life too precious for a German bullet.

Captain Mayberry said one morning:
"My work here is almost done."

"You belong to this outfit," Major Motes replied tenderly. "You helped build it up. . . . Surely you don't want to leave me?"

"It's not that, sir," Captain Mayberry said, stroking
220

his thin blond hair. "But I thought I might ask for a transfer to Caserta. . . . I am very weary. . . . I thought perhaps they might hide me away out there in some obscure little job in documents."

"Goddam it, what are you up to?" Major Motes cried like a stricken mother. "Don't think you'll get your majority any easier out at Caserta. Besides, they haven't even made me a lieutenant colonel yet."

"You know I don't think in terms of promotion," Captain Mayberry said. "But my ancestors were pioneers. I want something new."

"Well, just don't try to pull any fine Italian deals to get out of this outfit."

In the next few days Captain Mayberry drove often to Caserta in his jeep. He said AFHQ was no longer satisfied with the reports over which he slaved. Would Major Motes please transfer him to a quieter and easier job? He was terribly weary, he said.

"You're up to something," Major Motes said accusingly.

"Besides, sir, have you looked at your hair? It's almost white. When I knew you, it was still brown. . . . you have a terrible twitch too, sir . . . you're eligible for rotation to the United States . . . your wife . . ."

Major Motes felt his scalp prickle.

"Goddam it, how can anyone think of going home when the frightful war is still on?"

"We must all be selfish, even in our unselfishnesses," Captain Mayberry replied.

That very week Major Motes's heart broke. An order came down from Caserta returning him to the United States for rotation. He was relieved of all his command in Italy. Captain Mayberry and Captain Frank were transferred to Caserta. Stuki was to take over Major Motes's own duties.

"Sorry to see ya go, chief," Stuki said, taking his arm carelessly.

"Sure you can keep things running here?" Major Motes begged, stuttering more than ever.

"Oh boy, can I! . . . Let me say now that ya've been just a little too easy around here. I got a few new policies I'm gonna try on those Ginsoes after ya leave us. . . . After all, chief, ya didn't know the languages ya was workin with . . . maybe that's why they gave ya the air."

221

He wrote Lucinda that he was coming home to her for a little rest. Nervous exhaustion. He spoke of the perfidies of Stuki, of Captains Frank and Mayberry, to all of whom he'd given their start, out of pure benevolence. But then the army was full of opportunists and fingermen.

On his last night in Naples before sailing, Major Motes walked alone in the Galleria Umberto. It was after sunset, the first time he'd been alone with himself since that hotel room in Casa almost two years ago. The Galleria was full of Neapolitans, of Americans on leave from the hospitals at Bagnoli. The bars were full, even to the chairs on the pavements. Everywhere there were girls and old women screeching and selling and sweeping. Little boys tore around making deals with GI's, buying their cigarettes and selling them phallic charms and silver horsehoes. Major Motes saw himself in a mirror in one of the bars— white-haired, quite stooped, his walk unsteady, a tic under his left eye. On his left shoulder was the red bull of the 34th Division he'd sewed on when he thought he was going to inspect the front. He kept telling himself that men all over the world had died in this war, whereas he himself was only older and wiser and full of a bottomless grief.

"Goddam it," he said, fraternally clapping a lounging GI on the shoulder, "who started this war anyway?"

"Sir, if I was a major like you, I wouldn't even care."

Major Motes walked and walked in the Galleria Umberto till the moon rose over Vesuvius and a pale light rippled through the glassless frames of the domed roof. People came and went, drunks flopped against the archways, girls were chased into black alcoves. But for all the heat that remained over Naples in the dark, he felt icy and empty and alone. He lit a cigarette. His hand trembled and the nervousness under his left eye set up a crackling along the socket. His heart was broken.

"Guess I'm out of my time," he said to himself. "I'm a gentleman from Virginia. Such must suffer in Naples of August, 1944."

This thought comforted Major Motes. When he got home, he'd go to the Pentagon and sell them the idea of setting up censorship among civilians in the United States. Americans couldn't trust even one another in wartime.

SIXTH PROMENADE

(Naples)

I REMEMBER that Italy in August, 1944, lay off our port like a golden porpoise lapped in dawn. She had eggs and lumps on her outline which the sun and the light mist grossened into wens. From nearer I made them out to be the island of Capri and the volcano Vesuvius. I peered with more interest than I had at Africa, for I had precise and confused ideas of what Italy'd be like.

I remember how in my head and in my heart the city of Naples had always nestled like a sleeping question mark, as an entity gay and sad and full of what they call Life. I knew it would be a port town, but a port town over which lay a color and a weight peculiarly Naples' own, a short girl with dark eyes and rich skin and body hair. Motherhood. Huge and inscrutable as the feminine Idea.

In August, 1944, the port of Naples was a flytrap of bustle and efficiency and robbery in the midst of ruin and panic. Images of disaster lay about the harbor: ships sunk at their berths, shattered unloading machinery, pumiced tenements along the docks. And back of this lunette the island of Capri sheered out of the bay, a sunny yellow bulkhead. Vesuvius smoked softly and solemnly, the way a philosophic plumber does at a wake. The Bay of Naples was crammed with Liberty ships and boats with red crosses on their sides and decks. Out Bagnoli way among the laurels and the myrtles landing craft infantry thumped up and down in the water.

"I don't like to look at bombed buildings," the pfc said, putting polaroid lenses over his spectacles. "Not that this will shut out the view."

"Ten months ago," the mess sergeant said, "these greasy bastards were still hearin sirens and gettin pasted."

I remember how the blue of the Mediterranean shaded into gray or rainbowed oil around the berths. Everything floated near the piers: watermelons, condoms, chunks of fissured wood, strips of faded cloth.

"Europe drains into the Bay of Naples," the pfc said.

And I remember the jeeps along Via Caracciolo near the section of Santa Lucia and how Zi' Teresa's restaurant jutting on a small float was then a French officers' mess, and the tunnel to Bagnoli. I remember whizzing past the statues of the aquarium, the war monuments (Napoli ai suoi caduti) that stared out to sea in the sunlight as stiff and superannuated as warriors on the porch of an old-soldiers' home. The sunlight gives Naples a hardness and a mercilessness. It pokes its realistic fingers into the bombed buildings by Navy House. In the half shot houses what plaster yet remains in the eaves is as living and suppurating as human skin. And just over Naples stand the hills where the Vomero sits on its snaky terraces and flights of stairs like an old lady precarious on a trapeze. The houses of Naples as they swarm up the hillside are yellow or creamy or brown; they get lost in the verdure that mustaches the lips of Castel Sant'Elmo. I couldn't place Naples in any century because it had a taste at once modern and medieval, all grown together in weariness and urgency and disgust. Yet even in her half-death Naples is alive and furious with herself and with life. The hillside on which she lies, legs open like a drunken trollop, trembles when she turns on her fan bed. I remember too that at midday, when she was sleepiest of all in the lurid heat, she was a symbol of life itself, resentful and spiteful and cursing, yet very tender in her ruin.

"I don't care what anybody says," the corporal said, "this is a terrific town. Absolutely terrific. There's something here that makes me restless and drowsy at the same time. Naples ain't just a city, like St. Louis or Omaha. There's something moving in the air above Naples. . . . Poison gas? Perfume?"

"Ah, blow it," the mess sergeant said. "Look at them skirts jigglin over them rears."

I remember that along Via Caracciolo thousands of people strolled in the late afternoon. There came a hot wind off the bay that ruffled the buttocks and the marvelous breasts of the Italian women. It mussed their black thick hair. Everyone walked arm in arm, talking, laughing, crying, shouting, gesticulating. I remember the shabbiness of Neapolitan suits, different from the shine on the seats of American pants. I remember the mourning bands on the lapels of the Neapolitan men. I remember Neapolitan shoes—when there were any—cracked or sprouting or leaking, of sick flashy leather like the cheeks of the feverish. I remember the lipstick and powder that the women used—when they could get any—of the tint of fevered blood. I remember the dark pallidity of those girls who could get none. I remember the glistening damp underarm hair when the Neapolitan women put up a hand to their heads, and their legs, which seemed often to be skinned in dewy feathers.

I remember the walls along Piazza Municipio, stuck with movie posters and the yellow playbills of the San Carlo and the Italian review *Febbre Azzurra*, or "Prossimamente Greer Garson in *Prigionieri del Passato*," and Charlie Chaplin in *Il Grande Dittatore*, and *Napoli Milionaria*, and *Soffia So*. And the shops with their windows half-empty, with their scant goods cutely spread out to fake a display:

"Prezzi sbalordativi. . . .

"Riduzioni del 20%. . . ."

Or the bookstores where Louisa May Alcott became *Piccole Donne*, where paper-bound ocher books lay in carts like cheeses on their sides, where Benedetto Croce was bedfellow with old copies of *Life* and that bitching Roman periodical *Marforio*, with nude girls prancing on the cover. And in every street and vico the little rafts on wheels selling shoelaces, and combs that shattered when they touched my scalp. And how bottles were sawed down to make glasses and vases, and how chestnuts and oranges and tomatoes and spinaci stood wilting in the food stores.

"Oggi si vende. . . ."

"Si distribuisce sale. . . ."

"Non si riparano gomme per mancanza di materiale. . . ."

"Lo spaccio, la tessera. . . ."

I remember the San Carlo Opera House on the corner by the traffic island, across the street from a pro station —its 1743 A.D. arches, its lines sweating out opera and ballet at thirty-five lire. Near it the palazzo where the Limeys took their tea and the British officers got drunk on their roof terrace and poured gin on pedestrians passing into the Galleria Umberto. And I remember that every vico and salita had a different smell. Along Via Roma there was the color of movement: the OD's of the combat troops, the rusty shorts of the UK, the melting splotches

225

of the Neapolitan housewives' house dresses, the patter of sandals, the click of hobnails, the squunch of children's brown bare soles as they begged, pimped, screamed, tugged, cried, and offered. On Via Roma there was a smell, I remember, of fake coffee roasting, of ice cream with phony flavors and colors, of musty dry goods gloated over by the padrone behind his bars against thieves. Out of every alley in Naples the whiff of a thousand years of life and death and bed sheets and urination. The glass over the colored picture of the Madonna of Torre Annunziata. The clinking of the gratings on the balconies. And especially that small basket being hauled up and down many stories on its string, pulling up newspapers and groceries and the baby. Each alley had a different stench from many families with their own residual of body excretion, sweat, halitosis, and dandruff. And I remember alley after alley winding off Via Roma like a bowel, each with its off-limits sign. All I could see of them was the entrance, a flash of cobblestones, a turn of sunlight, and the scarred face of a wall shutting off further exploration.

"I'm lost in Naples," said the pfc. "Life has struck me in the face like a flounder. Cold, hot, ghastly, and lovely."

I remember making acquaintance with Italian. At first all I heard in Naples was asssshpett and capeeesh and payyysannn. But after a few days it broke down into something more articulate. Italian (not Neapolitan dialect) can soon be understood because it sounds like what it's saying. Italian is a language as natural as the human breath. Italian is a feminine and flowing tongue in which the endings fill up the pauses, covering those gaps and gaucheries of conversation that embarrass Americans and British. It's a language whose inertia has remained on the plus side. It keeps in motion by its own inherent drive. The Italians are never silent with one another. It isn't necessary even to think in this lovely language, for your breath comes and goes anyhow, and you might just as well use it to talk with. And good loving talk! If you've nothing to say, ehhh and senz-altro and per forza and per questo are always tumbling from your lips to prevent the flow from getting static. And then there were dico and dice, and the tumble of the Italian past subjunctive, like smoke turning on itself:

"Se io andassi o se tu potessi."
226

I remember that Italian used to amuse me till it caught me in its silken web. I remember how kind the Neapolitans were to me when I was learning it, the sweetness of their grammatical corrections, the look of joy on an Italian's face when you address him in his tongue, however poorly. Italian is the most sociable and Christian language in this world. It's full of a bubble like laughter. Yet it's capable of power and bitterness. It has nouns that tick off a personality as neatly as a wisecrack. It's a language in which the voice runs to all levels. You all but sing, and you work off your passion with your hands.

"Io andare a casa tua per mangiare e per fare amore ... finito capito amato andato venduto. . . . Capeeesh? . . . Molto buono, non buono, acqua fresca. . . ."

I remember that sometimes I used to wonder if so tender and human a language might disappear from the world because of the pattern of conquest. Italian is an atavistic language. All the rest have been visited by some torture or trickery or introspection. Italian alone is the language of the moment, cunning yet unpremeditated. I learned Italian in order to make love. And I found Italian feminine and secret and grave and puzzled and laughing, like a woman. Perhaps it came from the tit of Signora Eve in the Garden. For Italian is like milk and butter, sauced with some pepper lest it cloy you with its sweetness. Once Italian got into my palate, I remember, it never again left me. So I learned Italian in Naples.

I remember also the dialect of the city of Naples, which is Italian chewed to shreds in the mouth of a hungry man. It varies even within the city. The fishermen in the bay talk differently from the rich in the Vomero. Every six blocks in the squashed-together city there's a new dialect. But the dialect is Naples and Naples is the dialect. It's as raw as tenement living, as mercurial as a thief to your face, as tender as the flesh on the breast. Sometimes in one sentence it's all three. The stateliness of Tuscan Italian is missing in Neapolitan. But there's no false stateliness in Naples either, except in some alien fountain presented by a Duchess of Lombardy. Neapolitan dialect isn't ornamental. Its endings have been amputated just as Neapolitan living pares to the heart and hardness of life. Wild sandwiches occur in the middle of words, doublings of z's, cramming of m's and n's. When they say something, the Neapolitans scream and moan and stab and hug

227

and vituperate. All at once. And O God, their gestures! The hand before the groin, the finger under the chin, the cluckings, the head-shakings. In each sentence they seem to recapitulate all the emotions that human beings know. They die and live and faint and desire and despair. I remember the dialect of Naples. It was the most moving language I ever listened to. It came out of the fierce sun over the bleached and smelly roofs, the heavy night, childbirth, starvation, and death. I remember too the tongues that spoke Neapolitan to me: the humorous, the sly, the gentle, the anguished, the merciful, and the murderous. Those tongues that spoke it were like lizards warm in the sun, jiggling their tails because they were alive.

"I have hoid," said the mess sergeant, teasing a Neapolitan child with a chocolate bar, "that da wimmin are purtier in Nort Italy. But ya can't trump da build on da Neapolitan goils. Nuttin but rear ends bouncin like Jello and milk factories under dere dresses. I'm goin crazy for it."

I remember how the women and girls of Naples stood for all the women and girls of the world. There were girls like the Kresge and Woolworth pigs of Joisey City, with their hair not quite combed and dark and too long. Under this fluffy frowzy rat's-nest they had earrings too heavy for their ears, with some cabalistic design or jewel. And there were the girls of the Vomero, of the strangling middle class, who were rushed along Via Roma on their mothers' arms, girls who were locked up after nightfall when they'd come in from their classes at the university. Now they were studentesse, but soon they'd be dottoresse:

> Un libro di latino
> Per un giovinottino . . .

They were like pretty mice in cotton dresses as they whisked by me with their chaperones. Sometimes I caught their eyes on the oblique when Mamma was looking the other way, eyes demure and hypocritical, eyes shooting feudal disdain for the poorer Italian women, eyes masking jealousy and curiosity of those lower Neapolitan women who went with gli alleati. And there were also a few, very few Neapolitan women who reminded me of the blaring independence of American girls, who prom-

228

enaded slowly through the street, well made up, their hair a little lighter, their legs a little daintier, their dresses fresh and trim. And once in a while I saw a marchesa or a contessa who'd played ball with the fascists and was now doing likewise with gli alleati. These were slim and forty and chic. They could be seen all over Europe, not just in Naples. And there were also the widows of Naples with their canes and sober bags. But most ubiquitous on Via Roma were those signurrine who chewed gum and had forgotten how to speak Italian. These walked always in pairs, and they screeched American obscenities at one another, taught them by some armored force sergeant in heat. They called every American Joe, and they knew "Stardust" and "Chattanooga Choo-Choo." They knew the words better than I did.

But I remember best of all the children of Naples. The scugnizz'. Naples is the greatest baby plant in the world. Once they come off the assembly line, they lose no time getting onto the streets. They learn to walk and talk in the gutters. Many of them seem to live there. As the curfew was progressively lifted to a later and later hour, the children of Naples spent the evenings on the sidewalks. If I had to keep in my memory just one picture of the Neapolitan kaleidoscope, it would be of a brother and sister, never over ten years of age, sleeping on a curbstone in the sunlight with a piece of chewed dark bread beside them. Sometimes I thought that in Naples the order of bees and human beings was upside down that the children supported and brought up their parents.

Once I remember attempting to count the number of shoeshine boys between Via Diaz and the Galleria Umberto. I never could, for new shoeshine stands opened behind my back by the time I'd walked ten feet. Those incredible scugnizz'! They weren't children at all, the scugnizz', but sorrowful wise mocking gremlins. They sold *Yank* and *Stars and Stripes*. They lurked outside the PX to buy my rations. They pimped for their sisters, who stood looking out at me from behind the balcony of a primo piano tenement. They sold charms and divisional insignia in the streets. They hawked dough that looked like doughnuts or fritters, but tasted like grilled papier-mâché. They stole everything with a brilliance and furtiveness and constancy that made me think of old Ayrab fairy tales. They shrilled and railed at me in perfect and scouring American, as though they'd learned it from some sailor lying in a gutter and hollering holy hell to ease his heart. The children of Naples were determined not to die, with the determination in which corpuscles mass to fight a virus that has invaded them. They owned the vitality of the damned. And they laughed at me, themselves, the whole world. Often I thought that we, the conquering army, were weaker and sillier than they. I loved the scugnizz' because I had no illusions about them.

"Wanna eat, Joe?"

"Wanna souvenir of Naples?"

"Wanna drink, Joe?"

"Wanna nice signorina? Wanna piecea arse?"

"The kids are so dirty," the corporal said. "But they have such fine teeth and eyes and skin . . . like coffee with a little milk in it. . . . And they're smart as whips. Look at the way they've learned American just so they can buy an sell to us. . . . An, Christ, what can ya do when the poor little tykes stand outside ya mess and watch ya dumpin out GI food that somebody's wasted? The MP's won't let ya feed 'em. Why? Why?"

"I suppose," said the pfc, "that these children are responsible for Mussolini? that the babies of Naples supported Farinacci and Badoglio and the house of Savoy and the vested interests of Turin and Milan?"

"Ya go crazy if ya study on it too much," said the corporal.

"Las night," the mess sergeant said, "I seen two marines come outa the docks. An they met up with two signorinas of about eleven or twelve. Ya can't tell. They become wimmin so young here. . . . Start em young, I always say."

"Well, I guess the good must suffer with the bad," the corporal said. "That's what the Bible says."

"If the Bible says that," said the pfc, "Hitler should have burnt it too."

I remember the levels and terraces of Naples, slipping from the Vomero into the bay. I'd go from the bottom of the town to the top of the funiculars, which slide under the hillside on cables. Everybody fought their way into the cars in the stations. Then you skied along the wire. Sometimes you came into the light between two palazzi. Sometimes you scudded through a brief tunnel. Everyone's shoulder was against everyone else's gut. In the spells of darkness I'd reassure myself that my Ayrab wallet was still in my pocket. In the dark the storm of Neapolitan dialect went on:

"Dì, Pino, hai portato tua moglie Pina?"

Or I remember sometimes being stranded in the Vomero. For the funiculars stopped running at 2100 hours. The Neapolitans believed that the force of gravity ceased at sundown. Then it became a problem of descent down stairs that I couldn't even see, for Naples was blacked out. There must have been forty flights and levels. God help me when I got caught at the top without a flashlight! It meant groping along the dank walls of the houses, of gauging my step on stairs set at a pitch I couldn't walk or run: about one and a half times the normal stride. Each stairway had a different gauge, and each angle was different. It was like walking into a cellar of smells and secret life, for out of the houses over my head came the sound of GI's haggling for vino after hours, of women slapped and cursed by their husbands, of children eating their pasta. Sometimes I remember how across the path of my uncertain descent a light would fall athwart the mossy chipped stairs from an ill-closed door. Or a woman and a child would appear in the spectrum. Even as I stumbled down, I wondered what they were thinking. A piece of their lives had fallen across my way in an ax of radiation.

Sometimes around midnight I remember that a peace would hit Naples. The heat shifted gears for the hour of dawn. Only then did any silence come to the wrestling odorous city. There were stars over Vesuvius. The LCI's in the bay rocked and bubbled like ducks. The lights of the MP's kiosks and the glow from the pro stations rode in the hot dark like beacons. Then I'd twist under my mosquito netting.

"Napoli? . . . I've had it . . . or it's having me. . . ."

SEVENTH PORTRAIT

Giulia

IN 1943 THE Allied bombers hit Naples incessantly. They came in the afternoons with a noise like mad cicadas. But Giulia and her brother Gennaro rarely took to the shelters. It smelled foul down there. And Giulia and Gennaro had had enough of the stench of families living night after night at lap's length. They'd had enough of the screams of women giving birth to their babies in the ricoveri, those screams which could pierce the hum of the plane motors and the crunch of the bombs hitting the streets above their heads.

The English bombers made sorties almost daily from noon to fifteen hours. While families scurried screaming underground, Giulia and Gennaro would take to the top of their apartment house. In the sunlight on the roof they'd lean like connoisseurs on the parapet railing and watch the aircraft diving on the port.

"Se ci uccidono," Giulia said, clutching Gennaro's cool hand, "ci uccidono e basta, no?"

They'd boo fine hits. Often the American planes dropped nothing but leaflets, telling the Neapolitans that the Allies were coming as friends. Giulia and Gennaro had long arrived at the conclusion that it mightn't be such a bad thing to be liberated after all. They knew the score. Their Papa was a ragioniere, endlessly totting up figures in the employ of the state. He told them all the office gossip of the questura. Hence they knew that fascism, at least in Naples, was as bloated as those balloons sold at the feast of Piedigrotta, which exploded when their rubber saw the sun.

After the pamphlet bombings Giulia and Gennaro would gather up handfuls of the leaflets that fell on their roof. These they'd bring to Papa. They'd all sit around the dining-room table while the old man put on his spectacles and deciphered them. He read slowly and avidly under the stained-glass light. So Papa too came to the conclusion that it mightn't be such a bad idea for the Allies to

232

take Naples. He didn't tell this to his children, but they read his thoughts.

Giulia was nineteen. She had a pale little face under brown ringlets that hung over her forehead like spun sugar. Everything about her was tiny: her mouth, her throat, her breasts, her waist, her ankles. Her expression was always of contented repose, even when she was talking most animatedly with her chum Elvira, whom she'd chosen as her foil because Elvira was a dowd. Giulia dressed in gay cotton or linen dresses, with a tiny belt about her minute waist, tiny white sport pumps with heels that were almost too high. After every bombing she'd pick her way with Elvira or Gennaro through the streets of Naples. She avoided the rubble and the corpses. The sun danced on a segment of her honeyed skin and made a halo on her small beribboned straw hat. She knew she didn't look much like a Neapolitan girl. Possibly because her mother Rina had been a Florentine before Papa had induced her to settle with him in Naples. But Giulia was politician enough to speak Neapolitan dialect when she was with her chums. She'd had a better education than most girls of her class. She had almost as much book learning as Gennaro, who was in his second year at the University of Naples. When she was at the liceo, Giulia by some premonition had taken all the English courses she could get. Now she was teaching Gennaro English in the evenings after the dishes were done. From her maestra Giulia had an Oxford accent. She and her brother used to laugh over these lessons, his brown high brow crinkling over the difference between louse lice and spouse spouses.

Two years ago Giulia'd allowed her family to engage her hand for marriage. To a Neapolitan sottotenente with mustaches, spectacles, and serious intentions. But Pasquale became a prisoner of war. From his barbed-wire enclosure in Oran he wrote Giulia weekly a twenty-four-line letter on green American stationery, and the return address in Italian, German, and Japanese. He told her of his loneliness, of the American Spam he was eating. He hoped that the war would soon end so that she and he could settle down with his family on Via Chiaia, and he could go on with his career as an engineer. In her mind Giulia had already written him off as a liability. She wrote Carissimo fidanzato to him once a week. And like all

233

good Italian girls she led the life of a respectable fidanzata. She visited Pasquale's family once a month and mourned for him as though he were dead. She passed her time as a ragazza per bene, shut up in the house with Mamma or going to the cinema with her brother Gennaro or her chum Elvira, that simpatica dowd. Giulia lived in the vacuum and parenthesis that was Naples from July to October, 1943. Yet in her small breast she nurtured a hope.

The only excitement in Giulia's life (she'd never batted an eyelash at the bombings) was the periodic concealing of her brother every time the Germans came around to conscript him. In such moments coolness and resourcefulness shone forth all over Giulia. Gennaro would go white under his tan. Mamma would have a heart attack and lie moaning on the tasseled couch, praying that Papa wouldn't show up from his office, lose his temper with the Tedeschi, and get shot. Gennaro was also in danger of a fucilazione if they ever caught him. Such crises happened every other week. Only Giulia was capable of holding the entire Wehrmacht at bay at the door of their apartment. The Tedeschi respected her as she stood in the doorway, shaking her brown ringlets at them. None ever laid a finger on her, from Gefreiter to Hauptmann. Elvira however licked her chops over frightful stories of Neapolitan girls (always unidentified) whose nude bodies were said to have bobbed up in the Bay of Naples or been stuffed up a culvert on the road to Bagnoli.

Giulia's brother Gennaro was seventeen. She knew she had more influence on him than either Mamma or Papa. She doted on Gennaro. As she watched him comb his black hair over his white linen coat, she often told herself that Gennaro was bello: he wasn't dark or greasy like many Neapolitans. She wished he was a little taller, but everything in Gennaro's body was in fine harmony as he walked with her and Elvira, taking both their arms. Giulia loved him best when he was groaning over his English under the stained-glass lamp at the dinner table, his delicate face puckered into a cold passion, the rich undulations of his hair escaping down almost into his eyes. She noted that he'd a quick brain, though not so agile as her own. Gennaro kept his body to a whiplike temper by swimming, by fencing with other young Camicie Nere, and by dancing, which he loved dearly. And he was wise enough not to tie himself down by

234

going steady with a Neapolitan girl. The times were too unstable. Occasionally he'd disappear with a friend. Giulia knew where they went those evenings. To the casino of Madam Sappho. But then Gennaro was seventeen, and the heart that beat under his short-sleeved shirts and crisp summer jacket was the heart of a Neapolitan, which must make love.

Mamma had gained many chili since Papa'd brought her in 1924 as a bride from Florence. Once she'd been as slim as Giulia, according to her photos. Now she sat huge and bloated in her dark deep chair, listening to forbidden English radio broadcasts. Her heart wasn't good. Mamma was happiest when she heard jazz from London or when she ate a pizza prepared by Giulia to trick her appetite or when her cronies dropped up for coffee—a thing that didn't happen too often in these days of constant air-raid sirens. Every evening after supper she lectured her children on the vices of the world and reminisced on their one trip back to Florence to visit her relatives. Mamma hated Naples. She told the same stories over and over, but the children gave her her allotted hour every evening, sitting at her feet and listening to the hoarse gasping voice coming out of her chins and the mole on her lip. Giulia sat with her small feet tucked up under her buttocks, and Gennaro in the dim apartment smoked a Nazionale and nodded his head dreamily, saying:

"Eh sì, cara mamma. . . ."

And Giulia, in the thousandth repetition of the warning that Naples would be dangerous for a regazza after the Allies took it (as they eventually must) would study Gennaro's nose in the moonlight and feel a compulsion to tweak it. She wondered if at Madam Sappho's too the women loved and understood her brother.

Every afternoon at fifteen hours Papa banged up the five flights of stairs to the apartment. He came directly from his office in the questura, where he spent the day playing poker and adding up columns of lire and centesimi. He was always furious and splenetic till he'd had three cups of scalding caffè espresso. Then his spirits would rise and he'd bawl and mime in dialect for the rest of the afternoon. His gray mustaches and gray hair and small paunch quivered with apprehension. This apprehension was founded on the insecurity of all employees of the Fascist state. Till now they were doing all right. They

were the middle class with comfortable fixed stipends.
But after the Allies came (as they surely would) the
stipend would remain unchanged and the lira would go
down down down. Papa could always awake Mamma
from her doze by the radio by telling her that as soon as
Naples fell, she'd lose all her avoi dupois because there
wouldn't be anything to eat in the house. He also described with gestures his daughter earning her living on
the streets and his son withdrawing from the university
to work as a truck driver for the Allies, and at a wage
that wouldn't keep him in shoelaces. At this point Mamma
would awake with a jump, scream, say her rosary, caress her children, and say that Italia was rovinata and
they would be all rovesciati. Giulia and Gennaro, hearing of these predicted horrors, would merely smile at each
other. For they knew they'd get along somehow, even if
the Russians took over Naples.

In his youth Papa had been more progressive and socially minded than most of the employees of the Fascist
state, who simply pocketed their stipends and their bribes,
did as they were told, and played mad politics with the
questore at the questura. In 1919 Papa was returning
from under arms, sad and confused for the future of
Italy. Then he had met Benito Mussolini and had fallen
under the spell. Until the Ethiopian War Papa had been a
vigorous and intelligent Fascist. Papa knew so well the
good and the evil of fascism. Why hadn't the combines of
Torino and Milano let well enough alone? Why hadn't
they built up Campania and Puglie instead of distracting the public's attention with the Ethiopian War? Why
a dream of empire when Italy had only begun to be uni-
fied? So from 1935 on Papa had been as tepid a Fascist
as a ragioniere employed by the state dared to be.

"Ho smarrito a fede nel sognato destino," he said.

And with the outbreak of the Second World War Papa
in despair ceased to go to Mass on Sundays. In his home
he wept and railed against the farabutti who had brought
this on Italy. He predicted a speedy end to Europe. He
cursed the Italian middle class and the house of Savoy. His
curses were in his throatiest Neapolitan. In their hearts
his children agreed with him. Mamma wept continually.
Her heart condition got worse.

On 3 October 1943, Naples fell to the Fifth Army.

For a week Mamma kept her entire family about her in the house. She had a chain of cardiac attacks. The house was without light or gas. The sounds of the liberators in movement that came up from the streets were far more ominous than during the air raids or when the Tedeschi were in Naples. Mamma, with her feet in sheepskin slippers on the divan, was tended by all. She lamented that she'd ever lived to see this day. She said it was the end of the world for all of them. She lambasted Papa for not having consummated his plan of going to America twenty years ago. And every five minutes she made Giulia or Gennaro peer out of the apartment window into the swirling foggy streets to see if there were any New Zealanders coming. She remembered what Il Duce had said the Kiwis would do to all the women of Italy. She had Giulia fetch the carving knife from the cupboard. She promised that this knife would finish in Giulia's heart if ever a New Zealand tread were heard on their stairs. Then Mamma would turn the knife, smoking from her daughter's blood, on herself: for who knew that even a matron of her age would be safe from ravishing New Zealand soldiery? But peer and descry as they could, Giulia and Gennaro saw nothing but truck convoys tearing through the streets below. No New Zealanders came to their apartment to violate them. Over the nightly English lesson Giulia whispered to Gennaro that, while Mamma was keeping them all shut up like canaries, all the other Neapolitans were out hunting up choice jobs with the Allies.

A week later Mamma allowed Papa to return to his office in the questura. She also allowed Giulia and Gennaro to go out and try to buy some food. In their week of immurement they'd eaten up everything in the house. So Giulia, Gennaro, and Elvira sallied out to buy food. Gennaro carried the carving knife under his armpit, also a little biretta that Papa kept in a secret place. Elvira had also been kept locked up by her family. Her mousy face was unwashed, her hair all mad and atwirl. Giulia in her neat frock and little cloth coat with the fur collar thought privately that her chum looked a fright. When a girl isn't by nature attractive, she becomes a monster when she lets herself go.

In early October, 1943, Naples was a city of chaos, of movement with no purpose, of charnel smells, of rain, of army truck headlights coming out of the mist like eyes without lids. The shoe was on the other foot now: the Germans had taken over bombing the town as soon as they'd vacated the premises in favor of the Fifth Army. After the sun set through the fall rains, the few who dared go abroad stumbled their way over sidewalks in a close dreadful blackness. There wasn't a light, except from the truck convoys. Corpses were let lie where they fell, creasing and bloating from the rain. Living Neapolitans stripped the clothing from them: the living needed the cloth. The city's sewage had all backed up in a spasm of vomiting, like stomachs nauseated with war. What stench didn't renege from the bay wafted through the ruptured mains in the streets. There were red whispers of typhus, and prayers that it was true that the Americans had a new disinfectant. And in the daytime the poor sun squeaking through the rains showed a spectacle more ghoulish than you imagined by darkness. Clots of returning Neapolitans trekked in from their hiding places outside the city. Household furniture was pushed through the streets. Wagons and carts swamped the roads through which the army trucks were trying to pass. Horses and van owners were clubbed and kicked and screamed at by American MP's. They writhed and wrestled with the traffic like Laocoöns in a haze.

"La nostra città è morta," Gennaro said, his voice sickened and phlegmy.

"Non credo," Giulia said, but she too was ashgreen with terror as they felt their way through the vichi, where rubbish and foul moisture trembled on the walls like rotten emeralds.

Then she noticed that Elvira was chewing gum. Giulia whirled on her friend and demanded to know, her eyes narrowing into sparks, where that American gum came from. Elvira began to splutter and said that an American soldier had given it to her brother yesterday.

"Ebbene?" Giulia said savagely, elbowing her bosom friend against an archway.

"No, no, no, no," Elvira said bursting into tears. "Non ci pensare. . . ."

Giulia felt relieved, even though she despised herself for the thought that had popped into her head. . . . These were times. . . . She'd always sensed a weakness in Elvira,
238

but not of that kind which would send her amica out onto the sidewalks to proposition the Allied soldiers.

By a series of leaps across the streets, slinking along the narrowest and remotest alleys, they were approaching the questura. They arrived at a church slit in two by bombs. There remained the blasted portico with its picture of the Madonna under shattered glass, its candelabra twisted like a frostbitten branch. Under the tempera of the walls lay a cadaver in overalls. Its dead eyes turned upward and outward like buttons fearful of a buttonhook. A little way off, on another pile of slag, was the hat that the head had worn when alive. Elvira let out one cluck and fainted. Gennaro laid his head against the shattered wall and vomited soundlessly. Giulia desired to hold his head, but instead she knelt down to Elvira and chafed her hands. After a time of murmuring incantations and encouragement, the way her mother had when they were babies, Giulia got her partly restored and walking on again. She told Gennaro to use his silk handkerchief to wipe the corners of his mouth, from which dribbled a thread of slime.

"Vergogna," Giulia scolded.

She heard her small clear voice like a flute over the tympanum of sound that was Naples that morning. The pallor sank under Gennaro's olive skin, he resumed his spry gentle gait. Elvira pulled her shapeless hat over her eyes and marched on in a blind stupor like a pig to the slaughter.

At the main entrance to the questura, where her father worked, Giulia and her party came upon a long queue of screaming and buzzing Neapolitans, talking with hands and throats. At the side door cordons of MP's were hustling others under arrest to cells. The American MP's girdled the creamy stone walls of the entire questura building. In the glassed vestibule hung the sign:

QUI GLI ALLEATI IMPIEGANO
CIVILI COMPETENTI AL LAVORO

So Giulia told her brother and her friend to take heart; there were good jobs waiting for them inside with the Americans. She stood on Via Medina on the outskirts of the mob, trying to formulate some plan of action. But the yowling of the Neapolitans and the shouted orders of the MP's drove everything out of her head. She felt again that long-ago sensation when, as a tiny girl with sparkling ringlets, she'd take refuge in her mother's skirts if strangers spoke to her. But then she looked at her brother's sad proud face, at Elvira, who was beginning to jitter again. So she pulled her furpiece about her, took both their arms, and prepared herself to rush the line in the best Neapolitan tradition on trolleys.

"Where's this pretty baby goin so fast, huh?"

An American MP blocked her path. His sudden appearance, almost out of the ground, stopped them dead in their tracks. It was the first American soldier the three had seen at close range. Elvira burst into silly sobbing. Gennaro came to attention and gave the Fascist salute. Giulia stood her ground and simply looked at the MP. She was as tall as to his chest. Under his helmet she saw his yellowish face, pitted with the craters of his adolescence. His eyes were like oranges in blood. His mouth was a line of purple. He was in a tight olive-drab uniform and leggins. Over one shoulder and by his waist hung a burnished leather holster and a pistol. The blue and white MP brassard on his arm was pinned below the single chevron. He looked at her and she returned his glare until his eyes softened and netted into wrinkles. All her English flew out of her brain, then seeped back in. And Giulia spoke with her Oxford accent:

"Please, sir, please . . ."

"Ah, molto, buono," said the MP, "tu parlare americano?"

"I know English discreetly well," Giulia said. "And sir, we three desire a post with the liberating army. . . . We are good decent Italians. . . . My father is not an active Fascist. . . . We will do anything that good people ought to do to live . . ."

"A sharp mouse, a sharp mouse," the MP said, clapping his holster in a dour delight.

He put out his gauntled hand and with a finger lighter than she'd have imagined stroked the soft line below her ear to her chin. Giulia's impulse was to step smartly back out of his reach, but she stayed herself. Back of her she heard Gennaro's breath go into a snort. She hoped her brother would control himself.

"Please sir," Giulia said, "I am an honest young Italian
240

girl. This is my husband behind me. . . . We are recently married . . ."

"O scusate," the American MP said, himself stepping back. "I didn't know ya was married. . . . Well, baby, come around in a few more days and ask for Gibson. I might be able to help ya. But don't walk in that door now unless ya fixin to take a blood test an maybe end up in in Poggioreale jail. . . . But if ya wanta come back in a day or so, there might be somethin cookin. . . . Frankly, I like ya, baby. . . . Ya the first Ginso girl I could imagine goin for. . . . Why don't ya come to America? Ya smart enough to do all right for yaself."

"Thank you, sir," Giulia said.

She gathered her brood and hustled them around the corner of the questura to Via Diaz. Yet once again she looked back at the MP. He was still standing with his hands on his Sam Browne belt and gazing after her.

"An stay off these streets, baby," he yelled at her.

Giulia didn't tell her brother or her friend, but she liked the American MP for all his seamy looks. He had a brusqueness and a crudity that wouldn't be acceptable in an Italian man. But Giulia also knew from some core of insight that he would be incapable of doing her any treachery.

They walked up Via Diaz. Gennaro was lost within himself, murmuring something about the soldiering in the Italian Army and the fine manners of their ex-carabinieri. Elvira was sunk in a stupid terror; she'd retracted her head like a tortoise into her coat and was trusting only to Giulia's arm to guide her. From the rear of the questura, where the cells were under the ground floor, they heard the screaming of incarcerated ladies calling out Neapolitan obscenities and protesting that they'd never heard of syphilis.

On the façade of the neo-something Provincia - Building Giulia saw another advertisement for Italian help. At this portal were gathered petitioners of a different feather. She asked one of the hangers-on whose offices were here and was told that Allied Military Government was setting up its control of Naples. In the tense postulant faces Giulia saw most of the South Italian nobility. Contesse had risen early from their beds to get themselves a job as social secretary to a colonel; marchesi were ready to put their Ischia or Capri villas at the disposal of the

241

Americans and the British. All the elite of Campania were waiting here to prove that they'd never been Fascist, but had been just biding their time till they could give cocktail parties for the Allies.

"Razza di cani," Gennaro said and spat on the ground.

Giulia led him and Elvira away. She saw that there was no hope from AMGOT. She couldn't compete with really big operators—yet.

In a market of Naples where she'd always traded, Giulia found reality of a closer sort. There was almost no food on the shelves and no meat in the windows except a few chines of red runny flesh looking like no beef or pork she'd ever seen before. And what little there was of anything was selling for from four to ten times its price of two weeks ago. Giulia felt herself going sick and frightened under her gay dress and trim coat. She heard her voice shake on the brink of a sob as she asked Mr. Gargiulo if this weren't just a temporary shortage, if the Allies wouldn't soon be rushing food into Naples.

Thereupon Mr. Gargiulo, who'd always been so kind to her, seemed to blow up under his bloody apron. He delivered himself of five minutes' blistering Neapolitan rhetoric, of pleading and sobbing and suicide threats. He told Giulia that she was a cretin, then apologized to her; he called Elvira a ninny from Calabria, and he asked Gennaro in a burst of irony what good all that fine Latin and Greek were going to do him now. Then before Giulia's eyes, which were beginning to seep the tears she'd been suppressing all morning, Mr. Gargiulo waved a freshly printed one-lira note. He told them that this was the new currency of the Allies, and that it wasn't worth enough to buy a chicken with, no, not a whole bale of it. He told them that from now on Napoli was liberated—liberated from life itself, because henceforth money would mean nothing in the markets, nothing. He told them that the Allies had also liberated the lira of any value.

So all four of them cried there in the butcher shop with the rainy October air looking in on them. Then Mr. Gargiulo threw into Giulia's shopping basket some suspicious pasta, a few old greens, and a chunk of wormy meat. He said that he didn't want her money because it was the last time they'd see one another alive. They wept some more and cursed. Only Giulia stood a little apart from her own anguish and thought and puzzled inside her

242

small studious head. When they got home and told Mamma what Naples was like, she had a really good heart attack. For a week it was thought that Mamma wouldn't live.

From that time on Giulia and her family entered a desert of hopelessness. Since they'd kept alive all during the German occupation of Naples and the bombings, they looked back on those days as a rather gay paradise compared to their existence now after the city's fall. Then they hadn't minded living from day to day. But now it was a minute-to-minute struggle, in which any problem five minutes hence seemed a lifetime removed. Every evening they had bleak sessions under the stained-glass lamp on the dining-room table. They admitted that they hadn't been liberated from anything at all, that the war was just beginning for them. Giulia felt like the man who survives pneumonia only to discover that his heart has been weakened forever.

Worst of all she found that misery doesn't necessarily make strange bedfellows—or any bedfellows at all. Those other ladies in the apartment to whom Mamma, when they were ill, lent coffee and fruit and fresh meat now withdrew into chilly hostility when they discovered that the bounty was ended. Hence Giulia began to doubt whether privation and suffering unite people so much as they divide them. Each family went into a sniping war against all others. Everyone in Naples agreed only in saying that the Allies were worse liars than the Fascists. Everyone was divided from everyone else. Whereas the Neapolitans had known a certain dreary camaraderie when they all faced the war together in the bomb shelters, they now became one another's enemies, since each must go out and forage for food. And Giulia watched the comedy of her father's weekly stipend. Each week he collected the same sum of lire that he'd been receiving for ten years. But with it he could buy a day's ration of bread. It was like a child putting up his hands to stop a tidal wave.

The first weeks they managed only with the thought that this state of affairs couldn't last. For Papa was known and loved in Naples. He worked every angle and every connection, pulled every wire so that his family could buy in secret shops. His only luxury was that he smoked much. For a while his cherished cigarettes continued to dribble in: three from the Vomero, two from Torregaveta, four from Caserta.

In the third week typhus burst out all over Naples the way a rash seeps through after presages of itching. Momma said sta bene, it would carry her off quickly, then she wouldn't have to bother about her heart any longer, and there'd be one less mouth to feed. She rose from her sofa more than she should and spent time in the kitchen beside Giulia, trying to cook something into or out of the gray heavy pasta and the vegetables that seemed to have lain in the Sahara. She howled for the white bread the Allies had promised in their propaganda leaflets.

Then began the foul rectification of a foul situation. Everyone knew that you could buy in Naples any amount of American meat and medical supplies. If you had the price. Papa knew where these things were sold, for most of his friends had gone into the black market. The only catch was that the prices were ten to twenty times the normal level. Two weeks after its fall there was anything you wanted to buy in Naples. For two thousand lire a day a small family could live quite well. But Giulia knew no small Neapolitan families with an income of two thousand lire a day. She didn't know any millionaires.

One evening after a supper of dark bread, beans, and a potato soup Papa announced that they might as well bid farewell to honesty. He said that only two classes were destined to survive in Naples—the very rich and the very poor. The rich could afford to live through the parenthesis by selling all they had, to buy on the black market. And the poor stole more than they ever had because with the Allies here there was more to steal. Papa's mustaches were as stiff as iron. He described himself as a man tied to a plank and ordered to stand on his feet. Giulia listened. She wished she had more of the Italian woman's gift of tears. In her throat she felt only a pain as though there were a hot cauter there. After a while she went into the gabinetto. Her stomach wouldn't keep down what she'd just eaten for it was as delicious as grass and as palatable as cardboard. She stood over the bowl holding her hot dry forehead and feeling her stomach twitch oysterlike and deathly. Then she put on her coat and went out to find Elvira for a walk.

Elvira's family had already entered the bracket of the war rich. Papa Brazzi had closed his barbershop and had

taken a position as head waiter in an American officers'
mess. From the kitchen door of this installation there
streamed a small but precious rivulet of American meats,
coffee, sugar, and white bread. Enough of this contra-
band appeared on Papa Brazzi's table to keep his family
as well nourished as they'd always been. The rest he sold
or bartered. Actually Elvira and her family were living
on a slightly higher level than the prewar one for their
class, but in comparison to most other Neapolitans in October, 1943, they were princes. Elvira's posture was better, her eyes prouder, her complexion almost radiant. She
was now in a position to make a brilliant marriage, if she
chose.

Elvira greeted Giulia with condescension. She led her
friend into the Brazzi kitchen, remarking happily that
poor Giulia looked pale and faint. She set before Giulia
a plate of American spiced meat out of a can, two slices
of white bread, and a cup of chocolate which she bragged
came from American powder. Giulia ate every morsel,
trying to conceal how hungry she was.

"Ah, poveretta," Elvira squealed, watching Giulia as
though she were a canary breakfasting in a cage.

And Giulia, dizzy and enervated from her vomiting,
knew coolly that this was the moment Elvira'd been waiting for all her suppressed days—the chance to play the
queen at her own expense. Giulia tried not to listen to
Elvira's itemized boasting over Papa Brazzi's commerce
in the borsa nera, of the goods that lay in the Brazzi
cellar.

Arm in arm she and her new patroness walked in the
Galleria Umberto. The arcade was moist and dark after
the rains. On the pavement still lay the splinters of glass
that had been bombed out of the skylight. A few bars
were open. There was no electricity in Naples, but lighted
candles stood in their own wax on the marble bar tops.
By this wan light Allied soldiers drank vermouth. And
Giulia noticed that they were being whistled at in a casual
savagery that made a pain press on her eyeballs. It was
the first time in her life she'd been treated so. She tightened her grasp on Elvira's arm and forced her into a
swifter pace toward the Via Verdi end of the Galleria.

Suddenly there came to her mind in the midst of the
murk and the candlelight and the slippery pavement those
walks she'd taken here as a little girl with her Mamma

and Papa on Sunday afternoons. There was glass then in the dome of the Galleria Umberto; the sun dropped like a gay flag, the murmur of the Neapolitans talking was bright and sure. In those days Giulia wore small green coats and green ankle socks and a small straw hat fastened to her chin with a green ribbon. In those same bars where the Allied soldiers were now drinking, she used to reach up her little hand for the Sunday ice-cream cone. She was picked up and kissed by all, though Mamma didn't like compliments paid in her presence. Fifteen years ago! Out of the haze and the feeling of sleepwalking in a dank cellar, Guilia heard those voices praising her baby beauty:

"Ah, la piccina! Eh, che piccola regina! Com'è carina, signora, e ben educata pure."

But this memory broke off and mangled, for it was October, 1943, and Giulia and Elvira were walking through a changed Galleria. She observed—at first she thought it her imagination—that Elvira was gawking at the Allied soldiers, obviously turning her head as they passed concentrations of them chewing gum or passing around a cognac bottle. Giulia queried softly, Was it Elvira's plan to marry an American? Elvira replied with a coy casting down of her eyes, Well, she'd considered the matter. Then Giulia said with the tinkle of an icicle that the Americans were different from us and might easily break the hearts of us Italian girls. And Elvira gave a too loud laugh and stated that sentimentality was out of date; it didn't pay.

"Ah, ti prego," said Giulia, "di non dirmi più simili sciocchezze."

To which Elvira replied with heavy scorn that it was all very well for Giulia to talk big ideals when she hadn't enough to eat. For the first time in her tranquil life Giulia had the impulse to slap someone. But she merely tightened her hold on Elvira's arm.

In the exact center of the Galleria Giulia saw a sight that was new. It scored her with the fascination of a pimple on the back of one's neck. She saw many girls alone and in pairs, girls she'd never noticed on the streets of Naples before. Their attire, even in the dark, shone with a determined if shabby brilliance. They laughed constantly in a sound like crows jeering. They urged themselves boldly on the soldiers, who waited or pulled on their bottles. Through the night air tumbled estimates in lire such as one would hear on the stock exchange in Piazza della Borsa. Giulia'd never heard Italian women talking money so much before. The price of four thousand lire was much bandied between the soldiers and the girls. Then Elvira nudged her.

An American soldier was leaning against the slate-hued wall of the Galleria. He wore a fur-collared jacket and muddy leggins. In his hands were two tin cans which he pushed and retracted from the girl in front of him, who put out her tongue and wriggled the tip of her nose. Her dress was ragged. She was in hysteria of several moods. She seemed hungry and frightened and lewd all at once. Finally she seized the soldier's arm, pulled him along with a searing laugh, and they both ran out of the Galleria. Elvira tittered and revealed that in those tin cans was the food served to American troops at the front. Her Papa called it C-ration.

Giulia put two and two together. She began to quiver, standing still in the Galleria. Lightning raked across her eyes. There stormed up in her small breast a bitterness and a fury that frightened her and tore at her. She thought her heart was going to stop, and she was going blind with rage. And she heard her voice clang over her rigid lips like knives. She cried, not to Elvira or to anyone in particular, that a soldier who gave food to a hungry girl for love was outside the human race. Elvira tittered some more, said that this was war, and that Italian women could make riffraff of themselves if they chose. But then she stopped, for she saw that Giulia was crying.

Tears plopped down Giulia's cheeks. Sobs came from her small body in a series of waves, dry waves like sheaves of paper ripped by a mad hand.

"Siamo vinti. . . . In questa guerra sono morti non soltanto i soldati . . . ma l'anima, le donne, e l'onore di tutti quanti. . . . Che Iddio ci aiuti. . . ."

Still sobbing, she forced Elvira to quit the Galleria with her. She knew that if Elvira so much as giggled once more, she'd hurl her onto the wet sidewalk, though she was smaller than Elvira. Elvira suddenly took her leave and went into her own house. Giulia passed a church which the sacristan was just locking for the night. She told the sacristan that it was a gracious idea to lock Christ in and the people out of the churches when the sun set. The sacristan shrugged and stepped aside to let her

247

pass in. Giulia took water from the holy-water font and made the sign of the cross on her forehead. She was glad that Elvira had gone on home. She was still trembling, as a leaf remembers the wind.

After the black rainy air of Naples the church was glowing with vigil lights. These streaked out the offerings in the glass showcases, the cups of gold, the jewels, the token offerings for miraculous cures. Because of these treasures the church was locked at sundown. At a side altar a plump old priest was saying his rosary. Because she made some noise in entering, he looked at her testily and clucked.

Giulia knelt before the statue of the Madonna, which every year was borne through the streets on August 15 covered with flowers and smoked over with torches and incense. And Giulia prayed to Our Lady. She'd never really prayed before in her life.

She told Holy Mary Mother of God that she was a Neapolitan girl of nineteen. That she had her selfishnesses. That perhaps she was a little too proud for her station in life. . . . But (Giulia begged Mary) what are women put into this world for? Aren't they to make good wives to men. . . . at least in Italy. . . . Every good Italian girl wishes to be a wife and mother. . . . A woman doesn't fear suffering as much as a man does. . . . Having children isn't pleasant . . . but at least it's natural. . . . Mother of God, a woman can't cope with unnatural things like war, because a woman was put here to bring life into this world . . . women aren't interested in killing. . . . Giulia asked the Madonna to help her. Her lips formed most passionately around that word, help.

Then she left the church. It was only two minutes now to the door of the apartment. She rounded an alley and came upon a tableau. An American soldier was lying unconscious on a doorstep. In her reflex of flinching back Giulia saw that this drunk was being relieved of his lire and his packs of cigarettes. At her step the thief jumped up from bending over the unconscious figure. It was Giulia's brother Gennaro, all pale and with a murderous grief in his eyes. Her brother Gennaro.

Giulia discovered the consequences of sharing a secret which must never again be referred to, even with its imparter. This weight forced her deeper into herself and re-

248

moved her completely from this life. Hitherto her adjustment to living had been a sweet moderation: neither mad for society nor shunning it. She'd lived well in herself, but not with that intensity or misanthropy which marks the queer or the gifted. Now all was changed. The sight of her brother bending over the drunken American soldier and rifling his pockets had burnt Giulia's eyes, as though she'd looked straight at the sun. Often at night she saw this vision, asleep or awake, as a light remains on our retina after we turn away into the dark. With this there came to her moral and ethical nature a rift which refused to heal, which caused her night after night to cry into her pillow.

She knew that Gennaro had done what she saw him doing not through meanness or tendency to burglary in himself. He'd done what he'd done not for himself but because his family had to eat and because he could sell a pack of American cigarettes for three hundred lire. He had only to steal a few packs a week, and his family would revert to their former tranquil prosperity. All this Giulia knew, but the explanation didn't help any. And she knew too that in these times Neapolitans of the middle class could starve slowly, as effectively as if they'd willfully gone on a hunger strike. No it wasn't that Gennaro had stolen that brought agony to Giulia's soul; it was that he had had to steal, that there was no way out of doing what he'd done. Thus the worshiped figure of her brother became a symbol of that scabrous destiny which was debasing them all. He was no more her Gennaro, but a marionette whipped on by a fury and a fate beyond him. It wasn't fair. It was filthy. He was now much more and much less her brother. He'd become the projection of all that was diseased in Naples of 1943. To her dying day Giulia could never forget that figure crouched in the murky vico, that look of horror and fascination outstarting from her brother's eyes, that brown hand she'd so often spanked in their English lessons going like a shuttle through the pockets of the American soldier. Both their hearts broke at that instant—Gennaro's and Giulia's. They'd understood one another perfectly from the days when the little sister used to take the baby brother's hand. There could never again be between them that ripeness and gentleness, never, never. It was as though in a moment of madness they'd committed incest together, and

249

had arisen defiled from the act, resolving never to see one another again. For their love had been close. They'd collided and passed through and beyond one another, like shadows embracing in hell.

Mamma, noting that the family's diet had returned to its old level of abundance and variety, nodded sagely from her couch. She said, See, they'd done wrong to curse the Allies, for they'd kept their promises. Italians were overhasty in praise and in blame. She praised the American Spam and found that American coffee did her angina good. She hoped Gennaro'd make the acquaintance of an American and bring him home for dinner. In this way they might repay some of their debt to the Allies for liberating Naples and bringing fine American rations into the house. Giulia, when these things were said at table, would feel a knife go through her brain. She'd excuse herself from the meal and go to her room, for she knew that remaining at table would mean screaming. Her brother, the sad bent tool of injustice, simply sat in his place and stared at his plate. His dark hair seemed to have turned into sleek snakes hissing along his forehead.

Gennaro's own sorrow forced him into a kind of flagrance of bitterness, as those with skin diseases appear brazenly in public. In his room he kept cartons of American cigarettes. These Giulia would find as she did her morning dusting while Mamma chattered from the couch in the parlor. Then Giulia, in an ecstasy of horrid fascination, would pick up the shining cellophane packages with the red target in the center. She'd count them with loathing, letting each fall back into the drawer through her fingers. Each morning she would play with these American cigarettes till she had to sit on Gennaro's bed and weep. Mamma in the salottino would get peevish and restless and call out that Giulia was getting lazy in her housekeeping, and would make no man a good wife.

Giulia knew that Papa, anything but stupid, guessed what his son was up to after a few days' lying. So, living off the American food and the American cigarettes which he so passionately loved, Papa's mustache grew white. Giulia watched a metaphysical corset twine round Papa's plump chest that was strangling off his breath.

One evening in November Papa walked with Giulia to the door of her bedroom. All evening long he'd been ostensibly in high spirits, jesting of his Fascist youth, of

Mussolini's violin playing, of Edda Ciano's legs. He was as gay as one coming out of an anesthetic. But Giulia, inured to agony, saw his mirth for what it was, the abandon of a clown with a dying son. At her door Giulia's father kissed her good night so hard that she tasted the small onions he'd eaten with such bravura, the tart red wine he'd drunk with dinner, the stinging afterbreath of American cigarettes. And Papa's chest shook as he drew her head over his heart.

"Ah, cara mia, che bellezza! Abbiamo un figlio ed un fratello ladro. . . ."

And as she lay in her bed she sounded the depths of her father's bitterness.

Or sometimes Giulia tried to exchange a few words with Gennaro, those teasing sisterly sallies she'd always made. But their hollowness was obvious to her and, she knew, to him. Any conversation on their old level was as intolerable to both as a house hit by an incendiary bomb: only walls stood in the void where once were lovely rooms.

In December, 1943, Giulia sat under the stained-glass lamp over the dining-room table. She was reading *Risorgimento,* which she hadn't had time to glance over all day. It was full of news of the countless Neapolitan political parties and their diatribes against one another. Giulia thought of the line of steel and death to the north of her. The Germans were making Italy a shambles by retreating slowly to the north, destroying as they went. She wondered what other girls of nineteen were thinking tonight in Rome, in Firenze, in Milano. Then her eye hit upon an ad. It said that shortly a club for American officers would open in the Bank of Naples. They were going to hire Neapolitan ladies and gentlemen as cashiers and waiters.

Giulia arose from her chair, smoothing her somber dress and her hair. She was wearing also her cloth coat with the fur collar because the house was damp and cold. Nowhere in Naples could you buy wood or coal, even on the mercato nero. Giulia considered again. Then she went to her brother's room. She knew how she'd find him. And he was. Bent over their old English grammar. He lurched to his feet as she switched on the ceiling light. His passionate vitality at once wove an armor about

251

him. She felt it opaque and dense as a wall, but she kept walking till she stood beside him and took his hand. She put her index finger on the advertisement and pushed it to him to read as though she were forcing an invalid to eat. For a minute they stood there looking at one another with a fierceness that gathered and stiffened them both. Because it was the first time she'd brought herself to look upon Gennaro in months, Giulia saw how beautiful was his face, like the face of one with a wasting disease, where all the life and reserve passion pounds into the cheeks and sits there in a wildness of decision and husbandry, saying, Kill me if you dare. For a second she thought she was going to die. But some cyclone blew them into one another's arms, where they wept loudly for some while.

In the cold brightness of Naples in December Giulia and Gennaro and Elvira walked through the Galleria Umberto. It was nine o'clock in the morning. The night had brought the usual air raid. There were American ambulances in the streets, and Neapolitan plumed hearses were carrying those who'd died earlier. The winter of Naples has its own peculiar stink like the cursing in Neapolitan dialect. Giulia shivered and drew her fur about her neck. Since she had to wear it in the house too to keep warm, it mocked her out of doors. But she was soon distracted from her own discomfort by seeing the seat of Gennaro's trousers. He was wearing a gray pencil-striped business suit. A year ago it had been a quiet vessel for his beauty. Now the seat was shiny and the elbows the same.

For herself and her brother, however, Elvira more than compensated. The Brazzis were now rich. Elvira was getting a double chin from eating so opulently. She did her nails in various colors and painted her face till it was a mixed vegetable plate. She'd developed a mince in her walk that once was clumsy and nervous. Into her conversation, which had always been dreary, full of hot flashes and tremors and palpitations, Elvira now injected American words of whose meaning she wasn't precisely sure. Gennaro, who in his dealings knew a practical and earthy English, would correct her hastily and beg her not to use such expressions. Then Elvira would titter furiously and say, My Stars, she was getting as wicked as Countess Ciano, wasn't she?

Elvira wanted to see society, especially American. She'd developed a thirst for night life. And no matter how

252

rich Papa Brazzi got from the black market, he'd still lock Elvira in every night at curfew time unless she got a respectable job. Elvira was attempting to get this job to get away from her family. With a job in the officers' club at the Bank of Naples, she hoped to snare herself a handsome American officer. All this Giulia guessed.

Neapolitans said that the gray modern slate-colored Bank of Naples had escaped bombing because North Italian bankers had bought off the pilots of American and British bombers. It was the only clean and solid building on Via Roma. Its whole front was bricked and buttressed off from the street, against having its brass and glass doors shattered from detonations. The rear entrance was through a crypt with a subterranean car park. Inside this cave were many Neapolitans, wearing a suitable manner to be hired as waitress or cashier. They were all murmuring to one another, but they became demure and formal when they expected the officer in charge of the club to appear at the head of the stairs.

Would they be fed three times a day by the Americans? What were the wages? The Americans could afford anything. They ought to get together like a trade union and force the Americans to accede to their demands. Giulia noticed among the feminine applicants girls who swaggered on Via Roma. The males were nearly all Neapolitans with spectacles and greased hair and a classic air of exasperation as though they'd been whipped by their families out of the library of the University of Naples in the middle of their doctor's dissertation. Gennaro and Giulia and Elvira took their place in the queue and waited in silent listening. A queue is an unnatural formation for Neapolitans, who like to swarm and catch as catch can.

Late, very late, perhaps to show the Neapolitans that they were a conquered people and not patients at a charity dispensary, a glass door opened in the wall of gray granite. The hundreds of petitioners fell into reverent silence and arranged their clothes and hair. There appeared two American officers in short monkey jackets of green cloth. Their breasts were barred with colored ribbons. There was a major built like a duck, his beard like gravel along the jowls resting on his collar. A cheery stomach butted the high waist of his jacket. With him was a sad young lieutenant carrying a clipboard. The lieutenant's glasses drooped over his nose. To Giulia he seemed an unhappy grandmother commissioned by mistake in the United States Army. Beside these two an interpreter looking like an osprey took up his position. The major made a pass in the air past his paunch with his jeweled hand. There sounded in the half-cellar a voice as rich and persuasive as a pie bursting with suet. The major stopped after every sentence, which the interpreter then translated to the crowd. Giulia had never heard anything quite like the English that the major used. She listened only to him, paying no attention to the sentence by sentence rendition of the interpreter:

"Mah deah Neahpolitan friends . . . for you ah mah friends, each an every one of yo. . . . We ah openin this here little club to give ouah pooah American officers a place to relax in. . . . But this heah club is also a friendly gesture to you, ouah Neapolitan friends. . . . Those of yo whom we find competent we ah goin to hiah as waiters or cashiers. . . . For when ouah Uncle Sam liberates Italy, he also takes thought of her suffrin people. . . . Theah'll be no partiality shown in the hirin or in the firin. . . . We know yoah reputation for bein lazy, my deah friends, and we ain't standin for none of yoah nonsense heah. . . . But ah just want to ask yo to play the game with me, and ah'll play ball with yo. . . . Ah come from a state in the Union that is as bighearted as she is big. . . . Now yoah wages will be ninety lire a day, and you can take home what sandwiches and pastry they is left at the close of the workin day . . . if they's any. . . . All't ah'll say heah is, if theah is inybody heah who won't work for ninety lire, why they is just plain ingrates to Uncle Sam, that's all. . . . They can go to theah homes right now. . . . We don't want no truck with them. . . . Now my deah friends, just form an orderly line and wait yoah turn for interview."

Half of the Neapolitans broke away from the mass and went out of the rear of the Bank of Naples. Under their breaths they mewed and spat and cursed. Those who'd decided to stay pushed up the little stairway past the custode and turned left along the cool dark walls, cloudy with the veins and strata of the stone. Then they milled through another corridor where the doors were tall and bronzy. Then they mounted a stairway with sweep and curve where once Fascist bankers climbed with their briefcases. On the second floor more brass doors gave into a room where a faun played over a lighted foun-

254

tain. Then came the vastest room Giulia'd ever seen outside of the movies, and lastly a narrower apartment where benches had been linked on a trestle to make a long bar. The windows were all arched and hung with valances of cream and green. This led through a small reception room with a pink piano to a door that said Office—Off Limits.

They were oddly silent for Neapolitans as they sat down in the deep green leather divans and looked at one another with that mutual suspicion of outer offices. Giulia and Gennaro and Elvira found a seat close to the office door on a long sofa, in which they seemed to drop into a well of cushions.

Then a girl ran in with a shriek and collapsed beside them. She was pursued by a brilliant-eyed man in the belted jacket and the loud trousers of Italian racing drivers. They introduced themselves as Wilma and Gino. Giulia measured Wilma with interest and sympathy. Wilma wasn't young any more, but she balanced the equation by a mockery of everything, herself included. She began at once talking to Giulia. She told Giulia that Gino wasn't so rich as lovers she'd had in Trieste and Tripoli, but that he was shrewder. Wilma chain-smoked, thieving cigarette after cigarette from Gino's waistcoat and stabbing at her lipstick charred butts with violet fingernails. Her laughter was low and one inch this side of spiteful. And Gino talked over her voice, saying that Wilma was a vecchia strega, how he'd been an interpreter for the Americans since Salerno, how they were really quite nice to work for; and when they saw that you did a little feathering of your own nest, they took it all in the spirit of business competition. In the affection between Wilma and Gino Giulia noticed something as bitter and close as mint under grass.

Wilma kept grabbing Giulia's hands and caressing them as she reminisced of high life in Trieste and Tripoli. Gino got into a conversation with Gennaro on fencing and swimming and calcio. In track, alas, Gino had hardened his arteries before his time. Wilma's mouth, except when she laughed, was a long generous sphincter of carmine. During all this badinage Elvira just sat leaning her chins on her bosom and gasping with delight that she was at last getting a taste of high society. But Wilma, whatever she was or had been, was a wise woman. Love

255

and tricks and shrewdness and irony dropped from her lips into Giulia's ear as most women burble platitudes. She told Giulia that no woman need ever condescend in this life; no, not even if she worked in a casino. Giulia never forgot what Wilma told her that morning.

The Officers' Club of the Peninsular Base Section opened on an afternoon in late December, 1943. The light of winter Naples crossed Via Roma, cut the standards on the balconies, and grazed the parquet of the dance floor. Wilma and Elvira sat behind high enclosed cash desks and sold books of chits for drinks. Giulia's post was a small throne behind a long directorial table with a silver salver of Spamwiches and chocolate éclairs. For seven hours it was her function and her duty to lift up these refreshments on a silver spatula and put them into the wax paper in the hand of the purchaser. She could look across the dance floor and watch Wilma at her cash desk. Wilma's pose was to lean Sapphically on her hand and lazily to accept cigarettes from officers.

The major had ordered all his girls out of their pretty dresses and into Mother Hubbards of the hue of discolored wallpaper. He did this, he said, because he knew the desires of men in wartime. His aim was to make his girls as mouselike as possible. At first Wilma and Giulia raged because the faded Mother Hubbards made them look like graduates of the Pompeii orphanage. But Giulia soon found out that at closing time at the bar it would have made no difference if she'd been wearing a washed-out pea pod. The officers came around anyway.

Of all the major's employees only Elvira was sad. She moped and mulled behind her cash desk. Nobody came to her to buy chits. So at the end of two weeks the major fired her, advising her to go up to the Anzio beachhead, where it was darker and the men were less fussy about what they looked at. Elvira returned to her family, to be locked up every night at curfew time. She said she'd hated the whole vulgar job from the start, and had only been talked into taking it because she was too goodhearted.

More men than women worked at PBS Club. The major said that Giulia and Wilma were simply the dash of sugar in the staff. There was a corps of waiters, tricked out in white ties and tails. Two bars functioned simultaneously, for the major roared out that what American

officers wanted for relaxation was a combination of Radio
City Music Hall, Minsky's, Jack Dempsey's, and the Silver
Dollar. What he meant by this Giulia never learned. And
the major, his sleeves rolled up, personally schooled the
Neapolitan bartenders till he said they could get a job
anywhere in New York. They were Enrico, always melancholy and almost sweetly pockmarked; and Demetrio, that
acute little rat who couldn't stop having children; and
Luigi, who rolled his eyes on either side of his huge nose
and bragged of his friendships with German officers and
sang "Firenze Stanotte"; and handsome Sergio, who'd
somehow got trapped in Naples from Torino and never
talked to anybody, but kept a diary and lived in the
vibrant and closed sweetness of his own nostalgia.

Then there were the waiters who shot across the
polished floor with their coattails clanging like gossips'
tongues, banging their trays on the bar and calling for
Eight Jeeen e Jooos over the orchestra. Of these there
was first of all Giulia's brother Gennaro, who kept himself
aloof from the rest. She never discovered where he got
his tails. Gennaro had taken to brilliantining his hair,
which glistened like phosphorous. He now spoke perfect
American, bragged much with the American officers,
called his sister keed or mouse or butch. Giulia watched
the American nurses gasping for Gennaro. And there
was Furio, the tiny Communist who was once a tenente
di vascello in the Regia Marina and spent his Fridays off at
party meetings in the Vomero. And there was Alfredo
and his mustaches, who'd made what he hoped was his
pile in a Brooklyn barbershop and had come back to
Naples to die in peace. But a bomb had got the house and
the family for which Alfredo'd slaved in the Brooklyn
barbershop. Alfredo said grazie too many times for a tip
of cigarettes. His bows to majors and colonels made his
chin almost touch the floor and his coattails lash up his
spine.

There was also a troop of Neapolitan ladies and gentlemen who did odd jobs about PBS Officers' Club. They
didn't belong to the white-collar crowd. Giulia soon got
bored with seven hours' sitting behind her sandwiches and
looking like a madonna, as the major had instructed her
to do. So she watched everything. She observed Gaetano
the electrician climb ladders in his sandals and replace
burnt-out bulbs in the chandeliers. From her table she

might also observe the sales talks and outraged nobility of Signora Anna Negri, who stood beside her showcase on her aching feet and sold miniatures of Capri or cameos especially tailored to the mothers of Americans.

The major's retinue reported to work at 1630 hours each afternoon. They trailed chilled and peeved up the sharp noble stairs to the second floor of the Banco di Napoli, each carrying his or her supper mozzarella and black bread and tomatoes and an egg wrapped in last night's newspaper. Giulia used to listen to them talk as she held her own black market supper tight against her small sharp breasts and marched up the staircase. How they talked! They couldn't live on the ninety lire a day the major was paying, nor on the leftover smelly old cheese sandwiches, nor on the old chocolate éclairs which they were allowed to carry out of the club when the cream became like pus. As Giulia mounted that staircase every afternoon, all of Naples in the winter of 1943-44 was around her ears: babies freezing because there wasn't any firewood, American-issue pasta that turned to gray entrails when you put it in the pot, the sugar at wild prices, whose office boss (God love him!) was buried alive in last night's bombings, what girl had finally given up her reputation and gone with the Allies, the rate of Negro children born to Sicilian women. Giulia knew only that she was numb from it all. Then she would put on her Mother Hubbard and sit down behind her sandwiches and play tit-tat-toe with an American captain till her eyes sang with pain, or listened to an American colonel who resembled her Papa tell her why he hadn't won the mayoralty of Sioux Falls, wherever that was.

Both Giulia and Wilma had their own following. Around her cash desk Wilma attracted young airplane drivers whose tongues began to drip after their eighth Martini. For Wilma's benefit they fought all over again the bombing sorties out of Foggia. They gestured and goaded one another into new heights of theatrical enterprise in their tales, as little boys vie to entertain a little girl on the sidewalk. And Wilma also had a patronage that intrigued Giulia. These were bright and disillusioned parachute captains, majors from rich Baltimore families, lieutenants who wrote verses. With all these characters Wilma held court. She was magnificent, Giulia thought. Wilma knew what was in God's mind when He created
258

Woman. When Wilma entertained her boys at her cash desk, she leaned slightly back from them in tender hauteur, her eyes mocking and affectionate from inside their azure mascara shadows. Wilma's mouth was too big, but it was in such constant motion of eloquence that Giulia was never sure how large it was. And sometimes Wilma's laugh of protest came through the dance band, a trumpet all her own. Giulia saw that Wilma loved men. Therefore men loved Wilma. Or when no men were clustered about Wilma's cash desk, Gino would visit her from his office. He was liaison between all the Neapolitans and the mournful lieutenant who was the major's assistant. By privilege of his caste Gino wore only a turtle-necked sweater and tweed trousers. He'd talk long and low to Wilma, their faces scarcely apart. Often he'd make love to her with a speed and surety and intimacy which caused Giulia to turn her face away. The spectacle of this light bandit love made her sad for hours.

When Giulia first took her job at PBS Club, Mamma had all sorts of cautions to her daughter, reminding her that Italian girls were trained to handle men. Perhaps Giulia, to be on the safe side, ought always to carry a small dagger? Giulia laughed painedly and Wilma shrieked at the idea as they sat sipping coffee by Mamma's couch. For indeed Giulia did carry about her an armor deceptive as a cobweb. Officers used to lean over her by the hour. They asked her what was the Italian word for love. They told her that she was as lovely as their sister Elaine. Sometimes at closing time when they were tight Giulia noticed something painful and cruel in their eyes, but it faded when they looked at the down on her cheeks. She knew what they wanted of her, but no one ever framed it to her. And Giulia came to learn much of the world's men simply by observing them. She doubted that she'd marry Pasquale when he came back from his imprisonment in Oran.

One evening in August, 1944, she was sitting on her small enclosed throne, the cash desk of the bar at PBS Officers' Club. The boys were jammed up four deep at the bar; the air was silky gray with cigarette smoke. The officers kept up a roaring and a laughing over their drinks, a curtain which was in turn pierced by the public-address system piping in the orchestra from the dance floor. For the major was determined that in no place in the club should there be any silence. He told the sad lieutenant who was his office boy (and the lieutenant told Giulia) that they were endeavoring to avoid that stuffiness which always endangers a men's club. By now Giulia was used to American noises and to the American idea of living loudly and in public.

The dais on which she sat was so walled that in her six-hour shift she could cross or uncross her legs without anybody seeing the results. At her right hand she had a stack of chit books and a lined roster to be signed by all who bought her tickets. At her left was an English dictionary and a copy of *Uncle Tom's Cabin*. She'd make her sale with an automatic swift smile, then reimmerse herself in her novel. The tumult of the bar would die in her ears, and she could forget that she was the only woman in a vaulted roomful of drinking men. She was halfway through *Uncle Tom*. Next she'd line up *Gone With the Wind*, which she possessed in both English and Italian. By collating both copies she figured that in another month her English would have arrived at perfection. Long ago she'd dropped the Oxford accent she'd learned from her maestra at the liceo.

On this August night the officers hadn't bothered her. In eight months at PBS Club she'd polished up the brush-off tactics Wilma had taught her. But just now opposite her leaning on the bar was a most simpatico person. On one tab of his collar he had a silver cross. By a little questioning Giulia proved to herself what she'd guessed when she first saw him—that he was a priest. He was drinking gin and juice. He minded his own business, except that every so often he gave her a kind smile. He spoke to her in both English and Latin. When she got stuck on a word in her novel, he'd explain it to her, poising his brown finger on the pages of her book. This chaplain's hair was cropped to the bone. His face had the glow of a child. To Giulia he was a contrast with all the other American officers at the bar, whose faces were angry or soiled or lined or predatory.

"Have you many Simon Legrees in America?" Giulia asked, looking up from her book. Her forehead was resting on her hand.

"Oh lots," the priest said laughing. "But we've taken their horsewhips away from them."

"I take this book home with me every night," said
260

Giulia. "Last night I read where Little Eva dies, and I cried myself to sleep."

The priest laughed again and rocked back and forth on his combat boots.

"Giulia, you're great. I wish some of the bobby-soxers in my Boston parish could see you. They wouldn't believe you existed. . . . Crying yourself to sleep over a book! . . . American women used to do that fifty years ago . . . but not now."

She laid her novel face down and searched his face. The bar was weighted with the stifling August air. She felt the tiny ringlets fan over her moist brow.

"Am I so different, Father?" she asked earnestly.

"Well, frankly, Giulia, you're out of this world. . . ."

Then his face rushed a wild crimson, and he set down his glass and turned away.

"Good night, Giulia, and God bless you."

"Good night, Father, and thank you."

She watched him leave the bar through its lurid smoke. He was with the 3rd Division, which was crowding the streets of Naples. She'd heard that soon there'd be an invasion of southern France. That was why in August, 1944, you couldn't turn around in Naples for the americani. There were more of them here now than she remembered when the city fell in October of last year. Giulia sighed and resumed her novel. She found that her thoughts were still with the priest, not with Signora Harriet Beecher Stowe. So she shut her book and thrust it under her dictionary.

Then there came to the only open space of the bar a florid major clasping the waist of an American nurse. Giulia'd never got used to seeing women in officers' greens and wearing lieutenants' bars. Most of the American nurses had been gracious to her, saying that she was a dream. But this major and this nurse exuded an ugly reckless giddiness of alcohol. The nurse snuggled into the major and chuckled. She was a stout blonde, her cap set madly on her dyed hair. She had also a double chin. She began to size up Giulia, going all over her dreary Mother Hubbard with eyes like a parrot's.

"Sell me some chits, baby," the major said. "Don't just sit there and look like a doll."

"Please sign the paper," Giulia said, pushing it and a pen toward him.

"Well, just who does she think she is?" the nurse said, blowing cigarette smoke into Giulia's face.

Giulia's eyes watered, but she said nothing.

"A mighty pretty piece of quail," the major said to the nurse, indicating Giulia with a whistle.

"Herbert," the nurse said, "don't give me any of that crap that she reminds you of your daughter. I've heard that crap out of you before."

The nurse leaned her head on the major's shoulder and closed her eyes. Her double chin bobbled while she swallowed her drink. Then she leaned close to Giulia.

"Why don't you use lipstick, girlie?"

"I have naturally good color," Giulia said. "And lipstick is hard to get in Naples this year. And if I put too much on, my mother would have me wash it off . . ."

"Well, listen to that now," said the nurse. "Don't get on your high horse with me, girlie. I have to take enough crap on the ward in the daytime. I didn't come here to have the likes of you insult me. . . . I'm a commissioned officer in the American Army in case you don't realize it, girlie. I've a good mind to report you to the military manager. . . . I could have you thrown out on Via Roma with the rest of them . . ."

"Oh dry up, Mary," the major said. "Why don't you buy her some lipstick from your own PX?"

"I'd croak first," the nurse said, her double chin jiggling. "Let's get the hell out of this flea joint. . . . Get the jeep and drive me back to Aversa. . . . I'm all sweaty. I can't beat this damn heat."

"And just mind your *p*'s and *q*'s with me, girlie," she added to Giulia. "I'd hate to tell you what I think of you Ginso women."

The nurse and her major went out of the bar nudging one another, the major protesting that he hadn't made eyes at Giulia. Giulia watched their exit. Then she laid her head in her hands. Only for an instant, for the major insisted that his girls look sharp on duty.

Through the open windows of the Bank of Naples looking out on Via Roma the sultry music of the Neapolitan night came up to Giulia, an undertone discernible even through the rumble of the officers' bar. She could all but distinguish the press of the women's heels on the pavements beneath her, could almost see the Neapolitans lounging in doorways and the scugnizz' peddling things till they must leave the streets at curfew hour. This murmur of her own town had a certain meaning for Giulia. The simulated gaiety of the Americans in their bar had none. She was weary. The very repose of sitting and selling chits or sandwiches for eight months was beginning to fatigue her. Wilma and the other girls could break the monotony by ducking down behind the cassa for a quick cigarette. Lately she noticed that she'd a headache when she walked away from the club around midnight. Perhaps it was the war. Perhaps it was Naples in August, 1944. Perhaps she was what the americani called fed up. But it did seem to her that her life was assuming the quality of a grinning automaton who worked on the four-o'clock shift. She knew that she was giving nothing of herself, that she was turning into a slightly stale vase of flowers. . . .

"Buck up, Giulia," said an officer, buying some chits. "Life is real, life is earnest."

"Yes," Giulia said, lowering her eyes.

"So ye won't talk to me tonight?" the officer said, waggling a finger. "Okay, don't. I'll go and shoot the breeze with Wilma. She's naughty. . . . I like em naughty. Why don'tcha wise up and get naughty too?"

He left her in an irritation. Giulia sold more books of chits, but all the time her mind was running in its own groove. She thought of her fidanzato Pasquale. Every week his letters came from the P/W enclosure in Oran. They were flatulent and lamenting, living over the years 1940 and 1941. They were full of noble whining and quotations from Leopardi. He kept telling her that Italy and the Italians were done for.

And Giulia thought of the Neapolitan girls she'd grown up with. Either they'd gone giggling over to the Allies for what they could get, or else their mothers had locked them up for the duration. She knew that the lives of all Neapolitans had been cut in two. They might all be said to have died; yet she doubted if they'd had a rebirth, though their bodies went right on living. Only herself seemed unchanged, moving in some orbit of her own that had no relation to any reality.

On this night in August, 1944, Giulia was lonely. She was the only Neapolitan girl who was hewing to her own destiny, as though the war had never been. Thus now in her breast she felt a pulse of fierceness and resentment

263

when she looked at the Naples of August, 1944. There was nothing here now that offered her any consolation or the old quiet delight she once took from life: the sip of a glass of new wine, the walks with her girl friends (she'd none now, though she visited many), and that old pleasure she used to get from combing out her hair before going to bed. All these simple processes and habits had become routine and zestless to her. She felt like a starving person who has lost the taste for food. She wondered if she were dying of staleness.

"O Dio mio," she said fiercely to herself, "su, su! Coraggio! . . ."

She wondered to what a pretty pass she'd come that often now she carried on dialogues with herself. And it was all very simple, for she saw clean through the rhetoric of Italian. She wished to be loved. This craving had crystallized in Giulia during her eight months at PBS Club.

But she wished to be loved according to the old standards of honor passed down through generations of Italian mothers. She wasn't interested in something mad and fragrant for a few nights, such as she saw all about her in Naples of August, 1944. Before the fall of Naples she'd been on the right path to be loved according to her lights. She saw the purpose of her training, to be an Italian girl of softness and dignity. Nearly all Italian women had these traits. But many had abandoned them in the catastrophe that was rending Italy. Giulia had abandoned nothing. Now as a result of still living as she'd been taught to live, she found herself like an island, off by herself. She wondered if she were mad. She feared she'd schooled her soul for something that could never again materialize in Italy. She was objective enough to know that in a normal time she'd have had a quietly happy life. She'd have been a good wife and a good mother. That was what women did best. But how were these things to be now? Sometimes she got such a perspective on herself that she seemed a quiet feast set on a table to which no man would ever come. Now the food was growing cold, and all the loving pains of the cook were wasted. . . .

Giulia couldn't resist laying her face in her hands. She felt her tears squeezing through her tightly locked fingers.

"Why you're crying?" a voice spoke to her. "Ma Lei non deve piangere così amaramente. . . . Perchè?"

She looked up and made a grab for the handkerchief that an American captain whom she'd never seen was holding out to her. She peered swiftly up and down the bar. Everyone was drunk and talking wildly. No one had noticed her disgraceful giving-way. The tears in her eyes stopped quite suddenly. She turned away her head from the American captain and blew her nose. Reality returned to her in wave upon wave of mortification.

"Metterei volentieri mille fazzoletti Sua disposizione," the captain said.

Her joy at being addressed in formal Italian by an American made Giulia weak. She gripped both sides of her cash desk, smiled stupidly, and returned his handkerchief to him. She reached blindly for her green bag to take out her own.

"You mustn't speak Italian to me," she said. "Among my American friends I speak American."

"Now who taught you that pretty speech?" the captain said. "I know you're too sharp a girl to think that the people who come to this club are your friends. So don't begin with a hypocrisy . . . let's be honest with one another from the start, shall we?"

"Yes," said Giulia, "I do so want someone to be honest with."

The brazen sound of this speech in English (she still thought in Italian) stunned her. She felt her color coming up over the shapeless collar of her Mother Hubbard.

"Yes," the captain said, setting down his glass, "let us be completely honest with one another. . . . I'll be honest with you. You're the loveliest girl I've ever laid eyes on. And your loveliness comes . . . from being . . . just there. . . . I walked into this smelly strained room; expecting to find nothing. And I find you . . . just . . . there . . . how wonderful. . . . And I'm not drunk either."

This American captain was the ugliest man Giulia had ever looked upon. His face was square. In his combat boots he looked like a wooden robot. His hair was gray at the temples. Yet when he smiled or gestured with his long gentle hands, or when he spoke, it seemed to her that granite dissolved into music. He was so hideous that he made her want to laugh, as at a gnome in a fairy tale. Yet her laughter at him turned back on herself. In his first contact with her this captain had beckoned her into a peace in which he himself moved. This peace wasn't spe-

265

cious. Giulia sensed it was a solid block which only his death could shatter. Within five minutes she thought that this captain had always been resident some place inside her, had chosen this moment to step out and introduce himself. For he had a way of allaying her doubts before she uttered them. He knew her, and she knew him, as though all their lives they'd instinctively been preparing for one another.

"You're smiling now," the captain said. "That's better. Tell me that you never smiled at anyone that way before."

"No," said Giulia, hardly daring to look at him, "I never have."

For the rest of the evening till the bar closed Giulia and the American captain talked together. Quietly, when the spirit moved them to say something; casually, without effort. He leaned opposite her on the bar. Never too near or too familiar, because the externals weren't necessary. Something else in them was touching. And there was respect for each other's privacy, like two civilized people bowing in a maelstrom. The bar ceased to exist for them. Giulia continued to sell chits. Even when she took her eyes from him to count chits or change or to speak to the officer purchasing, she knew that this captain was with her. From this moment on he wouldn't leave her. Some force had come up under her and was buoying her up as she'd never swum before. And she'd look into that face with no redeeming trait of beauty to make a man desirable. Then a laugh of the wildest joy would seem to smother her. He responded to everything she thought or said as though, well, that was exactly what he'd expected her to think or say.

"We're not mad," the captain said. "Sanity is so marvelous."

Yet Giulia in her bed that night was sure she was mad. She laughed and cried till the sun came up over Naples. Looking at her sorry face in the morning, she laughed again and fell back on her bed.

"Sì, sono pazza," she said. "Non potrei essere così felice. . . ."

That afternoon Giulia knew she'd gone mad, but in a precise and scheming way. She put on and took off nearly all her dresses. She experimented with her hair, ending by doing it the old way with the delta of ringlets around her brow. Mamma from her couch kept calling out, Whatever on earth was the matter with Giulia? And Giulia only smiled from before her mirror, her mouth full of hairpins. Finally she put on her green frock, her green shoes, her green Meravigliosa hat with the green bow. Then she tucked under her arm the copy of *Uncle Tom's Cabin* and the English dictionary. Mamma, inspecting her, pointed out that today was neither Sunday nor a giorno di festa. To which Giulia replied that, given the right frame of mind, every day was a giorno di festa.

She went down into the streets of Naples. In August, 1944, the city had a smell of baking stone shot through with spicy tang of mandarini sold in the corner wagons. In that salita where Giulia lived the corrugated iron walls of the public urinal impregnated the air with an acrid fume poignant as history. She walked quickly along humming to herself that tune "Polvere di Stelle" by Hoagy Carmichael. She swung her green bag so gaily that shoeshine boys in the public garden of Piazza Municipio turned round at their stands and called out to her invitations that had an American tone of provocation. She had also to pass the palazzo where an American port battalion was quartered; the GI's were hanging out of their balcony windows in their undershirts, chewing gum and swapping with one another observations on current events and Neapolitan girls with whom they were shacking. Giulia's passage provoked a madrigal of whistles. The sentinel at the barbed wire, a GI of more feudal heritage, presented arms to her. Ordinarily she'd have cast down her eyes and felt her body go taut, but today she smiled and looked him straight in the face.

"Come stare? Tu molto buono," the sentinel said, shifting his carbine back to its shoulder sling.

"Grazie assai," Giulia said.

Wilma and Gino were living together in two rooms on Via Diaz. They were quite comfortable by pooling their salaries from PBS Club and by drawing American rations that Gino'd promoted from the quartermaster. They were easily the happiest unwed couple in all Naples. Their prosperity and their love were supported by the Americans, whom they both cherished with the cynical devotion of people below stairs.

This afternoon Giulia found them where she'd hoped she would, taking the sun from their second-story balcony, leaning on the railing and holding hands. They talked in-

267

cessantly to each other, Gino's mouth against Wilma's hidden ear, whispering ironies and passions. Gino was wearing his turtle-necked sweater and a pair of white flannels. His brilliantined curls wriggled like garter snakes in the Neapolitan sunlight. Wilma had on a blue silk kimono. The white globes of her breasts twinkled in the sun. Her blue hair was low over her forehead; her rouged and mascaraed face made her features sharp and clear to Giulia, who was standing thirty feet below the doting couple. Wilma sent up her scream of welcome.

"Ho bisogno di te," Giulia called up to the balcony, beckoning urgently up to Wilma.

"Giulietta, aspetta un po'!" Wilma cried and vanished from the balcony, roguishly tucking her kimono about her creamy shoulders.

"Ciao, Giulietta," Gino said, leaning out over Giulia.

"Ciao, Gino," said Giulia.

After a while Wilma appeared on the sidewalk and took Giulia's arm. They waved good-by to Gino on his balcony and whisked off along Via Medina at a businesslike clip. Wilma'd put on a dramatic hat with a veil and had applied more paint so that her generous flamboyant face glistened like porcelain under the veil. With her breezy tact she didn't even inquire what Giulia wanted of her. Obviously she remembered her ancient promise to be Giulia's chaperone in any emergency.

"Come mai sei così cambiata in una notte?" Wilma said chuckling.

By this one sentence Giulia knew that this wise girl was in on her secret. Wilma smoked a cigarette through the mesh of her veil, giving her the appearance of a network on fire. They turned up Via Diaz, arriving at the Intendenza di Finanza Building. In August, 1944, this was the headquarters of the Peninsular Base Section. Without any difficulty they got by the MP and into the cool foyer, for Wilma had a pass. As they seated themselves on the bench by the information booth, Giulia suddenly asked what would Wilma think if she married an American? Wilma gave out a jolly cackle, patted her hand, and said that Giulia for quite some time had been spoiling for an American.

They didn't say much while they waited. Giulia's body went into her usual meek relaxation. Inside however she felt like a faggot of dynamite. Wilma smoked two ciga-

268

rettes. At all officers who passed by she gave a benign look. For by now Wilma and Giulia knew every American officer in Naples who drank at PBS Club. Some stopped and kissed Wilma's hand and exchanged veiled obscenities with her. And they bowed and said Hi to Giulia. Wilma held a little salon in the cortile.

At seventeen hours the court filled up with officers and GI's coming down from the offices above. The GI's went shooting out into the streets of Naples for their mess and the long questing Neapolitan evening. The officers carried themselves more stuffily. They moved in tight groups, talking shop and vengeance and promotions. For the PBS officers were quite different from the combat officers who descended on Naples for their leaves from the front. Giulia watched them all go by from under her green bonnet. It was like counting sheep. She peered quickly at the faces of each, then lowered her eyes to the green bows of her tiny slippers.

"Dov'è, dov'è?" Wilma whispered nervously.

She was taking it almost as hard as Giulia herself.

After a stretch of watching faces and confessing to a sinking feeling that maybe He wasn't coming after all, and wondering whether she'd gone too far, Giulia suddenly planted her elbow against Wilma's fruity flank.

"Eccolo che viene," Giulia said.

Wilma gave a sigh and gathered herself up in her noblest manner.

Her Captain came gravely toward them. He'd been planting his khaki cap over his right ear. Catching sight of them, he dropped his hands to his sides, then squared out in a gesture of surprise and welcome. His ugly face fired into a smile. Giulia heard Wilma sigh again, gustily.

"Ma! . . ." said Wilma, and Giulia had no idea what she meant by this.

Giulia made Her Captain a curtsy of humility and joy. She introduced him to Wilma, who broke out into praise and effusions. It was one of those things that Wilma did gorgeously well, pretending that she was merely renewing the acquaintance of the person presented to her. But all the while (Giulia knew) from under the veil Wilma's merciless witty eyes were giving Her Captain an appraisal like the last judgment. Nothing escaped Wilma. It was for this reason Giulia'd brought her along: to comply with South Italian standards of decorum, and also to check on her own perceptions.

"Ma parla così bene italiano!" Wilma squealed graciously.

For a few minutes they all three spoke in Italian. Wilma and Giulia's Captain outdid one another in gallantries and compliments. Giulia just watched and listened, her gray eyes going from one face to the other. Inside she felt proud and gay, for it was already clear the Wilma and Her Captain liked and respected each other. Buon indizio. Both excelled in a mellow worldly Italian chatter of the formalest sort. Both realized that conversation of this civilized order was a means to an end. Giulia herself was by no means so glib. She was accustomed to sit in a corner and reflect gravely to herself. Yet she derived a delight in watching Wilma and Her Captain hit it off.

Then Her Captain took Giulia's arm ever so lightly, as though a feather had insinuated itself into the crook of her elbow. And he observed to Wilma in English.

"I've been thinking of my girl all day long."

"You are making no mistake," said Wilma, whose English was slow and stately.

There was a pause, seemingly contrived by Wilma, in which Giulia and Her Captain looked at each other. Their eyes interlaced in hunger and questioning, and Giulia's small doubts were again put at rest. There came to her again that odd mad peace, that sense of being pulled out of the tempest and the dark, of flying upward into the sun. Giulia felt giddy, and she heard Wilma laugh at Her Captain:

"Carina la nostra bimba, eh?"

"Ma sì," said the captain. "Ma sì. Un tesoro. . . ."

"Ciao, Giulia," the captain said.

"Ciao, capitano," Giulia answered. The words came from deep within her.

"I invite you both to tea," the captain said.

He placed himself in the middle, took both their arms, and they walked out into Naples. For Giulia the sun had never been so warm, the browns and grays of Napoli so rich. She looked at the thousands of Neapolitans scurrying on Via Roma, screaming and gesticulating and worrying; and she found herself blessing them all: the weary widows, the frenetic scugnizz', the anxious studenti and

270

studentesse burbling about their examinations and the spleen of their professori. All the while during their walk Her Captain and Wilma chattered of tiny nothings and amenities. Giulia didn't feel as though she were left out of the conversation, but rather that with their words they were making a garland for her. They were both aware of her.

The three entered the Galleria Umberto and made for a café. The bars were just opening. In the center of the Galleria, the focus of the cross that was its floor plan, a Neapolitan in the middle of a crowd talked against Russia and Il Communismo. A trio of Italian soldiers hissed and made scissors motions toward the hair of a girl in conference with American GI's. Children scooted along the walls selling cameos and carrying trays of fried fish and dough. And through the Galleria ran a rumble as though they were all underground. For the first time in a year Giulia could look at all these human faces and feel that maybe there weren't too many people in the world after all.

They sat down at the wicker table of a café on the pavement of the Galleria. Giulia had never appeared in public before without Mamma or Papa. Her Captain helped her shed her green coat over the back of her chair. For Wilma and herself he ordered a torta, a dish of ice cream, and an orangeade. Wilma lit into whatever was put in front of her, gossiping without pause. She and Giulia's Captain discussed Badoglio, Hitler, and American movies. It wasn't the sort of discussion in which Giulia was at home. But she listened and smiled and shifted her eyes from one to the other as though she were a spectator at a tennis match. In former times she'd have thought herself a nitwit not to be able to engage in their repartee, but now she knew it wasn't really necessary. She felt like closing her eyes and just listening.

"This is a conversation piece," Her Captain told her.

"A what?" Giulia asked, reaching for her dictionary.

"A way for ladies and gentlemen to pass their time when they've nothing better to do."

"Must I learn how to do it?" Giulia asked worriedly.

"I wish you wouldn't," the captain said gravely. "I don't want you to be a blue stocking."

"Blue stockings?" said Giulia, looking down at her own. "Do American girls wear those?"

She suddenly felt frightened. Both of them might be playing with her.

"You just be Giulia," the captain said. "No American girl could do that, you see."

Then Wilma changed her rhythm and got off into a long Italianate speech of set pattern, in which she enumerated Giulia's qualities, as though she were preaching a funeral sermon. She spoke feelingly of Giulia's reserve, piety, industry, and frugality. Then she finished off with a conundrum twist, that she doubted whether Giulia would marry an American. They weren't fine-grained enough for Giulia, Wilma thought.

"No?" said the captain, lighting Wilma's cigarette.

Giulia saw herself as a statue in green hat, green dress, and green shoes, perched on an auction block. She began to feel ill at ease and wished that Wilma would stop talking. She began almost to wish that Her Captain weren't there either, that she could be alone in her room and brood for a little while. It seemed to her that an issue was being forced and shaped by conventions, when on the face of it it was so easy and so natural. Then she began to wonder if there weren't something more than a little mad about herself, too secret and private and egoistic. But at this very moment Her Captain reached over, took the tips of her fingers, and squeezed them lightly.

"Giulietta is not of this world," Wilma said laughing.

"She's not worldly," the captain corrected.

And they walked in their threesome back along Via Roma. It was time for Giulia and Wilma to climb the stairs of the Bank of Naples, slip into their chaste Mother Hubbards, and go on duty for the evening. But at the entrance to the club Wilma suddenly said grazie and arrivederla to the captain and dashed upstairs, leaving them alone together. Giulia was dazed and embarrassed. She prepared to say arrivederla to Her Captain and follow Wilma. But Her Captain laid his long hands on her shoulders. She saw a convulsion cross his dark hard features. Then he kissed her fingers.

"My darling," he said, "it mustn't frighten you that I love you."

Giulia turned slowly away in hot tears. She groped her way up the stairs like a blind girl.

Reversing the principles of Italian courtship, Giulia

took the initiative because Her Captain was a straniero. She suddenly found herself so strong and resourceful that she feared she might be wearing the figurative pants, like those American women who appeared on the streets of Naples with slacks emphasizing their buttocks. In this period of Giulia's love Wilma was her second, embodying all the traditional functions of duenna, cicisbeo, and arbiter. It was a role that Wilma loved because her nature gloried in all duplicities. At thirty-one Wilma had a heart as rich and scheming as a dowager or matriarch of eighty. If Giulia in her poised timidity made the balls, it was Wilma who aimed them and fired them to their mark.

The process was simply this: gradually to lead Her Captain by threads of silk into Giulia's house, where his intentions would be sounded out. If he passed all the Neapolitan tests, he'd then be secured to the household with chains of steel. Her Captain, knowing Italian and the Italians, saw clearly what was going on behind the scenes and grinned within himself. He suffered himself to be led to the slaughter, as cheerful as a sacrificial heifer. He never made any of the breaks or gaucheries perpetrated by most Americans when they enter the European marital labyrinth.

Giulia's brother Gennaro was the first hurdle to leap, a prickly one in his position as Younger Brother. Gennaro still worked evenings as a waiter at PBS Club. In one year Giulia'd seen him change from something adored and gilded into a bitter and handsome Neapolitan, out for Number One. He dealt in American cigarettes and food. He was now quite rich. Giulia believed that he was the lover of an American WAC captain. He kept his job at the club only to maintain some respectability in Mamma's eyes. Giulia of course (and Papa to a lesser extent) had no illusions about Gennaro.

It was Wilma, the great fixer, who delivered the first coup and forstalled any nonsense from Gennaro. In the major's office at the Bank of Naples she presented Giulia's Captain to Giulia's brother. Five minutes later she reported to Giulia that the encounter had been as economical and efficacious as lightning. The captain had offered Gennaro a cigarette and lit it. They'd looked at one another like boxers in their corners. Then, Wilma said, Gennaro had folded his hands on his breast in Neapolitan

273

exhortation and had said in his brand-new business Americanese:

"Captain, you know my sister is strictly a ragazza per bene?"

"That fact has always been uppermost in my mind," the captain said.

"And are you going to take her to America with you as your wife?"

"I don't look upon your sister as a week-end vacation," the captain had said, bristling at the directness, yet aware that it was necessary.

Two days later things got going like a clockwork juggernaut. Giulia's Mamma invited Giulia's Captain to coffee. The affair followed the rules for the first formal encounter of all parties to the imminent transaction. There were present Papa, Mamma, Gennaro, Giulia, Wilma, Gino, and Elvira the dowd. To mark the austerity of the occasion Giulia's ninety-year-old paternal grandmother was brought in from Caserta. This old lady was there to play the role of devil's advocate, lecturing on the risks of marriage and citing fearful examples of Neapolitan girls who'd been betrayed by Americans and Negroes. In honor to the occasion, angina or no, Mamma got out of her sheepskin slippers and rose from her couch. She forgot about her heart condition and rustled about the apartment in black silk, giving instructions on the disposition of the coffee service and reminiscing on how such matters were carried off in Firenze when she was a girl. Wilma brewed the coffee (American) strong and black. She'd also stolen from PBS Club several dozen éclairs and sandwiches made of Spam. These were all set formally on silver trays of Mamma's dowry.

When Giulia's Captain, precisely at sixteen hours, knocked on the apartment door, he was admitted by Gennaro to a scene as stylized as a Chinese play. On the couch sat Mamma her double chin and moles propped over her black silk gown, her fingers queenly with rings. She didn't look at the captain till he was presented to her. At Mamma's right hunched the grandmother in mauve lace, muttering to herself the part she was to play and peering about with bleary Cassandra eyes. Papa paced up and down the salotto with a thick bitten cigar in his hand. He wore his gold watch chain. Giulia sat demurely by herself on a leather ottoman. She must pretend that she had

274

nothing at all to do with the ceremonies, that she was a timid and nubile slave girl about to be sold to the highest bidder. She'd known this role since she was a tiny girl. But she'd never imagined that some day it would come her turn to play it.

The introductory sallies and pleasantries took five minutes. Papa in his excitement was lordly and dictatorial. Once he wept. The entire trope was conducted in Italian, everyone using the Lei form, which is sometimes thorny for Neapolitans of the middle class. The paternal grandmother kept lapsing into dialect. Gennaro occasionally lapsed into choice Americanese. Papa, as a kind of marital toastmaster, made his introductory remarks, keyed to Naples in August, 1944. He spoke of the collapse of fascism, of the liberating Allies. Then he became eloquent on prices and the black market. This second section of his prepared discourse was punctuated by comments and illustrative examples from Gennaro and Gino.

Next it was Mamma's turn. She folded her delicate hands in her great lap. In her wheezy voice she confessed that Giulia had been engaged to a Neapolitan sottotenente called Pasquale. But that person was to be considered dead because he was an unrepentant Fascist and a prisoner of war at Oran. Pasquale's family had released Giulia from her bond. Then Mamma launched into Giulia and Giulia's upbringing. She gave a picture of Giulia's fault's and virtues. But since Giulia was a ragazza seria, her virtues outweighed her faults. The captain was invited to form the opinion that whoever wed Giulia was getting a treasure.

To all this Giulia's Captain smiled and nodded whenever Mamma gasped for breath:

"Ehhhhh, sì, gentile signora. . . ."

Then there was the third and grim act before the refreshments could be served. The paternal grandmother talked for twenty minutes, with gestures, on vice among young women. After its initial hoarseness her voice was as great as Duse's, falling in periods and strophes through the dingy apartment. She sniffed at Neapolitan trash that walked Via Roma, but discounted these girls as having always been cattive. Then she mentioned a higher percentage of girls who had once been good, but now prostituted themselves to the Allies per qualche scopo. She whispered of a lurid marriage in which a Neapolitan girl had

275

imagined herself legally joined to an American MP, only to discover that they'd been wed outside the church, and now had a child on the way without any legal proof of who was the father. But the paternal grandmother finished in radiance and optimism, picturing a tiny percentage of good Italian girls who'd shut themselves up in their houses waiting till the right man came along. And to all of this Giulia's Captain made the proper comment: "Ma si figuri un po', che strazi, che sofferenze. . . ."

Everybody relaxed after the speeches were over. Giulia from her ottoman smiled on Her Captain. The captain and Papa and Gino and Gennaro had some men's talk, weighty and discerning. Giulia and Wilma withdrew to the kitchen and whisked out the coffee and the sweets. Mamma allowed the captain to kiss her cheek, under a mole. Everybody praised everybody else. The air twittered with Italian delight. The world was good after all. And the paternal grandmother, in reaching greedily for her ninth éclair, fell into the hammered silver tray and got chocolate icing all over her lavender lace.

Now that she'd complied with all the formalities, Giulia was free of certain restrictions, though she was bound by others. The worst machinations were over. She might now, for example, take walks with Her Captain if Wilma came along. Once even Mamma, angina and all, turned up as the captain's guest in a box for *Rigoletto* at the San Carlo. But O Dio mio, Giulia could go neither alone nor in company to Her Captain's apartment on Via Santa Brigida. In point of fact she shouldn't be alone with him anywhere anytime. But Wilma was an indulgent and winking chaperone. Often she contrived to relieve Giulia of her cash desk at the club for one hour at a time. Then Giulia would slip out the back way and meet Her Captain in Piazza Municipio, in the public garden full of rustling figures aimlessly wandering, full of moonlight and queues before the urinals. Then Giulia had one full hour alone with Her Captain. They'd walk hand in hand along Via Caracciolo. The bay was cobalt under the August moonlight. He'd point out to her the shipping that teemed on the water, the landing craft for infantry, sharp metal wedges that rode low on the tide, the sulking hospital ships.

It was on Via Caracciolo that Giulia got her first kiss.

"I think often at night," she said, "that I must lose you. I'm too happy. . . ."

They were leaning by a little altar to Neptune in a niche with sculpted conch shells. Below them the fishermen had beached their boats on a mole, wooden-bellied crescents of tar piled along one another like dead whales. Sometimes the light of a motorboat slashed their faces. In an interlude of darkness he tilted up her chin and covered her mouth with his. He drew in her lower lip like a little fig. Giulia was inundated by a new sensation. Concentric circles flowed out from her heart till her whole small body shook. Her hand went around his neck, and they swayed together in the hot darkness. His fingers slipped up from her waist. She felt she was being invaded with a warmth terrible and sweet, a presentiment of dying with delight. Her breath choked up in her throat; she felt that she was being crushed. Something red and beaconlike flickered in her mind, crying Not Yet, Not Yet. With a violence, not of revulsion, but to keep her mind intact, she released herself.

"Puritan," he said. "By God, you'll be both wife and mistress, Giulia."

"We must be getting back," she said in joy and terror.

In the next days Her Captain seemed to have sloughed off most of his marvelous peace. He chafed at the politics and meanness of base section life. He said he hadn't been happy since he left his tank outfit. Each day he told her of friends killed a few hundred kilometers to the north of them. Then he began to lecture her on her adjustment to American life. He told her sadly that to be happy as his wife in America she must convert her personality. He said she was too utterly dependent on him. That an American wife was something quite different from an Italian wife, shut up in the house with her children. His words hurt her, though she never told him so.

"And it's this paradox that saddens me," he said. "I fell in love with you, Giulia, because you're something apart from all cheapness. You're everything that women have always insisted that they were, yet rarely succeeded in being. I wonder if in America you could stay that way."

"You think I'm not real?" she said hotly. "You think me incapable of being myself anywhere?"

"I know, I know . . . but the noblest Italian life doesn't belong in the twentieth century at all. . . . There seems to be no more room for flowers in this world."

"I may be a flower," said Giulia, puzzled and piqued, "but I think I have roots . . . and . . . what you call in American . . . guts."

"It's the guts of woman," he said moodily, "that ability to be proud without insulting, to stand childbirth and sacrifice. . . . But you scare me because I can't find a trace of bitchiness in you."

"Do you want there to be?"

"God, no, my darling," he said, sighing and pulling her against him.

And Giulia saw with a comic relief that she was stronger than he. That was the way it was decreed to be. She looked detachedly at her superiority with an odd wistfulness. It might be something given her to serve her in the long years ahead.

One night he came to their meeting with an air restless and sheepish. It didn't become him. Hand in hand they walked for fifteen minutes along Via Caracciolo. She waited, listening to him with a new ear that had been born in her. At last they stopped and looked out at the bay from the railing.

"Sei nervoso," she said reproachfully. "Hai qualche segreto . . . ?"

He took her hand and rubbed her fingers.

"Yes, Giulia, I have. . . . Tomorrow I'm leaving for the front. I put myself in for it. I thought it over for a long time. I'm going back to the tanks. . . . It's not fair to you, but it's the way I feel. I'm going up there with all the others. . . . For that's where I belong. . . . I'm sick to death of all the Americans in Naples, with their villas and their jeeps and their mistresses."

Something snapped in Giulia's heart. She gushed with a woe she hadn't dreamed possible in this world. She felt that God had tricked her shabbily.

"You must do what you think is right," she said gently, controlling herself.

"Is that your heart or your brain talking?"

"Don't be cruel to me . . . it's both."

They had a long silence. Vesuvius glowed weakly on both its peaks.

"Giulia . . . you must stay with me tonight. . . . Get

278

Wilma to tell your mother you're visiting your grand-mother in Caserta."

She felt her nails gouge into her palms.

"I thought you were different from the rest," she said.

"I thought so too. But I've got to make love to you, Giulia, and tonight. . . . Suppose . . . up there . . . they got me . . . and I died without ever having had you?"

"Then that's the way it would have to be," she said.

"You must be made of ice," he said.

"I'm not made of ice," she answered, feeling her cheeks scalding. "When you touch me I know I'm not made of ice. . . . I want your love . . . all your love . . . just as much as you want mine. I mean some day to give myself wholly to you . . . and not to any other man . . ."

"You and your codes of respectability," he cried. "In wartime they don't mean a damn. . . . All that matters is that we love one another."

"I am what I am," Giulia said. "I love you. Do you doubt that? This is the first and last time I'll love. I'm made that way. . . . But I won't stay with you tonight. Not . . . brutal as it sounds . . . if you were to be killed next week . . ."

"Thank you, my dear," he said roughly.

"Oh I know it's all a game," she said. "But I'm so made that I must play that game . . . call it what you will . . . stuffiness . . . respectability . . ."

"You're a fool," he said.

"I'm anything but a fool," she said and began to cry. "I know all the arguments and all the answers. All women do. . . . We have to hold you off till we get a ring on our fingers. . . . My mother and her mother before her played that game. . . . And I shall do so too. . . . Don't you see, my darling? The world is built on such games. Most of those games are invented by women for their own protection . . . for their children's protection. . . . In every woman there are two things all mixed up . . . her heart and her head . . . but that's what makes her a woman. . . . And you, my darling, will never know me in love till I'm your wife."

He said nothing further. They walked back along Via Caracciolo by the statue of Pompey in the little garden with the white railing. Giulia was in agony, yet she smiled to herself. She'd gladly pass with him one night in which all their love was rolled up into one knot. But against

279

this, something merciless and logical in her saw the possibility of a lifetime of bitterness and loneliness and aridity. It was a gamble she was willing to make. On such odds her whole life had been predicated.

They entered the Gallería Umberto, where the life and the motion had died. There remained only the black heat of Naples in August, 1944. Their loitering footfalls were prescient and austere.

"My God, Giulia," her Captain said, "you're a fiend."

"Why, every woman is," she answered.

For she knew he'd be coming back to her.

SEVENTH PROMENADE

(Naples)

I REMEMBER that my heart finally broke in Naples. Not over a girl or a thing, but over an idea. When I was little, they'd told me I should be proud to be an American. And I suppose I was, though I saw no reason I should applaud every time I saw the flag in a newsreel. But I did believe that the American way of life was an idea holy in itself, an idea of freedom bestowed by intelligent citizens on one another. Yet after a little while in Naples I found out that America was a country just like any other, except that she had more material wealth and more advanced plumbing. And I found that outside of the propaganda writers (who were making a handsome living from the deal) Americans were very poor spiritually. Their ideals were something to make dollars on. They had bankrupt souls. Perhaps this is true of most of the people of the twentieth century. Therefore my heart broke.

I remember that this conceit came home to me in crudest black and white. In Naples of 1944 we Americans had everything. The Italians, having lost their war, had nothing. And what was this war really about? I decided that it was because most of the people of the world didn't have the cigarettes, the gasoline, and the food that we Americans had.

I remember my mother's teaching me out of her wisdom that the possession of Things implies a responsibility
280

for Their use, that They shouldn't be wasted, that Having Things should never dominate my living. When this happens, Things become more important than People. Comfort then becomes the be-and-end-all of human life. And when other people threaten your material comfort, you have no recourse but to fight them. It makes no difference who attacks whom first. The result is the same, a killing and a chaos that the world of 1944 wasn't big enough to stand.

Our propaganda did everything but tell us Americans the truth: that we had most of the riches of the modern world, but very little of its soul. We were nice enough guys in our own country, most of us; but when we got overseas, we couldn't resist the temptation to turn a dollar or two at the expense of people who were already down. I can speak only of Italy, for I didn't see France or Germany. But with our Hollywood ethics and our radio network reasoning we didn't take the trouble to think out the fact that the war was supposed to be against fascism— not against every man, woman, and child in Italy. . . . But then a modern war is total. Armies on the battlefield are simply a remnant from the old kind of war. In the 1944 war everyone's hand ended by being against everyone else's. Civilization was already dead, but nobody bothered to admit this to himself.

I remember the crimes we committed against the Italians, as I watched them in Naples. In the broadest sense we promised the Italians security and democracy if they came over to our side. All we actually did was to knock the hell out of *their* system and give them nothing to put in its place. And one of the most tragic spectacles in all history was the Italians' faith in us—for a little while, until we disabused them of it. It seemed to me like the swindle of all humanity, and I wondered if perhaps we weren't all lost together. Collective and social decency didn't exist in Naples in August, 1944. And I used to laugh at our attempts at relief and control there, for we undid with one hand what we did with the other. What we should have done was to set up a strict and square rationing for all goods that came into Italy. We should have given the Neapolitans co-operative stores.

I remember watching the American acquisitive sense in action. We didn't realize, or we didn't want to realize, that we were in a poor country, now reduced to minus zero

281

by war. Nearly every GI and officer went out and bought everything he could lay hands on, no matter how worthless it was; and he didn't care how much he paid for it. They'd buy all the bamboo canes in a little Neapolitan shop, junk jewelry, worthless art—all for the joy of spending. Everywhere we Americans went, the prices of everything skyrocketed until the lira was valueless. And the Italians couldn't afford to pay these prices, especially for things they needed just to live on. For all the food we sent into Italy for relief, we should have set up some honest American control by honorable and incorruptible Americans. Instead we entrusted it to Italians who, nine times out of ten, were grafters of the regime we claimed to be destroying.

I remember too that an honest American in August, 1944, was almost as hard to find as a Neapolitan who owned up to having been a Fascist. I don't know why, but most Americans had a blanket hatred of all Italians. They figured it this way: These Ginsoes have made war on us; so it doesn't matter what we do to them, boost their prices, shatter their economy, and shack up with their women. I imagine there's some fallacy in my reasoning here. I guess I was asking for the impossible. This was war, and I wanted it to be conducted with honor. I suppose that's as phony reasoning as talking about an honest murder or a respectable rape.

I remember that the commonest, and the pettiest, crime we did against the Neapolitans was selling them our PX rations. We paid five lire a package for cigarettes, which was a privilege extended to us by the people of the United States. To a Neapolitan we could sell each package for three hundred lire. Really big business. A profit of 6,000 percent. Of course the Neapolitans were mad to pay this price for them, but I don't see that it made our selling any the righter. I don't believe that these cigarettes were legally ours—ours, that is, to sell at a profit. They were only ours if we wanted to smoke them. If we didn't smoke, we had no right to buy them. Though there was no harm in *giving* these cigarettes away.

I remember that we went the next step in vulturism and sold our GI clothes to the Neapolitans. Then we could sign a statement of charges and get new ones, having made meanwhile a small fortune out of the deal. This was inex-

282

cusable on any grounds whatever. There are loopholes in my cigarette syllogism, but none that I see on the clothes question.

Then I remember that there were not a few really big criminals who stole stuff off the ships unloading in Naples harbor, stuff that didn't belong to them by *any* stretch of the imagination. For all this that I saw I could only attribute a deficient moral and humane sense to Americans as a nation and as a people. I saw that we could mouth democratic catchwords and yet give the Neapolitans a huge black market. I saw that we could prate of the evils of fascism, yet be just as ruthless as Fascists with people who'd already been pushed into the ground. That was why my heart broke in Naples in August, 1944. The arguments that we advanced to cover our delinquencies were as childishly ingenuous as American advertising.

"If a signorina comes to the door of my mess hall," the mess sergeant said, making a salad, "and she says she's hungry, why, I give her a meal. . . . But first I make it clear to her Eyetie mind that I'm interested in something she's got. . . . If she says ixnay I tell her to get the hell out."

"Of course the only reason I sell my cigarettes," the corporal said, "is because we're gettin creamed on the rate of exchange for the lira. . . . What can I buy in Naples on the seventy bucks a month I'm pullin down?"

"You've got enough to eat and a place to sleep," said the pfc with the glasses. "That's better than most of the world is doing in 1944."

"I didn't ask for this war," the sergeant major said. "I didn't ask to be sent overseas. Guess I've got a right to turn a buck when I see the chance, ain't I?"

"You must make the distinction," said the pfc, "between so-called honest business tactics and making money out of human misery."

But he was only a Jewish Communist; so no one paid any attention to him.

Yes. I remember that being at war with the Italians was taken as a license for Americans to defecate all over them. Even though most of us in the base section at Naples had never closed with an Italian in combat. Our argument was that we should treat the Neapolitans as the Neapolitans would have treated our cities presumably if they'd won the war. I watched old ladies of Naples pushed off the sidewalks by drunken GI's and officers. Every Italian girl was fair prey to propositions we wouldn't have made to a streetwalker back home. Those who spoke Italian used the tu on everyone they met. And I remember seeing American MP's beating the driver of a horse and wagon because they were obstructing traffic on Via Roma. I don't think the Germans could have done any better in their concentration camps. I thought that all humanity had gone from the world, and that this war had smothered decency forever.

"These Eyties," the mess sergeant said, "ain't human beins. They're just Gooks, that's all."

"All I know," the corporal said doggedly and worriedly, "is that they ain't Americans. . . . They don't see things the way we do."

"They'd steal anything," the mess sergeant said, stuffing a turkey, his mouth crammed with giblet leavings.

I remember that other arguments against the Neapolitans, besides the cardinal one, that they'd declared war on us, were that they stole and were filthy dirty. I only know that no Neapolitan ever stole anything from me, for I took pains to see that no temptation was put in their way. Though once my wallet was lifted in a New York subway. And for those Neapolitans to whom I sometimes gave an extra bar of soap, I noticed that they used this soap joyfully on themselves, their children, their clothes. I've buried my face in the hair of Neapolitan girls. It was just as sweet as an American girl's if the Napoletana had the wherewithal to wash it.

I remember that in Naples after my heart broke I decided that a strictly American point of view in itself offered no peace or solution for the world. So I began to make friends with the Neapolitans. And it didn't surprise me to find that, like everyone else in the world, they had their good and their bad and their admixtures of both. To know them, I'd been working on my Italian. That lovely supple language was kind to my tongue. The Neapolitans were gracious in helping me with it.

I met agile dapper thieves who'd steal the apple out of my eye if they could sell it on the black market. But this tribute I must pay even to the crooks: when I answered them in Italian, they'd laugh and shake my hand and say they were going to try someone else who didn't know their language quite so well.

I met studenti and young soldiers just fled from the army, baffled and bitter, with nothing but a black bottomless pit of despair for their future. Perhaps I'd have been like them if I'd been on the losing side?

I met Neapolitan whores who charged a rate a countess couldn't have earned from her favors in the old days.

And I met ragazze and mamme so warm and laughing that in Neapolitan dining rooms I thought I was back in my own house, hearing the talk of my mother with my sisters.

This forced me to the not original conclusion that the Neapolitans were like everybody else in the world, and in an infinite variety. Because I was an americano the Neapolitans treated me with a strange pudding of respect, dismay, and bewilderment. A few loathed me. But from most Italians I got a decency and a kindness that they'd have showered on any other American in Naples who'd made up his mind to treat them like human beings. I'm not bragging. I'm not unique. I'm not Christlike. Many other Americans in Naples made friends they'll never forget. Thus I remember that in Naples, though my heart had broken from one idea, it mended again when I saw how good most human beings are if they have enough to eat and are free from imminent annihilation.

I remember that I came to love the courtesy and the laughter and the simplicity of Italian life. The compliment I pay to most Italians who haven't too much of this world's goods is that they love life and love. I don't know what else there is, after all. Even in their frankness the Italians were so seldom offensive. An Italian mother told a friend of mine that he could never marry her daughter because he had the face of a whoremaster. And we all laughed. No one was hurt.

I remember the passion and the understanding of Italian love. There's no barrier between the lovers. Everything is oxidized at the moment, without rancor or reservation.

"Fammi male, amore mio. . . . Fammi godere da movire. . . ."

And I remember the storms and quarrels of Italian love, mostly rhetorical. The going to bed is all the sweeter for the reconciliation.

For I thought that to this people, broken and saddened and dismayed, there yet remained much of that something which had made Italy flower—though not as a nation of warriors. To this day I'm convinced of Italy's greatness in the world of the spirit. In war she's a tragic farce. In love and sunlight and music and humanity she has something that humanity sorely needs. It's still there. Something of this distillation of noble and gentle grandeur seeps down through most of Italy's population, from contessa to contadina. I don't think I'm romanticizing or kidding myself. In the middle of the war, in August, 1944, with my heart broken for an ideal, I touched the beach of heaven in Naples. At moments.

I remember how the children of Naples pointed my dim conception of American waste. They'd stand about our mess hall quiet or noisy, watching the glutted riches from our mess kits being dumped into the garbage cans. I remember the surprise and terror in their faces. We were forbidden to feed them, though I heard that combat soldiers, gentler and more determined than we, took the law into their hands and were much kinder to Italian children than we were allowed to be. When I watched the bitten steaks, the nibbled lettuce, the half-eaten bread go sliding into the swill cans in a spectrum of waste and bad planning, I realized at last the problem of the modern world, simple yet huge. I saw then what was behind the war. I'll never forget those Neapolitan children whom we were forbidden to feed. After a while many of us couldn't stand it any longer. We'd brush past the guard with our mess kit full of supper and share it with Adalgisa and Sergio and Pasqualino. They were only the scugnizz' of Napoli, but they had mouths and stomachs just like us. I remember the wild hungry faces of those kids diving into cold Spam. But our orders were that since America was in no position to feed all the Italians, we were not to feed any. Just dump your waste in the GI cans, men.

But I remember even then thinking and fearing that we'd come to a day when we too, we rich rich rich Americans, would pay for this mortal sin of waste. We've

always thought that there was no end to our plenty, that
the horn would never dry up. Already I seem to hear
the menacing rumblings, like a long-starved stomach. But
in Naples in August, 1944, we were on the crest of the
wave. We? We were Americans, from the best little old
country on God's green earth. And if you don't believe
me, mister, I'll knock your teeth in. . . .

And I remember well our first facing of the problem
that we couldn't live in Naples as though there were a
wall between us and the Neapolitans. There were American clubs and American movies, but only a blind man
can carry his life around with him quite that much. Perhaps in Washington the generals had their doubts about
the perfect probity of the American way of life and
wished to make sure that overseas we wouldn't come in
contact with any other. Consequently we were flooded
with American movies and with Coca-Cola to distract
our wandering attention and to insure that we shouldn't
fall into dangerous furren ways of thinking. But some of
us wondered none the less.

The main leak, I remember, was in sex. It just isn't
possible to take millions of American men and shut them
off from love for years on end—no, not with a thousand
other American distractions. Sooner or later every man's
thoughts start centering around his middle. The cold and
scientific solution would have been to have brothels attached to all our armies overseas, as other nations of the
world have always done. But the American people
wouldn't have stood for that. I mean the American people back home. Too many purity lobbies from old ladies
who have nothing else to do but form pressure groups
to guard other people's morals. And there were few
women in our army as compared to our own percentage.
There were WAC's, to be sure, but in such a tiny ratio
to us. And with the nurses we couldn't go out because
they were officers. Thus our perfect chastity was theo-
retically assured. From the hygienic point of view there
were pro stations on every corner of Naples. This was a
nice paradox in that every interesting alley was off limits. The army took the point of view: You absolutely must
not. But if by chance you do . . . Finally they had a re-
striction on marrying overseas.

Then we started casting our eyes on the Neapolitan
girls.

287

"These Gook wimmin," the mess sergeant said. "It's so easy with em. You just walk down Via Roma and some signorina does all the rest."

"But," the corporal said, dreamy in his shorts, "I don't wanna hafta pay for it. I just wanna little girl all my own to love."

"There's something very nice about Italian women," the pfc with spectacles said. "No funny ideas about fur coats and higher income brackets and silk stockings, like American girls. And they don't feel they have to discuss books with you that they haven't read . . . not that women shouldn't be emancipated . . . to a certain degree, as companion to man and as his helpmate. . . . But the Neapolitan women are so down to earth. First they cook you a spaghetti dinner. . . . Then . . ."

I remember that we GI's were used to women in a different tradition. American women, with their emancipation, had imposed their own standards on us. In America most Nice Girls Would . . . if you knew them well enough. Nearly all college girls Would, and waitresses too, if they thought there was a reasonable chance of your eventually getting spliced. And as for the separate career women of America, with their apartments—well, they'd abrogated to themselves all the freedom of single men. A Career Girl would keep you, or you kept her, depending on the financial status of one or both. And in America there were lots of rich middle-aged ladies who liked their young chauffeurs or gardeners, but didn't dare marry them for fear of what Cousin Hattie would say.

But to us GI's the girls of southern Italy fell into two tight classes only. That's where we got stymied. There were the girls of Via Roma, whom the Neapolitans, mincing no words, called puttane. These girls asked fixed prices in either lire or PX rations. They satisfied for a while as long as we had money, but their fee was steep for a GI unless he were a big operator in the black market. And then too something in a man's vanity craves something other than a girl who's shacking with Tom, Dick, and Harry. American men are so sentimental that they refuse to have a whore for their girl—if they can help it. That's the schizophrenia of our civilization, with its sharp distinction between the Good Girl and the Bad Girl.

Consequently after a few tries, with the fear of VD

always suspended over our heads, we began to look at the Good women of Naples. And here entered the problem of the GI Italian bride. I remember that Italian girls began to look sweet to us early. Perhaps because their virginity was put on such a pedestal. There were few of us who didn't have access to some Neapolitan home, where we were welcomed, once our entree was definite and our purposes aboveboard. We usually got in through a Neapolitan brother. Then we discovered that there were girls in the family, carefully kept and cherished as novices in a nunnery. It was obvious that these girls were interested in us . . . if we proposed marriage to them.

"I don't get a minute alone with Rosetta," the corporal said. "They treat me swell at her casa, but Mamma doesn't trust Rosetta out her sight for one minnit. An after midnight Papa's always remindin me what time it is . . . as if I didn't have a wrist watch."

"Ah, I keep to Via Roma," the mess sergeant said. "You can't lay a finger on the others."

"But north of Rome," said the pfc with the spectacles, "a girl once she's engaged will do anything to satisfy her fiancé . . . short of the real McCoy. I don't get these fine distinctions in tribal ethics."

"These Ginso girls," the sergeant major said, "never forget that they're women. That's their strongest and weakest point. They know how to get in ya hair and under ya skin with wantin em till ya have to slide that gold ring on their finger."

"Onelia told me quite frankly," the corporal said, "that she was interested in a passport to the States as my wife. . . . I liked that honesty in her. I guess she likes me too."

"Us GI's is so hot," the mess sergeant said, "that once we leave Italy, these signorians will never be satisfied with the Eyetie men . . . never again. . . ."

I remember that we Americans brought heartbreak to Neapolitan girls in many instances. There were Negroes who told their shack-jobs that they weren't really black, just stained that way for camouflage and night fighting. There were mess sergeants who told nice Neapolitan girls that they owned chains of restaurants back in the States. I've often wondered at the face of some of those girls of good faith, arriving in the States to discover they'd live in one cabbage-smelling room over the stairs.

There were, I remember, American GI's and officers who most cruelly betrayed and seduced Neapolitan girls, concealing from them and their families that back in the States they'd a wife and kids. These girls weren't in the position of an American girl, who knows the language and can make her own investigations. For the heartless deceit of such as these I sometimes felt shame that I was an American because the life of a pure woman is like a mirror, and can be smashed but once.

But I also remember instances of love and good faith on both sides. GI's and officers met Neapolitan girls, fell in love with them, and married them. I see no reason why such marriages shouldn't be happy and lasting, once the girls have learned English and made the not easy adjustment to American wifehood.

I remember Lydia, the gay shy mouse who sang in the chorus of the Teatro Reale di San Carlo. She was courted and won by our medic. I remember their wedding at Sorrento and their honeymoon at Taormina in Sicilia. Unless the world falls apart, I think that little Lydia and her capitano medico will be as happy in their lives together as human beings ever are outside of fairy tales.

I remember Laura, to whom a GI killed at Cassino made two presents. He gave her a baby and a white spirochete. When I see flowers lying crushed in a muddy street, I think of Laura.

I remember plump and smiling Emilia, who thought she'd married an MP. The MP disappeared forever after the wedding, and Emilia just sat in the kitchen night after night and wept so bitterly that her heart would have broken if it hadn't already been in tiny pieces. Her mother kept cursing her and asking where were all those allotment checks from America? And her brother yelled that he'd put a razor into the first americano he met on a dark night.

And I remember Wanda, stately and blonde, who used to sit by the stove and feel the life stirring within her. We all said she was too big to be having just one. And sure enough she came out with twins whom she christened Mario and Maria. They were brilliant gay babies, the way Italian children know how o be. Wanda hoped they'd grow up strong in St. Louis. She got me to point out that city for her on the map of America.

I remember that in Naples in August, 1944, for all the

red tape and the army regulations and the blood tests and the warning talks by chaplains, there was still a great deal of human love. And this rejoiced me. For all the ruin and economic asphyxiation we'd brought the Neapolitans, we also in some cases gave them a new hope. They'd been like Jews standing against a wall and waiting to be shot for something they'd never done. And I began to think that perhaps something good might emerge or be salvaged from the abattoir of the world. Though in the main all national decency and sense of duty might be dead, I saw much individual goodness and loveliness that reassured me in my agony. I saw it in some Neapolitans. I saw it in some Americans. And I wondered if perhaps the world must eventually be governed by individuality consecrated and unselfish, rather than by any collectivism of the propagandists, the students, and the politicians. In Naples in August, 1944, I drowned in mass ideologies, but was fished out by separate thinking and will. I remember watching the mad hordes in the streets of Naples and wondering what it all meant. But there was a certain unity in the bay, in the August moon over Vesuvius. Then humanity fell away from me like the rind of an orange, and I was something much more and much less than myself. . . .

EIGHTH PORTRAIT

Queen Penicillin

AWAKENING these mornings in Naples, he'd turn on his canvas cot, shove aside the mosquito netting, light a cigarette, and look out at the bell tower of Maria Egiziana. His consciousness was clear, the way he used to come to as a child and start thinking of what he'd do today.

But the deliciousness of those awakenings had gone. Up till last week he'd known them with Marisa. But now she'd gone to Rome. And for days there'd been something in his mind, something crouching that he could escape only when he slept. All day long it sat on his shoulder whispering the red doubts and fears into his ear. He was free only in those first instants of awaking. But with

the first few puffs on his cigarette the Idea came back.
This morning It was especially pressing. Today he'd
Know.

He got up and groped down to the latrine. The sunlight hadn't yet come into this corridor, but he knew the
passageway drunk or sober. In the latrine he voided his
bladder and stood looking at his naked body in the mirror. By the early August sunlight of Naples he looked like
a Moor. Marisa'd loved this color of his skin. He examined his flesh, peering over himself with a wild hushed
interest. He knew every inch of himself. Then the Idea
broke over him more viciously than in the past four days.
His dark skin globuled with sweat.

Back in the room he dressed himself quickly. He was
shaking. He heard his heart say yes yes yes. And from
the other cot Roy was regarding him with sleepy compassion.

"Goin to find out this mornin?"

"Yup."

"Good luck, boy. Ya been sweatin this one out."

His boots clattered on the stairs of the palazzo. Naples
too was awakening in the August morning. By the windows the sandflies hung poised in their clouds. And he
heard the clatter of the carts in the street and the
prickly whispering of the women's brooms as they swept
the sidewalks.

He walked through the screen door of the mess hall,
taking more than his usual pains not to let it slam. The
mess sergeant sat at a wooden table littered with lettuce.
He looked up with an iron petulance.

"Now what, Jo-Jo? Ya feelin hungover?"

"Nope. Got any black coffee?"

One of the Neapolitan kitchen help poured him a mess
cup full of scalding java and passed it to him.

"Grazie, Joe," he said.

"Niente, Joe," the Neapolitan said.

The metal lip of the canteen cup singed his lips and his
tongue, but the coffee flooded down his throat. Again the
sweat seeped out through his shirt. He felt the cup teeter-
ing against his teeth from the trembling of his wrist.

"Ya ain't feelin good, Jo-Jo?" the mess sergeant
said. "Ya ain't been on the beam since ya quit ya
shackin . . ."

"Nope," he said, setting down his cup, "I ain't feelin well."

"Knock her up or somethin?"

"Nope. Me and Marisa just broke up."

"Well, they's plenty more where she came from," the mess sergeant said, shoving a mound of lettuce wearily away from him. "Plenty more."

"I don't want no more."

Now in a lewd sweat from the steaming coffee and the reeking Neapolitan morning, he plowed along, his cap on the back of his head and his hands in his pockets. Seeing Vesuvius and the barbed wire around the port enclosures, he decided to smoke a cigarette. As he was lighting his butt with fingers that wobbled, an officer passed. He lowered his eyes.

"Say, soldier," the lieutenant said, "don't ya salute officers any more?"

"This ain't a salutin area, sir . . ."

"Shut up and salute me," the lieutenant said. "I don't know why I don't take ya name an serial number. . . . Wearin ya dogtags?"

"Yessir."

"Well, get on ya way. Next time watch ya step. Not all officers is as square as me."

He saluted again and walked on, replacing his hands in his pockets. He put his cigarette in the farthest angle of his mouth. He felt that his shoulders were sagging. He didn't care. He dragged along with his eyes on the ground. For he wished that he could pass out quietly some place, that the March eruption of Vesuvius had buried both Naples and himself under lava as stiff as molasses. He cussed and spat against a tree that grew from the sidewalk in his path.

There was no one in the Galleria Umberto except some children asleep like sweaty kittens, and little old men who went over the pavement searching for cigarette butts. From the cornices the weather-eaten angels looked snottily down at him from behind their trumpets. He saw the canvases in the art shops as daubs of vermilion and ocher and cobalt. The bars were all shut behind their rolling corrugated blinds. The new sun filled every nook of the arcade, microscopically adumbrating the smears on the walls, the peeling posters, the chipped mosaics in the pavement. And above him the empty skylight criss-crossed the sky like veins in an eyeless socket. He re-membered the Galleria in past evenings: blots of light leaking from under the bars till curfew time, the smell of bodies in movement, the shrill laughter, and the voices promising annihilation from the heat and the pain. And like a flashlight into his dark hot misery he saw the figure of Marisa swaying in the August darkness, the cleft of her breasts in her gray figured cotton frock, her tiny brown feet. He heard her voice:

"Vieni, amor mio . . . fammi tua per sempre. . . ."

Thinking of the past, he walked across the Galleria into Via Roma. A Neopolitan kid asked him if he wanted to eat; so he told him what he could do with himself. On Via Roma there was the sparrowy life of Neapolitans hurrying to work, old ladies fanning themselves with their morning paper, the screams of the cameo dealers as they set up their displays in the porticos of abandoned shops and ruined tenements. British and American con-voys rumbled in the pinched street. In the gutters lay squashed oranges and spent rubbers that had been hurled from the windows above.

He turned, crossed Via Diaz, and entered PBS building from the side. For a while he stood before the red and white canvas sign that read FIFTH GENERAL DISPENSARY. He laid his hand on the bronze maniple of the door. It was as hot as a molten ingot to his palm. He was listening too to his heart throbbing, opening and closing like a spastic fist. It had beat like that when he lay in Marisa's arms after their lovemaking. . . . Marisa. . . . He felt his knees begin to shake. There seemed to be a pool of ice water in his belly. But he stiffened his legs and pulled the door of the dispensary open.

It was cool in there. The floor was a pepper-colored parquet. The GI's who worked there stood behind glass wickets like bank tellers. And in the coolness there was a reek of phenol and antiseptic. As they set up their cages for the day, the Gi's called out to one another their pissin and their moanin. They yelled back and forth criticisms of the breakfast they'd just eaten.

"I've *had* Naples! O Mr. Roosevelt, can't I please go home?"

To stop the trembling of his knees and the turbine in his chest, he sat down on a bench near the door. He wondered were his eyes bloodshot. He felt like an ulcerous scarecrow sitting alone in the middle of that cool noisy dispensary, with the click and hum of the dental clinic just beyond. The other GI's were unconcerned and gay.

Finally he got up, clutching his cap, and walked to a window that said ADMISSIONS. He ran his tongue over his lips and looked at the floor.

"Ya too early for sick call, sarge," the corporal back of the plate glass said. "Go outside and wait a while . . ."

"But I took a blood test . . . five days ago," he murmured.

"Oh ya did? Imagine that! Blood tests is SOP in Napoli . . ."

"Will ya please do me a favor an look?" he said, giving his name.

"Okay, okay, sarge," the corporal said. "I hate to see a guy sweat."

Out of a pigeonhole the corporal took a sheaf of small pink slips and leisurely ruffled through them. With tormenting indifference.

"I don't seem to find ya name, sarge. . . . Oh wait, here it is. . . . Outa alphabetical order . . . damn that lab. . . ."

Through a swimming mist he saw the pink slip thrust at him along the counter. A kettledrum was beating in his ears, thudding out Yes Yes Yes and No No No in acceleration. He saw the manicured fingers of the corporal holding the upper edges of the slip. He read down till he saw the brash rubber stamp and the red crayon comment:

Wassermann—Pos
Kahn—Pos

Everything inside him seemed to whirl up and go down in a crash. Besides the drumming there now came a ringing in his ears. His knees buckled. He gripped the marble counter to keep from dropping to the floor.

"Tough luck, sarge," the corporal said.

"What do I do now?" he said, his vision clearing.

For his previous weakness there was now substituted an icy surety of horror that carried him out to a pinpoint in space. And he saw Marisa's face, her mouth open, her eyes closed, murmuring:

295

"O come sai bene amarmi, tesoro mio. . . ."

"Just step into number four," the corporal said briskly and professionally.

He stumbled along by the cages, clutching the pink slip in his palm, which seemed to be gushing hot butter. He steered through a railing and into a long corridor with clinics and rooms opening off it. He knocked on the door of number four. At a call he opened to find a medical captain washing his hands in a sink and chewing gum in rhythm, with the oscillation of his forearms.

"Mind waiting outside, sergeant?" the doctor called sharply.

So he all but lay down on a bench, the slip dangling from his hand. He tried to close his eyes and swallow the searing sensation in his eyes and throat. Finally the sound of running water stopped and the doctor beckoned him in. He thrust the pink slip into the cool moist hand.

"Well, got the dreadfuldreadful at last, hey? You're one of the bright joes who thinks that signs and films are for everybody in the army except himself. . . . And you won't be sergeant much longer, boy."

"Yessir," he said.

"Well, we'll start treatment at once. . . . We don't mess with this."

"Is there . . . any hope, sir?" he said hoarsely.

"I'm no great believer in this new treatment. . . . Take down your pants."

Then began the questionnaire, which the captain wrote down.

"Take a pro after your last exposure?"

"Nossir."

"Italian girl, I suppose. . . . Give me her name and address."

"Don't know, sir."

"Don't try to protect her through any mistaken notions of chivalry. She gave you a nice burning, and she'll do it to others. I advise you to give me her name and address."

"I told ya, I don't know, sir. . . ."

He went outside the dispensary and hung around the several waiting ambulances, holding in his hand an admission slip to the hospital. One of the ambulance drivers, a tech five, had one of his boots through a window of the ambulance cab.

"What hospital ya goin to, sarge?"

296

"Twenty-third General."

"Then hop in. Ya can ride in front with me. Just like an officer."

He climbed into the front, to the right of the driver's seat. On the line he'd never had to ride in an ambulance. Now in the rear area of Naples, here he was going to the hospital in style, but not for a wound or for trenchfoot. The tech five pulled his boot inside the window and started his vehicle.

"What are ya goin to the Twenty-third for, sarge? Hepatitis? VD?"

"Nope, neither . . . just a general checkup."

They drove along Via Caracciolo toward Bagnoli Tunnel. And, seeing the Bay of Naples in the August sun, seeing the fishermen already far out in their skiffs toward Ischia and Capri, he thought of how he and Marisa used to walk and dally here in the bright open moonlight. They'd lean on the parapet by the docks of Santa Lucia and watch the British sailors coming over the ramp on liberty. . . . But now he was riding in an ambulance with a tech five who talked all the time, having lit a cigar. The tech five made him listen to all the details of his last night's shacking.

"I get me one gal an I stick to her," the tech five said. "Then I don't stand no chance of pickin up nothin nasty. See my point, sarge?"

"Ya never can tell about them things," he answered vaguely.

He wished Marisa would quit his thoughts. He pressed down on his thighs and peered through the ambulance windshield. He knew that Marisa was very much with him. She was even in his veins.

They pummeled through the dark dripping gloom of the Bagnoli Tunnel. The overhead inset lights barely pierced the dusty gloom kicked up by the truck convoys. Marisa and her family used to sleep in this tunnel during the air raids. . . . And at Bagnoli they turned by the old tenements with the washing on the balconies, the arrows to direct traffic and show the way to the staging areas.

Then he got his first look at the Medical Center. Long low modern buildings with friezes and dominant stairs, like WPA American high schools. Unexpected gardens and trellises, phallic arches, and parapets skirmishing like roller coasters out of the pine trees. Excavated rifts piercing white and unfinished out of the hillsides. The tech five explained that Musso had built these grounds for a world's fair or something, that now the Americans were using them for a concentration of hospitals. They passed plaster statues of ripple-thighed naked young men in Fascist attitudes of victory. A couple of swimming pools. The whole Medical Center had an air like an exhibition: sheets of windows, inscriptions everywhere.

The tech five stopped his ambulance on an avenue near an MP gate.

"That's the Twenty-third right over there, sarge. Just walk straight up to that barbed-wire enclosure . . ."

"Barbed wire?" he said. "But I ain't no prisoner."

"Just wait," the tech five said, wisely chewing off the tip of a fresh cigar.

He got out of the ambulance and walked up a flight of stairs to the barbed wire, over which hung the leaves of low trees and vines. Inside was a great press of people moving around. He thought of the courtyard of a jail during exercise period.

"No visitors here, Joe," the MP said, raising his carbine to port arms.

"I ain't no visitor," he said, presenting his admission slip.

"Then welcome," the MP said. "This the place where shackees repent their shackin. . . ."

There was a series of arrows showing new patients where to go. It was as methodical and cold as his induction into the army. He entered first a long low hut where pfc's sat at typewriters. In a window a major sat with bored but catty stare. To this medical officer he presented his admission slip. The major scanned it quickly, with the air of a movie usher seeing a picture for the hundredth time.

"So you got burned?" the major said. "And you'll be losing those three stripes too."

"Yessir."

"I don't say: Welcome to our hospital. You're not going to have a good time here. Our whole setup is guaranteed to make you hate everything about us. We don't want men coming back here, do you see? There's no excuse for getting VD. No excuse whatever. We give you treatment here, but we do it in such a way that you won't care to

298

come back as a repeater. Yet I see the same faces again and again. Well it's their skin. . . . Take down your pants. . . ."

"Pretty sight, aren't you?" the major said after the examination. "Just as pretty as you saw it in the movies. I'll bet you said: That'll never be me."

"Nossir."

After the major had got through with him, lashing softly and insistently with his tongue, he was sent over by a wall where there were chairs with armrests, rubber compresses, and a lot of little glass vials with red stuff in them.

"Roll up your sleeve," the pfc attendant said.

"But I already had a blood test," he said.

"Roll up your sleeve. You'll be takin blood tests from now on like you would a bath. . . . An you can't give none of your blood to the Red Cross an get ten dollars for it, neither. . . . Make a fist."

He did as he was told. He felt the rubber hose go about his upper arm and the pressure mount as though an anaconda were squeezing. His blood began to bang in his arm. Looking down, he saw that a blue vein was bulging from his elbow. The pfc took a needle and inserted it into the obvious blood vessel. He felt the cold point go in, and he watched his crimson blood seep into the syringe as its handle was drawn back.

"At this point," the pfc said, "the jigaboos usually faint. . . . Now go an draw ya clothes."

He got up from the chair, crooking his elbow against the patch of cotton to stop the slow ooze of his blood into the elbow joint. The GI took the vial of his blood and pasted his name to it on a piece of adhesive tape. This he put into the rack along with the other vials.

"Looks just as pretty as new wine," the pfc said, indicating the file of vials. "Only no wine has got what these tubes have."

Next he filed past a counter where another GI leaned on his belly cushioning it and picking his teeth. He had that spleen of all supply sergeants.

"Take off ya clothes, boy."

He undressed himself there in the half-light of that corridor. Outside swarms of men milled in what looked like a desolate and unweeded garden picked with pyramidal tents. All his clothes went into a little barracks

299

bag tagged with his name. In return he got a set of frayed but freshly laundered green fatigues, shirt and trousers. On the back of his jacket and on the trouser legs were painted these large smeary letters:

V D

"Guess this is about the last time y'll be wearing ya stripes," the supply sergeant said. "There ain't no rank here in them green fatigues. Ya'll sit down next to a major an never know it . . ."

"Take it easy, take it easy," he said, buttoning up the fatigues, which were a casual fit and chafed his crotch.

"Ya shoulda taken it easy yaself," the supply sergeant replied.

"Where do I go now?"

"Ya'll hafta see about accommodations, I guess. We're full right up in this hotel. An ya never wired us for a reservation."

So he walked down, stumbling a little in his fresh fatigues, to another window, where a pfc in harlequin spectacles was reading his *Stars and Stripes*.

"What can we do for you? Have you got number one or number two?"

"I got the worst ya can possibly get," he said.

"Well, lawsy. That entitles you to our very best accommodations. The kids with clap get stuck in tents all over hell. But our guests with syph are put in the bridal suite. You'll get the very finest attention. Every three hours, rain or shine, for a hundred and eighty hours. . . . You'll find the bridal suite in the first door on your right off the court."

He went out into the hot light of the courtyard. Now he understood clearly the confused and mobbed movement he'd seen through the barbed wire. Among the tent pegs walked hundreds of men in green fatigues like his own. It seemed a holiday crowd promenading at a canival. But those who had their backs turned showed VD signs on their jackets and pants in letters high enough to be read half a mile away. They were like a chain gang without chains.

He entered the indicated door into a long shed, half-ruined and rambling as a cattle barn. Canvas cots with

300

mosquito netting tied up over their racks stretched as far
as his eyes could see. On these cots more men in green
fatigues stretched reading or playing cards or shooting
craps in small knots. He knew that they were set apart
from all the other men in the world, though they looked
perfectly healthy. When he crossed the threshold, a
shout went up. Nearly all who weren't asleep turned to
look at him and yell:

"You'll be sor-ry! Only a hundred and eighty hours
more!"

He flushed, cast his eyes to the ground, and walked between the cots looking for an empty bed. He found one
between a Negro who lay looking at the ceiling and an
Ayrab in a red fez.

"They ain't no pick on the sacks," the Negro said, rolling his eyes slowly around. "Ya cain't never get moren
three hours sleep at one time anyhow, boy."

"What's that Ayrab doin here?" he asked in a whisper.

"Mohammed? Oh all the Allied GI's gits their shots
here . . . we got Goums and Eyeties too. . . . Lend-
lease. . . ."

He sank down on his cot and looked at his shoelaces.
He was casting about in his mind for some way to enter
into conversation with the Negro and get answered some
of the questions that flopped like flounders in his brain.
The Negro may have been waiting, but he merely looked
at the low ceiling of the shed with his deep eyes.

"Is it . . . rough . . . here?" he asked, untying his shoelaces and frigging with the buckles on his boots.

"Well, it ain't no rest cure," the Negro said. "But it
done me a good turn in takin me away from mah woman.
Ah'd a shot her. She gimme bad blood, bad blood . . ."

"What I mean is, do they . . . cure you fast here?" he
pressed.

He was conscious of a fluttering fright now that the
panic and fever of first discovery had ebbed.

"They claims they does. But man, them needles . . .
every three hours. Ah feel like mah Aunt Delilah's pin-
cushion . . ."

"Needles?"

"Sho, boy. What does yo think they does to yo here?
They sticks yo an then they sticks yo again. Every three
hours. Sixty times in all. . . . But it ain't doin me no

301

good. Ah can't do thout mah lovin. So ah'll go right out and do it agin. . . . Yessir . . . but them needles sure does go over big with us colored boys."

He had a dozen more questions to put. But he was confronted by a sharp sergeant standing by his cot.

"You. Didja just come in?"

"Ya."

"Then get down to the lab for ya first Dark Field."

"An that ain't no grope," the Negro said, rolling his eyes up to the ceiling.

He went past the double file of canvas cots out into the sunlight. He passed through the crowds of men in fatigues who walked alone or together, brooding or laughing aloud. He crossed the clearing of the pyramical tents to the swinging sign that said LAB. Inside was another long room with desks where microscopes stood in their metal frames like scrubwomen resting on their brooms.

"You've come for your first Dark Field?" a sergeant asked him.

"I guess that's what they call it," he said.

He had visions of being smothered in black gauze, or pain and probings.

"Then down with your pants," the sergeant said.

The sergeant's face assumed the expression of one who handles the entrails of a sick rabbit. He put down his cigarette and drew on a pair of rubber gloves. Into his shiny false fingers he took a large toothpick wadded with cotton on its tip. Then he bent over and went to work.

"Whaddya doin? . . . Hey . . . you're openin it up . . ."

"That's what I mean to do . . . and if you think I enjoy doing this . . ."

"But ya hurtin like fire . . ."

"I'm swabbing. . . . Okay, up with your pants."

The sergeant straightened up, brushed the swab against a glass slide and dribbled on the square of glass some drops of staining chemical. This he slipped under a microscope near him.

"Now," he said, "I want you to see what death looks like."

The sergeant stepped aside blandly, allowing him to apply his own eye to the lens of the microscope.

"Focus it to your taste," the sergeant said languidly, picking up his cigarette.

He finagled around with the brass screw till he saw the

field of the slide clarify and harden like setting Jello. He was looking at a shifting orange horizon that seemed to be clouds at sunset. There were strata that buckled and changed their densities.

"That," the sergeant's voice said, "is your own polluted blood. Keep looking."

Then he saw something swim into the pink blobs. At first he thought it was a sunfish. He maneuvered the focusing screw some more and found that it was a tadpole. It passed across his field of vision, delicately rowing, and disappeared gaily from his sight with a flip of its tail. He wondered if it hadn't winked at him like a goldfish on the make.

"And that," the sergeant's voice continued like a lecturer's in a darkened room, "is Sophie Spirochete. Just one of the girls, but what she can do to you! . . . Better than a bomb, though somewhat slower."

"Have I got many of those?" he asked.

"Millions. They're multiplying all the time. And brother, they'll eat you up alive!"

"Tell me what I must do," he implored, running his tongue along his lips.

"Every last one of them," the sergeant said, "has got to be killed. That was just one dear little specimen I took off you."

"Well, thankya anyhow . . ."

"Oh don't thank me," the sergeant said coquettishly. "You didn't get it from me, you know."

He'd just got outside the lab when an electric bell went off. All through that dense field of roaming men a mobilization became apparent, as in a factory after lunch hour. Soon there wasn't anybody left in the tent area. He decided that he too must be concerned in this; so he followed the last straggler round a corner.

On a long lading platform hundreds of men in green fatigues were arranging themselves into two files, one much longer than the other. At the end of the platform, by the screen door to what seemed a dispensary a tech sergeant stood with rosters in his hands, adjusted his glasses, and read aloud in a shout:

"Hardfield! Jones! Miozza! McCauliffe! Mahomet Ben Ali! Get the hell up here for ya shots? Don'tcha wanna be cured?"

The two lines quickly evened out till the longer reached

back to the end of the platform. He wasn't quite sure what the lines were for, and which was which. So he stepped cautiously up to a fellow with glasses:

"Maybe ya can tell me what cooks here . . ."

"Je ne comprends pas. . . . Pardon. . . ."

He tried again and this time got an answer from a pimply fat boy:

"This here's the clap line. We get stuck first. Those with syph come after us."

He thanked the joe and walked quickly away, placing himself at the tail end of the shorter line. The tech sergeant appeared again at the door of the dispensary with his rosters and hollered through the entire area:

"Shots! Shots! For Chrissakes come an get em! Ya'd be late to ya own funerals! An I ain't going through the whole area to rout you lazy bastards outa ya tents!"

Tentatively he touched the shoulder of the man in front of him, handsome and blond and shy:

"Say, bud, am I in the right line?"

"Depends on what ya got," the blond boy replied, appraising him languidly.

"Same thing you got, I guess."

"Well," the blond boy said, "this ya first shot? Ya get only fifty-nine more after this one. One every three hours. I don't envy ya much. Ya got a week an a day ta go. . . . Christ, ya'll never sweat out anything like ya will these shots. . . . Three hours . . . three hours . . . forty-eight, forty-nine, fifty. . . . They even wake ya up in the middle of the night. . . . An if ya miss one, they make ya start all over again. . . . I'm gettin' out tamorrah. Hope a hope a hope."

"Where do ya take these shots?"

"In both shoulders an in both cheeks a ya butt. Ya get ta feelin like a sampler. Ya get so ya can't sleep on any part a ya. An still them damn shots go on. Like a pile driver. . . . But ya lucky. They just started this new treatment last week . . ."

"New treatment?"

"Ya. Pencil somethin. Before that they gave ya shots for six months. Useta make fellers puke all over the place. Now they give ya sixty shotsa this new pencil stuff, and it usually cures ya. The clap boys get only four. They get out in a day."

304

"I'll never come back here again," he said piously.

"That's what they all say," the blond boy said. "But they get repeaters here just like in reformatories. Buddy a mine's been in here four times. He gets all cleaned up, then he goes out and picks hisself up another dose. . . ."

The first and longer line began to press forward with rapidity. He thought to himself it was just like all the other lines he'd sweated out in the army—for movies, for PX, for passes. Soon the second line, his, began to urge up on the screen door. Inside the dispensary there was a wild cry.

"Either he's fainted or it's his last shot," the blond boy explained.

Finally it came his turn at the end of the file to enter the dispensary. Inside the screen door the line had forked into two prongs and was being funneled past two GI's, each with a hypodermic in his hand. Along the walls of the room were electric iceboxes. And on the tables glittering with hypodermics and blunted needles were many little glass ampoules of an amber fluid. Into these the GI's plunged their hypodermics, filled them like fountain pens, and squinted at escaping bubbles of the yellow liquid. Ahead of him were men with either arm bared or with their buttocks offered like steak to the needle.

"They give ya a choice on where ya want ya shot," the blond boy said. "If ya take it in the arse, they'll use a longer needle to get through the fat. My advice is ta take ya shots round the clock. Then none of ya four parts gets too sore. Ya'll be hurtin' anyhow . . ."

"Come here," a voice called to him. "I haven't seen your face in line before, boy."

He disengaged himself from the line and went over to where a sergeant with gentian-blue eyes sat at a field desk. This sergeant's sleeves were rolled up to his elbows. Rosters were spread out in front of him. He gave the sergeant his name, which was last on the list.

"You're too nice-looking a guy to get this crap," the sergeant said. "Why don't you stay away from women, like I do?"

"I'm takin my medicine without any sermons from you," he said doggedly, looking down at his boots.

He wanted to be cured, not played with.

305

"Sure, sure, kid. . . . Look, every time you come in here, be sure to stop by and see that I check your name. . . . Otherwise if you miss a shot . . ."

"Ya, I know all that," he said impatiently, rolling up the right sleeve of his green fatigues and preparing to advance into the line for the needle.

Then the sergeant thrust out his fair delicate hand and flipped the miraculous medal that nestled with his dog-tags among the hair on his chest.

"This didn't help you much, did it?" the sergeant said. "You're a mockery of purity."

"I promised my mother to always wear it," he said, again avoiding the cool blue eyes.

"You've got nice brown skin too," the sergeant continued. "Too bad to think of soiling it with crap like you've got. . . . Tell me, did you love that signorina?"

"Shut up an let me alone," he said and walked into the line.

"You'll see me sixty times," the sergeant called after him.

He offered his brown right upper arm to a GI who stood waiting with a hypodermic. He felt the antseptic go all over his flesh like slippery ice. And then a swift stab as the needle went in.

"We ain't interested in making these shots painless," the GI told him.

He felt the needle's charge going into him in a compressed enema of spite. Then he knew a stinging worse than he remembered from tetanus shots. The needle was pulled out and his arm wiped again. On his skin he saw many lemon drops shimmering, raised out against the brown.

"What's that stuff?" he asked, lowering his sleeve.

"Penicillin . . . and more precious than gold, boy."

Being the last to get his shot, he was the last to leave the other door of the dispensary. Barring his way stood the gentian-eyed sergeant, hands folded on his chest. That open neck reminded him, with a jump of memory, of Marisa's throat, glistening and tight in its cords after he'd kissed it.

"Look," he said to the sergeant, "I just wanna be alone. I just wanna take my shots an be left in peace, see?"

"I was wondering," the sergeant said, recrossing his arms, "whether you got it from a one-night stand or from

306

love. Because you seem so bitter. . . . Yes, you must have been in love with her. And now you look like a lamb that can't understand why it's being led to the slaughter. Why don't you want to talk with me?"

"Ya got some ax ta grind with me," he said pushing through the screen door.

The sergeant followed him:

"You know that I'm in a position to do you dirt. I might forget to check your name on the roster. Then you'd have to take all your shots over again . . ."

"I wouldn't advise ya to mess with me," he answered.

Outside the dispensary there was another corridor leading back to the tent area. It had lighted doors leading off it, with the names of medical officers and their rank printed in curly letters. Along the other wall were tin sinks in which GI's were washing their parts. Under these sinks were tin cans stuffed with bloody gauze. The running water and the septic smell and the pungency of dried blood made him dizzy, so he went out into the open air. The tent area had filled up again with men walking or talking or reading. Now he knew the rhythm of the place. They'd walk or talk or read for the next three hours. Then the bell would ring again. Then . . . he felt already the stinging in his other shoulder. All his life telescoped down to three-hour periods and a hypodermic needle with yellow drops dribbling out of it. What was it called? Pencilin? Penisssilin? Pencillllin?

In the shed the syphilitics had resumed their poses. They didn't walk in the courtyard among the tents with the others, for theirs was the scabrous aristocracy of venereal disease. Between shots most lay on their canvas cots dozing. One boy with horn-rimmed spectacles was reading Plato. And his own Negro neighbor still rolled his eyes slowly at the ceiling.

"Ah was a numbers man in Harlem," the Negro began.

But in order not to encourage the Negro's reminiscences, he threw himself on his own cot and closed his eyes.

"It's bad in the moanin," the Negro's slow voice dribbled through, even past his shut lids. "Ya know how a man wakes up. Well, now it'll hurt. An at night the thoughts yo has! Ya feel lak cryin. Least of all ah does . . ."

He emitted a soft feigned snore and the Negro shut up.

307

His brain kept turning over the sibilant secret name of his disease. It was a word that he'd always thought of in connection with others, like leper. He was trying to get used to the idea of having it himself. It was as strange now, in the peace of aftershock, as imagining yourself dead. He kept trying to figure out what there was in the name of this disease, its very sound, that was so frightening. It had a whistling slide when you pronounced it, like a toothless old woman dragging her skirts in a black corridor. Or it reminded him of girls' names like Phyllis. Only with this girl he saw the skull showing.

He thought also of his mother and his sisters in Pittsburgh; their bathrooms with the embroidered cover on the toilet seat, the hems on their towels, the white soap in the rack by the washstand. He remembered how his mother got panicky when she found a speck of dust anywhere. Then he peeped through his eyelids at his own brown body, tense under its shameful green fatigues. And under his flesh he seemed to see microscopic rats running in his blood, squeaking and nibbling as they did their work of demolition. Till finally the house fell apart with a screaming clatter.

He thought also of the army posters against VD. He imagined himself addressing a V-mail to Pittsburgh:

Dear Mother,
You'll be surprised to know that I'm writing you from the syphilis ward of the Twenty-third General Hospital . . .

"I've got a new secondary," a bright lecturing voice said from somewhere down the shed. "Not very nice. Just a rash on the inside of my arms and legs. And a few little blisters containing a rather nasty kind of pus . . ."

"Me and my buddy sweated out the clap for five days," another voice said. "Were our faces red when we found out what we really had! . . ."

"Why, it takes twenty years to kill you," another voice said.

Lastly he thought of Marisa. He remembered yet the brown still fragrance of her body, the round sucking bite of her lips against his shoulder. She'd told him to give himself to her, as she was giving to him, without reserve of fear. She'd said that gli americani made the act of love as

308

sanitary as brushing their teeth or gargling with mouth-wash.

"Ma perchè mi tratti così? Hai forse paura ch'io sia malata? Godi, godi, e non torturarti con certi pensieri. . . ."

It had been the first time he'd fallen in love. He remembered how he'd wait for her evenings in the Galleria, longing and hot, yet in a peace that was tender, and how he'd been gentle with her. Each evening he'd brought her candy or cigarettes or a handkerchief such as she loved. And he remembreed how, after they'd spent their love, they'd lie together talking and laughing. It had never been so with him before. With all the others, after his fever was cooled, he'd only wanted to pay them and kick them out of the door. But with Marisa he'd known a sense of joy and well-being. Thus he'd given her his heart like a piece of fudge in his open palm. He couldn't yet associate this disease with her name. Only over her face there now hung a veil that blotted her features.

Yes, he was sick. It didn't feel like much of anything now. But this sickness was like being told definitely just how long he had to live. There was something mocking and foul in his disease, because it was a legacy to him from the happiest moments in his life. He remembered the idiots he'd seen in county jails, leaning out from behind their bars, lolling their tongues and screaming. He remembered old men helping themselves along the sides of walls with their canes, so that every step took half an hour to accomplish. All this had nothing to do with Marisa. Yet it had. . . .

Someone was tapping the sole of his boot. He opened his eyes. At the end of his cot stood a red-cheeked chaplain, arms loaded with tracts and colored leaflets. So he sat up respectfully.

"Well, son," the chaplain said, "I guess now we see what the wages of sin are, don't we?"

"What sin?" he said, turning his eyes to the other row of cots.

"My boy, my boy. We mustn't be unregenerate in our hearts. Our disease is the punishment of God for fleshly sin."

"I happened to be in love," he said, standing up from his cot, putting his hands into his pockets, and whistling a little.

"Love!" the chaplain said with shining eyes, lifting his plump pink hands. "Love brings little children into the world. Not death. We should have saved ourselves for some fine clean American girl. These Italians are all sinful and diseased . . ."

. "Then they should all get some of these here pencil shots," he said sullenly.

"My boy, if there were no disease in the world, there would be no decency. The fear of God. Our illness is a sign of the disapproval of God for what we did . . ."

"I was unlucky, that's all . . ."

"And the army doesn't approve either," the chaplain said, searching for further backing. "After we leave this hospital, we'll lose our rating, if we have one."

"I know that too."

"Well, I'll just leave some of these pamphlets, son. Let's all think of our mothers . . ."

"I have."

"I'd like to shake hands, son," the chaplain said, withdrawing. "But God has made certain diseases highly infectious. . . ." The chaplain went on to other cots. He lay down again and covered his face with his hands. He still saw Marisa's face, but he heard too a crowing laughter. Even her voice now seemed clotted with slime.

He soon got used to the simple reality of life in a syphilis ward. Three hours was the boundary of all his consciousness. He lived only for his next puncture. Every needle meant another x on the roster opposite his name, and three hours nearer to his release. Forty-seven, forty-eight, forty-nine, fifty. Night or day had no longer any distinct meaning, for he couldn't count on uninterrupted sleep for more than three hours. Then the fleering jangle of the electric bell. At 0300 hours in the morning, having just got to sleep after his midnight injection, he'd hear that silvery rattlesnake in the court outside. All the tents would come to life, with men groping into their fatigues and tottering out sleepy and cursing to where the threads of light poked out from the dispensary. The sergeant in charge of shots yelling for order. The beams of flashlights thumbing through the dark. The uproar lasting about twenty minutes. The files forming and going through like an assembly belt. Then the voice of a sergeant speeding up slackers who might be still in their cots. He didn't un-

310

derstand how people could take their time about their shots. Here they had death in their blood, yet they were leisurely and dilatory about receiving from the needle's point those yellow drops that meant life to them, life truer than the amber drops of gasoline or bubbles of molten gold.

He got into the habit of waking by reflex a few seconds before the electric bell exploded. He'd lie under his mosquito netting with an arm under his head, thinking: Now what did I wake up for? Oh, number twenty-two. And as soon as he heard the tingling dissonance he'd be bounding off his cot, buttoning his fatigues and sliding his feet into his boots, which he never bothered to lace or buckle. And he'd go rushing down the line of cots with their shadowy dressing figures. He usually managed to get to the dispensary among the first. Not that it made any difference. The gonorrhea boys always went through first. They took their own sweet time in forming their line. The syph patients were more eager beavers and would stand with their file already in order, cheering and booing the stragglers. For nobody got pincushioned till both lines were formed.

Needles around the zodiac of his brown body. At first he tried taking them in alternate arms. But soon the flesh of both shoulders was so raw that he couldn't sleep on either side. By the twentieth shot he was ready and eager to have them jab him in the buttocks. This called for a longer and heavier needle which bit him like a hornet. After a while both of his tight brown cheeks were so sore that he couldn't sleep on his back any more. He asked if he could be shot in the bulging calves of his legs, but they told him it would hurt worse than a cramp. So he finally evolved the least agonizing of many torments, which would carry him through half a day: a shot in the right shoulder, a shot in the left, a shot in his right buttock, a shot in his left. This meant that every twelve hours his compass was boxed. The stings felt worse all the time in his mincemeated flesh; he'd stand watching the penicillin ooze down his skin like the yoke of an egg. And always in the dispensary the ampoules of penicillin stood in a pretty druggist's window display of bottles, and the trash barrels outside the dispensary were overflowing with the dead ones, like small jars that had contained a lemon preserve put up every fall by his mother.

"I wonder how much the government is forking out for my sixty shots?" someone asked.

"When ya see it in a refrigerator," another said, "the stuff looks just like sherry wine on ice. They hafta keep it cool. . . ."

He had to go for his second Dark Field. Again he met the sergeant with the rubber gloves who scraped some fluid off him and put the film on the slide under the microscope. The sergeant indicated he should look again through the lens. He saw his salmon-colored blood; but try as he might, he didn't see a solitary tadpole wriggling. One floated by in the field, but it looked curled up and lifeless.

"Your spirochetes are pretty well done for," the sergeant said dryly.

"Ya mean I'm cured?" he asked, raising his eyes, dazzled.

"You'll take your full sixty shots, just like everyone else."

But he walked on air back to the shedlike ward and told everyone within range that the tadpoles in his blood were kaput. The Negro in the next cot just lay and looked at the ceiling for the doctor had told him to expect a circumcision tomorrow. The Negro had been saying all day in his dreamy voice that no army doctor was going to circumcise *him*. Hadn't he still his razor with him?

The last shot of the night vigil was given just as the dawn came up over Mussolini's fairgrounds at Bagnoli. Nobody slept much between the three o'clock shot and the six o'clock. The sun would leak up with a lemon and creeping pace. He'd totter out into the yellow and gray light, his eyes foggy, pulling his fatigues about him. The lines would form and the needles would start pricking. This was the time when the night shift of butchers went off duty to be replaced by the day shift. Their tempers were frayed and they did their jabbing with a vindictive spite, hating all who were so stupid as to catch diseases which would keep them out of their beds all night long on a hypodermic line. The six o'clock shots were characterized by blunt needles which tore his flesh jaggedly. Then there was the pulsing orgasm of the penicillin pumping into him like a piston.

Then he'd limp back to his ward, flexing his stinging

312

arm. By his cot on the mosquito netting bar with his towel and soap hung his mess kit. He'd gather up this metal gear and head for the chow line. It was now fully light.

He'd made a friend in the ward, a shy guy who said he was a staff sergeant in ordnance. They waited together in the chow line. His new buddy talked about this nurse, and how he never suspected she would have passed It on to him. They dipped their mess kits into the GI can of boiling water.

"I wonder if they sterlize these things with each next batch of patients?"

"Nah, what with the scaldin water an that pencil stuff, ya can't catch a damn thing here. They even have Ginso barbers to shave ya if ya want it."

He got three meals a day of hot C-rations ladled into his mess kit. Back of the steam tables stood Neapolitans who leered knowingly at them as they dished out the steaming powdered eggs, the scalding coffee, and the chunks of bread. They jested with the patients:

"Whassamatta, Joe? Signorina malata?"

"Ah, fungoo and ya signorinas," the patients answered, helping themselves to marmalade and sugar.

He and his buddy sat down at the long planked tables, which filled up in order as the joes came off the chow line. Occasionally he saw a guy dressed in OD's instead of fatigues. That was a sign his shots were finished and he was going in the world outside the barbed wire. Opposite them was a little redheaded man morosely eating his powdered eggs and bacon. He had a burst of friendship for this sad little man. After all they were all members of the freemasonry of penicillin.

"Doin all right?" he nodded at the little redhead.

The little man didn't answer but moved himself and his mess kit to the other end of the table.

"They say that's a first looie," his buddy whispered to him.

"Oh they get it too, huh?" he said, poking some bread into his face.

Nobody talked much in the mess hall, except to agree that penicillin was a wonderful thing. Dried you up in no time. Or they compared their symptoms or told one another how many more shots they had to go. A few bragged that they were repeaters in this dump. Some came back

constantly in order to keep out of combat, where they'd
only get killed. But most held up their hands over their
coffee:

"No sir! I ain't never comin back to this concentration
camp!"

"Wait till ya get outside the barbed wire," the minority
said, "An ya meet another signorina an she shakes it at
ya. That's all it takes. . . . You'll be back."

Over their coffee he and his buddy lit cigarettes and
looked at each other. All the meals were the same here.
Three a day. Then you waited for your next shot. They
went outside into the sunlight and dunked their mess gear
into the GI cans of scalding soapy and clear water. The
tent flaps were up all over the area now; the new sunlight made weird curlicues of the monuments, mosaics,
and shafts of Mussolini's fair grounds at Bagnoli.

After breakfast he made up his cot, rolled up his mosquito netting, and waited for his turn for the broom to
come by him. Bedmaking was easy, for he had two GI
blankets, nothing more; sometimes it got chilly in the
early mornings at Bagnoli in August, 1944. Then he'd
sweep the kittens of dust from under his cot into the aisle
and would pass the broom to the Negro on his right. He
knew now who were the officers in the ward, in spite of
the incognito of their green fatigues, because when the
morning sweeping was in progress they leaned against the
wall and tried to look nonchalant.

"Hey, sirrr," the pfc wardboy called to one, "there's no
rank in a syph ward."

After the policing he'd lie on his cot and wait for the
doctor to come. Each morning they showed themselves to
this medical officer, who discharged those who were going out that day. For others he prescribed circumcisions
or made little notes in their Syphilis Registers. Each had
his own little scrapbook in which the progress of his disease was recorded. This doctor felt their glands or said:

"Rash fading nicely, isn't she?"

He was a fat little captain with a face like a doughnut.
His eyes had frozen into a perpetual revulsion from looking at men's genitals and thinking in terms of spirochetes
and gonococci. He was forever tearing off his rubber
gloves, washing his hands, and peeling on the gloves again.
Each morning he made a set speech to those who were
going out upon completion of their sixtieth shot:

314

"Ninety percent of you men will be permanently cured
. . . if you don't get another case. . . . And if you do have
a relapse, there's always that nice long-term treatment
with mapharsen and arsenic. . . . In three months come
back for your spinal."

It was always the mention of the spinal tap that sent a
shiver and a whispering through the rest of the ward, who
always listened to the doctor's baccalaureate sermons
even when they weren't included in them. The Negroes,
at that word spinal, would roll their eyes and gibber at
one another:

"No, boy, ah ain't takin no spahnal . . . no suh . . . if
dey ties me to dis cot, ah still won't take no spahnal. Dat
needle sometimes slips and dere you is, paaaaahlahzed
for de rest o yo natcherl life. No spahnal fo me. . . ."

Hearing this as he lay on his cot waiting for the captain
to call out his name for the morning checkup, he'd imagine the needle at the base of his spine, the slip as the
target was missed, and all his nerves jolting into paralysis.

Or sometimes to relieve the tedium of his morning examinations, the probing of groins and armpits, the questioning about the state of the chancre, the medical captain
would bring specialists into the ward with him, colonels
who peered at the patients as though they were guinea
pigs.

"Look, colonel, sir, he had a rare kind of rash. I had
him photographed. With a mask, of course. . . ."

"This man insists he never had a primary lesion. . . ."

There was everyone on that ward: Negroes, Ayrabs,
Italians fighting for the Allies, one Hawaiian Japanese.
They waited three hours, took their shot, then waited
again. They all wore the green fatigues with VD painted
on the back. They all lived eight days inside the barbed
wire. They all sat on the long planks in the mess.

After the medical inspection he was free till 0900 hours,
the time of the next inspection. He'd take his towel, razor,
and toothbrush and go out into the sunlit courtyard where
the patients walked. He crossed the area of the tents of
the common ordinary twenty-four-hour patients who were
here for only four shots. He passed also the barbed wire
within the barbed wire where prisoners with VD were
treated under the eyes of their individual MP's. These
real prisoners slept on the ground under the pup tents,
issuing forth every three hours with their armed guard

315

to get nipped by the penicillin needle. Then he'd arrive at the latrines, these too in sheds. Then began his one joy of the day. He'd brush his teeth and shave. Then he'd strip away the hateful green fatigues with the advertising on the back and step under the shower. He'd smear his long dark body with soap and let the tepid water gush over his flesh. At such moments he still thought of Marisa's arms that had given him this death. He'd lift his hoarse voice and sing an Italian song she'd taught him. For between the soapsuds and the penicillin something was being washed away from and out of him.

Close to 1500 hours he was lying on his cot reading a comic book. His thighs were crossed and his boots were up on the rack for his mosquito netting. He was sleepy, but it was almost time for the next needle. In the cots near him were people different from those who'd been here when he came a week ago. In this ward life went on by relays, constant as to the disease, but different in respect to personalities. He laid down his comic book, aware that someone was coming toward him. It was the gentian-eyed sergeant of the rosters. He sighed. The sergeant was carrying a parcel wrapped in wax paper.

"You again?"

"You weren't very glad to see me," the sergeant said, sitting on the edge of the cot and undoing a package.

"A roast-beef sandwich. . . . Are ya gonna eat it right here in front of me?"

"It's for you. We get good chow in the detachment mess. You must be tired of that C-ration they give you three times a day. I got the mess sergeant to make this up for me special. I didn't tell him I was giving it to a friend."

"Well, thanks. . . ."

He sank his teeth into the hot red flesh. The soft bread rose round his gums in a contrast of textures and tastes.

"Ya shouldn't bother with me," he said. "I'm just another syphilitic."

"You're not," the sergeant said.

He edged over on his cot to make room for the sergeant. He buried his face in the roast-beef sandwich to finish it, but he knew that those strange blue eyes were on his face. It made him squeamish to be watched while he was eating.

"Ya got some ax to grind with me," he said again, putting the crusts into the wax paper.

316

"Why?" the sergeant asked brightly. "You don't know me . . . yet."

"Well, it don't add up somehow," he said, shaking his head and placing his boots again on the rack for mosquito netting. "Ya must meet thousands of VD's coming through here for their shots. I'm just another one with the dirty bug . . ."

"I've watched half the Fifth Army taking shots," the sergeant said. "But when I saw you, I knew you were different."

"I snafu'd just like the rest of them," he said warily.

Besides reminding him of Marisa, something in this sergeant's blue eyes touched him, the way a lame bird would.

"You should come out to dinner with me once in a while," the sergeant said. "I know a black market restaurant on Via Chiaia. Do you like pasta asciutta?"

The words thrilled him with a pang of remembrance. He seemed to be with Marisa in a cramped kitchen in Sezione, San Ferdinando, she with an apron on standing over the stove. In those days he'd come up behind her and slip his hands over her loins. And she'd turn her face to be kissed. . . .

"Ya don't wanta be bothered with me," he said, wrenching himself from this memory. "I'm no good. Can't even take care of myself. Accordin to the posters the army puts out, I can never get married now nor have kids. I'm just a old pieca meat gathering flies in the streets."

"You'll get cured," the sergeant said. "Just don't think you are till you know you are, that's all. . . . But you *are* different. . . . I need a friend, you see. Being a dancer has given me an unreal view of life. I'm so fed up with the arty boys. I want to know just one real person. You're good and you're decent. . . . I'm so bored with sitting around in cliques and drinking and talking poetry and scandal. . . . Do you like to swim? We could go to Torregaveta and Mondragone for sun baths . . ."

"I don't get much time off," he said.

"I need a friend who's real," the sergeant continued softly. "Someone who lives quietly and thoroughly without pointing out that he's doing it. I'm fed up with the idea of sex without love and ideas without deeds. . . . You shouldn't run with these Neapolitan girls . . . the ones, on Via Roma, I mean. They don't offer you any-
317

thing without a price. There are nice Italian girls, but you won't stand a chance of meeting any . . ."

"When a guy needs a woman," he said, "he needs a woman . . ."

"That's the great old myth of the American male," the sergeant said wearily, picking up the wax paper from the cot. "And you see what you've got out of it. . . . Look at yourself in the mirror sometimes. That fine coffee-colored skin you've got and your black eyebrows and your straight nose. You're a very good-looking man . . . too swell to end up with spyhilis from some bitch who didn't give a shit for you. . . . When I first saw you, it was like looking at a statue covered with mud . . ."

"I was crazy about Marisa," he said, surprised that he wasn't sore at this sergeant.

"I suppose you thought you were," the sergeant said. "That's all part of the mystery and the pain of life to me . . ."

"Say," he said, sitting up suddenly, "don't you like women?"

"When I don't see through them," the sergeant said, rising from the cot. "Will you come to dinner with me next week? Then we can go to the ballet at the San Carlo. The Italians can't dance, but they call it ballet anyhow. . . . Will you come?"

"I don't stand to lose nothin," he replied, trying not to sound calculating. "I won't be lookin' at no women for some time now . . ."

"You're crazy if you do," the sergeant said hotly. "And do you think it would be fair to take any chances? Right now you're not infectious, but you can never be sure until you've had your spinal. It can come back on you at any time. Would you want to pass it on to somebody else?"

"I been thinkin of that," he said. "I ain't so low that I'd do to another girl what Marisa done for me."

"She's doing it for others right now."

"No," he said, closing his eyes. "I don't believe that."

"Did you give her name on the questionnaire?"

"Get out."

The sergeant with his bright hair and blue eyes and delicate figure stood irresolutely at the foot of the cot. He seemed to want to stay and to go. He looked almost as if
318

Marisa had dressed herself in GI suntans and a blond tight wig. "

"Willya do somethin for me?" he asked, already knowing the answer. He didn't believe in putting friends to the test, but he had an overpowering compulsion to do this. "Bring me some of that penicillin?"

"What for?" the sergeant asked in a quick whisper. "Do you want to sell it? Do you know what an ampoule of penicillin is worth on the black market? What do you want it for?"

"I ain't gonna sell it," he answered stiffly. "I just want it for myself . . . like people keep their appendixes and tonsils in a jar."

The sergeant shot a swift look along the ward, where as usual the patients were snoring on their cots or playing cards. He darted off. Shortly he was back carrying something in the same wax paper.

"You realize," the sergeant said, passing the wax paper into his hand, "that if anybody finds out about this, they'll throw the book and the DTC at me . . ."

"I ain't never done no one dirt in all my life," he replied, returning the sergeant's stare.

The ampoule with its amber fluid was still icy and misted from the refrigerator. He thrust it into the chamois bag containing his toilet articles.

"What a world," the sergeant said. "The mold of yeast turns out to be more precious than gold. . . . I've got to go, boy. It's almost time for the bell. . . . Meet you day after tomorrow at 1900 hours in the portico of the San Carlo."

"Okay," he answered.

A little later the electric bell began to split the air. He went out to stand in the second line. He had two more shots to go. Fifty-nine, sixty.

Next morning when the 0600 bell pealed for shots and the shadowy men in the first orange of dawn groped from under their mosquito netting into their fatigues, he remembered and smiled to himself and turned over on his other shoulder. His butt and arms still felt like hamburg, but it didn't matter any more now.

"Hey, Joe," the guy from the next bed was prodding him, "get out of that fartsack and take your needle."

"Ah, go way," he murmured, "I had my sixtieth."

He fell back into a delicious sleep during which he sensed an electric excitement in his belly. He awoke again when the others came trooping back from breakfast with their dripping mess kits.

"Powdered eggs?" he asked dreamily.

After a while without hurrying he got out from under his blankets, made his cot, and swept beneath it. He had a sense of victory over all the others, bending over their housekeeping with the painted letters VD on their backs rippling as the muscles in their shoulders moved. He felt particularly affectionate toward a tiny Negro two cots over who'd just come in.

"Boy, ah's scared. Does them needles hurt much?"

"Ya'll faint sixty times," he answered, sweeping under the tiny Negro's cot.

"O Lawd," the Negro said, fainting on his blankets.

When he'd revived his small friend, he took his chamois bag and went down to the latrines. Here Italian prisoners of war were swabbing the wooden frames and the corrugated urinal with chlorine. He rejoiced in its clean acridity. Before he seated himself, he reverted to his old fastidiousness of placing clots of toilet paper all around the wooden hole. It was a practice he'd dropped during his treament here. Now he was beginning it all over again. Cleanliness was no longer a mockery. One Italian P/W called to the other as they mopped:

"Sa che cos'è la sifilde? Un' ora con Venere e dopo sei mesi con Mercurio."

Shortly he arose in great satisfaction, brushed his teeth, and shaved. He'd observed that the brown skin along his thighs was paler for the eight days he'd spent out of the sun. Then he took a shower, soaping himself with gusto and dodging the Italians as they turned on the other sprays to damp down the floor planking. And his body was once again immaculate. He passed both hands along his loins in a wringing motion to force off the tire of soap.

He dressed himself for the last time in the tight green fatigues and walked up among the pyramidal tents. The gonorrhea patients were still making their beds. They had no floor to sweep, for it was of clay pounded down hard. They were rolling up the flaps of their tents to let in the Neapolitan sunlight: Ayrab soldiers under the red fezzes they insisted on coupling with their ignominious fatigues, French soldiers and officers from Alger and Oran, Italian

320

sergenti maggiori who worked for the Allies, and that greater percentage of Americans. Occasionally one would run out to the Lyster Bag and swallow his sulfa tablets.

In the great clearing girdled with barbed wire he paused to look at the bulletin board. On typewritten sheets were thumb-tacked the list of dispositions for that day. He found his own name in alphabetical order under American Personnel. At first he had a feeling that perhaps they might never let him out of this place, that he'd stay here till the end of the war in Italy, being jabbed with millions of units of penicillin. But there was his name. He was getting out today. After each patient to be discharged was the rank and serial number, followed in the last column by the diagnosis: These read: Syphilis, Old, Secondary, Relapse; or Gonorrhea, New Acute. He noticed also that some people he'd met (he'd never guessed from their fatigues) were first lieutenants or majors. But most were GI's of all the Allied armies.

He returned with his toilet kit into the shed. They were lining up for inspection by the nauseated-looking medical captain. He unbuttoned his own green fatigues and waited his turn in the queue.

"You're going out today," the captain said, looking at his revealed middle and sounding his lymph glands. "Take a blood test every month. And come back for your spinal in from three to six months. Come even if we don't send for you. . . . And behave yourself, understand?"

"Yessir," he said slowly, then swallowed. "An' I wanna thank ya for all ya've done for me."

The rubbery face contorted into another knot.

"Don't thank me. Thank penicillin. Thank Dr. Fleming."

The medical captain then wrote out in an acid hand a discharge slip from the Twenty-third General Hospital. Then he consigned to him the little bound Syphilis Register with his name on the cover, like a diary, and two copies of a letter to his commanding officer making it quite clear why he'd been in the hospital—not in the line of duty.

"And don't try to tear up that letter," the doctor told him. "Because we mail a carbon to your CO anyway."

Then he went out into the sunlight among the pyramidal tents where the men in their green fatigues were milling and talking and waiting for the next electric bell. He

321

went first to the supply sergeant to draw his own clothes. It was the first time in eight days he'd had them on; they were rumpled and a little mildewed from lying in the barracks bag. Then he had an inspiration. He took his razor from his toilet kit and sliced both sets of sergeant's stripes from his sleeves. His chevrons fell to the floor, trailing thread, twisted like crinkled tin foil.

"Might just as well bust myself right now," he said to the supply sergeant, handing across the counter the green fatigues with those huge letters painted across the back of jacket and trousers.

Next he went into the large office with the typists and the vials and the chairs with armrests. He sat down against the wall and let a tech five leech more blood from his arm.

"Of course this proves nothing," the technician said, emptying the dark blood into a test tube taped with his name. "Penicillin turns ya blood negative anyhow."

Lastly he went to the barrier in the barbed wire and presented his pass to the MP.

"See ya back here in about another week," the MP said, looking down at his sleeve, at the light triangular patch where his stripes had been.

"Not me, boy," he answered.

He walked slowly down the macadam drive of the Medical Center at Bagnoli. Once he turned in his tracks and looked back at the barbed wire behind which the hundreds of marionettes in green fatigues paced like lifers. He saw also the kiosks, the glittering façades, the nude muscled statues under their helmets, and the swimming pools that Mussolini had laid out for his world's fair. He couldn't forget that here he'd passed eight days of his life in three-hour intervals with a hypodermic needle waiting to prick him at the end of each period.

On the Bagnoli-Naples road a pfc in a weapons carrier picked him up. They rumbled through the Bagnoli Tunnel. In the August morning the town of Naples stretched golden on its hillside. Ischia and Capri struck like honey-colored thumbs out of the Mediterranean. He had an urge to talk.

"Say, that penicillin sure is marvelous stuff," he confided. "I was nearly dead from pneumonia an it pulled me out of it."

"Ah, it may have worked for you," the pfc said, biting on his cigar. "Me, I always say that penicillin is still

322

to be put to the test. It's probably the latest racket of the medical profession. They say it cures VD too. Me, I think it just conceals the symptoms and arrests the disease for a while. But we don't know nothin about its future reactions on the human body. Ten years from now you'll probably find cripples and people dropping dead all over the United States. Victims of the great penicillin swindle."

"Nah, it works," he answered in a dreamy sort of happiness. "It's great stuff, boy. . . . Cured my pneumonia. . . ."

In Naples he dismounted from the weapons carrier at the end of Via Roma. He entered the Galleria Umberto, where the girls were walking and the children screaming and bargaining in the August sunlight. He walked to that corner of the Galleria that he remembered best. Though it was noon he seemed to see Marisa standing there with her arms out to him. So he took the ampoule of penicillin out of his pocket and hurled it against the wall where her ghost flickered. The glass smashed; the yellow liquid ran like bright molasses to the pavement.

EIGHTH PROMENADE

(Naples)

I REMEMBER that in Naples of August, 1944, I came again to realities I'd all but forgotten. There are three of them: tears, art, and love. Most people in the world live their lives with at least two of these realities. But between Casablanca and Naples I'd lost all three by watching what was going on around me. So when they came back to me, I felt like one whose heart begins to beat again when he was despaired of.

Naples, I remember, is a good city for relearning the reality of tears. Americans assume that tears are wet and that life should be dry. Consequently crying in America is done usually by women and babies. Life as we Americans have made it is presumed to be a gay affair. Even when it wasn't gay, a man mustn't cry. But the old maxims tell me to take the bitter with the sweet. So I reasoned that life isn't so gay as the advertisments pretend it can be—if I'll only use their product. And where is the place of tears in the scheme? When may even a man cry?

"Ah," the mess sergeant said. "They spend half a their time bawlin. It's all part of the act. But I see through these Eyeties."

"Once every hour," the corporal said, twisting his GI handkerchief, "the Neapolitans cry. They cry when they're happy an they cry when they're sad. Don't make sense."

"But it does," the pfc with the spectacles said under his mosquito netting. "Look at a face laughing. Then look at the same face crying. . . . Which do you think is the truer mask?"

I remember thinking of this point. In tears there's something very old and very young. In between is the vacuum that laughs or smiles. I decided that Americans cried less because they lived mostly in that vacuum. They weren't close enough to birth or close enough to death. After some time in Naples I saw that by the Mediterranean it's more human to weep than to laugh. More reasons to. I got to love the Italians because they were still able to do some of both.

I wasn't satisfied with the easy song and dance that Italians are just volatile. If people cry easily, perhaps they're gentler. Perhaps they acknowledge the truth of life more honestly. Crocodile tears aside, of course. So often when I was alone in Naples at midnight and saw the moon on the bay, and Capri like hope turned to stone, I saw that too much laughter was a mockery of our own precarious state, a spiting of God, as though to show Him that he couldn't pull these incongruities over *our* eyes.

"I had a signorina las night," the mess sergeant said. "She bust out bawlin after it was all over. But I know she oney did it to screw me for a hundred lire more. . . ."

I saw the women of Naples cry. But I'd seen women cry before. The Neapolitan women wept for strong reasons. They couldn't get food at black market prices. Their two rooms had been blasted by a bomb. Or their man would never come back to them, for the Germans had shot him in North Italy. I saw Neapolitan mothers pass

324

me on the street and suddenly begin to cry. I saw a Neapolitan girl great with child rolling on a doorstep where till recently an American had been billeted. I saw a girl from the Vomero shoot a British captain on Via Roma and fall weeping on his body. Then I began to understand the reasons for tears.

I remember I wept once myself, in Algiers. Because I couldn't figure out the mess I and other Americans were in. That crying of mine was like a boy kicking his bicycle or tearing up a crossword puzzle he's too stupid to solve. Mine was selfish weeping because my pride was baffled. Thus I learned the difference between crying over a broken heart and crying over a principle. On this difference depends whether tears lift or debase. Tears can flow from the heart or merely from the eyes. In the first case they're like blood. In the second, just so much salt water.

I remember the farmers out Caserta way standing in their fields and crying over the drought. In 1944 Italy needed food. But the war had dried up even the heavens; the fields even down to Bari and Puglie were scorched.

I remember a scugnizz' on Via Roma crying in the August noon because the American major confiscated his can of shoe polish, saying that he stole it from the americani. When this kid cried, I thought his heart was spilling out of his dirty thin body.

I remember Aïda, arrested on the streets where she was walking and not bothering anybody. They jailed her in the questura till her blood test turned out negative. Today in Naples Aïda must still remember how the americani treated her. I saw her in her pink cotton dress and sandals, rolling up her sleeve for the needle. Her tears fell on her brown chest. We Americans stood around laughing and asking Aïda how much she charged.

I remember the family Russo: Papa and Mamma and Valerio and Salvatore, looking at the place where they and their blood had lived for two hundred years. In that palazzo Mercadante wrote his songs. After a bomb it looked like a pile of chalk. I remember how the mother put her face on the father's shoulder, how both of them rocked together, how Valerio and Salvatore simply sat down on the dust of the place where they'd been born.

I remember Gerarda of the hair that never stayed in place, of the smell of lace and oranges, of the hands that

325

were folded in front of her—but not in resignation.

"Una volta," Gerarda said, "ero un' ottima pianista, al Conservatorio. Anche la maestra me lo diceva. . . ."

Gerarda wept sometimes out of fury and a refusal to accept her own destiny. Her tears taught me that the individual is never so responsible as the moralists hold, that by August, 1944, the Italian personality had long been stymied by collective hell.

And I remember an American USO actress weeping because the QM laundry hadn't ironed the pleats into her skirt. Or myself moaning because our cigarette ration got cut from seven packs a week to five.

"These Ginsoes are softenin me up," the mess sergeant said. "They do so much turnin on of the water works that I'm meltin away myself."

"When Rosetta left me to spend a week in Rome," the corporal said, "she puts her arms around my neck and she busts out bawlin. . . . So I did too. Just dig that. . . . They better get us GI's outa Italy before we all go to pieces."

And I remember seeing wounded soldiers in the 300th General cry when they thought no one was around. Except for them I don't believe most of us Americans in Naples of August, 1944, had much real reason to cry. But we did when we'd got a skinful of vino. We were feeling sorry for ourselves. But we were doing all right compared to the Neapolitans. Then I saw that those who weep honestly had simply come to a point where they must cease acting or break.

I remember that in Naples I began to observe a dreadful harmony among the sorrow, the hunger, and the filth. I heard how Neapolitan music was this common denominator. It was music, not to amuse or to distract, but to comment on the life of Naples. This music was more than sounds coming out of the air. It was a voice focused from the horror and squalor that I saw in the streets. It didn't need program notes. I knew it for a consciousness of the Neapolitans. I found out where this awareness came from, for I saw poets and painters and musicians by themselves, watching the city of Naples from a distance. They were not followed by publicity agents who took down everything they said, for release to the world the following morning. They just stood and looked and

326

thought. They were sponges sucking in whatever there was in the air in August, 1944. I was seeing the isolation of the artist. His mind runs along in its own time, and no one can tell him for sure whether he has anything to say. He can only watch and listen and himself become transparent. Everything he sets down is at the focus of the crosscurrents. He feels the fret and push of currents and forces, but he cannot express them except in his own medium. This negating and expanding of himself lets him know that he's great and infinitesimal all at once. He's so occupied with life that he's incapable of living it himself, for that would ruin the barometer in him.

I remember that Italian artists are different from American ones. The Americans always announced that they're artists. They were glib about their techniques and their souls. They told me also that they were making money —not that I should pay much attention to that. They told me a man could be either very rich or very poor from his art. Look at Shakespeare; look at Mozart. But I might as well know that in the twentieth century a good artist had a 90-percent chance of making scads of money. They told me so. And they assured me that the most successful artists neither wrote down to their publics nor retreated into meaninglessness. They often blithely referred to such phrases as It Sells, and Giving the Public What it Wants. So I decided that these American artists were craftsmen in the plumbing of the soul. Chromium and plastic.

But the Neapolitans never informed me that they were artists. Nor had they a press agent to tell me so. They looked like any other Italian when they came into a room. Only when I'd got to know them did I learn that they'd written or composed or painted. I saw no romantic hunger in their eyes. But I was aware in them of a reserve and a delicacy, as though they were playing with fire, and knew it. Often they were inaccessibly melancholy. And except in the Cafés (where there was no coffee) they talked of many other things than the problems of the artist. They told me that they worked from their hearts, after they'd tested those hearts. They said that every human heart contained a key to other hearts. But the artist's gaze must be within, after a long time of looking about outside. These Neapolitan artists told me that a man knows if he ever puts down the truth. It hurts as

327

it's being torn out of the heart. But once set down, un-deformed and whole, it will lie on the paper forever—more or less. It should never be warped into what the artist thinks *may* or *should be* the truth. The Neapoli-tans told me that a bad artist cooks up what people want to believe. They told me that in August, 1944, I must listen hard to pick up the least murmur of truth.

I remember that the Amerian artists had no such counsel to give me. They spoke of fitting oneself into movements. They talked of periods and tendencies and lucky shots and literary agents. They wouldn't read any-thing I'd written, but they liked to have me around as audience:

"Got a minute? Here's an amusing little thing I just dashed off. . . ."

The Neapolitan artists taught me by knowing them. They said that the artist is also a teacher. The striving must be done with his material. And the highest and hardest striving of all with himself. No one, they said, could help him in this secret battle. No one but himself for that first carving and that last polishing. They told me that if the artist didn't believe in some worth in life, there wasn't any point in trying to be an artist. For art was an act of life and love, with some of the violence inherent in each. There was no excuse for titillating or frustrating. Just let pen and paper and brush alone for a better man. Good art had been accomplished before and probably would be again.

"These Italian buildins," the corporal said, "like they grew from the ground without even tryin."

"Ah," said the mess sergeant, watching a signorina watch him, "when these old mousetraps was new, they looked as shiny as Rockefeller Center does now."

"I wonder," the pfc said.

"Yuh, Naples is too fulla monuments," the corporal said. "Oughta tear em down. All slums."

"My boy," the pfc said over his spectacles, "you must make the distinction between old lumber and old jew-els. . . ."

I remember wondering what there was in Italian music and Italian painting and Italian architecture different from anything we Americans had given to the world. And I decided that the best were complete projections of incomplete human life into a dead medium. In them

328

all I found a regret, a sense of something transitory caught on the wing, a humility and a pride inextricably mixed. I saw that, the better succeeding ages had judged these pieces of art, the more fully did they partake of a discipline that man wishes he possessed, of a sweetness such as he rarely has the strength to sustain. But most of all these tunes, these statues, and these poems had an air as though everyone had felt them but had been too lazy to write them down.

There's something in these memorials of the human spirit that cheers and terrifies at the same time. Death is coming, but it can't be so awful because everyone goes through with it. And out of death this art speaks to the living. It smiles. With the smile of a mother who knows what her child has to look forward to. But she never speaks of it. This is the crystallized wisdom of art. Nobody heeds it, yet everyone admires it on one plane of taste or another. I remember that in Naples of August, 1944, I found that art achieves what man hopes for and what religions promise.

And I remember that something in the air of Naples or in the Neapolitans brought me and other Americans back to the strength of human love. In the middle of a war it's easy to forget how to love, either another's body, or just humanity. War throws out of kilter that part of us which delights in a kiss, the feel of skin, a smile. Our emphasis falls on sheer physical release taken hurriedly and brutally.

I wondered why Americans must be taught how to love. Perhaps it's because in our country there is felt to be something shameful in two human beings taking their pleasure together. In America I remember a tension between the sexes. Human love is a disease for the isolation ward, not at all nice. Thus love in America is often divided into the classifications of Having Sex and Getting Married. Neither has much to do with love. It was the Having Sex which began to strike us in Naples as being so cold-blooded. What caused this? The Italian scenery? The Neapolitan women? But after a while I and many other Americans ceased to be satisfied with passion without affection. I'd known Americans who'd lost their virginity without ever kissing or making love in the old sense of the word. So we came to look upon this

Having Sex, this ejaculation without tenderness, as the orgasm of a frigidaire. There was no place for it in the scheme of human love. It wasn't so much bestial as meaningless. For Having Sex meant that the two bodies involved never really knew one another. They just rolled and arose strangers, each loathing the other.

For I remember that many of us Americans couldn't fit love into our lives. Before marriage we knew the double date, that negation of intimacy and privacy. Two men and two girls go out for an evening. The men talk between themselves, the girls between themselves. After four hours everyone is so bored that the only escape is a physical one, as a book is torn to bits by a reader who can't understand it. There were no overtures, no epilogues. I watched Americans when I was on double dates with them. They hadn't much sense of how to lead up to the act by conversation, of how to stir the woman's mind before their fingers touched her body. Their kisses, if they kissed at all, were rough and fumbling. They did outrage to the gentleness of women. I wondered why many Americans kept their love of women in a tight compartment. And the women in their turn thought the men graceless bulls.

"I was standin in the park," the mess sergeant said. "An she starts to cry an scratch my face when I wouldn't kiss her."

"Rosetta tole me I necked like a butcher," the corporal said. "But I caught on fast, with the lessons she gimme. These babes know somethin. . . . She taught me to kiss slow, to take my time. I useta close my eyes an just jab, hoping for the best. . . . Rosetta kisses sleepy-like. Sometimes she puts her tongue in my ear. Or just brushes her lips along my throat. Gee . . ."

"Neapolitan women know how to hold their men," the pfc said, wiping his spectacles. "They've had centuries of training. You don't need divorce when you can cook and make love. Love's a lot simpler than some people make it out to be. Quite natural, you know . . ."

"Damned if I do know," the tech sergeant said. "Wouldn't it sorta embarrass ya to be married to a gal that responded too well? Wouldn't ya feel she knew a little bit too much to be ya wife? . . . If ya had a mouse in ya house that really knew how to love ya up,

330

ya might feel like handin' her five bucks before ya went
to sleep."

"You'd get used to it," the pfc said. "And you wouldn't
be nervous or dissatisfied half the time."

For though we Americans were a conquering army,
when history is written it will show that the Neapolitans
conquered many of us. They beat us down with love.
They loved love. There were Italian boys and girls who
slashed their wrists for us, whether we deserved it or not.

The Italians regarded romantic love as what it really
is: a virulent disease. And we only jested about it. They
taught us the anatomy of this extraordinary madness.
They showed us that it should be enjoyed and feared,
that the rules and science of love are at least as worthy
of consideration as the laws of hygiene, football, and business ethics.

The Neapolitans taught us that love's as necessary as
eating and excreting. It's a game in which music and
cruelty and peace are all at stake. People are only admir-
able in ratio to their susceptibility to love. Laughter and
good manners and wit are all trappings of love. Even
when they aren't in love, the Italians ape the mannerisms
of the lover. Thus they can be joyous at eighty. Italian
love is both articulate and silent. The lovers quickly
knock down any barrier between them. It's the only time
in a man's life when he can forget that people are really
alone in life, that actually there's no way to bridge the
chasm between hearts. Those physical manifestations of
love, the touches and glances and kisses and confessions,
are all deceits that we invent to hide our own loneliness.

"When ya walk down Via Roma," the corporal said,
"ya can tell by their eyes whether they will or won't. They
make no bones about it over here. . . . Christ, what eyes
they giveya."

"Back home," the pfc said, "they'd call it unbridled sen-
suality."

"I can have any Ginso I want," the mess sergeant said.
"Any age, any sex. They all love, it. It's the one good
thing I'll say for em."

I remember that love in Naples was both wild and
disciplined. When two people enter into this madness,
they can't stop short at any point, saying: There, I've
loved you enough. Yet this madness of giving and pleas-

ing and reciprocating is governed by strict rules that the lovers seem instinctively to understand. The only evil you can do to love is to thwart it by purely intellectual rules or by betraying what your own heart tells you to do.

I remember how easy and fluid the beginning is. That first entrance into a room, that easy lounging on a street corner, that first sally of eyes, those first words that awakened a suspicion or an echo in my cellar. I couldn't believe it was happening to me. Yet I'd always dreamed this was the way it would be when it came. At first I tried to hold off and watch my own mind. But I ended by tumbling into the stream I was charily testing with my toe.

I remember the next stage of my disease. Something I've been looking for is here for the asking. Everything we say to each other means more than our words denote. For love is understanding. And the solace! For a night, for a week, for a month, for a year two people are able to forget the riddle of being alive in the greater delight and torment of being lifted out of themselves and married on some island where nothing else in the world may come.

"Dimmi che cosa pensi, John."

"Same thing you are, of course."

I remember that then I found the difference between love and Having Sex. There's none of the blind preoccupation with my own body and its satisfaction. The first aim is to please my love. And I end by being pleased too.

"No, penso a te. Voglio sentirti contento fra le mie braccia."

"Don't you feel that I am? If I could keep my lips in your hair forever. . . ."

For the act of love is only the continuation and the resolution of a desire and a mystery already set up in two minds. The blueprint becomes the working model, the raw stone the statue. I remember lying there, lost and wondering. I put my hand out to encounter another hand, already reaching for mine. My mouth went out exploring, only to meet another mouth working toward mine in the darkness. In that kiss I felt as though my tongue had at last articulated a word I'd been striving to pronounce all my life long. In those long kisses there was nothing brutal, nothing rapacious, as mad love is said to

332

be, so that the lovers lacerate one another's lips. I think we were both a little sad when we kissed. In those kisses we tried to heal each other's souls.

And I remember the sweet slowness of undressing one another, the longing and the languor. The clothes dropping whispering to the floor, the shadowy bodies gradually revealed, the secrets even more secret and removed that they lay under our hands. It seemed that in our lethargic and compassionate caresses we were trying to console each other for every hurt the world had ever inflicted: I am with you to comfort me, and I will comfort you. For I love you.

And I remember how exquisite was our leisure with one another. If there was passion—and indeed there must have beem much—it only carried us slowly and steadily up to that place where there is understanding. Higher and higher. We didn't say much, only one another's names in rising intensity of pain and delight. And for one instant we were in a place where there was no difference between us. We melted into all those who've ever loved and lived at all. But then the hand that had buoyed us to these places slowly set us down again on earth. For no one can live very long up there.

And after a while of nothing to say out of the huge peace, it's time for sleep. Sleep's a part of love. No man should rise from the bed after loving, button his pants, and run to catch a train. For that's a denial of the peace that love brings. I remember how we turned to each other, to sleep all night long with our arms about each another:

"Buona notte e sogni d'oro. . . . Dormi, John. . . ."

Thus in Naples I and other Americans loved. In a war one has to love, if only to reassert that he's very much alive in the face of destruction. Whoever has loved in wartime takes part in a passionate reaffirmation of his life. Such love has all the aspects of terror and surprise. I am bitter when my love seems cold. Nothing can equal the malice with which I plot to pay back every slight, real or imagined. And nothing can match the tears and vows with which we are reconciled for the second or the hundredth time. All my conduct is analyzed scruple by scruple with an ethical nicety which I can never carry into my daily living. If men could live all their lives as

333

virtuously and introspectively as when they're in love, we'd all be gods, and there'd be no need of promises of heaven or of hell.

"I deliberately insult Rosetta," the corporal said. "An when I've said my piece to her and see the expression on her face, I'd give a month's pay to take back my words. . . . Yet I won't apologize to her. Why's that?"

"Those minutes of waitin," the mess sergeant said, "wonderin will she show up tonight."

"In love," said the pfc with spectacles, laughing for the first time overseas, "is the only time when the human race is amusing or good or anything else but scheming beetles . . . and it's the only time when we get a true perspective on ourselves, for we can't stand ourselves. . . ."

I remember that in Naples I learned that everything in life is a delusion, that all happiness is simply a desire for, and unhappiness a repining of, love. Nothing else matters. All of life is a preparation for, or a retrospection on, those brief hours when two people are together and perfect in each other. Then we're the slaves of a power outside ourselves, that brings us together for its own ends and tricks us into a joy and an equality.

And finally I remember that the Neapolitans, because they were human beings and concerned with being nothing else but, carried their loves into their relations with others. I suppose that Christianity is only a code to expand your personal love to all the world. Your desire and your potency are supposed to touch all people. On the lowest scale this means simply good manners. On the highest, Jesus Christ. I wondered sometimes why the Italians struck me as kinder and gentler than many Americans. Perhaps it was because their lives were more fixed economically, because they knew they could never make a million dollars or be President of the United States. Therefore their energies turned inward: to the enjoyment of life as it could be lived within their own possibilities, to the acquirement of those graces and kindnesses which make life different from the whirring of a machine.

"She brought me to her house," the mess sergeant said. "I didn't wanna go, but I went because I thought there was a chance of her ending the night shackin with me an Jacobowski. Christ, what a welcome I got! Ya'd think I was a visitin fireman. . . . Well, those Ginsoes treated me
334

so white that me and Jacobowski decided not to shack with her after all. . . . Say, maybe that was in the back of their heads all the time."

"Maybe," the pfc said. "Or maybe they just liked you as a human being. That's not impossible you know."

"Nah," the mess sergeant said. "They wanted somethin outa me. Just what they wanted I ain't yet figured out. But I will."

"Maybe they didn't want anything at all from you," the pfc said.

But no one ever listened to him.

And sometimes I wondered why the Neapolitans, with some exceptions, seemed so good to me. Their motives were so unmixed; their gladness so bright, their grief so terrible. I decided that it was because they were living for their bare existence. They'd never had much, and in August, 1944, they'd given up every nonessential and quite a few of the essentials. We Americans were still thinking in terms of nylons and chromium and that raise from fifty to sixty dollars a week. The Neapolitans weren't always sure they'd be eating that evening. But instead of inducing a squalor and envy in them, in most cases this bleak reality brought forth in them a helpless gaiety, a simplicity, and a resignation that touched me and many other Americans. This even though they'd lost their war. The fact remained that these people must and would live, the only important fact after the nonsense and cruelty of the moment have been wiped away. There'll be Neapolitans alive in 1960. I say, more power to them. They deserve to live out the end of their days because they caught on sooner than we to how simple human life can be, uncomplicated by advertising and Puritanism and those loathsome values of a civilization in which everything is measured in terms of commercial success. What difference does it make if a man has BO from honest work if he can't buy soap? And does a wife care for the hair on her legs if her children aren't eating regularly?

I remember that this generalized love of the Italians for life and other human beings brought them to a functionalism that we Americans have so far realized only in our machinery. I don't speak as a romanticist. What complicates human life unbearably is the unequal distribution of goods and favoritism. But the last is far more human and understandable than the first. People aren't born equal intellectually. But that's a truism. All have a right to work, to eat, to sleep, to make love, and to dress, if they choose. Everything else in life has been introduced into it by the so-called ruling and intellectual classes, who in 1944 were too aware of themselves and too little cognizant of their responsibilities. By August, 1944, they'd failed completely. It was time for a new order and straight thinking. The alternative was obvious.

I remember that I knew and I saw that the Italians were a more cohesive social group than the Americans. Then that is all to their credit. Have we Americans, for all our preaching, done much to assimilate our minorities, to control vested interests, to distinguish between talent and ballyhoo, to understand the world in which we live? In the future there'll be no satisfaction in saying: I am an American, as the Italians used to tell me, with the pride of an inferiority complex: I am an Italian. So what? Perhaps we must soon all come to the point where we're proud only to say: I am a human being, a citizen of the world. For in Naples I and other Americans learned by a simple application of synecdoche that no one, in himself and by himself, is much better or much worse than anybody else. And we Americans were only fortunate. Our good fortune should be shared, or we'd lose it and ourselves and our humanity. In Naples I and other Americans were reduced by watching the effects of the war to that cipher which is the beginning of wisdom and love. Who am I? Why, only a more or less sensitive piece of chemicals and reactions. I shall live for a part of a century. And it's to my own interest and to the interest of my children that others in the world shall know that life can be as good as *I* have found it to be. This is utter idealism. It is also utter practicality, such as Americans like to talk about.

And I remember that in Naples I relearned that man is more than a physical being. The religions of the world have been saying this for several thousand years. But the world has never settled on a dogma to define the spiritual nature of man. No one ever will, except for himself. That belongs to liberty of choice. It's at any rate a question that can be settled without murder. All that matters in the twentieth century is that millions of people must never again be thrust out of life through no fault of their own.

336

It seemed, against American rules of A Good Fight and Fair Play, that the Italians should hate us and that we should hate them. Then in twenty years we can all have a Return Engagement on the Home Field. In Naples I saw that this need not necessarily be so.

"Dovete aiutarci," the Neapolitans said.

This meant that we ought to help them.

Why not? I don't remember noticing that most Europeans were content to sit back for the rest of their lives and receive American food and medical supplies. This is the newest form of vicious propaganda. Some, of course, were. But then there are also Americans who'd be only too happy with a dole.

In August, 1944, I remember that there were many Americans in Naples. They learned from Italian life. They learned the things that were good and bad in both American and Italian life.

I remember the Italian women, brought to situations that even the men couldn't cope with. I remember that they still laughed and loved their men and their babies. I remember the wonderful beauty of Italian women, outside and inside. And even the whores had a certain beauty of logic in them. These Italian women were often gentle without weakness, gay without giddiness, and loving without gumdrops. These principles of conduct seemed to be rules for life which held even when life was at rock bottom. They were learned thousands of years ago. Yet we forget them through too much comfort and through bad art.

I remember also the Italian men. There were thieves and liars and misanthropes among them, of course. There are everywhere. But I remember Italian men who moved in sober brilliance of purpose—that nothing like this would ever happen again. They studied things outside Italy, endeavoring to discover what good had been done in the world since 1922, in what respects the outside world has surpassed Italy in science and humanism and government. I remember how much they gave me when they thought they had nothing left to give: a sense of tragedy, a sweetness, and an easiness toward little problems. All this for a few cigarettes or an occasional meal. Or for nothing. I remember their dark faces when anyone was kind to them. The gentle and noble Italians (and there are many) never envied me.

"Caro John, ti consiglio di dire a tutti quel che hai visto in Italia . . . Perchè, sai, gl'Italian: non vi odiano, non vi odiano, voi altri americani. . . ."

Thus I walked often in the Galleria Umberto Primo, that arcade in the center of the city of Naples. Most of the modern world could be seen in ruins there in August, 1944.

I remember that Galleria as something in me remembers my mother's womb. I walked backwards and forwards in it. I must have spent at least nine months of my life there, watching and wondering. For I got lost in the war in Naples in August, 1944. Often from what I saw I lost the power of speech. It seemed to me that everything happening there could be happening to me. A kind of madness, I suppose. But in the twenty-eighth year of my life I learned that I too must die. Until that time the only thing evil that could be done to me would be to hurry me out of the world before my time. Or to thwart my natural capacities. If this truth held for me, it must be valid for everybody else in the world.

This is the reason why I remember the Gallery in Naples, Italy. . . .

NINTH PORTRAIT

Moe

ALTHOUGH he was a second lieutenant, there was both indolence and nervousness in the way he leaned against the wall of the PX on Via Diaz. He had a toothpick in a corner of his mouth, and he was watching the people going in and out of the PX. In brown paper packages was all their wealth for one week: seven packs of cigarettes, a cake of soap, five razor blades, and some candy bars. And they carried their packages fearfully cradled in their elbows, as though they were smuggling something. In the gutter stood Neapolitan kids who bid for the contents of these paper bags. An MP sometimes came up and chased the kids away. But just around the corner from the PX the Americans and the Neapolitans would get together again to engage in trade or barter.

A GI with an armored force shoulder patch came side-
ways up and saluted him. He spat out his toothpick,
straightened up, and returned the greeting. This GI wore
the Purple Heart on his shirt, which didn't prejudice the
second lieutenant one way or another.

"Lieutenant, sir," the GI said.

"One or the other," he said. "But not both."

"Ya givin me a hard time, sir. I got mine at Salerno . . ."

"So did I," he said, "and I don't wear anything to show
it. . . ."

And for the GI to see he spread out his right hand,
which he'd been keeping in his pocket. He let the GI see
how one finger had been bent on itself, how the flesh on
the back of the hand was mottled and taut like melted
rubber.

"And I liked to bang out a tune or two on the piano,"
he added, "when I wasn't driving my taxi."

"Well, that's not all," the GI said. "Last week I got
nicked at Poggibonsi. I'm just gettin outa the hospital . . ."

"So am I, boy, so am I," he said, changing the cant of
his legs. "But I can't show you my other wound. Not
here in public on the streets of Napoli anyhow."

"Ya givin me a hard time, sir," the GI said. "I thought
ya was one of these PBS commandos."

"Tell me what you want," he said, wiping his forehead.

"I need some shirts . . . an I didn't sell my others
either. The Ginsoes hocked em. Or some kike sold em
while I was in the hospital . . ."

"I'm a kike," the second lieutenant said.

Nevertheless, telling the GI to wait outside, he went
into the PX. It was hot and crowded inside the glass
doors. Some officers were fighting over the last wicks and
flints left on a counter. Others were knocking one another
down to get at the shoe counter, where three pairs of low
oxfords waited for the victor. Others sat at card tables
spread with brown paper, drinking cokes and coffee or
eating sugar doughnuts. He looked at them all for a minute. Then he went upstairs to the officers' clothing store.
It hurt him a little to climb. His combat boots scraped
on the marble stairs.

The Neapolitan girl behind the clothing counter was
pressing her temples and squeezing tears out of her eyes.
She looked at him as though he were the newest rat come
to gnaw at her.

339

"Say, maybe you need an aspirin," he said. "What did they do to you?"

"O Dio," she said. "It's this rush rush rush . . . The Americans are always in a hurry . . . they yell at me . . . Maria, Maria, Maria . . . I'm their servant . . . and they are driving me crazy. . . ."

He took his right hand out of his pocket and laid it on the counter as he leaned toward her. She saw his proud flesh and his twisted fingers. Then she took a handkerchief from between her breasts and started to dry her eyes.

"Your servant, lieutenant."

"Have you got a size fifteen suntan shirt?"

She got him one from a dwindling pile on the almost empty shelves. While she was wrapping it, he signed the old business on the yellow sales ticket:

"I certify that this clothing was bought by me for my personal use; Moses Shulman, 2nd Lt, Inf. . . ."

And while she was making change from his thousand-lira note, he went downstairs and bought a wax-paper cup of coffee and two sugar doughnuts. These he carried back to the girl Maria.

"They never let us buy these, you know," she said.

Then she stepped into a recess and drank the coffee and ate the two doughnuts. He watched her shiny black smock, which all the Neapolitan PX girls wore over their print dresses. He saw the glint of the earrings under her profuse hair. He watched her throat swallowing. Then she came back to the counter, wiping her mouth and looking at him dubiously.

"I want you to smile for me," Moe said, picking up his package. "I got a feeling there's something you haven't showed me of yourself."

"I have no reason to smile," she said, staring at the brown paper on the counter.

"Neither do I."

So she wiped her lips once more. Her mouth widened. He saw her teeth and the tongue behind them like a frightened polyp.

"But that's no smile," Moe said.

And suddenly he tweaked her lightly in the ribs. Again her lips parted and she laughed. And he felt his heart sicken and flower all at once.

"Maria what?"

340

"Maria Rocco," she said, "of Naples, Italy. Di una razza vinta e inferiore."

"Ah," said Moe, "and what conquered and inferior race do you think I come from?"

"But you're an American," she said, glancing at his frightful right hand. "You should be the happiest man on earth. The world is at your feet . . ."

"Do you think so?" he said, putting his hand back into his pocket. "Look, Maria Rocco, will you meet me tonight at eight? At the Via Roma side of the Galleria Umberto?"

"Well, why not? You're the first man today who treated me like a human being."

"Take a look at my nose and my dark skin," Moe said. "I might almost be a Neapolitan."

"At eight at the Galleria, then," Maria Rocco said.

He looked at her for a second, then with his package under his arm he went downstairs and out of the PX. The August sun in Naples was broiling. The GI was waiting for him and took a roll of lire from his pocket.

"Gee, lieutenant, thanks. Ya gimme a hard time there at first. How much?"

"I won't be needing money for quite some time," Moe said.

The GI saluted him and took off down Via Diaz toward the questura. Moe looked after him, put a toothpick in his teeth, and slowly turned onto Via Roma.

He turned into the Galleria Umberto. In the heat of August, 1944, he felt the cauterized lips of his new wound murmuring like the gratings of a thirsty mouth. A tremor ran up his side along his ribs. He thought maybe the medic had left a wick inside him. He walked till he was in the very center of the Galleria, under the dome. Slowly he spun round in his boots as though he were the needle of a compass orienting itself on the grid lines of a map. Thus he was the very center of that afternoon crowd in the Galleria. He was the nub of hundreds of persons, American, British, French, Polish, Moroccan, and Neapolitan. He smiled and said to himself that this was the first and last time he'd be the center of the world.

As he stood poised, a young Italian in a white linen suit came up. He limped on a cane. Out of his handsome head stuck an unlighted cigarette.

"Please," the Italian said. "I'm not asking for a cigarette, you notice. Just a little fire for my own . . ."

"Why certainly, Joe."

He put out his zippo lighter so suddenly that the Italian ducked and fell to the pavement of the Galleria. In helping him up Moe saw that one white linen trouser, disordered by the fall, bared an aluminum leg.

"You're too used to getting hit," Moe said.

"In Ethiopia I was a tenente pilota. I used to strafe the Ethiopians in the fields. According to orders, you understand. One day my plane was forced down. The neri started to cut me up. You see what they did to my leg . . ."

"That's enough," Moe said. "Walk along with me."

The handsome Italian took his arm and they cut diagonally into the Galleria, away from its center under the dome. Moe had to walk at half his usual pace. The Italian helped himself puntingly along on his cane. One white linen shoulder hunched up and down.

"I have always wanted to know an American. How did you know my name is Joe? It is; Giuseppe Brasi from Taranto. . . . For one week now I have been standing by myself every afternoon in the Galleria, waiting for an American to whom I would feel costretto to speak. One whole week I waited, with the excuse of the unlit cigarette in my lips. And then today I saw you. . . . I don't want anything of you; cigarettes, black market. I am rich, as Italians go nowadays. But I wanted to talk to an American. The right American. . . . What is there in your face that I find so simpatico?"

"Damned if I know," Moe said, feeling the Italian's weight rising and falling on his arm. "But Hitler probably would."

"Well," the Italian said, "you Americans have some secret we Italians have missed. So you will pardon me if I make you my friend. At once."

"Not at all," Moe said. "Let's sit down at this table and have a vermouth."

"First," the Italian said, laying a hand on Moe's arm, "I must do something for you. I cannot stop giving presents to those I like. . . . Do you love women? I know an actress from Gorizia here in Napoli. I never kiss her on the mouth. But I buy her food when she meets me on the street and says, Ehhh, Pinuccio, I am hungry, cousin. . . . Or can I take you to the casini? I go often there for pleasure. The girls give me special attention because of my leg. They cannot tire me out. . . . At fifteen I was

342

mad for ballerine. I went every night to the revista to look at one Wanda. In those days I didn't have much money from my father, so I bored Wanda. Over her I used to cry myself to sleep. At fifteen. . . . Now I am in Napoli from Taranto on business. Marriage business. I am affiancing myself to a dottoressa of a good family. A serious girl. We fight every day. I leave her in tears and walk into the streets of Napoli. I amuse myself. . . . Mi piace tutto. . . . For you I will do anything."

"Thank you," Moe said, ordering two vermouths. "Thank you very much, Joe."

"But," the handsome Italian said, laying his cane across his lap, "you must tell me what you know that I do not. I must learn your secret. Is it just that you are an American? . . . I think not. I find many of them offensive. . . . Look, caro, I have an apartment on Via dei Mille. You must come and live with me for a week. As my guest. We will have cene and pranzi such as you have never eaten. We will have women in the moonlight. I will fight with my fidanzata for one solid week in order that I may be always with you."

"But this time tomorrow night," Moe said, "I'll be north of Napoli. I'll be seeing the houses of the farmers up in Tuscany. Walls spattered with holes. I'll be running with my carbine. . . . Think of me up there if the sun is as bright as it is this afternoon. . . . You see why I can't accept your hospitality."

"Beh, caro mio," the handsome Italian said, shrugging a shoulder as though he were still limping, "you mean you are going back to fight?"

"I'm only an infantry platoon leader," Moe said. "Lean and mean . . . maybe you'd like to fly me up in your plane?"

"But the Duce told us," the Italian said, ordering two more vermouths, "that Jews did no fighting in the American Army . . ."

Then he checked himself and added:

"Of course you will agree with me that your Roosevelt started this war?"

"Look, Joe," Moe said. "Let's talk like two friends, huh? It's too late in my life for arguing. . . . I argued for twenty-five years. I saw that somebody had to be the grist for the mill instead of just talking about it. . . . So here I am . . . I have a hand that looks like a claw, and a

343

rip in my chest. I'm no good to any one any longer. All those fine dreams I once had are gone. . . . The world will never be what I thought it could be. I used to dream at the wheel of my taxi while I waited for a stop light to change. I listened to what people were talking about in back of my meter. . . . Nothing they said made any sense to me. . . . So here I am in Naples, Italy, in August, 1944. It makes a little more sense to me than a drunken dowager in an evening gown. . . . Anyway I'm almost happy and almost calm . . . I'm seeing the world, like you do in that last look around before you go blind. What more can I ask?"

"Mi dica un po'," the handsome Italian asked. "Are you such a strange man because you are a Jew or in spite of it?"

"I've hungered and I've thirsted after something," Moe said. "And it took a war to show me what that something is. . . . I've lived all my life in insecurity. I feared it and I fought it. I saw what it did to my father. I saw how it embittered my sisters Audrey and Rebecca and Elaine, even as they sat at their typewriters. I saw how only the sweetness of my mother was able to hold out against it. . . . But now that I accept insecurity I find a weight has been lifted from me . . . It means that in this year I must die."

"You are a perfectly just man," the handsome Italian said, and tears came into his eyes. "You are a good man in 1944 . . ."

"No, not good," Moe said; and he smiled to counteract the Italian's tears. "But I see that it's nothing to give up my life. It's easier to do than be slowly smothered."

"Spend the rest of today with me," the Italian said, wiping his eyes and smoothing his white lapels. "I shall give you a night in which no pleasure will be lacking."

"No thanks, Joe. It would be forcing the issue. I've never been able to do that. And everything now is so natural to me. Like one of those dreams in which you want something and it happens . . . without any effort on your part."

The handsome Italian put the toe of his cane on the pavement of the Galleria. He stood up and wiped his eyes again.

"Ah," he said, "I too have a good heart, even though I strafed the Ethiopian contadini. Under orders of the Duce,

344

of course. . . . I had also an amante, a Libyan black girl.
I had two children by her. It broke my heart to leave my
cugina di guerra and my bambini. . . . But I feel that I
shall see you again. Otherwise . . . morirei de dolore. . . ."

"Well, take care, Joe," Moe said, putting out his hand.
He watched the Italian go along the Galleria on his cane.
He limped through the crowds, one white shoulder rising
and falling as his weight hit his aluminum leg. Then Moe
took out two sheets of V-mail stationery and a pencil
and began to think what he would write to his friend
Irving, driving his taxi in Brooklyn. He bit on the pencil.
The sun was dropping outside the Galleria Umberto. A ray
of it smote his chest, and he seemed no longer to be in
August, 1944, and the Italian campaign called Rome-Arno
like a soccer match. There was just himself close to the
Mediterranean Sea. Something specific in himself had
come from this sea long ago. He didn't quite know why
he felt so at home.

Somewhere in Italy
14 Aug. 1944

Hullo, Irv,
This is that matzoth man talking to you again—I'm writing to you because I could always tell you nearly any ole gunk
that came into my head—you just happen to be *it*, that's all
—right now I'm sitting on my fanny in a city in southern
Italy and you know dam well I'm not allowed to tell you
what the name of it—doesn't matter anyhow—I got out of
the horsepital this morning and tomorrow I'm going back to
the line—I have been away too long from my boys—I keep
wondering what they are doing up north of me and how
many of them are still with us—right now I'm drinking vermouth—it's late afternoon—anyhoo I'm glad you aren't sitting across from me at Hymie Hamilburg's because then I
couldn't tell you what's on my mind—you'd keep butting in
with your corny humor (?) like you always do—everybody
says this life is unreal—the executive officer of our battalion
told me that in the middle of a war everybody contracted a
bad case of irrelevance—did I spell that right?—I dunno and
I don't much care—what I started out to tell you is that this
life, I mean me being a platoon leader in the infantry, is as
close to anything real as anybody ever gets—you suddenly
see how simple and terrible everything is—and beautiful like
a bolt of lightning—
    (this V-mail is continued on another sheet—I hope they
photograph the two together hope a hope a hope)

345

#2. I have got it figured out this way—the Americans, including us taxidrivers (smile), have been living in a vacuum that they thought was paradise—but it wasn't really anything except chromium plating and drunkenness and hunks of sex like a Thanksgiving dinner—it bored us even when we were in the middle of it—and that's the reason millions of us have got to pay—through the nose—I think I'm going to be one of these millions—I feel it like you know you're going to have a toothache—somebody has to pay the piper and if everybody takes the attitude "it won't be me" it will end by being everybody—don't get me wrong boy—I don't think of Me as a burnt offering—but in the world there's a surgical operation going on—a lot is going to be cut out—I wonder if the world will be a better place when it comes out of the ether—think about what our battalion executive officer said—a bad case of irrelevance—if we had to have this war, it kind of looks as though everything we stood for meant nothing—or maybe you can tell me why I can shoot a Jerry without feeling anything, but a dirty deal or a starving kid makes my stomach flop—it must be the vermouth—Irv, keep yours where it belongs and gib ein Kuss for me to Mamma, Sadie, Audrey, Rebecca, Elaine, Anna, and Lilian that works at Cantor's—and tell Mr. Feingold that there's no Ghetto here—the whole city is one—

Be good—
Moe

Moe didn't feel like drinking any more vermouth in the Galleria Umberto. He wasn't much of a bibber anyhow. Alcohol mounted to his brain in a spiral of screams and complaints, like charwomen panting into an attic. Alcohol divided something in his head against the other half. After a few drinks he always felt as though he ought to rise to the defense of something. He didn't quite know what. So he pulled at his belt and went out into Via Roma and the heavy sunlight of the Neapolitan afternoon. He strolled into the piazza by the San Carlo Opera House, crossed it, and walked along the palace where in the niches stood brown statues of Carlo d'Angiò and the kings of Naples and Sicily leaning on shields and looking like idealized politicans in armor. After the palazzo he came into a little railed park on an escarpment. He could see over the bay, golden in the sunset and thumping with LCI's and hospital ships. He saw the sulphur on the sides of Vesuvius and the dotted stretch down to Amalfi and Sorrento. This afternoon he could see al-

346

most to Salerno, where he'd come ashore eleven months ago. Naples wasn't so far from Salerno. So little progress in eleven months. Inching up this sunny sad peninsula. Tomorrow he'd be farther north, in Tuscany. Hearing that cracking and crunching and clumping and roaring, feeling that floating uncertainty, seeing the running dots of men who fired and ducked and sometimes didn't get up again. And occasionally the arch of a church, with a Jerry rifle peeping like a perioscope around the pastelled cornice. Himself running running running or looking back as he ran to see where his boys were. . . .

Moe loved the city of Naples. It must be like Jerusalem, in contrast to Tel Aviv. Those corners that gave onto nowhere, the sunlight slanting on a pile of rubble, those faces looking out laughing or weeping at him—all reminded him that his heart was a hinge, not a valve. And most of all he loved the titter or hum or roar of Naples, saying to him things older than 1944, things that reached back into a time when men were more united in their chaos, willing to be put against a wall for something they believed. It seemed to Moe that in Naples there had somehow survived the passion and coherence of an old faith. All this he only felt, but the city of Naples comforted him. There was a poultice in its dirt, a natural humanity in its screaming.

Holding onto the low balustrade, he walked along the path above the street. It was beyond the palm trees on the edge of the escarpment. There were shoeshine boys along his way. Sailors—British, American, French, and Italian—leaned on the balustrade and looked over at Vesuvius. Moe walked till the path turned back on itself round a statue of Pompey and the railing was ornate with low white pot-bellied pilasters. Here to his right Via Caracciolo began and went on for miles around the bend of the bay. And here Moe stopped, for an American officer of the field artillery was sitting on the railing, back to the bay, lighting one cigarette from the stump of another. Moe and he recognized each other with the must of minorities. This captain had a beaked nose, a heavy close-shaven beard, and a narrow chest, and hairy slender wrists. He nodded rapciously yet shyly and offered Moe a cigarette.

"And only dis mornink I vas sayink to Marcus dat a soitin frient of ours iss too bright to be a Christian. . . ."

347

Moe refused the cigarette but stood next to the artillery captain. He waited politely, looking at the huge nose and the resentful eyes.

"Oh it's silence then he's eskin," the captain said, gesturing pathetically at the Bay of Naples. "Zo maybe I should be shuttink the mouth? I got vound up in my garment business and the big mouth I haven't shut since."

"If you want to come out here and talk," Moe said, "that's all right too. It's your privilege."

"It's a great country ve got," the captain said, "dat both of us coicumcised persons should be officers in its army. If ve vas livink in Poland . . .".

"I know, I know," Moe said, and he leaned on his elbows and belly to watch the sunlight on Capri.

Then the captain brandished a copy of the *New Republic* in Moe's face. Even with his chain-smoking he couldn't sit still on the wall. He blinked as he talked. There was an agony of the pursued about him.

"And dis I'm readink," the captain said, "to improve my English. Den my GI's von't be leffink at me. Dey are fine kids, but sometimes dey're leffink ven I tuk."

"You mean they make an issue of . . . ?"

"Dis I don't say. But sometimes I see funny looks. Den dey're sayink, He's a Yid and he's got two silver bars and he can't tuk American. So who is this Yid to be commanding us? Let him go back to his pawnshop . . ."

"I don't think that's a general attitude," Moe said. "I've never had any trouble with my boys . . ."

"Ah but you vouldn't, you vouldn't. You're tukking a perfect American and in da dark, pardon, you could be pessink yourself off as a Yenkee."

"It's quite obvious that I'm not," Moe said.

"Ah, but pardon, you vasn't born in Vienna like I vas," the artillery captain said.

"When did you leave Viennea?" Moe asked softly, looking back to the bay.

"In January, 1938."

"Then you weren't in on the worst of it," Moe said. "You've got no cause to complain. The country took you in. As you said yourself, it even gave you a commission in its army. No other country in the world except the United States . . ."

"Lissen a vile. Pardon, but you're tukkin almost as much as me or Marcus. . . . Only dis mornik I'm tellink

348

Marcus dere's no vun like us ven it comes to tukkink. Dot's how ve sell. .... Zo I'm come from Vienna in 1938. And me just a student. Ach, vat a time to learn American. And I'm not spikking it perfect. . . . But lissen. I arrive vid Reichsmarks in my pocket. I take a job as dishwasher. I go to Columbia. A kind Jewish lady takes an interest in me. She hears I have degrees from a gymnasium in Vienna. Zo translations from Rainer Maria Rilke I'm makink for her at three in da morning in place of sleepink. . . . Zo kind she vas to me. . . . But listen. Dey kilt my fader before ve leafe Vienna . . ."

"I'm very sorry to hear that," Moe said.

The artillery captain slid down from the wall. He took hold of Moe's arm, forcing him to look him full in the face. His skinny figure towered upward; his eyes flashed; he shook his finger under the hot soft Neapolitan sky. A bloodstone leered on his index finger. His nasal voice peaked up into a scream:

"He's sorry! . . . Lissen a vile. . . . I'm going back to Vienna . . . Dis year or da next . . . ven falls the Stadt to our army . . . because I spik good Deutsch, I have a high position. . . . Lissen . . . I pay back those Viennese for everytink dey do to me and my fader. . . . I cut them up in liddel pieces if I can. You hear me? . . . Dey pay. Vait and see. Dey pay. I pay back dose doity bastards. I spit in deir faces, I'm mekking dem eat deir vord Jude . . ."

"That wouldn't be wise," Moe said, offering the captain a stick of gum.

"Vise? Vise! . . . Zo much he's sayink wid a liddel vord. . . . Lissen to him tukkink."

"Don't you think," Moe asked, raising his voice a little, "that there's already enough hatred in the world without you settling a private grudge! . . . We must wipe the slate clean and start all over again."

The artillery captain stopped buttonholing Moe long enough to light another cigarette from the stub of his latest. Then he screamed:

"He's tukkink! Da most dangerous man in da vorld! Everybody, everythink he's sellink down da river . . . his own race. . . . Zo I'm goink avay before I'm losing da temper."

"You've already lost more than the temper," Moe said, and firmly he turned away from the captain to look on the Bay of Naples. The captain took one more frenzied puff on his cigarette and tore away up the promenade. He shook his head and muttered to himself. Once he turned back and looked at Moe and shook his head. Even from the distance his eyes glittered like a vulture's.

Moe paced slowly back in the direction he'd come. Near the palace were stairs going down to a urinal. At the entrance to this subway an Italian boy of eighteen in dark blue shorts and a monk's-cloth shirt open at the neck was lounging. For a swift instant he looked steadfastly at Moe, then dropped his eyes. His face had the removed contemplative beauty of women beyond the moment of their spasm of love.

"Let us not waste any time," the Italian boy said, looking past Moe out into the bay. "Will you give me a cigarette or will you not?"

"I don't care for your salesmanship," Moe said, unbuttoning his breast pocket. "But you can have this whole pack. I don't smoke myself."

He put another toothpick between his lips and watched how the boy took the pack into his fingers and stroked the cellophane. The boy's lips moved but nothing came out. Then his eyes veered from the bay over Moe's shoulder to Moe's face. They were black Italian eyes, calm yet full of a passion of ink when it falls into words.

"You know of course," the boy said, "that Neapolitan boys would do anything for this pack of cigarettes. I would or I would not, depending on how I felt toward you. I am a Lucchese, you see."

"If you think that cuts any ice with me," Moe began. Then he saw no point in heightening the wall between the boy and himself. It had been flung up by the boy himself, a hasty reflex masonry of sorrow and pride and fear. "Who taught you to speak such perfect English?"

"You Americans. . . . You Americans taught me everything I know of evil and hate. Last month you shelled our house at Viareggio. And you killed my mother, who would not leave the house because she loved it. . . . And you Americans have taught me things I never dreamed of. . . . Best of all, you taught me that hate is stronger and lasts longer than love. For all the things you Americans have done to me and wish to do to me and with me are hateful. Every time I see you or touch you, I hate you more . . ."

350

"And you hate yourself too," Moe said. "We didn't teach you that . . ."

"I don't care any longer," the boy said, accepting the flame from Moe's lighter. "None of us Italians does. We've been bent this way and that. . . . So all we want to do now is live, just exist, however shamefully and ambiguously. We will live off you Americans. Off your food. Off your drunken spending. And we will yield to your desires, no matter how beastly they may be . . . for a price, you understand. . . . But you should hear how we talk about you among ourselves. We sear you and we scald you. Because we hate you. To hear Italians talk about you when they are together, you would think we were discussing a pen of pigs and vipers. Because we hate you. And no matter how you degrade or possess or kill us, there is always our laughter at your vileness. Laughter so scathing your cheeks would burn up and your bowels explode to hear . . . There is nothing in the world sweeter than Italian love. And nothing fiercer than Italian hate. . . . Don't you sense it everywhere about you? . . . But I make no pretenses. I am a Lucchese from Viareggio. I do not smile and fawn on you like the Neapolitans. I tell you frankly that I hate all Americans, and Americans desire me even in my hate. That's the depth to which you all have sunk. . . . Razzi di porchi, di finocchi e di mostri . . ."

"You mother should hear you now," Moe said, turning away. "And I guess she must have been a very beautiful lady."

"Wait, please," the boy called, crushing out his cigarette and running after Moe. "I have some photos of her. When may I show them to you . . . signor . . . mister . . . lieutenant?"

"After the war," Moe said increasing his pace.

"But may I see you tonight?" the boy begged, the coolness of his voice breaking into a whimper.

"I'm afraid not," Moe said. "But enjoy the cigarettes. . . . Tomorrow night I may be near Viareggio. I'll think of you and your mother. . . . For I'm sorry, very very sorry . . . believe me. . . ."

Turning back at the San Carlo, he saw that the beautiful Italian boy of eighteen was standing with his face in his fingers, weeping like no one who hates.

351

After his chow Moe circled around the Galleria Umberto in the growing dusk. It was still hot, but a sly change had crept over the city of Naples. The roar had dropped to a whispering, but it was still asking subtly for the same thing it had been growling for all day long under the sun. Moe had eaten Spam for supper. He'd taken a slice of it from his plate and laid it between two pieces of bread. With this sandwich in his hand he walked down Via Santa Brigida. The flies of Naples followed the arc of his sandwich. He couldn't bear to hand this food out to a whole crowd of children, to see them dismember it and one another. He was seeking a lonely soul and a lonely stomach. He walked toward the gates of the port till he saw a little girl standing with her hands behind her back, regarding the MP at the gate. Moe called out to her till she came slowly. Her admiration had already been fixed on the MP. Moe held his sandwich behind his back.

"Tu come chiamare?" Moe asked her.

"Perchè?" the girl said, backing off. "Vuoi mettermi in galera, come tutti gli altri americani?"

Gently he spread his boots apart, leaned back a little, and extended the Spamwich to the little girl. She had black matted hair and a pink stuck coyly in her ear. Her feet were nude, scuffed and stained with a dung and the fruit juices of the pavements.

"Mi chiamo Adalgisa," she said in a voice tinier than herself, putting out her hand to the bread and meat and drawing it back again.

"Adalgisa's always hangin around here," the MP said. "We stuck her mother in jail at the cuestura. An her pop got his in Eritrea. That's her story anyway, lieutenant . . . she's always around here."

"She'll continue to hang around," Moe said, "as long as she's alive. Of course we'll do our best to get rid of her. It would be more convenient for us if Adalgisa had never been born."

"Well, I got enough to worry about, lieutenant," the MP said, unslinging his carbine. "I got a wife and kid in Sacramento. I figure it don't pay ya to look too deep into all this crap that's goin on in the world."

"No," Moe said, "you're right . . . it don't pay . . . not one cent."

He took Adalgisa by the hand and walked along with her while she tore at her Spamwich. Her left hand lay in his like a warm robin while her right fed the food to her mouth inexorably as a machine-gun belt.

"I didn't know I was going to meet you, Adalgisa, I'd have brought two."

"Uno, due, tre, quattro," she said with her mouth full.

They sat down on a bench in Piazza Municipio. The courtyard arch of the City Hall palace yawned in the rising moon. Behind them were the laurel trees. The urinals sent out their shrill acid. In and out of these men moved, plucking at their buttons as they emerged from or entered the iron screens. And Adalgisa, after she'd finished eating, licked her teeth and her lips and sat placidly beside him, looking at the moon. Sometimes he felt her eyes tickling his face like a cat's whisker. They were round and unblinking, as though she wondered what he would do next. Finally she climbed into his lap and began to explore the colored divisional bandanna about his neck, the buttons of his opened collar. Her small skinny body smelled like a new olive.

"Sei triste stasera," she said, looking up into his eyes.

"Sad?" Moe said. "I'm always sad. . . . I was sad when I was pushing up the lever on my meter so it wouldn't register during waits. I was sad when I saw fat old ladies in furs going into the Astor. I was sad when I saw the snow in Brooklyn, smutted over in the alleys. . . . You're sad too, Adalgisa . . . but you don't know there can be anything else."

She was a tiny child for one who, he guessed, must be about eleven. He didn't know whether it was because she was undernourished or Mediterranean. She got off his lap and walked once around the bench where he was sitting. Her feet whispered in the grass behind him. Her ragged dress crinkled as she walked. Then she seated herself beside him again.

"What are you thinking about, Adalgisa? . . . Cosa pensare?"

"Ehhh," she said, "un bel piatto di pasta asciutta . . . che bellezza!"

"Sure, sure," he said, taking her hand. "Your world would be full if only you weren't hungry. . . . Me, I want to live. . . . I'd like to have some kids of my own . . . three or four maybe. . . . I wonder if I could teach them anything . . . how not to hurt others . . . how to understand them. . . . I've been wondering if there's some method of

353

hurting kids when they're a couple of months old, so that their meannesses would be burnt out of them early in life. . . . I guess not though. . . ."..

"Ho ancora fame, sai," Adalgisa said, pressing his hand more tightly.

"I know, I know."

Without taking his eyes off the climbing moon, he undid his breast pocket and gave her his two remaining sticks of gum. Then he stood slowly up from the bench and pulled the bottom of his pants down over the saddles and buckles of his boots.

"Good-by, Adalgisa," he said. "Remember me when you grow up. . . . Because I know you will grow up . . . somehow. . . . You'll live to be eighty. . . . Don't sit by the fireplace with your hands folded and tell your grandchildren about the americani, how horrible they were . . . Try to remember that there were many of us who looked at you and loved you in your helplessness and despair. And we said: My God, how cruel. . . . If I live, I'll do something about all this . . . something. . . ."

Then he walked quickly away from the little girl toward the Municipio. He was trembling. His loins vibrated with something fiercer and more durable than the excitement of love. For Moe saw that he hadn't so much time left, that the sweetness was dribbling away from him as from a broken jelly jar.

Moe went to the Red Cross motor pool off Piazza Carità. There were jeeps and command cars behind the barbed wire. Through the area walked Italian soldiers in American issue uniforms dyed green and green helmet liners with MIG on their visors. Even their leggins were a washed-out emerald in the moonlight. They were sweating softly but they saluted him. He went in at the gate and was saluted also by the American GI in charge.

"Listen, Joe, I've got to have a jeep for an hour or two."

"No can do, lieutenant. These are Red Cross vehicles . . ."

"Listen," Moe said, "my brother's grave is near Caserta and tonight's my last chance to visit it. . . . That's a lie, of course . . . but don't get chicken on me, Joe . . . you hate chicken as much as I do. . . ."

Then the MP saw Moe's ruined hand, extended in supplication. He thought a little more and then he scribbled out a trip ticket and waved at a jeep at the end of one of the parked rows.

"Okay. Willya promise me to have it back by 2300 hours, lieutenant? That jeep belongs to Genevieve, who I happen ta know is at Capri tonight with a colonel. . . . But 2300 hours for sure, lieutenant."

"Thanks," Moe said, sticking the trip ticket in a pants pocket.

He unlocked the steering wheel of the jeep, started it, and drove into Piazza Carità after another wave at the MP. He saw his own hands guiding the wheel of the jeep, one with the thumb delicately dangling as it used to in his taxi, the other yellow and macerated in the moonlight.

He cut sharp left into Via Roma. It was now dark, but on either sidewalk of that straight street crowds were pushing along in the blackout and the heat. Over his turned-down windshield Moe saw those thousands of faces, stuck on bodies being pushed along by the momentum of more people behind them. In the moonlight they looked like flowers and stalks being carried down to some sea, flowers dumped down from the balconies above them. There was much talking, shouting, whistling, and jerky singing. There were still in the gutters old women vendors and kids selling peanuts or love. Thus the whole August night murmured on Via Roma as the faces pushed aimlessly yet steadily in the current.

Moe drove slowly till he came to the Galleria Umberto. There in the moonlight, a little detached from the crowds on the left-hand sidewalk, Maria Rocco stood. Her head turned this way and that, and she glanced at her American wrist watch, sometimes shaking it or laying it to her ear. He called out softly to her and waved that she should cross Via Roma. She got in beside him without his bringing the jeep to a full halt. She was wearing a black silk dress that buttoned from her throat to the hem of the skirt. She wore no stockings. From under her rich hair escaped the pendants of silver earrings that tinkled to her shoulders.

"If you did not come," she said, "I had resolved never to go with the Allies again . . . except at an enormous profit. . . . Già mi dicono venale."

"I wasn't sure whether you were beautiful or not this

afternoon," he said. "Now I know. . . . Why do they make you put on that other smile in the PX?"

"Why?" Maria Rocco asked. "Because the world is now so terrible that people have to be ordered to smile. They pretend to kindness. It is something that brings in more lire."

"You don't have to say those things to me," Moe said. "And you're natural with me . . . I think. . . ."

"I shall not be natural much longer. . . . Have you got a stick of gum for me?"

"I did have, but I gave the last to Adalgisa."

"Adalgisa?" Maia Rocco's eyes began to glitter. "Vergogna. . . . Adalgisa! . . . And I spent an hour making myself pretty for you. Although my sister Bruna said that no American was worth it . . ."

Moe reached over, lifted her left earring, and let it fall to her shoulder.

"Adalgisa is the name of a hungry child . . ."

"I'm sorry," Maria Rocco said. "I'm sorry."

And she tilted back in the stiff seat of the jeep and raised her chin to the moon.

He drove dreamily along Via Caracciolo. The August moon was one quarter way up now; the Bay of Naples was slit with streaks of light that broke where the islands reached up from the water. Moe and Maria in their jeep passed the Aquarium. Then he turned by Soldiers' Park and steered up towards the Vomero. The jeep twisted and turned. Moe chose streets that were steepest because he liked the way her head jerked back when they began to climb.

"I think I know most Americans," Maria Rocco said. "They are for the moment. . . . What moment? . . . I worked for them at the QM. They ordered me to be cheerful, so I smiled as I counted out smelly drawers of officers' laundry. And I smiled as I handed out dry cleaning to your GI's. . . . Then I went to work at the Red Cross. With an ice-cream scoop in my hand. Here too I was ordered to smile. . . . I shall go on smiling for the Americans till my teeth drop out. . . . The Americans like smiling people. Why? A smile is hideous unless it means something. . . . For five years now none of my smiles has had any meaning. . . ."

When they'd got to the top of the city of Naples, Moe found a little park backboarded with mimosa and scrub

356

pine and a few olive trees. It was really a small balcony between two palazzi, and it looked down over the moonlit city, which stretched beneath them like a dihedral angle filled with towers and terraces. After he'd run the jeep up to the railing of the balcony, he parked and they sat for a while in their stiff metal seats looking at the town below them and the black or silvery bay. Then he put his hand into his pocket, took out a little hinged box, and gave it to Maria Rocco. She opened it to find a cameo pendant on a gold chain. He fastened it around her neck. As he clasped it, her hair fell on his hands, both the whole one and the scorched one. Maria Rocco's eyes became moist; she ran her fingers down the chain of the pendant and held the medallion of the cameo up to the moonlight and looked at it.

"It was my mother's," Moe said. "She said I should give it to some nice Jewish girl I was going to marry. Don't waste it on just anyone, she said."

"And now you're wasting it on me," Maria Rocco said. "I wonder what your mother would think of me."

"Oh," he said, finally snapping the clasp of the locket, "you serve your purpose just as well as that nice Jewish girl my mother had in mind."

"What purpose?" she asked, drying her eyes.

"Being something . . . very . . . necessary to her son. . . ."

Maria Rocco took up Moe's right hand, the mangled one, and laid her mouth against it. Then he, by maneuvering his boots and his position on the seat of the jeep laid his head down in her lap. Looking up at her, he saw the flange of her chin, her nostrils, her eyelashes, and the dangling ornaments of her earrings. It seemed to him that lying in her lap he lay at the roots of a living tree. He sighed and rolled his head about so that the buttons on her dress dented his hot cheeks. He smelled the dark warmth of her lap, of earth and silk and flesh.

"Did you ever look up into somebody's face from below?" he asked. "Then all the things you like about people's faces are upside down."

She laughed and chafed his hair.

"You are stronger than I, even though now you lie in the position of a little boy who runs to his mother's lap when he is afraid . . . for comfort from the world that has frightened him. . . . What comfort can *I* give you? . . .

357

Tell you that everything in this world seems mean and ugly to me, except you? . . . For there is a shadow over all the earth, with no promise that it will ever lift by the cloud's passing away from the sun. . . . Only from you have I ever sensed what hope could mean. And soon you too must leave me. . . . It has always been so. . . . When I was a little girl, I used to watch the others being merry. And I would run off and cry. . . . Now I know why. . . . The light on the Bay of Naples . . . the laughter that I heard in the streets at night . . . the mandoline and serenate . . . all seemed to me such a mockery, as though people were deluding themselves that they were happy, that anything could last."

"You were just waiting for something holding yourself in readiness," Moe said, smiling up at her.

"Waiting," Maria Rocco said. "What is a woman waiting for? Listening and hoping. . . . Why must a man like you die? Why can't they just take the rotten Italians and the rotten Americans and the rotten of the world and take them out and shoot them? . . . Then the decent ones could make another start and try to make a go of it. . . . Aren't you afraid?"

"Not very much," Moe said, taking her hand, that lay upon his chest. "But I have been afraid. . . . I was afraid when I was a kid and Ma said to go down to the delicatessen and see if there were any leftover sausages. . . . And I was afraid when I first started to drive a taxi. . . And I was afraid that first day on the line. . . . You never really get over being afraid, until you're not alive, and then you've found out there isn't much to be afraid over. . . . Now I know that a lot of all this doesn't matter. What does matter is my Ma in Brooklyn and my friend Irving and a girl like you. . . . It all seems so sweet, even if it has to end like an ice-cream soda at the end of a straw."

"No, it all seems so ghastly," Maria Rocco said; and she shook her head with such vehemence that his head bounced in her lap. "There's nothing fair or decent from the beginning to the end. . . . If you have too little, you pass your life in envy and aspiration. All your energies go up in smoke, simply trying to convince your neighbors that you exist. . . . Or if you have too much, you become like a crazy squirrel laying away nuts for a future that

358

will never materialize. . . . O Dio, mio, we have all lost the way. One loves too much and breaks his heart. One loves too little and lives in his own petty world, respected for what he has and dying unwept. And each is a fool. . . . We have all lost the way."

"I don't think I've lost the way," Moe said. "Just being alive now is good to me. . . . And you're not lost either. And most of the people in the world are like us. We just have to find what not to put our faith in. Most of the people who try to tell us what to do are wrong. . . . Look, you and I are together tonight. We're happier than most of the others. Because we know one another. We've confessed to one another that we're frightened and puzzled. But the point is, we have confessed. We don't pretend to know the answers."

Maria Rocco began to cry again. Her tears fell on his upturned face. He put out his spoiled fingers to catch a few of the drops.

"I am a whore," she said. "You are not the first man I have been with. . . . Your mother would hate me. . . . Thank God she is five thousand miles away and cannot see you with me."

"Why, you don't know yourself," Moe said, taking both her hands in his and imprisoning them, for they were fluttering above him. "You're kind . . . and sweet. . . . I don't know what else there is to be. . . . To me you're like a light in a dark noisy passageway. . . . I've seen plenty of faces of dead Americans and dead Krauts . . . Their eyes were wanting something. In death they looked surprised and hurt. . . . But when I watch your eyes, I see the difference."

She ran one of her fingers across his lips as he lay looking up at her. When she bent over him in their cramped quarters on the seats of the jeep, the cameo swung out into the air above his face. He threaded the path of buttons, hummocking out over her breasts.

"Don't you go north tomorrow," Maria Rocco said quietly but eagerly. "I know a place where I can hide you. I'll bring food to you. . . . Don't worry. I will save you. This war must soon be over. . . . Let them kill off the others. But men like you must not die in it. Stay with me. Rather than give you up, I would shoot all the MP's in Naples who came looking for you. I would fight for you. . . . And humanity, if it still exists, will end by being grateful to me. . . . Women have preserved great and good men before."

Moe laughed softly in her lap. The moon was laced through her hair.

"Thank you, my darling. . . . But the funny thing is, I wouldn't be happy in our hideaway. Can you understand why? . . . My place is up north of here. Fighting. . . . It doesn't matter what the war means or who wins it. But I'm tied up in a set of circumstances I've got to follow through. . . . I'm going back to the line tomorrow. I don't have any ideas that the world will be any better for me living or dying. . . . It's just the way things have panned out for me. There's been a logic in my life. A crazy logic. And this is part of the logic. . . . People spend most of their lives saying: This can't be happening to *me*. Even on their deathbeds they say it. They're surprised to find themselves dying on account of they could never quite accept the fact that they were alive. . . I accept everything. . . . This is *me* lying here and above me is *you*. . . . This is Naples. . . . This is August 14, 1944. . . . My name is Moe . . . yours is Maria. . . . And I love you."

"Maria does not understand Moe at all," she said.

She bent down and laid her mouth against his temple, passing down to his lips. There was no pressure in her kiss, but it sealed a wild peace he'd been feeling with her all evening. Her kiss made him hers more than any passionate one ever could have. Her hair fell into his closed eyes. He raised his arms and twined them about her shoulders, where the black silk soothed his fingers— the good ones and the bad ones.

"You understand me very well," Moe said against her cheek.

"Something keeps looking over our shoulders at us. . . . We have so little time and we need so much of it."

"Okay," he said.

He raised himself out of her lap, keeping one arm round her neck. He looked out over the Bay of Naples. By Ischia he saw a motorboat turning on the water. He looked at her body rising and falling on the seat beside him. Then he began to unbutton her dress, beginning at her neck. She wore nothing underneath the tight black silk; so as it was released by the parting fabric, her skin gushed to his hand like a living sponge. At last her dress

360

was open from neck to skirt. She lay with her eyes closed. Her breathing was inaudible. In the open shell of black silk, her naked beauty seemed to have burst from a ruptured pea pod. She seized his hands and brought them down on her breasts, beehives in the moonlight.

"Baciami . . . abbracciami, amore!" Maria Rocco cried.

At her cry he trembled with recognition. It was something he'd been listening for all his life.

There'd been no firing since dawn. Moe and his platoon were crawling along a country road in Tuscany. They were looking for some protected trees where they could sit down and eat their K-ration. This countryside was hilly and brown. Ahead of them on a cliff a castle with spires looked down into the valley. Nobody knew where they were. The cultivated terraces all looked alike, alternating bands of green and umber.

With it the platoon had three Krauts, captured at dawn. One had chest and arm wounds and never stopped groaning. The platoon wanted to do away with this Kurt. He staggered along in bandages and doped with sulfa, saying over and over again that Roosevelt was a Jude. The other two Krauts walked with him, but didn't help Kurt or pay him any attention. Moe never took his eyes off his platoon this morning. They were more than lean and mean riflemen. They were ugly. He watched especially his medical aid pfc, Dimplepuss, who occasionally prodded the moaning Kraut named Kurt.

"Dimplepuss, listen to me," Moe said. "All you're here for is to get that Kraut to battalion aid . . . if we ever find it."

"I ain't supposed to do anything for the bastard," Dimplepuss said.

"Oh shut up!" Moe yelled. "You're goddamn triggerhappy for a medic. Tonight I'm turning you in for an NP."

Thus they drooped and stumbled along in the dust till noon. Throughout the uneven and smoking landscape there wasn't a sign of regiment or battalion or company or any other platoon. They passed an overturned Kraut tank under a laurel tree. And in some bushes a mortar and three Krauts, kaput beside it. Moe's section sergeant edged up from his place in the demoralized march.

"Listen, lieutenant. You can see they're pretty pissed off. Not at you. They better eat chow. But fast."

361

"Wait till the next turn of this road," Moe said. "We're really lost."

So they plowed on farther in the heat and the yellow smoke that arose from the vegetation and from their own boots. Around a bend in the road they came upon a tiny village. Every house but one had at least a wall and roof off. A cat poked around in the one street, the main one.

"That's what the artillery done las night," one of the men said. "All that poppin too. . . . Git off the pot, Mister Dupont."

The jagged glass windows of a store still sustained a swinging hinged sign: Vino. Onto the pavement in front of the shop was a settled pool of red around a blasted wine cask.

"Vino with our chow," Moe said. "That cat has been licking it up all morning."

The platoon carried out of the shop bottles of red and white vino, some flasks of cognac. Then most sat down under the bowl of a stone fountain in the piazza. It gave a shade for their heads. Others possessed themselves of the church at the other end of the tiny square. The bell tower and three walls were standing. They threw off their packs and disposed themselves round the splintered baptismal font or at the feet of a fresco of Christ feeding the multitude with loaves and fishes. This fresco too was cracked and missing sections, like a ruined billboard advertising tires. As the platoon opened their K-rations, two of the Krauts began to whimper. The one named Kurt started yelling Roosevelt and Jude in a splitting howl.

"Shut your lousy mouths!" a corporal bawled, clanking his helmet and carbine down. "Ya interferin with my digestion."

"O my aching back," the section sergeant said, grinding out of his pack and sitting down next to Moe. "Lieutenant, it would be so goddam simple to dispose of those three supermen . . ."

"Ah, forget it," Moe said. "The divisional cages must be somewhere around here. Those Krauts have got to be questioned. . . . They won't bother us much longer."

But Moe stood up again and walked over to where the three Germans were blubbering by a watering trough. Kurt, the wounded one, lay face down on the pavement near the spilled wine, moaning and jabbering Roosevelt. His chest wound had now put a wheeze into his noise.

362

Moe took another carton of K-ration out of his musette bag and set it down near the three. Then he walked back across the piazza to his noncom, without watching to see what the Kriegies would do. He ate his canned ham and egg and his biscuits and washed them down with water. All around the stone fountain and in the battered church the rest of the platoon were silently finishing off the liberated vino and cognac. Moe watched their throats as they swallowed one bottle after another. From his K-ration carton Moe gave the three cigarettes to his section sergeant, who lit one, stowing away his own. And Moe settled back and stuck a toothpick between his lips.

"Lieutenant," the section sergeant said, accepting a light for his cigarette, "ya look beatup since ya got back from the hospital in Naples. Ya ain't ate out nobody's arse except Dimplepuss. Ya ain't give none of us a bad time. Didya get all the shackin ya wanted?"

"Only once," Moe said. "And it wasn't really shacking. It was in the open air. In the moonlight in a jeep. Looking down at the bay. . . ."

The section sergeant sighed. He blew out a puff from a lesser-known brand of cigarette, such as came in K-rations. He looked at the dust of the road, at the checkered hillsides of Tuscany, at the platoon, which was still drinking or lying down in the piazza with their heads resting on their packs. Their M-1's were beside them like dwarf stiff bedfellows.

"When we git to Florence," the section sergeant said, "I'm gonna git me a signorina and I'm gonna sweep her off her feet. I hear that the signorinas in Florence are different from the ones in Naples. Who knows, I might marry her? . . ."

Moe took the little cans that now were empty, stuffed them into the rent carton, and shied the whole package over the fountain. It flew into the doorway of the battered vino shop. Then he spied a public urinal just off the piazza.

"I'm taking a little walk," he said to his sergeant. "Keep your eye on Dimplepuss and the three Jerries. It's just like you said. I don't like my boys much today."

With his thumbs in his pistol belt he walked slowly through his sprawling platoon. His boots clacked on the stone flags. Dimplepuss was nursing a cognac bottle and watching the Krauts tear into the box of K-ration, Kurt, the wounded one, had turned on his side, groaning Roosevelt.

"Characters like you should only drink on pass," Moe said. Dimplepuss looked at him around the bottle, which had its neck in his mouth. He winked at Moe like a cat.

"I ain't feedin these bastards."

"I don't expect you to."

Moe walked leisurely out of the piazza and around the corner. It was hemmed with low slant-roofed Tuscan houses. All the windows had been blown out by the barrage. Washing was still hanging in one courtyard. In one house he saw a dinner sitting cold on the table. Through a window he saw a mussed bed and a colored picture of a blond girl. All the inhabitants, Moe knew, were in the hills. He wondered if they'd start coming back this afternoon, now that all was so quiet. He expected to meet a child someplace in this shambles. It had always been so—at Formia, at Cisterna, at Velletri. In empty Italian villages they'd always come upon at least one child, playing unconcernedly as though it had been born out of the rubble. But here there was no life except the cat that had got drunk from licking spilled red wine.

Moe went to the urinal. From under its porcelain bowl were heraldic streaks like the corona of the sun, violet and yellow; the stains of generations who'd here done their business after leaving the vino shop at midnight. Moe reflected on the relation between your personality and the color of your urine. Thoughtfully he began to button his trousers. Then he heard his men shouting and the crack of a M-1. And he heard the words, "Nein, nein!"

He took off on the run, still buttoning his fly. He got his revolver into his fist. Back in the piazza all his platoon were on their feet, in a cluster. Some were holding the arms of the two Kriegies. Dimplepuss was standing straddle over Kurt, the wounded one. Moe saw him fire another round into the belly of the outstretched P/W, who kicked up his legs in answering spasm.

"Are you dead yet?" Dimplepuss asked calmly. "Tot? Tot? Tot? . . . Say ja and be damned!"

"Nein, nein," the German choked. "Nein. . . . Gott! Gott!"

"Not yet, huh?" Dimplepuss said in a cold scream. And he fired again from the rifle he'd got somewhere.

364

The Kraut's legs kicked again and spun over on his belly. He was still lying between Dimplepuss' legs. His wounded arm flailed like the wing of a thrush, and he lay still.

As Moe came racing in, cocking his revolver, the rest of the platoon shambled back to their places with their eyes down and sat again on their packs.

"You're all gone!" Moe cried sobbingly. "And I hoped and prayed you weren't! Jesus Christ Almighty!"

"This bastard was groanin and I lost my appetite," Dimplepuss said calmly to Moe. He moved the muzzle of the M-1 away from the Kraut's belly.

Moe hit him three times in the face, and Dimplepuss went down on the corpse, whose blood welled leisurely forth from three holes in his coveralls.

"You can go back to the States as an NP!" Moe screamed. "You're under arrest. . . . And when you get to New York start shooting off your face to reporters about the sorrows of combat infantrymen!"

Dimplepuss laughed like ripping steel. Two of his buddies lifted him off the body and took charge of him. The three sat together in the nave of the ruined church. His guards lit a cigarette for Dimplepuss, made him put on his helmet to ward off the sun of Tuscany.

"Lie down and shut up!" Moe yelled again at his platoon. "See if you can remember that you're still alive and human beings! . . . Twenty more minutes and then we take off."

He went back and sat beside his section sergeant, who was scratching the stubble on his chin.

"That's the way it is, lieutenant," the sergeant said.

"Is?" Moe said. "Are you sure all this *is?*"

And he noticed that his chest was heaving stabbingly, as though he'd run miles. It was panting from some windedness outside himself.

Four of the platoon made up a burying party and proceeded to shovel the dead Kraut under in a sandy space off the piazza. The other two Germans sat glumly down and ate the K-ration. They murmured to one another. Then there was the sound of the entrenching tools clawing up the brown sand. One of the platoon took two two-by-fours out of the lumber debris of a smashed kiosk with a fallen sign that read *Corriere della Sera*. Out of these planks he fashioned a cross which he thrust into the hummock of the new grave. Moe watched for a while. They knew what to do and were doing it like dolls wound up. Then he took a wrinkled and dirty V-mail form and a bitten pencil from his pocket. He proceeded to write a letter to his friend Irving in Brooklyn. It was automatic writing:

Somewhere in Italy
27 August, 1944

Hullo, boy:
   Your little chum is in that state like in nightmares where you're surprised to find yourself doing things—and yet you do—you think that nothing more terrible can happen to you but it always does—but you don't mind because you know that pretty soon you'll wake up—I know the censors will never let you get this letter—but I'm writing it anyhow—gotta talk to somebody who's outside all this—does that other world exist?—I can't remember the time when I was a part of it—what I just saw now seems sorta natural—so I'm scared that I'm accepting it—I wonder if I really exist at all—last night the colonel of our battalion turned an Eyetie family out of their farmhouse—he hadda use it for an OP—but the family diddn't take to the hills like sensible Ginsoes—they just moved into the chicken house—the woman was far gone and she gave birth to her kid at midnight out there among the manure and feed—the kid died and the woman did the same three hours later—then the Ginso father blew his top and spat on our colonel's feet, which is what I've always wanted to do myself—then he ran away into the night crying and cursing —but there was still that dead Ginso woman and her dead kid in the chicken house—

   Then Moe found another sheet of V-mail stationery in his musette bag and continued to write the second sheet. The letters formed under his tight fingers without his thinking:

   #2 Because I'm crazy I can make a distinction in my mind between killing Krauts, of which I've done plenty, and doing a lot of the other things that go on in a war—I can't see this crap about war criminals—we do all right at the game too once we get started—the only thing that's safe from us is the women—because they play safe and take to the hills as soon as their town becomes a combat zone—so what do we do?—we loot—we call it liberating material—Irv, I'm so sick of signing my John Hancock on the lower left-hand
366

corner of packages that are being mailed home—our officers and GI's take anything they've a mind to out of the houses and mail it home as a souvenir to their folks—pictures—jewelry—money—blankets—anything they can lay their hands on—how in the name of God are these Eyeties supposed to live after we Liberators have passed through?—have we no mercy whatever on these people?—last week we captured a Kraut dump—we looted that too—millions of dollars' worth of stuff—Lügers—silk stockings—cameras—radios—cognac —they took all that—and the higher the officer's rank, the bigger his cut—is the world so rich that we can take everything, even though it's our enemies'?—and my GI's expected me to sign my name in the lower left-hand corner of the package—meaning that I'd censored it and it was OK to mail back to the States—we've all lost our souls—we're just like everybody else in the world—worse, because we have everything we need—how can we ever get our hands clean again?—how can we ever look anybody in the eye and brag about being Americans?—there's a rifleman in my platoon that reads and writes poetry—he says: To the pit with us. To the pit with us all—we're there already—you may get this letter after the war.

Moe

In the late afternoon Moe and his platoon were still walking through the countryside of Tuscany. Ahead of them the shelling had resumed. They walked with their heads down, in single files on both shoulders of the road. They could see umbrellas of brown spray opening on the horizon ahead of them. The two remaining Kriegies trudged by themselves. Dimplepuss shuffled along laughing between his guards. They'd passed another of the castles on a hillside like those Moe remembered in the sunny background of Italian paintings. Ahead of them on another hill was another castle. The August sunlight cast some of its towers into shadow. Moe looked at it, then lowered his eyes to the dust his boots were kicking up. He shifted his carbine to the other shoulder. He looked down at his mottled right hand nestling in the carbine sling. His life now appeared to him as a stagger through one Tuscan valley after another, with sunny castles looking down at him from their hilltops with the pity of history. In this same Tuscany there had been beauty and laughter. Once.

Moe felt someone in the rear file edging up on him. So he turned with a wariness he hadn't always had. He

367

found one of his corporals close behind his shoulder staring at him with the penetration that people use when they will someone to turn and look at them. This corporal was a blond kid from Wisconsin who used to work in a cheese factory. Moe dropped back so that he was walking to the right of the corporal, both of them on the left side of the road.

"Maybe ya can explain somethin to me, lieutenant. . . . I . . . keep thinkin of myself like I'm a was . . . not a is. . . . See what I mean, lieutenant? . . . I think about myself an I say: He did this or he thought this way. . . . Right now in fact I can see myself walkin alongside a you like we was both in a movie. . . . See what I mean? Why is that?"

"I guess . . . The present doesn't exist for us," Moe said. His tongue was pricked by the toothpick in his lips. "Or we don't want to think about it."

"Well, that would be all right too," the corporal said. "Except I can't think of the future either. . . . It's all past. Past tense like in grammar in school. Like an old man. An I'm just twenty-one. . . . Christ, lieutenant, I don't wanna have any memories yet . . . or be one."

"And I," Moe said slowly, "keep thinking of when I was in Napoli two weeks ago. . . . I see it all so clear cut and finished—as though I was reading ancient history."

"Gee, maybe this is the end for us, lieutenant?" the corporal asked almost hopefully. "Maybe the war is over and we don't know it yet?"

"I guess we're just bogged down in today," Moe said. "You know how it is, boy. . . . The moment just seems there, that's all. . . . You don't feel you ever lived at any other time but now . . . not yesterday . . . not tomorrow. . . ."

"Well, I don't understand ya, lieutenant. But I see what ya mean. . . . Say, lieutenant, I keep havin cravins . . . cravins for simple things. But if I could satisfy em, I'd think I was in heaven. . . . Just a bite of cold apple again . . . or to take an cut a piece of yeller cheese with a sharp knife and watch the peelins . . . or to see my steady lookin at me after I've kissed her."

"I think I understand," Moe said. "And I think I see what you mean. . . ."

Moe peered over his shoulder at his platoon and the two Kriegies. He signaled them all to slow down. For

368

they were approaching another curve in the yellow and green Tuscan road. They spread out and scattered and he went on ahead with the section sergeant following at his heels. Ahead was a hamlet of six houses, a demure concentration such as they'd seen a thousand times in Italy from Salerno on up. Smoke was snaking from a chimney in one of the yellow farmhouses. Moe and his sergeant dropped behind a tree.

"Pretty damn peaceful," the sergeant said. "Like Indiana. . . ."

After half an hour of noiseless observation of these six houses, Moe sent a scout ahead, who loped and dropped from tree to tree. The way he held his M-1 as he alternately trotted and took cover made him look like a scissors. Later he came back, calmly walking upright.

"Hell, lieutenant, they's nothin but Ginso farmers there. All cookin supper."

"Too perfect," Moe said. "I don't believe a word of it. And I'm not calling you a liar. Wait here."

Himself approached the six houses, running and dropping, as the scout had gone the first time. There were seven trees between the turn of the road and the nearest dwelling. Over its door was the sign:

PODERE DI ANACLETO SPADINI

With his carbine across his chest in both his hands, Moe stood for a long time before the low oak door. His shadow fell across its threshold. Finally he kicked with his boot three times at the lintel. He heard a voice inside cry out, "Avanti." Then the door swung inward. All he saw of the house was the wide main room and fireplace. In front of this sat an old woman sewing. She stared straight at him with unblinking eyes.

"Buona sera, signora?" Moe said politely, himself and his carbine bowing. "Io tenente americano . . . avere molti soldati . . . un po' di vino?"

"Sì, sì, sì," the old lady said, laying down her work and rising slowly. "Noi abbiamo molto vino per americani liberatori."

" . . . niente tedeschi?" Moe asked cautiously after a pause, peering about the shadowy room.

For there were places where the afternoon sunlight didn't hit. Chairs in shade. A curtained closet. A door leading somewhere. The old lady spread her hands out calmly and supplely and smiled again.

"No, signor tenente . . . abbia fiducia . . . niente tedeschi."

But still her eyes looked through him. Her glance was the well-wishing of the dead toward the living. Moe, still holding his carbine across his chest, walked silently and quickly up to her. He passed his hand over her face. Those gray gentle eyes didn't blink.

"Oh," he said in a gush of relief and pity, "you're blind. . . . You know you look something like my mother in Brooklyn. . . . Oh excuse me . . . la mia mamma . . . she's a Jewish lady and you're Italian . . . same difference, I guess."

He laughed. He put his hand on her shoulder and gently made her sit down in her place. There was no terror in her eyes, only a shining kindness as though she wished she might focus her blindness on him. But again she bounded up with something of a hospitable bustle. She put out her hands and made to go out of the room. Then she turned and made Moe a low curtsy.

"Ora vi porto il vino," she said. "Quanti soldati avete, signor tenente?"

"There are thirty-seven of us," he said. "Trenta e sette. . . . But don't hurry, ma'am."

Then she turned from the door and came toward Moe without hesitation, as though she smelled or felt where he stood in front of the settle. She put her arms about his shoulders and kissed him lightly. Her cheek smelled of eggs and linen dried in the Tuscan sun.

"Figlio mio," she said. "Figlio mio. . . ."

"Why, I'd just as soon be your son," he said, sitting in the other chair by the fireplace.

Then she left him and went into the next room, which he saw as the door opened under her sure pressure, was the kitchen. He watched her cut the light of the kitchen window, which opened onto a little garden of her own. He watched her take down from a shelf a decanter of ruby wine. He began to relax in his chair and smile to himself; for somehow he felt that he was at home here. He looked down at the dust on his boots, coating even the buckles.

At this moment there was a burst of firing all around the house. He recognized the splitting bark of American

370

M-1's. And another sound. In the kitchen as he leaped to his feet he saw the old Tuscan lady fall to the stone floor. The decanter of red wine she was still holding splintered in her hand and hit the pavement before her body did.

Moe spun around. A Kraut lieutenant was standing behind him in the fireplace. There was a Lüger in his hand. Under his low helmet his lips drew back into a smile of something like welcome. And he bowed to Moe as though he desired to continue the graciousness of the old Italian lady. Moe returned the bow.

"Very pleased to meet you," Moe said.

Then he knew he was lying on the floor by the fireplace, hit harder than he'd ever been hit before. He looked into the ashes on the hearth, and he looked at the boots of the Kraut officer, towering up by his broken right hand. The German was still looking down at him with that smile, not bitter, not sweet. The Lüger now pointed down along the Jerry's thigh, a twirl of smoke coming out of its barrel.

"Grüss Gott," the German said. "Heil Hitler. . . ."

And Moe realized that he was fading fast, as one does on the margin of sleep. Himself was ebbing away from himself with a powerful melancholy, with no hope of recall. For a moment an agony plucked at his brain. He sensed a longing and a regret such as he could never have imagined. But then he saw his mother and Maria Rocco, and he knew he'd come a long long way. It wasn't really so long. But it was farther than most. So Moe smiled back at the German, and he felt his face dropping toward the floor.

THERE'S an arcade in Naples that they call the Galleria Umberto. It's in the center of the city. In August, 1944, everyone in Naples sooner or later found his way into this place and became like a picture on the wall of a museum.

The Neapolitans came to the Galleria to watch the Americans, to pity them, and to prey upon them.

The Americans came there to get drunk or to pick up something or to wrestle with the riddle. Everyone was aware of this riddle. It was the riddle of war, of human dignity, of love, of life itself. Some came closer than others to solving it. But all the people in the Galleria were human beings in the middle of a war. They struck attitudes. Some loved. Some tried to love.

But they were all in the Galleria Umberto in August, 1944. They were all in Naples, where something in them got shaken up. They'd never be the same again—either dead or changed somehow. And these people who became living portraits in this Gallery were synecdoches for most of the people anywhere in the world.

Outside the Galleria Umberto is the city of Naples. And Naples is on the bay, in the Tyrrhenian Sea, on the Mediterranean. This sea is a center of human life and thought. Wonderful and sad things have come out of Italy. And they came back there in August, 1944. For they were dots in a circle that never stops.

Naples   18 June 1945—23 April 1946
Caserta
Florence
Leghorn
Milan
Boston, Massachusetts
Windsor, Connecticut

MORE OUTSTANDING SELECTIONS FROM THE
ARBOR HOUSE LIBRARY OF CONTEMPORARY AMERICANA

AIKEN, CONRAD
Great Circle
Introduction by Graham Greene $8.95

ALGREN, NELSON
The Devil's Stocking
Introduction by Herbert Mitgang   hardcover $16.95
paperback $8.95

ANDERSON, SHERWOOD
Kit Brandon
Introduction by Christopher Sergel $8.95

BASSO, HAMILTON
*The View from
Pompey's Head*
Introduction by John W. Aldridge $8.95

BOURJAILY, VANCE
The End of My Life
Introduction by John W. Aldridge $7.95

CAIN, JAMES M.
Past All Dishonor
Introduction by Thomas Chastain $7.95

CALISHER, HORTENSE
*The Collected Stories of
Hortense Calisher*
Introduction by John Hollander $10.95
Standard Dreaming
Introduction by Richard Howard   hardcover $13.95
paperback $5.95

COATES, ROBERT M.
Wisteria Cottage
Introduction by Brendan Gill $8.95

DAVIS, CHRISTOPHER
*A Peep into the Twentieth
Century*
Introduction by Anatole Broyard $8.95

FAUST, IRVIN
Willy Remembers
Introduction by Elmore Leonard   hardcover $15.95
paperback $7.95

FRIEDMAN, BRUCE JAY
Stern
Introduction by Jack Richardson   hardcover $13.95
paperback $5.95

GALBRAITH, JOHN KENNETH
The Triumph
Introduction by the author $7.95

GOLD, HERBERT
Fathers
Introduction by Jerome Weidman   hardcover $16.95
paperback $8.95

HALL, OAKLEY
The Corpus of Joe Bailey
Introduction by Herbert Gold $10.95

HARRINGTON, ALAN
*The Revelations of Dr.
Modesto*
Introduction by Vance Bourjaily $8.95

HEINZ, W. C.
The Professional
Introduction by George Plimpton $8.95

HOAGLAND, EDWARD
Cat Man
Introduction by Roger Sale $7.95

HOBSON, LAURA Z.
Gentleman's Agreement
Introduction by Jacqueline G. Wexler
hardcover $16.95
paperback $8.95

HUNTER, EVAN
The Blackboard Jungle
Introduction by Stephen King $8.95

LEVIN, MEYER
Compulsion
Introduction by Merle Miller $9.95

LOCKRIDGE, ROSS, JR.
Raintree County
Introduction by Joseph Blotner $12.95

MAILER, NORMAN
St. George and the Godfather
Introduction by John Leonard   hardcover $14.95
paperback $7.95

MARCH, WILLIAM
Company K
Introduction by John W. Aldridge $7.95

MILLER, ARTHUR
Focus
Introduction by the author $7.95

PURDY, JAMES
In a Shallow Grave
Introduction by Jerome Charyn $6.95

ROUECHÉ, BERTON
Black Weather
Introduction by John Brooks $8.95

SCHAEFER, JACK
The Collected Stories of Jack Schaefer
Introduction by Winfield Townley Scott $8.95

SOUTHERN, TERRY
Flash and Filigree
Introduction by William S. Burroughs $7.95

WEIDMAN, JEROME
I Can Get It for You Wholesale
Introduction by Garson Kanin $7.95

WILSON, SLOAN
The Man in the Gray Flannel Suit
Introduction by the author $8.50

All titles of this series are available at your local bookstore or directly through the publisher, Arbor House Publishing Company, 235 East 45th Street, New York, NY 10017.